I0773075

THE WHIP IN THE WAVES

EMMA G. PEARL

INDIE FORGE
PUBLISHING HOUSE

Copyright © 2025 by Emma G. Pearl

All rights reserved.

No part of this publication may be reproduced, distributed, or transmitted in any form or by any means, including photocopying, recording, or other electronic or mechanical methods, without the prior written permission of the publisher, except as permitted by U.S. copyright law. For permission requests, contact Emma G. Pearl

The story, all names, characters, and incidents portrayed in this production are fictitious. No identification with actual persons (living or deceased), places, buildings, and products is intended or should be inferred.

Without in any way limiting the author's exclusive rights under copyright, any use of this publication to "train" generative artificial intelligence (AI) technologies is expressly prohibited. The author reserves all rights to license uses of this work for generative AI training and development of machine learning language models.

No part of this book may be reproduced in any form or by any electronic or mechanical means, including information storage and retrieval systems, without written permission from the author, except for the use of brief quotations in a book review.

Book Cover by Jasmine Kendall at Indie Forge

First Edition 2025

To Darla, you'd make a great Whip

TRIGGER WARNINGS

- Depictions of death, blood, and gore
- Mention of parental abandonment and abuse
- Mention of sexual violence and abuse (off-page)
- Intimate partner abuse
- Sexism and misogyny
- Alcohol consumption and allusions to abuse
- Suicide and attempted suicide
- Allusions to hunting

LISTEN ALONG

TO THE WHIP IN THE WAVES PLAYLIST

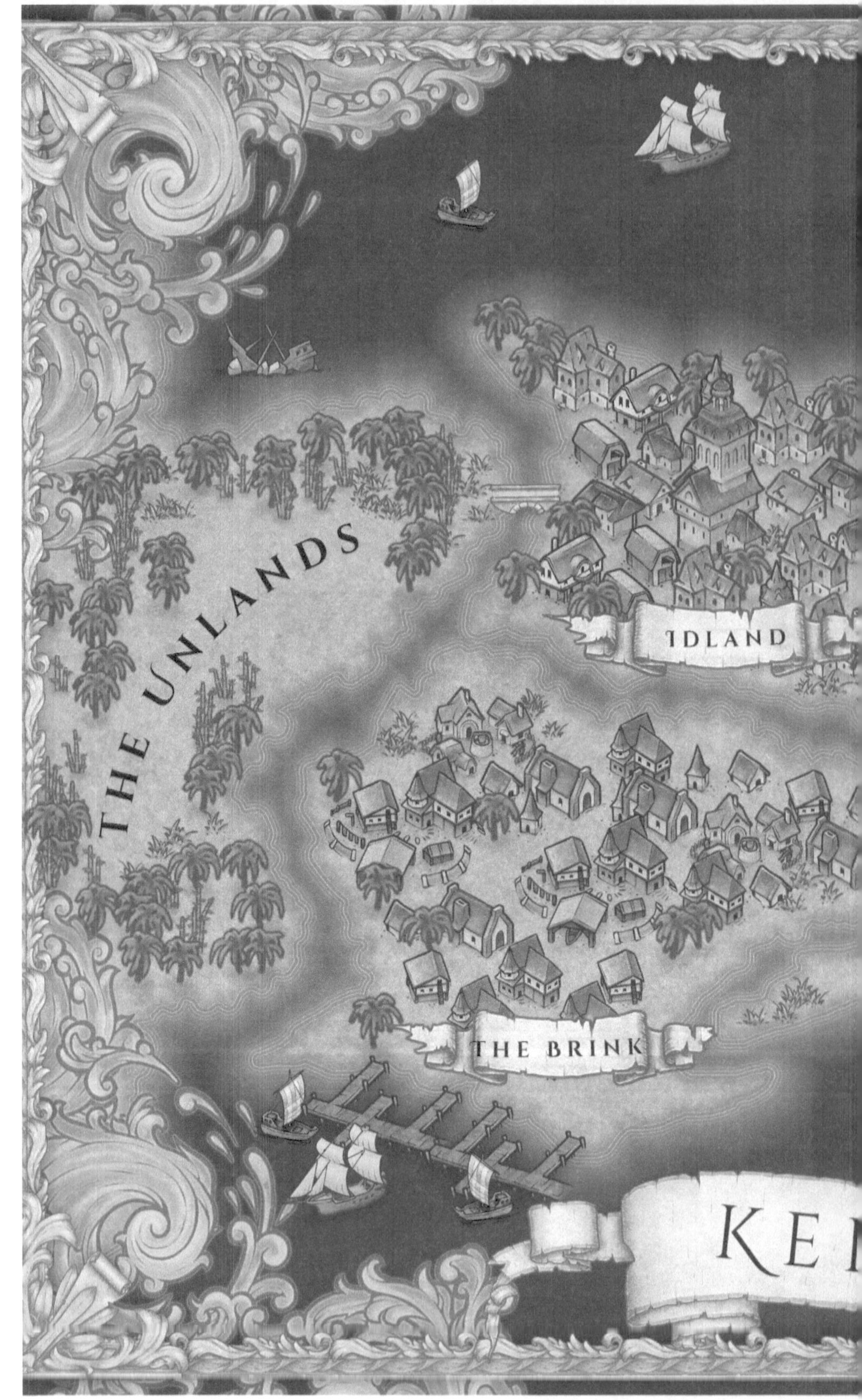

THE UNLANDS
IDLAND
THE BRINK
KE

THE LEES
HOUSE OF WHIPS
SIN DISTRICT
WOOLHILL ESTATE
THE LODE
N
NW
W
ESA

CHAPTER ONE

S he wasn't sure why she'd had to cut out the sailor's tongue but Wyna Bryant wasn't in the business of asking questions. She knew she could just as easily end up like the second mate if she asked the wrong ones. Besides, Wyna told herself she didn't want anything Madame Orinna didn't want to give her. You earned your keep in the House of Whips and when the Madame was ready to bring you into her chambers...well, that was when all the sought secrets would pour.

No, for now it was enough for Wyna to dip her bloody hands into the brine of the Dracan Sea and watch the red curl away, knowing she was involved in something much bigger than herself. She pulled her hands out of the water to wipe them on her skirts, noticing the crease of dried blood stuck under her fingernails, and reminded herself to steal one of Madame Orinna's many letter openers to use as a pick.

Maybe she wouldn't accept secrets she wasn't supposed to have but Wyna was far from opposed to taking objects she didn't think anyone would miss. And sometimes, maybe, ones they would. Surely, Madame Orinna wouldn't object to anything that aided Wyna in her duties.

Wyna stood and stretched out her aching muscles before

turning and starting back towards the House of Whips, the faint beat of drums in the distance. Her ankle smarted. The second mate of the *Etana* had put up more of a fight than she'd anticipated and, in the struggle, her ankle had folded at the perfect angle to give her pain for the next week or so. She practiced her faces as she walked, pretending she didn't know what pain was, let alone that she felt it. She thought she did a decent enough job but, without a mirror, there was really no way to tell.

Really, she just hoped Thessa had finished her portion of the second mate's warning. When Thessa had told Wyna to wash up in the Draca, she'd done a good job of pretending it was only concern for stains in Madame Orinna's basins. Wyna suspected, though, it had more to do with the secrets being kept from her. If Wyna didn't know why the sailor's tongue had to be cut out, who was to say the sailor had any better of an idea?

The walk back to the House was short. Madame Orinna prided herself on their seaside view and had ensured her House had been constructed with massive, double-paned windows. She made sure, too, she had plenty of rooms free of the view of the Draca. After spending weeks—or months—on those waters, their clientele might not be so interested in staring at it while they buried themselves in Madame's Whips.

Not that most of them got that far.

Regardless, none of the other brothels in the Sin District were quite as nice as the House of Whips. Wyna was sure that was only because very little of the House's income actually went towards keeping their girls healthy. The Whips didn't have to worry as much about spermicide draughts or the fancy medicines the apothecary swore up and down would keep the girls from syphilis. So far, they hadn't worked but Wyna wouldn't deny the girls their hope. And Madame Orinna wouldn't dream of keeping her Whips away from any potion or salve they could conjure if they asked for one. Some did but the Whips all knew that wasn't the kind of business they were running. A sailor here or a noble there

—just enough to keep up their good name and never if a Whip didn't want it.

Wyna hadn't served the House in that way quite yet and, frankly, she wasn't sure if she wanted to. Not out of any sense of taboo or distaste for the job. Plenty of the girls of the District were more than happy with this way of life and it was a consistent way for them to earn a living and a roof over their heads. But Wyna also saw the aftermath of the bad nights, of the girls who had no choice in the matter. She was unsure if she was prepared to handle those consequences and it felt foolish to acknowledge her own desires until she was.

The parlor was empty when she finally tramped back through the doors of the House. Not even Maren could be seen lounging about, pretending to man the desk. It was hardly a problem. No ships were set to return tonight and any other patrons would be too caught up in Keresa's festivities to make it over to the Draca whores for hours.

She wished she could go downtown and join in. There would be so many opportunities for dropped coins or expensive wrist-watches that wealthy men took off when their lager splashed too much. She would even be happy to sit on a rooftop somewhere and just watch the dancing and the chaos. Maybe even tap her foot to the reverberations of the drums.

Wyna sighed and crossed her arms, leaning her back against the wall next to the entrance. Took some weight off her ankle. Thessa had told her to stay in the parlor when she returned and not to budge until Thessa came out to retrieve her.

Wyna wanted to consider Thessa a sister, to confide in her like family she never had the pleasure of knowing. But Thessa made that pretty damned hard. She was Madame Orinna's star pupil, a perfect example of everything the Madame wanted her Whips to be. Thessa was not the first to know all her secrets but she was the one trusted with them the most.

Wyna had not been waiting long when Thessa did finally emerge from Wyna's room. Her skin was mildly pallid, as it always was after she'd had a brief panic, and it was a stark contrast from its usual olive glean. Thessa was tying her dark, unruly locks into a pile atop her head as she fixed Wyna with a weighty hazel stare. Wyna straightened immediately, forcing weight back onto her ankle so Thessa wouldn't see and report back. "How'd it go?" she asked.

Thessa sighed. She was always sighing. "Fine, now that I'm through with him. What happened in there? None of his fingers were broken."

Wyna's cheeks burned and a hearty knot formed in the pit of her stomach. Madame Orinna had given her a very specific set of instructions. Instructions Wyna thought she'd followed perfectly.

Lure the second mate: *check*.

Give him the special wine—the one with the sleeping aids crushed up inside: *check*.

Cut out his tongue so he can never speak again: *check*.

Break his fingers so he couldn't hold a quill: *not check*.

The sleeping aid had taken so long to kick in that, when Wyna finally heard the grate of his snoring, she'd wanted to jump at the opportunity. Unfortunately, he had just fallen asleep because he was tired, *not* because he was medicated, and woke up as soon as she'd had her fingers in his mouth. She'd panicked when she'd seen the sultry glint in his eye and had thrown his head against the corner of her bedpost in the hopes of knocking him out a little more violently.

But the second mate was a weathered sailor and Wyna was only a seventeen-year-old girl. She hadn't exactly had the training the other Whips had and wasn't prepared for a plan to go so off-course. He had swung his arms up to grab Wyna and flipped her so he was on top. She'd been frightened for a moment that he would resort to more than just violence but whatever carnal desires had been on his mind before were lost in his string of curses as he tried to hold Wyna's struggling limbs in place. She'd managed to free a leg and cracked it down on his spine, crumpling him into her.

Rolling out from under him had, surprisingly, been the hard part and she'd twisted her ankle when she finally tumbled free.

When she'd turned around, he'd been holding a hand to his back where her foot had been and she used the opportunity to lunge for him once more, shoving him even harder into the lip of the windowsill than she had her bedpost. The crack had made her stomach queasy but she'd tried not to show it. At that point, it'd only been about getting the tongue out and she hadn't spared a thought for the fingers.

Wyna would get hell for this.

"I—"

"I'm not interested in your excuses," Thessa interrupted. "I took care of it. The Madame doesn't have to know."

"Thank you," Wyna breathed. "It's done, then? All of it?"

Thessa's lips parted to answer, interrupted by Madame Orinna stepping out of the office to their left. She settled for a small nod to Wyna. The Madame gave the girls the twinkling smile of a mother whose daughters had just returned with goodies from the market. She was not the type of woman one would expect to run the kind of operation she did. She was tall and she was warm, more of a mother than a killer. Her red hair twisted every which way around her head and her shoulders, complimenting the cherry oak tones of her skin. Some of the girls in the other brothels had taken to calling her Mama Red. It was a more familiar address than any of the Whips were allowed but the Madame didn't mind. "Red is the color of desire, no?" she would say. "Is that not what we're trying to sell?"

Her accompanying smirk was smug and large because Madame Orinna wasn't interested in selling anything but a promise.

"Finished?" the Madame asked, echoing Wyna's question.

Thessa nodded. "Tongue is resting on his lap for now but Wyna said she'd throw it off the pier once the night begins." She fixed her eyes on the gleaming moon through one of the many windows as she spoke. "Fingers are broken but we'll have to keep re-breaking them to make sure they don't set correctly."

"Nothing we can't handle. And he knows his crimes?"

"Yes."

Wyna didn't opt for the moon, instead staring straight ahead, not wanting Madame Orinna to think she was too interested in their conversation. It was better if she thought Wyna was merely reporting back. Mama Red might not look deadly but Wyna would not be the one to cross her.

She noticed anyway.

"And Wyna?" Madame Orinna asked Thessa.

Wyna's heart sank in preparation for Thessa to expose her failures. She blinked twice to banish the tears before meeting Madame Orinna's gaze head-on.

"Perfectly executed."

Wyna didn't dare spare Thessa a glance, no matter how much she wanted to express her gratitude. She wanted no reason for Madame Orinna to question the validity of Thessa's statement. Perhaps Wyna had only forgotten to break the second mate's fingers but, if there was any doubt at all, Madame Orinna would make Wyna go back to cleaning the House.

"And is she ready?" The tone of the Madame's voice was sweet but the question piqued Wyna's interest. "Ready" had a different connotation in the House. She wasn't asking if Wyna could handle her job—barring this evening, she'd proven she could. "Ready" meant knowing what Thessa knew. What the rest of them know.

"I'd say so," Thessa answered.

"Send the girls downtown. We need ears," she told Thessa. "You two'll meet me in my office once you're done."

Wyna had to ignore the pangs of disappointment and envy that overtook her. She didn't think it was quite fair the rest of the Whips got to go downtown while she was stuck at the house but she hoped whatever Madame Orinna had in store for her would well be worth it.

"Thessa," Madame Orinna started as she turned away. "I trust you'll never lie to me on behalf of the girls again. And fetch a compress for her ankle before you come to my office."

Wyna had to give credit to Thessa for not looking cowed. She couldn't say how she'd react to the Madame personally reprimanding her, especially for lying. But Thessa only responded with a cool, "Yes, Madame," and made her way up the stairs next to the office.

Wyna started towards her bedroom before she remembered the unconscious sailor still strapped inside. She darted up the stairs after Thessa.

"Thank you," she whispered once she felt they were far enough away.

Thessa did not lecture her on how she could never make a mistake again, did not ask Wyna to lie for her in return. Thessa knew Wyna would feel just as guilty about her lie as she did—her point had been made.

"Well?" Wyna pushed, though she was certain she already knew the answer. She simply wanted validation for her excitement. "What do you think Madame Orinna wants?"

Thessa shot her a look that made Wyna remember why the other girl was second-in-command. "You know what she wants."

"So soon?"

Wyna'd told herself never to hope for things. She tried to follow that fiercely. At that very moment, though, she couldn't quite help it.

Thessa turned to face her completely. "She calls Whips into her chambers for two reasons, and two reasons only: to dismiss you or to promote you. We've got a sailor downstairs with his tongue in his lap and dozens of others who've heeded your warnings. Somehow, I doubt she's dismissing you."

She didn't say what hung in the air between them—that Madame Orinna didn't dismiss her little contracted murderers. She did what she had to do to keep them quiet and Wyna had heard that the quietest place of them all was the bottom of the Draca. But she wouldn't let her fears get to her now.

Thessa was right.

And Wyna knew it.

She hopped behind Thessa as she dismissed the other girls to go join in the festivities. The brittleness of her salt-dried skirts was starting to bother her but she didn't want to risk being late to see the Madame. She settled for checking herself over in a window's reflection, made by the candlelight against the black night beyond. Passable, but she still had blood under her nails. When the two of them finally made it back downstairs, she pilfered a letter opener from the cup on top of the front desk, making quick work of cleaning under her nails as Thessa ushered the Whips outside and wished them a safe and merry night of espionage.

Wyna needed no prompting once they were gone and bounded stupidly towards Madame Orinna's office chambers. She rapped against the door twice, letting it creak open to show the Madame seated at her desk, poring over books of ships' logs. Wyna noted abstractly that she practically skipped over all the inventory and focused solely on the short diary entries that sailors sometimes left in the margins of the pages.

She'd often catch glimpses of Madame Orinna through the crack in the door when she hadn't quite swung it hard enough to latch. She couldn't be sure what those logs held or what they had to do with Madame Orinna's work but Wyna did know that every time she got a new case of those logs in, the Whips had a fresh list of names to pick off, most of them sailors like the second mate holed up in her room.

She was sure whatever she didn't know, she would find out tonight.

"Shut the door," was the only greeting Madame Orinna offered. Thessa obeyed instantly and when she took her place again at Wyna's side, she slid a compress silently into Wyna's hands—a forgotten injury, truthfully, with the excitement. "I've been impressed with your work, Wyna. Other than the small slip up this evening, you've completed every task I've set for you with a precision I usually only see from Thessa."

"Thank you, Madame."

"Tonight was unfortunate. You got lucky. Lucky that Thessa was slotted to come finish the job. Lucky you didn't know the secret we're trying to keep. Do you understand that?"

"Yes, Madame."

Madame Orinna's lips pulled tight. "When you know the secrets people kill for, Wyna, you can't afford to make mistakes. You can't afford to forget. That's how we wind up dead or, gods forbid, worse off than the tortoise—than Sher's girls."

Wyna flinched at the unfinished name for the girls on the other end of the District. Only one of them had ever crafted a brassiere out of a tortoise shell but the name stuck for them all. The men found them to be feral, barbaric. They liked that. Liked having something they might tame. Or, at the very least, a reason to punish when taming wasn't possible. Madame Sher's brothel hardly made any money at all. They couldn't afford to turn down the men who would come and pay to put the tortoise girls on their boats, entertainment for their voyage. It wasn't work. It was—

Wyna didn't want to be a tortoise girl. She nearly whimpered. "Are you dismissing me?" she asked, focusing only on trying to keep her voice even.

The Madame laughed. "No. But you need to understand the severity of our work. Do you understand it?"

"I think so, Madame."

"Well, you'll know so soon enough. That is, if you want the responsibility."

Wyna did, desperately, clawingly, achingly. "Yes, Madame."

"Then I suppose it's time."

Madame Orinna stood and crossed the room to the left side of her desk. The wall housed a collection of books Wyna was confident Madame Orinna never opened. She could only detect one book whose spine had ever seen the light of day, its edges weathered and oft-touched. The Madame plucked the book off the shelf and let it fall open in her hands. She saw that Madame Orinna—or someone—had hollowed out the center of it to hold a key. The ironwork of the tool was nothing overly impressive and gave no nod to creativity but Wyna could tell that it was heavy and well-made. Madame Orinna notched it into a hole Wyna could not see and gave it a turn, dispelling a muted click.

Nothing happened.

Nothing, at least, until Madame Orinna shouldered her bookcase and Wyna watched it tear from the wall. Rather, tear from where the wall should be because there was only blackness behind the case. The Madame slipped into her secret room and gestured for Wyna and Thessa to follow, uncaring that Wyna's heart was beating right into her throat. Choking her.

She followed.

THE UNDERDRAKE

The infant sank in a cocoon of sea foam and, when it landed in the sediment, it made no sound. This was not unusual this far under the surface. But the underdrake knew. Disturbed from its slumber, the underdrake glided towards the foam and the child within, nudging at it with the scales of her snout. She recoiled as the foam dispersed, leaving the child—sleeping and quiet—exposed to the will of the currents.

The underdrake had never seen a human child with her own eyes. She no longer even dared to explore the surface of the sea, though she saw shadows of little boats pass overhead. She had awareness of the people above. But those people were not for her to know, not for her to study. Not anymore.

Her magic was a magic of the water. People did not live in the water.

Not, at least, until the child.

The underdrake approached the child again, curious at the muted blue tinge of its skin. It was not skin like hers, and yet it held the same colors. She turned and used the fin on the end of her tail to swipe at the child gently. It did not move. The underdrake harrumphed, disappointed that this strange creature was not there to offer her entertainment.

It was only after staring at the child for many moments that the underdrake understood the child could not breathe.

With a nonsensical declaration of delight, the underdrake called her magic to her and bestowed upon the child the ability to breathe in her domain. But why stop there? The child's limbs would do her no favors in the water, should she choose to swim, so the underdrake made the child a tail to match the blue of her skin. She did not alter the arms, for what was the fun in having a human if she changed it entirely?

The child awoke as gills rippled and tore through its skin. It opened its mouth, reaching for a sucking breath, and the under-drake sensed organs inside that yearned to expand with air. And though the underdrake wished to keep the child with her forever —so long as she did not grow bored of it—she decided to leave them unaltered. Perhaps the child could investigate the land in a way the underdrake could not.

When the child realized its sucking would do nothing and the gills began to accept and filter the water that moved against them, its skin abandoned its aquatic hue. The underdrake growled quietly in frustration, seeing her creation no longer matched as beautifully as before.

And then it began to cry. Its eyes, the color of the sand below them, stared at the underdrake as it did so, as if it expected her to cure and correct the source of the tears. The underdrake only cocked her large head to the side. As she did so, the child caught sight of the underdrake's whisker-like protrusions and silenced itself. The eyes followed the whiskers as they trilled in the water and the underdrake shook her head about to test the child's attention.

The child paid no heed to the horn atop the underdrake's head. Its twin had long since been gone, stolen by a whaler and his sharp stick with the magic to cut through surf and bone. But the underdrake was still quite proud of her remaining horn and preened, wishing the child to take notice. When it still did not approach the horn, she swam forward and jutted the bone into the child's vicinity, only for it to wrap its small, incapable fingers around the horn. When the underdrake lifted her head, the child held on, setting onto her neck and straddling her as if it expected the underdrake to take it where it wished.

Complying, she flew through the water. Used the intricate, muscled fins on her back to push her forward and her magnificent tail to steer. The underdrake showed the child the yawning expanse of the sea—of her empire—and the child laughed and babbled, reaching for every copse of reef and every school of fish.

CHAPTER TWO

The scrunching awe on Wyna's face was worth all of Madame Orinna's dramatics.

While Thessa was entertained by the twinkle in Madame Orinna's eyes, Wyna was busy taking in the pure magic of the secret chamber. Covering the walls of each side of the room were bookcases much like the one that slipped aside for the women to enter. These shelves hid the Madame's ship logs that she employed Theo to painstakingly recreate and send back to the captains. But Madame Orinna had been in business for years and two shelves—even if they were ten feet wide and spanned from floor to ceiling—simply weren't enough. Madame Orinna had begun stashing the logbooks in some old crates and had set them up in front of the shelves as a makeshift set of stairs, though she hardly needed the extra height.

A squat table sat in the middle of the room. Thessa thought it looked entirely too cluttered but she knew Theo would swear the mess was only a product of careful organization and categorization. The books started tall on the edges of the table, steadily crawling into the center, right under the hanging candles Madame Orinna had installed. Burned into the middle of the wood and covered in drops of fallen wax was the image of a scaled tale slapping back into a wave.

Thessa had always been curious as to who the Madame had commissioned that bit from, if it had been one of her girls or a reckless request from a local artist. In fairness, the image on the table alone was not enough to give away Madame Orinna's secrets. Its sister image that Beckett had painted on the back wall of the secret office did well to clear things up. Wyna couldn't take her eyes off of it and, honestly, Thessa couldn't blame her. The Whips weren't strangers to the arts and they had seen many a rendition of mythological creatures, ethereal and deadly. But Beckett's painting looked less like an artistic rendition and more like she had ripped the creature out of the Draca and pinned it to the wall.

The image, of course, was that of a mermaid. Weightless in water and staring at whoever dared to enter Madame Orinna's chambers. Her tail was muscled and stocky, a powerful weapon against the waves and currents. It was covered in iridescent scales that seemed to glitter impossibly in a light for which there was no source. Where the tail met the creature's torso, the scales spread up to the human skin as if it were ivy devouring a building, the longest of the strands winding their way to her clavicle and meandering to her back. They trailed down to the inside of the mermaid's wrists and caressed her jaw.

The mermaid's hair, suspended in the water and floating around her like a striking halo, was a stark white that seemed to reflect the glittering of the scales. Beckett had painted the hair so it covered the mermaid's body very little. Thessa had always thought it would have been easy enough to cover the nipples for those with more modest sensibilities but Beckett had insisted on crafting the mermaid's breasts in great, heaving detail. The sight made Thessa blush but no matter how many times she tried to avert her eyes out of some proprietary sense of politeness, they always found their way back.

"Beautiful," Wyna gasped. Thessa almost agreed out loud but

Wyna was talking about the image as a whole. Not that Thessa didn't think that was beautiful, as well. Gods, it was distracting. "Why do you hide this?"

The Madame snickered. "Take a guess, girl."

"I've seen you working with the log books but I didn't know you stockpiled them," she said. "And I still don't quite understand why it's such a secret. What are the sailors doing? Some sort of financial fraud?"

Like Madame Orinna, Thessa wanted to laugh at Wyna's inability to comprehend the mythical. But hadn't she had a similar reaction when Madame Orinna had first brought her in? Even at eleven years old, Thessa hadn't been foolish enough to think the fairy tales were real and didn't dare to hope. She had seen too much to believe in the facilitation of happy endings.

But the fairy tales were real and no amount of tragedy would change that. Or, perhaps, tragedy was a more frequent affair because of it.

"The mermaid, Wyna," Madame Orinna said, very suddenly serious. "Though I'm sure the sailors dip their hands in their investor's books, we aren't interested in those kinds of crimes. At least, that's not why we cut out tongues."

"Whips. Mermaids. What's the difference?" Wyna asked. "I thought that was just their name for us."

"It is," Madame Orinna conceded. "They call you girls 'mermaids' and they have no idea why."

Wyna peered down at the russety, wet driftwood color of her skin. She lifted her skirts as if to ensure her legs were still there. "I don't think I do, either. We don't look like that."

"We aren't the real mermaids, Wyna," Thessa sighed, speaking for the first time since entering Madame Orinna's chambers.

Wyna only stared at her. Then at the painting. Then at the table. Then at the logs. Then back at Thessa. She wouldn't meet Madame Orinna's eyes.

"You can't be serious."

But Wyna looked doubtful and Thessa knew it was because Wyna thought Thessa was always serious. Thessa said nothing.

Madame Orinna spoke for her. "She's serious," she said, trying to coax Wyna's attention back to her. "And so am I. You think I would worry about these sailors at all if there wasn't something other than money at stake? I am not a greedy woman, Wyna."

The younger girl had the sense to look rattled. "I never meant to imply—"

"I know you didn't. We all say silly things when faced with the impossible."

"It *is* impossible," Wyna insisted.

"It is, is it?" Madame Orinna raised an eyebrow. "Come."

She ushered Thessa and Wyna out of the room and when they cleared the bookcase, she returned the key to its hole and the heavy wood slid back into place with only a small creak. It was ritual, methodical, the way she replaced the key in the hollowed book and, in turn, settled that to its spot on her shelf.

"Come," she said again. Thessa knew she was included in the command.

The Madame led the girls down to the pier behind the House, electing to go under the wooden slats rather than atop them. Right where the sand met the water swayed a small boat, only big enough for maybe four at a time. Thessa eyed Madame Orinna's looming form warily and then glanced down at herself. It wasn't often Madame Orinna invited more than one of the Whips onto her little boat. It made Thessa nervous every time. But she wouldn't let Madame Orinna see her hesitate. She was the first to step onto the boat and settle. Wyna followed her lead and clamored in after her, tucking herself into Thessa's side.

Thessa wondered if she was asking to be comforted.

The older woman retrieved the oar she'd strung up to one of the posts before untying the boat and giving it a hard shove out into the water. She led it like a stubborn dog, not bothering to hike up her skirts to avoid getting wet. Thessa braced herself for the boat to tip when Madame Orinna finally climbed in but she was experienced and graceful.

They were off.

Wyna stayed silent, matching not even the slow hum of the waves knocking into one another. Thessa knew Madame Orinna was keen on building the suspense of proof and Thessa certainly wasn't going to be the one to break the silence.

The water calmed her. The Dracan Sea was a dangerous one —that, at least, she well knew—but this close to the shore, Thessa wasn't worried about peril. The sea held a secret she knew and, right then, she didn't have to worry about anyone finding it out. That relaxed her.

The slaps of the oar into the water slowed as the women approached their destination. A destination which Thessa was willing to acknowledge looked like the middle of nowhere. The sea wasn't incredibly deep here but it was enough that the chain of the anchor pulled entirely taut when Madame Orinna dropped the heavy metal out of the boat.

"Can you swim?" Madame Orinna asked Wyna.

The question reminded Thessa of her own attire and she cursed. Though, absently, she'd known she would have to swim, changing into a dress she didn't care for as much hadn't crossed her mind. She resolved to salvage what she could and reached behind her to try to unstring her skirts and pull them off. The blasted things somehow took up more space in the boat off her than they did on and Thessa stepped gingerly over them to begin the work of unstringing Wyna's laces.

Wyna flinched at her touch.

"Yes," she answered warily, eyeing Madame Orinna and Thessa in turn. "Why?"

With great patience, Madame Orinna said, "Because you'll be swimming."

Finished unraveling, Thessa released Wyna to stand and let the skirts fall to her ankles. They weren't undressing for one another —though a brothel House was no stranger to the act. Rather,

Madame Orinna had procured for them a tight pair of trousers, ones that conformed to their skin and moved when they did. The Whips were to wear them under their skirts on the ever-likely chance something went sour and they were forced to do something proper clothing wouldn't allow.

Madame Orinna didn't bother with hers since she'd already gotten it quite wet during takeoff.

"Don't take too big of a breath," Madame Orinna warned. "We aren't going far."

She dove off the little boat and disappeared into the night-blackened waters. Thessa nudged Wyna forwards, choosing to take up the rear and ensure Wyna didn't get lost. She dove, Thessa close behind.

Thessa could just barely see Wyna's flapping feet and hoped Wyna had the same vision of Madame Orinna. It wouldn't matter much if Wyna did lose her, really. Thessa had swam these waters hundreds of times and could easily direct Wyna if it came down to it.

But Thessa wanted to enjoy her swim.

She could neither feel nor see ground below her but seaweed wrapped itself around her legs as she swam. Though it was fanciful, she sometimes liked to pretend *she* was a mermaid, trying to propel herself forward by clamping her legs together and fluttering them behind her. She tried it now and grinned when she gained a bit of speed, almost catching up to Wyna entirely.

Wyna wasn't a terrible swimmer, either, and Thessa had to give her credit for that. She gave her credit, too, for diving into the Draca blind, no ideas about where they might be going. Thessa thought if she could return to Wyna's position, she probably would have figured it all out by now.

But Thessa had still been a child when Madame Orinna had showed her hand. She'd taken in when she was only ten, after Thessa had come to her in the wake of tragedy. The Madame hadnt hesitated in accepting Thessa as one of her own, taking only a year to trust her enough with her secrets and Thessa had held the treasure for seven now. But perhaps, despite the aging of the trauma, Thessa had still lived in the world of fantasy and fancy when mermaids had entered her life. When she grew into adulthood, she'd never been forced to abandon them. That was what made her job so simple: the grown citizens of Keresa didn't want to believe in the supernatural. Not if they didn't have to. And those who did believe were easy enough to silence.

Of course, that wasn't to say every aspect of a Whip's job was effortless. Thessa had found physical violence to be quite straining, even when she used the specialized daggers Madame Orinna had crafted for her.

Lost in her mind, Thessa crashed into Wyna in the weightless, gentle fashion that could only be achieved under water. She tried to look past her only to see pure blackness and no sign of Madame Orinna. Lucky she knew where to go from here. She found Wyna's hands with one of her own in the dark, the other reaching into the blackness until it collided with a once-rough stone, since smoothed by the movement of the water and the smacking and rubbing of tails. Thessa used the stone to propel herself upward, dragging Wyna behind her. She'd just used up the very last of her breath by the time they broke the surface. Beside her, Wyna gasped and sucked in air and hardly saved any effort for treading water.

The blackness of the sea did not end with breaking the surface and Thessa had to rely on her other senses to get her bearings. Something that was definitely not seaweed but just as slimy brushed her ankle and her wrist, stinging her skin when it met again with salt. She guessed Wyna was having a similar experience based on her frightened cry.

Sloshing that had nothing to do with Wyna's splashing sounded behind her and Thessa knew light would follow. One at a time, Madame Orinna lit candles placed ritualistically around the surfaces of the cave.

She'd led the girls to a small, natural grotto with no access to the outside world, save for the underwater entrance. Thessa had never measured but the pool couldn't have been too much wider than the table in the Madame's secret chamber, surrounded by narrow slivers of solid ground where Madame Orinna stood. Now that her eyes had adjusted, Thessa could see the tiny flecks of moonlight that snuck through the holes in the rock. She turned to Wyna to take in her reaction but Wyna wasn't staring at the rock, at the moon, or at Madame Orinna.

She was staring at the faces across the pool and they were staring back. Thessa swallowed her laugh, her humor lost as her gaze landed on the women across from them. She'd seen the mermaids plenty of times, considered them family for years. But she was never quite immune to the awe they inspired.

Thessa couldn't see their tails in the low light but she could recite the colors of the scales with their names as if she were reading it off a scrap of paper. Dinah's tail had the soft, blushing pink of a newborn, though the depth of the color and the glimmer of it in the moonlight were more breathtaking than a baby could ever be. It paired beautifully with the mass of scarlett hair falling down her back.

Rose's tail held the exact color Thessa'd thought the sea should be: the color of nature lost in the chorus somewhere between blue and green. It was a compliment to her miraculously still-tanned skin and an ode to the cooling tones of her dark hair.

Edonie, of course, was the mermaid depicted in Beckett's painting. Thessa'd spent so many hours studying it, Beckett may as well have painted it on her eyelids.

It was lucky, Thessa thought, that the three of them were all there to greet Wyna. She suspected Madame Orinna had organized the whole affair in advance. It wouldn't have surprised her. Rose, Dinah, and Edonie were not the only mermaids to swim these waters but they were the friendliest to the humans—to the Whips—not taken as much to grudges as some of the others close by were.

"Hello." Rose broke the silence, amusement ringing clear in her sultry voice.

Thessa returned her greeting in kind, speaking their names for Wyna's benefit and because she liked the taste. "Rose. Edonie. Dinah."

"Good evening, ladies," Madame Orinna said. "I thank you for being here tonight instead of the festivities."

Dinah wrinkled her nose. "You couldn't catch me near the town center. The canal water is full of sewage." She swam closer to the girls. "Besides, I love meeting the new ones."

Wyna did not move, save for the slow bob of her head as she kicked her legs to stay afloat. Dinah gave her a peculiar look, possibly a cruel one, before slipping behind the girls and stealing Wyna's hand away from Thessa's. Dinah dragged Wyna over to the edge of the pool, under where Madame Orinna stood and watched. The Whip did not take the cue, only stared, so Dinah took her arms and propped them on the ledge so she didn't need to use her legs. When Dinah turned back, her overgrown brows were raised.

Smiling, Thessa turned from Wyna and swam to Rose and Edonie, offering them a warm embrace. "It's been quite a while," Thessa gushed, thrilled to again be in the presence of her friends.

"Too long," Rose agreed. She gave Thessa a damp kiss on the cheek. Thessa felt Rose wrap her tail around Thessa's body and she relaxed her legs, using Rose's tail as a makeshift chair.

Edonie's smile was tighter. She was friendly and otherworldly but she was a bit older than the others and wasn't as comfortable around them as she was Madame Orinna. Still, Thessa did her best to ensure she knew she was loved and appreciated. Through the water, she snatched Edonie's hand and gave it a squeeze.

Dinah had returned to the others before Wyna spoke at all. "How?" was all she asked.

Madame Orinna lifted her shoulders. Dropped them fiercely, though Wyna wasn't looking at her. "Sometimes we know. Sometimes we don't," she explained. "Most times we just blame the sea."

"The sea's never turned me into a mermaid!" Wyna said.

"Not yet, it hasn't," Madame Orinna laughed. "There's only one common thread we've been able to find all these years."

They all waited a few beats for Madame Orinna to finish her thought. Thessa'd done this enough to know she had no intentions of going on without prompting.

"Oh, just tell her," Thessa urged with a roll of her eyes. "What's the common thread?"

"Betrayal."

CHAPTER THREE

She'd never had parents tell her it was rude to stare so Wyna had no qualms about keeping her eyes locked on the mermaids in front of her. She wanted to listen to Madame Orinna with the kind of attention one would expect from an employee but she'd barely heard her when she said something or another about betrayal.

"Apparently, that's not news to her," one of the mermaids—Wyna thought Thessa had called her Rose—laughed. "But then again, is it really news to any of us?"

The mermaid beside Rose was solemn when she shook her head and Wyna clocked the sorrowful stare she directed to the third mermaid. Gods, she couldn't remember their names. In fact, Wyna could hardly remember her own name as her mind swirled with all the impossibilities in front of her.

"Wyna," Thessa started, reminding her of just what she'd forgotten. "Are you alright?"

She wanted to say *no*. Say she'd never be alright again. That proof of something she'd only dreamed about was sitting—swimming—right in front of her and she didn't know what to do about it.

How was she meant to keep the wonder out of her voice when she replied?

"Yes."

"Do you understand now?" Madame Orinna asked from behind her.

It cracked her right out of her wonder. Her boss—the woman who both employed and housed her—had brought her to the mermaids. But why?

"Well, no," Wyna said. "So the sailors aren't forging the logs or stealing. What do they have to do with mermaids? What do mermaids have to do with maiming?"

Madame Orinna crouched down so that her mouth was closer to Wyna's ear. "Do you plan on running and telling everyone what you've seen here tonight?" Wyna wasn't sure what that had to do with her questions but she shook her head. "Good. And you shouldn't. This secret is the burden only a privileged few can bear. The men you 'maim,' as you say, are threats to the secret."

"Why must it be kept a secret at all?" Wyna asked, feeling perhaps she knew even if she couldn't articulate why.

"How many men do you know would kill a creature just to see its blood run out? How many men do you know would stop at nothing to get the answers they seek? Or to get the glory? I know too many. These women are not their experiments and they are not game to be hunted. We prevent that from happening."

The Madame's words were haunting. All the same, Wyna knew them to be true. She had seen too many of the upper class of Keresa boasting about trips all over the world and the carcasses they brought back to show off. She had once been tasked with luring a man of science away from one such welcoming party and she knew Thessa had taken his life later in the evening.

Six months of carrying out tasks she never understood slipped into place in Wyna's mind as she considered both what Madame Orinna said and what she now knew. Yes, this was indeed a secret that needed keeping.

"I wish I had known of the Whips while I lived in Keresa." the mermaid with platinum hair sighed.

"You lived in Keresa?" Wyna asked. "In the canals?"

The mermaid laughed. "No, I had legs once. Nice ones, if I can recall. Though I suppose it's been about fifty years."

Wyna scrutinized the mermaid and her glowing skin. She didn't look to be fifty and Wyna said as much.

"I'm long past fifty. Closer to eighty, really."

"How?"

"I suppose the aging stopped when the tail came. I'd been young. More than ready to face the world. But I never wanted to face it like this."

"Edonie, enough," Rose snapped. "None of us would have chosen this but surely it's better than the alternative."

The mermaids were skilled at dancing around topics without really answering any of Wyna's questions so she asked them directly. "What happened to you all?"

Edonie was the first to answer. "My husband happened to me. I had married a man who fancied himself quite important to Keresa—I've been assured he's long perished. As self-important men do, he'd of course had a mistress when he was alive." Her eyes flitted to Dinah. "When I found out, he took a knife to my throat and threw me in the Draca."

"He killed you?"

Edonie nodded.

"You always make me say it," Dinah grumbled. "And I was his little mistress." Her words seemed to mock Edonie—not to insult her but to share in her laments and laugh at the life they once lived. "I'd heard he had mistresses in and out constantly. I thought his wife—I thought Edonie wouldn't mind. I'll be damned, she minded. He didn't, so much. I found out what he did and confronted him but I suppose I should have known better than to come at a man who'd just killed his wife."

Wyna didn't have to ask if the man had killed Dinah, too. She turned to Madame Orinna. "Is that what you meant by betrayal?"

"In a way."

"Were you murdered as well?" she asked Rose.

Rose shook her head, the tips of her hair swaying about her in the water. "I was swept into the tide."

"Who betrayed you, then? The Draca?"

"My father," she said. "I woke up at the bottom of the sea and I knew nothing other than that I could breathe and I could swim. So I did. But when I finally found the shores of Keresa, there was no returning to land. I tried the canals but the closest I could get was right outside my family's home."

"Tell her what you heard, Rose," Madame Orinna instructed.

"I heard my father. Screaming at my mother and blaming her for my disappearance. He said he would never get his money now if he couldn't deliver me to the docks."

"He sold you?"

"Into an arranged marriage. Claimed he needed the money to pay off his gambling debts." Her tone took a positive turn and the mermaid winked at Madame Orinna. "I have it on good authority that he never got his money."

"He doesn't need it anymore," Madame Orinna told her, a bloody image entering Wyna's mind as she considered the words.

She was beginning to unravel these threads. It wasn't the act that changed these women but rather the concoction of their sorrow and the sea. It was easy enough to understand the Draca had magical properties—Wyna'd always felt that was so—but she never knew why or exactly how. To her it seemed the sea took these women, insisting if the land wasn't going to treat them right, then they'd belong to her. And with each ounce of under-standing came the weight of the secret. Knowing now these mermaids used to be people. Used to be just like Wyna. Like Thessa and Madame Orinna.

That changed everything.

Tickling the back of Wyna's mind was a nagging thought. One that was jealous her own familial abandonment hadn't been enough to give her immortality and a tail. She felt guilty for her pettiness, for hoping she had suffered enough for this kind of reward when she should feel lucky she was alive at all. Lucky Madame Orinna had taken her in and given her an opportunity to right the wrongs in Keresa. Perhaps she could do more for the mermaids if she were on land, anyhow.

Madame Orinna had different ideas.

"Now that you know, it's time to talk about your assignment," she said, her voice void of any of the sugar and comfort it sometimes deigned to provide. "I need to send you out to sea."

"Me?" Wyna flipped her body over in the water so her head was level with the Madame's feet. She stared up at her. "Why?"

"I've got the other Whips tied up in assignments for two months after the last batch of logs. And you aren't going to have the same association as the other girls. The men won't fear you. Not yet."

"What, exactly, is the assignment?"

"Are you familiar with Alastor Woolhill?" Edonie sucked in a breath and Madame Orinna shot her a sympathetic look. "Yes— your nephew."

Wyna nodded. "Noble merchant. Handles sixty percent of trade in all of Keresa," she recited.

"The very same. I met with him earlier this week. Managed to convince him having a Whip on one of his ships wouldn't impede business. It's a rare chance and an important job, Wyna. But I won't lie to you and tell you it isn't dangerous."

"You still haven't even told me what the job is," Wyna said, annoyed with Madame Orinna for being so elusive.

Madame Orinna narrowed her eyes at the challenge but went on anyway. "The work we do here in Keresa is good but it would be better if the reports of our seafaring friends never made it into the log books at all. We've never been given the opportunity to cut off the rumors right at the source and I certainly wasn't about to refuse the one that was presented to me."

Wyna tried to manage her emotions but she couldn't quite tell how she felt about the assignment Madame Orinna offered her.

She, of course, was willing to jump at the chance to be trusted with her very own assignment—and a vital one, at that—but she didn't yet know if she *could* be trusted. She had so far held her own against all her victims, yet she'd never been allowed to deliver the final blow. What if that was required out at sea and she wasn't prepared for it?

There was also the matter of the other girls Madame Orinna had mentioned. Wyna wanted to be chosen for assignments because she deserved them, not because everyone else was caught up with their own. She couldn't imagine the disappointment on Madame Orinna's face if she turned to her in desperation and Wyna couldn't deliver.

Not to mention Wyna still didn't know everything she needed to know about the mermaids. She understood now that they existed and why it was so important to keep them a secret. What she did not understand were the rules of these creatures and how to spot them—or, rather, how to keep others from spotting them. She twisted back to study the grotto around her, tried to memorize the glimmer of the scales crawling up the mermaids' bodies and imagine how they might look from the deck of a merchant's ship. She'd still not been able to see their tails but, if they were anything like the painting in the Madame's secret chamber, she could only guess at how difficult they were to hide.

Jealousy plagued her again, shivering through Wyna's body as she caught sight of Thessa, still perched right up with the mermaids. *Wyna* wanted to get that close, wanted to befriend them like Thessa had. And why hadn't Thessa ever treated Wyna with that same fondness? They had known each other for almost four years now! She wondered what kind of assignment Madame Orinna would give to the star. If the ship job was oh-so important to the Whips then what was so important here in Keresa that Thessa had to stay?

It was only when Madame Orinna spoke again that Wyna realized she'd never responded. "Wyna? Are you the right Whip for the job?"

All that consideration and she still hadn't wrapped her mind around the work. But she met Madame Orinna's eyes and responded in the affirmative anyway.

The Madame clapped her hands together under her chin and grinned, that sugar nestling right back into her voice. "Perfect! You leave tomorrow."

Wyna didn't have time to register the tightness of that time frame before Madame Orinna insisted the girls were due back. She thanked the mermaids for their presence and let them exit the grotto first, on the small chance anyone out on the water noticed their little boat. The mermaids gushed their goodbyes, Rose swimming over to Wyna to offer a slimy embrace.

"Thank you, Wyna," she said. "I already feel so much safer knowing you're a part of this family."

Wyna's heart soared at Rose's words and they banished all her fears. If they—the mermaids and the Whips—were going to be her family then she would stop at nothing to ensure they were protected. It didn't matter if she had never actually killed before and it didn't matter that she knew so little about mermaids. This was her assignment and she was resolved to complete it successfully. No more questions asked.

Well, maybe one or two more. Like, for example, what she should pack.

Rose released Wyna and sank into the water, whipping her tail up as she dove deeper. The disturbance splashed Wyna's face and she wasn't able to get a great look at the tail. She dunked her head and tried to search for it underwater but the mermaids were too quick.

They were gone.

When she popped her head back out of the water, Madame Orinna and Thessa were staring at her, expectant looks in their eyes. Wyna blushed. For how long she'd spent wishing to have their attention and affection, she now felt it was too much. She wasn't prepared for it. Wyna peered down and treaded water while she waited for them to speak first.

"I think we've given them enough time," Madame Orinna finally announced. "Let's get back to the boat."

The older woman blew out all the candles she had lit, subjecting them to complete darkness once more. A slew of water droplets hit Wyna's face, a splash sounding as Madame Orinna dove into the middle of the pool. Wyna was contemplating how long she should wait before following when Thessa's hand slipped into hers once more, tugging her under but giving her enough time to correct the direction of her body.

She tried to enjoy the swim this time around. Tried to be content with her new knowledge. Tried to be excited about her new assignment. And she was, in a way. She knew, if nothing else, she would make her way back home with the secret intact. What she was unsure about was what exactly would transpire between then and now. It was hard to look optimistically towards the future when she could hardly see in front of her in the present.

She wished she'd taken a bigger breath before she let Thessa take her away.

The other girl led Wyna's wrist to smack into a rough, rusty metal and Wyna could make out that it was the anchor Madame Orinna had dropped. She tilted her neck, finding the outline of the Madame directing herself to the surface and using the chain as her guide. Wyna did the same and, this time, instead of waiting for her to go first, Thessa swam up right beside her.

Madame Orinna pulled Thessa into the boat and began to tug on the anchor. Wyna was too busy marveling at her strength to notice Thessa's outstretched hand offering her the same passage aboard. It was an ungraceful act, getting back onto the boat, but they managed and were soon on their way back to Keresa's shores. The ride was not nearly as silent as the way out and Madame Orinna filled her head with instructions on how she should behave on the merchant ship and what exactly her role would be. She even answered all of Wyna's questions on how to spot the mermaids and the best ways to cover up a sighting. And as they pulled closer to the shore, Wyna let herself feel giddy for what might be the first time in her life.

Their discussion left her restless with anticipation for another reason, as well. The subject of mermaids had put Thessa and Madame Orinna in a more talkative mood than Wyna had ever experienced. She felt as though she'd finally entered the inner circle of the Whips and she never wanted to leave it. Even on a ship miles and miles off the shore, Wyna would be one of them, truly and forever.

CHAPTER FOUR

Thessa found it rather difficult to not grow jealous of Wyna's assignment. She would have given anything to be allowed free passage away from Keresa. There were too many people and too many memories here. She'd thought maybe her assignments would create a new trauma that would melt away the old. But it was never the case. Every time she closed her eyes to sleep, her senses focused on how close she was to people she only wanted to leave behind. Thessa loved the Whips and she loved her job—she only wished she could do it somewhere else.

Or maybe she just wished for someone else to leave.

But Thessa knew Madame Orinna had her reasons for sending Wyna on Woolhill's ship. She wasn't blind to how the Madame favored her and she knew there was likely a task much more pressing here on land. She hoped it would be enough to soothe the nasty emotions rising inside of her but those hopes were not high. What was important to Thessa wasn't always what was important to the Madame.

The House of Whips was just as still when they returned as they'd left it and Thessa noted that the rhythms of the drums had only increased in volume as the night grew darker. But Thessa could hardly hear anything over Wyna's excited chatter and her questions about the mermaids, the Whips, and her assignment. She kept asking Thessa what she should pack, as if Thessa had ever taken a trip on a merchant's ship. She almost snapped and told her to ask one of the actual brothels up the road but she bit her tongue. She didn't want her envy to ruin her relationship with her new sister.

After all, a found family was much more useful than a dead one.

As soon as the three of them stepped through the doors, Wyna rushed to her room, emitting the tiniest squeal. Thessa remembered the second mate still tied up inside. She sighed, giving Madame Orinna a parting roll of her eyes, and set to work. The second mate was conscious and his eyes widened when Thessa crossed the threshold. It would have been nice if his eyes had widened because of the vastness of her beauty but she supposed fear was as good a reason as any. A muffled groaning came from the depths of his closed mouth—he was in too much pain to open it, it seemed. Thessa wondered if there might be some whiskey around that she could pour down his throat to help ease the pain.

It wasn't his fault he was in this position, not really. He had been in the wrong place, at the wrong time. Had seen more than any man should. Thessa couldn't fault him for that. And maybe he would have kept their secret if they had asked it of him. But Madame Orinna wasn't the type of woman to give people chances to disappoint her. She was the type of woman that yielded results. And cutting out a tongue? Well, that yielded results.

Thessa tried to convey her sympathy for him through her eyes but she could tell every look she gave him seemed only threatening. He flinched as she bent over him to unravel the ropes. Poor fellow.

"Up," she commanded.

He got to his feet hesitantly, the flesh of his missing muscle slapping against the wood floor—yet another thing she'd have to take care of in Wyna's stead. He paused as if he were unsure whether he was actually free to go. She pointed at the door and he took small steps towards it until she flung her hand out to catch his arm.

"This was your warning," she told him. "Punishment will be worse."

Wyna thanked Thessa under her breath as Thessa followed the second mate out to the parlor, making sure he left without trouble. It was only after the heavy wood of the doors thunked behind him that Thessa allowed herself to sink into the counter. Her wet clothes were starting to itch under the skirts she'd had to put back on for the walk back to the House. She smiled to herself when she realized what it might have looked like to the second mate. He had lost his tongue for his discussion of mermaids and then the Whips had shown up with wet hair and mostly dry clothes? Yet, even if he somehow found his voice again, no one would believe the mermaids he claimed to see were anything other than the girls from the peculiar brothel by the shore.

Thessa was sure of it.

Madame Orinna's voice snapped Thessa out of her thoughts. "My office. Please."

Thessa straightened and smoothed her skirts before following Madame Orinna back into her office. She made quick work of opening the secret chamber and ushering Thessa inside. This time, she inserted the key into a hole on the other side of the bookcase and it slammed into place behind them. Locked them in. It occurred to Thessa that she was one of very few that felt most comfortable in private with the Madame. There, she was free from the responsibility of acting as a role model for the other Whips.

Madame Orinna sank down into one of the high-backed wooden chairs sitting around the table and looked expectantly at Thessa. Thessa remained standing and began undoing her skirts again, eager to lose the extra weight, and waited for Madame Orinna to begin. She dared to hope Madame Orinna would tell her to accompany Wyna on the ship, as even playing nanny to one

Whip was surely better than mothering them all. But she knew better. She had lost her chance to go to sea.

"I have an assignment for you, as well," Madame Orinna said. "Related to Wyna's."

Or perhaps she hadn't lost her chance.

"Alastor Woolhill's status in Keresa cannot be overstated and I am sure you can see the victory it is to have Wyna on that ship. But that is not all he has agreed to. Not only is he considering a permanent position for the Whips on his voyages—should all go well—he has agreed to entertain our presence at his estate."

So. No ship.

"I think it would be wise to send you to his estate regularly," Madame Orinna continued. "Gain his trust. Get to know his staff —whether they can be trusted, what they know or do not know. The closer you grow to him, the more influence we might be able to have over his trade. Perhaps we could get our hands on his books without theft."

Thessa could see reason behind Madame Orinna's request but she held back a groan. It was an important assignment, to be sure, but Thessa couldn't help but feel her talents were better suited elsewhere. Of course, she couldn't say any of that. Not to Madame Orinna.

"Yes, Madame," she said instead.

"Wonderful! There is a bit more to it than that, naturally." Thessa did not hold back her groan this time. "Oh, hush. Woolhill has made some great concessions in our dealings but he doesn't want to commit to a partnership with us quite yet. Unfortunately, that means he would like to keep his reputation intact. He will not be visiting the House of Whips anytime soon and he would prefer the public not see a mermaid traipsing back and forth between here and his estate, despite my assurances that I'm sponsoring you, not employing you. To put it plainly, he still thinks you're a whore." The Madame swallowed pointedly. "But he doesn't want you to look like one."

"Meaning?"

"We're relocating you."

Thessa talked her heart down from soaring and dared to ask where. Keresa was small for a merching port but its peninsula shape allowed docks to cover every side. The House of Whips and its sister brothels existed at the point of the peninsula in the Sin District—after all, what better place was there to store pleasure? Thessa pulled up the maps of Keresa in her mind and pinpointed Woolhill's estate about halfway across the southern border of the peninsula. Her breath caught in her throat, a sense of doom settling over her as she remembered the seaside shack on the outskirts of the estate. Logically, there was no reason for Madame Orinna to say what Thessa thought she would and there was no reason Thessa should suspect.

But Thessa did suspect it.

And Madame Orinna said it.

"I've been in contact with a family on the outskirts of Wool-hill's estate and they graciously agreed to offer you room and board while you carry out this assignment."

"What family?" Thessa asked through gritted teeth.

"The Gillbridges."

Thessa flinched, a ruddy face covered in freckles flashing across her mind.

"I'm not oblivious to your history with them, Thessa." The words weren't quite consoling and the Madame wouldn't pretend them to be. "But they're good people and they're a convenient way in."

"Of course," Thessa nodded. She wasn't going to argue with Madame Orinna. There was no point in it. That didn't mean she had to be happy about any of this. "Whatever you need."

"I know where you would rather be," Madame Orinna sighed. "But I need you here. I need you for this. And I know I don't have to tell you to take this seriously."

"No, Madame," Thessa agreed and pulled out one of the chairs across from Madame Orinna. She sat. "What do I need to know?"

LORELAI AND SAMUAL GILLBRIDGE were lovely people, really. Samuel made an honest living loading the ships at the yards and supported his family on a modest wage that allowed them the comforts of their small home. They were kind-hearted and generous with what little they had and they had always welcomed Thessa with open arms. But the Thessa the Gillbridges knew was not the Thessa the Whips knew. Not even the Thessa that Keresa knew. They were unaware of her occupation and even more oblivious to what said occupation actually entailed. She felt guilty to have known them, for now she came only to soil their home and potentially their reputation.

Madame Orinna had told Thessa she'd not given the Gillbridges a name in their initial communications and the only detail the family knew was that the Whips were sending over a girl in need of lodging. Madame Orinna assured Thessa she had been vague enough in her wording that the Gillbridges could have easily assumed Madame Orinna was only turning away a potential employee. Thessa wondered if they'd told their son. Knots twisted her entrails at the thought. She hoped they hadn't. She wasn't sure if she could handle Huxley's reaction, no matter which way it leaned. Wanting her there would only make it harder but rejection was a quiet hurt. Thessa felt it daily but she had never quite built up a tolerance.

Madame Orinna dismissed Thessa to her room after a long discussion that quickly derailed from her assignment to helping Madame Orinna line up the other Whips for theirs. It felt as though hours had gone by when Thessa emerged from the office. The House was still quiet, save for the faint shuffle of Wyna floundering about in her room and singing songs to herself. Thessa almost turned to ask Madame Orinna if she could send Wyna downtown but she thought better of it. Wyna's ship was leaving quite early tomorrow and Thessa wasn't convinced the festivities would even be done by then.

She'd always felt like her room was in a private wing of the House, up the stairs and on the far left end, facing a stretch of beach rather than docks. It was a simple pleasure but it meant the world to her. She threw her skirts on the bed and stood over her chest of clothing with her hands on her hips. Hardly any of this would do. She would obviously need the trousers she hid under her skirts— she never dressed without them—but the rest of her clothing was everything that embodied the brothels. Madame Orinna would have no problem purchasing better clothes for the girls but cheaper, simpler fabrics didn't bring as much attention and Thessa knew the sailors could spot the quick-release skirts from a mile away. Dressing like the other ladies of Keresa would blow their cover.

It looked as though a shopping trip was in Thessa's future. She tried not to get too excited. Perhaps she couldn't escape into the waves of the Draca but at least she could dig into Madame Orinna's pockets for some new dresses. The other Whips would be jealous. Maybe Thessa could distribute them once her assignment was over.

There was nothing to be done about her wardrobe tonight so she resolved to packing only what she felt completely necessary. Getting to her knees next to her bed, she reached under and pulled out a folded swath of velvet. She opened it up for a peek at the beautifully-crafted daggers inside, making sure they were all accounted for. One of the slots in the case was empty but that was only because Thessa had tucked the smallest of the daggers under her breast. It was an emergency dagger.

So far, she hadn't run into any emergencies.

The daggers had been a gift from Madame Orinna when Thessa first started her role as second-in-command. They'd been a gift of good faith and a promise of the potential Madame Orinna insisted Thessa held. She told her they were just as beautiful as daggers should be for a girl like her and Thessa had thought it was a compliment. They were like a piece of gifted jewelry for a woman who was never meant to wed.

She had always wondered what it might feel like to be loved like that. It simply wasn't her place to know. Not now, at least.

She wrapped the daggers back up in their sleeve and shoved them into the bottom of the bag Madame Orinna had purchased for her years ago. Looking around her room, it wasn't hard to see that everything she had, she owed to Madame Orinna. She was the mother that had been robbed from Thessa and Thessa wouldn't trade her for the world.

She would never admit it aloud but Thessa was haunted by her history. It had been almost a decade since she had seen the blood fall out of her mother's stomach onto the sand but the colors were burned into her mind. She had been hiding under one of the docks, splashing privately in the freezing water, when she had heard the commotion. A man dragging a woman through the sand by the back of her neck, her hair wrapped tight around his fingers. Thessa'd heard the ripping of the hair from the scalp, even so far away. The woman hadn't made a sound. It'd been impossible to tell in the dark but Thessa wouldn't have been surprised if there weren't even tears falling down the woman's face.

The couple didn't fight. There was no screaming or shouting or accusations to cut through the air. There was only the calculated violence of the man and the shore. The primitive knife in the stomach. The detached rage of discarding the body in the sea. It was only when the man began walking up the beach, back to his home, that Thessa understood the couple to be her own parents. She never went back to her father but she never tried to find her mother, either. She had seen a tail in the waves as she stood and stared at the spot the woman had been dropped and Thessa, in all her youth, had convinced herself it was the silhouette of a starved creature feasting on her mother's corpse. But she found her way to the Whips anyhow, had survived on the hope that maybe there was something to the nickname, and Madame Orinna had shown her there was.

Thessa hadn't seen her mother since that night. Edonie had told her she'd left the others only a day after her death. Had vowed to rise above her desire for revenge. It had hurt Thessa to know her mother's bloodlust was stronger than her love for her daughter and she'd let Madame Orinna hold her while she cried for hours.

A child who would never be chosen.

She refused to cry about it now. There was no sense in shedding tears over those who would never shed them for her. She tried to grow detached from the atrocities she committed—hated how she reminded herself of her father. Every drop of blood was the blood of her mother's in her mind and, as much as she didn't want to care about the woman who had abandoned her, she couldn't help but mourn each man she killed. Their lives were in her hands and she squeezed them between her fingers until they darkened. Sometimes she fancied herself a sort of angel of death. Yet, when she recalled the faces of those she had let perish, she knew nothing about herself was angelic.

Thessa wasn't far enough into her musing to access the emptiness and the dread when those weighty wooden doors to the House flung open and the Whips poured in, their victims in tow. She decided then that this would be her night off. She wouldn't check the girls' work or correct any more mistakes. She would lock herself off from questions and requests for guidance. It was her night to prepare.

A crash and a yelp ruined her fantasy instantly and she pulled her skirts back on with a guttural groan she did not care if anyone heard.

A Whip's work was never finished.

CHAPTER FIVE

She wasn't convinced she'd closed her eyes that night at all.
Wyna had stared at her ceiling, envisioning fanciful
scenarios to fill up the blank spaces for hours until the dark
recesses of her room were bathed in Keresa's morning light. When
the first shadow disappeared, Wyna leapt from her bed, forgetting
entirely the pain of her ankle from the night previous. She never
had used the compress Thessa had retrieved for her.

A stinging joint was nothing to her now.

She was sealing her bag when a knock sounded at her door.
Not a closed fist of question, rather an open palm expecting the
door to give at its behest. Wyna flung the door open to see the
Madame hovering in the hallway. She had in her hands a bundle
of black velvet though it was nothing so big as a new ensemble.

"For you," Madame Orinna said, extending the bundle to
Wyna. "An assignment like this requires some tools of your own."

Wyna accepted the bundle without hesitation and rushed it
over to her unmade bed to uncover whatever was held inside.
Madame Orinna followed her into the room, nudging the door
closed behind her, as Wyna undid the ties with the nimble fingers
of the thief she would never admit to being. Falling open, the

fabric unshrouded a set of weapons. She let herself feel special for only a moment, let herself believe Madame Orinna didn't do this for all her girls, even though Wyna had seen velvet cases tucked around the House where the girls thought no one else might find them. She forced herself to get over the sting of *not* being special and instead told herself to be thrilled Madame Orinna would give her anything at all.

The weapons were breathtaking. There were two of them—sisters, clearly, but not twins. Each hilt had its own design, carved meticulously in heavy wood. Wyna half expected to see the scales of a mermaid but she knew the Madame would never be so conspicuous. Instead, each had its own rendition of Dracan waves. Inset into the hilts were lightweight blades, jutting out before curving into semi-circles. The tips were narrow, pointed like needles. She imagined setting the sickles into an enemy's neck, pinning them against the wall by their throat. She did not need to pick them up to feel their power.

She may not be a pirate—like in her many fantasies—but these blades went a long way towards helping her feel like one.

"Thank you," Wyna breathed out.

"A Whip must have her weapons," Madame Orinna told her. And Wyna didn't need her to say any more to understand.

"I'm honored to be one."

Madame Orinna nodded and retreated, leaving Wyna alone with her new toys. Not wanting to see them ruined before ever being put to use, she took painstaking measures to place them back into their velvet homes. Her pinky brushed against a bulge in the pocket where a hilt was meant to go.

Maybe she was special, after all.

Inside the pouch was a cinched cloth bag and Wyna didn't need to pull it out all the way to know what was inside. The scent of herbs hit her nose and with it came flushing cheeks. Wyna appreciated Madame Orinna's dedication to making sure her girls were safe—truly, she did—but she couldn't help but feel agitated Madame Orinna would assume she was so easily given to distractions. Wyna wasn't going to board this boat simply to flirt with a sailor or two. She was going to do a job and she was more than determined to do it well.

No distractions.

Of course, that didn't mean she took the herbs out of the velvet case.

She was out the door as soon as the sickles were tucked into her bag. Thessa stood by the front entrance, posture perfect in Madame Orinna's presence. Wyna didn't think Thessa did it to impress the older woman—she did it because she seemed to hold herself to an impossibly high standard and wasn't about to let anyone else have reason to doubt her. Wyna straightened her back to match Thessa, the bubbles between her bones popping loudly and giving her away.

Madame Orinna smiled tightly. "I presume you're set."

It wasn't a question.

"Yes," Wyna answered. "Are you walking me to the harbor?"

She felt silly to ask, like a child hopeful to have their parent's guidance. It was necessary though, considering most of Keresa's perimeter was harbor. And though Wyna was sure she could find it, it would save her a lot of time if the Madame just delivered her directly to the ship.

Madame Orinna nodded. "Thessa and I will accompany you until the ship departs."

Wyna glanced down for the first time and noticed the bag at Thessa's feet. Clearly, Wyna's mission was not the only one that required a departure from the Whips. She was wise enough to know the news she'd received the night prior was likely the extent of the information she needed, though. She was back to no questions.

When the doors slammed behind them, it occurred to her she should be sad to leave the other Whips behind without goodbyes. They were the closest she had to friends and to family. But she had to remember she wasn't leaving them behind forever. Only until she could come back, knowing she had kept them and their secrets safe.

She didn't anticipate the walk to her ship to be so long. Most ships preferred to dock just west of the tip of Keresa's peninsula—it was why the Sin District had started there. But Woolhill preferred his ships to dock and depart as close to his estate as the Draca would allow. Unfortunately, that meant the women had quite the journey ahead of them. Thessa suggested walking along the edge of the peninsula. Madame Orinna only smiled and told the girls she had arranged other transportation as a buggy pulled up outside the House. It wasn't extravagant, by any means, but Wyna felt like royalty. What a privilege to not have to use her legs.

The thought had hardly formed in her mind before she felt the guilt of it. She wasn't so sure the mermaids would have the same opinions about the usage of legs.

Madame Orinna pitched her voice low when they were settled inside. "You'll have the most issues with the Crow. They'll be the first to see the mermaids and you'll probably be the last to know."

Wyna nodded.

"You'll also have to keep close watch on the captain. His quarters will offer the perfect view of the sea. That might mean keeping him busy and out of his quarters. You'll want to ask for a tour of the ship once you're aboard. If they oblige, great. If not, I know you're more than capable of making the tour yourself. Now, if you can give me a list of the most vulnerable points of the ship when you return, that would be great. Even better if you can draw a picture."

"I'm no artist, Madame."

"There's always one on board. Tell them you want it for posterity's sake. You can label it yourself."

Wyna was starting to feel overwhelmed by the task but she shook off the queasiness in her stomach. By the gods, she would not get seasick before she was even on the water. There was a reason Madame Orinna had chosen her for this. She spent the rest of the ride in silence, listening and gulping down whatever information she could get from the Madame. She didn't want to take the chance she might miss something useful.

"That's all I can give you for now, Miss Bryant." Wyna was startled by the formality. "I trust you have what you need."

"I do," she said confidently, though she was missing the actual feeling behind it.

The harbors on the southern side of Keresa were much more industrialized than on the north and Wyna could tell Woolhill spared no expense in his trading business. His shipyard was made up of the hard lines of the coming age, a smooth surface to contrast Keresa's crooked edges. The salt of the Draca didn't hit Wyna like it usually did here. She supposed she would have plenty of time to breathe it in in the weeks to come, time to let it seep through her skin into her bones. Madame Orinna whispered gently to Thessa before ushering Wyna out of the buggy and following. Thessa stayed. They made it only twenty paces before Wyna asked Madame Orinna if she could say goodbye.

When she swung open the door of the buggy, Wyna had enough sense to ignore the tear ambling down Thessa's cheek. "Thank you," she said. "I'll miss you."

Thessa, too, ignored the tear and flattened her lips in something like a smile. "I should only hope you have the time to miss us at all."

"I'll make you proud," Wyna told her. She wasn't sure why.

She couldn't read Madame Orinna's face when she fell in step beside her again and she wondered if she should feel embarrassed for that sudden swing of emotion. But she had seen the way Madame Orinna cared for Thessa. Wyna liked the think the Madame would have done the same.

She eyed the largest ship in Woolhill's fleet as she approached, suddenly feeling quite wary of her charge. But it was not bustling with the life of a vessel about to take to sea. Madame Orinna directed her attention to the next ship over—smaller, indeed, but still quite a lot to take on by herself. She would not let herself be cowed.

"The *Volia*," Madame Orinna announced. "Not his most beloved, to be sure. We'll work our way up to that. This one moves faster and has a smaller crew. I think it'll serve our needs quite beautifully."

"Yes," Wyna agreed, stifling the hurt that made its way into her skin with the announcement. She read between the lines of what Madame Orinna told her. The *Volia* wasn't chosen for Wyna's benefit; it was chosen because it was expendable. Easier to manage and therefore harder to ruin. Clearly, Madame Orinna's faith in her only went so far.

Wyna would prove her wrong.

"Do they know I'm coming?" she asked, refusing to take her eyes off the shuffling crew.

"Wollhill has assured me he's informed the captain. I can't assume he's told his men." Madame Orinna stepped in front of her, Wyna's eyes suddenly level with the cinch of Madame Orinna's skirts. She tipped her neck to meet her eyes. "Listen to me, Wyna. You have not earned their respect yet and I cannot promise you ever will. You are not boarding this ship to sit about and wait for a problem to occur. The problems will find you if they do. If not in the form of a sea creature, in the form of these men thinking they're entitled to you simply because you've entered their territory. Tell me—what do you do when you find yourself in someone else's territory?"

"You make it your own."

The answer came easily to her. She had heard Madame Orinna's rallies before the Whips left for a night in downtown Keresa. The city was not meant to be theirs but they would make it so.

"Good," Madame Orinna nodded. Then asked again, "You have what you need?"

"Yes."

"Then you are not mine to worry about any longer. Luck to you, Wyna."

"Luck," Wyna echoed, unsure of what endeavors she was wishing the Madame luck with.

She steeled herself, adjusting the bag slung across her shoulders and straightening her spine as she ascended the ramp that had been slapped on the dock from the ship. She soaked in the puzzled stares as she moved forward, reassuring herself no one would have the gall to stop her. She felt the buzz of victory as soon as her foot left the ramp and connected with the deck of the *Volia*.

"Oi!" A shout sounded from across the deck and a hefty man departed from a group of young sailors to make his way to Wyna. "You're Swither's girl?"

It took Wyna a moment to understand the man was referring to Madame Orinna, but in that moment she took the opportunity to assess with whom she was dealing. He wore the scarlet of Woolhill's estate in his coat, the buttons and the shoulders bearing the gold pins she'd come to recognize during her time as a Whip. She flicked a short glance to the pin on his lapel that labeled him Captain of the *Volia*.

"Yes, sir," Wyna said.

A sailor that had followed the captain over to Wyna whooped and clapped the man on his back. "You got us a mermaid, Cap?"

The captain shifted his weight. Wyna guessed he might be uncomfortable at having his crew display such friendliness towards their better in a woman's presence but any discomfort he felt was quickly drowned by the full force of his pride. He tugged on his lapels, a small, smug smile doing the same to his lips.

He turned away from Wyna slightly, tucking his thumb and his pointer finger between his lips before releasing a splitting whistle. The crew faced him like a well-trained pack of dogs.

"This mer—" he stumbled, an important man caught using the slang only those intimately familiar with the whore houses in Sin District would know. He corrected himself and continued. "This Whip will be accompanying us on route. Orinna Swither has been so kind as to lend us one of her girls for the journey and we will not do a thing to compromise a Whip's presence on any future voyages. You can thank our employer for this luxury."

Wyna wasn't so sure why he even bothered to correct himself

after calling her a mermaid if his speech made it clear why she was on this ship—made it clear he had intentions to partake. She bit her tongue. She wouldn't undermine his power so soon.

The captain gave her his full attention once more. "I captain the *Volia* but you needn't address me by any titles as my men are instructed to." He paused, letting the friendly sailor know his stance before baring his teeth to Wyna in a confusing sort of smile. "I'm called Felix but I expect you'll call me whatever you'd like. Whenever you'd like."

Wyna took his extended hand. "Felix," she repeated with a nod. He seemed elated by the contact and she wondered how long it must've been since a woman gave him any sort of touch without promise of immediate payment.

"I presume you'd like to make acquaintances with our crew?"

Wyna knew this was the moment to craft herself aboard this ship. She didn't have to be a Whip that was still learning the ropes. She didn't have to be the girl who'd never dealt the finishing blow. The one whose insides roiled at the thought of it. She could be the strongest version of herself, not tied down to who she'd been or what she knew. The opportunity for reinvention had already been handed to her on a silver platter once when she'd been left for dead in the middle of Keresa without a home, without a family, without any title other than the name she'd heard people call her.

She wasn't about to let it go again.

"I'd like to see my quarters first," she told him, a demand hiding conspicuously behind her polite tone. "Be rid of this bag."

Felix jumped to remove the bag from her shoulder and she flinched when she heard the tiniest clink of her sickles as their tips met in the movement. Felix didn't notice, too distracted by the outline of her body under the clothes, now unaddled by the weight of her belongings. Wyna ignored the feeling of nakedness.

"We've displaced an officer for you...I'm sorry, I didn't quite catch your name."

"Wyna," she told him, kicking herself for not having the time nor the guts to come up with a lie.

"Ah, well, we've moved an officer to the crew quarters. Puts you closer to me and farther from the rest of this unsavory lot," he said with a laugh. "Not that I—I just meant that you might find it more comfortable to put the men to work if they wish to seek you out. If a sailor finds that something comes easily to him, he'll never work as hard. Can't breed lazy on the *Volia*. Woolhill'd never stand for it."

She let Felix ramble as he led her below deck into the dark. Away from the others and away from people. She wasn't sure why she would feel safer to be above deck among these men, especially when these men were the only other souls around and especially when it seemed their leader worked to craft their habits. The tension in her muscles tightened with each step they took until Felix used his elbow to turn the knob of the door and shoulder it open.

The quarters weren't large and Wyna shouldn't have expected them to be—not on a ship the size of the *Volia* and not in quarters meant for men who were supposed to be working. She couldn't quite quell the thirst for luxury, though, even if she'd never known it. Felix dropped her bag onto the cot and Wyna sidestepped the brush of his body as he retreated back into the doorway. He watched her, the mud of his eyes exposing his expectations. She let him believe she was either oblivious or simply didn't care.

"If I could take a moment to get used to the water, I'd be quite grateful." She hoped he was too distracted by the empty promise of her words to mention how they hadn't left the harbor yet.

"Of course," Felix said, bowing out of the room.

Wyna wondered how long this act would last. How long until he dropped the guise of the gracious captain and began to treat Wyna how so many thought her kind deserved? She shook off her concerns even while the swirls of dread danced around her organs, tangling them and making her feel sick. She knew she only had these short moments to herself before she would have to show her face on deck, meet the sailors, and pretend she wasn't only here to protect a secret.

It was only when she opened the door to her quarters to see the gathered faces of hungry men that she truly felt the weight of what Madame Orinna had asked her to do.

CHAPTER SIX

Thessa was sure to rid herself of the signs of tears well before Madame Orinna returned. She couldn't say why she was crying, really, and didn't want to bother parsing it out if it didn't matter anyway. All that mattered was doing what Madame Orinna needed her to and she would without complaint. Verbal complaint, at least.

She knew she hadn't given Wyna the goodbye the girl wanted and she felt sorry for it. Selfish. But there was nothing to be done about it now and Thessa was fairly certain Wyna was more than capable of handling herself aboard a ship so long as no one's fingers needed breaking. Regardless, no matter how confident Thessa was in Wyna's abilities, she had been unsuccessful in ridding herself of the jealousy. Every piece of advice Madame Orinna had offered the girl on the ride over was knowledge she wished she could have hoarded for herself.

Thessa schooled her expression when Madame Orinna finally yanked open the creaking door. The older woman clapped the side of the buggy as she settled in and they were off again. The ride this time would be much shorter and Thessa wished she could think of a reason to go back home first.

She couldn't.

They'd only gotten halfway around Woolhill's estate, riding the edge that bordered Keresa's shopping district, when Madame Orinna tapped the side of the buggy. Thessa's body jerked forward at the abrupt stop. The Madame's remained stable.

"I'll return in a moment," she told her, leaving Thessa alone once more.

The delay was welcome and Thessa felt the overwhelming urge to make something of the moments she had been given to herself. She ran through the possibilities in her head but Madame Orinna was back in the buggy before Thessa was able to land on anything suitable.

"I think you'll require these," Madame Orinna said, extending a bundle to Thessa and gesturing for her to stash them away in her bag. Thessa recognized the seal on the ribbon as belonging to a high-end clothier that usually specialized in preparing Keresan ladies for courting season. She thanked the Madame, hiding her excitement. "They should serve you as well as anything else but if you run into any issues with the fit, please send word."

"Thank you, Madame," Thessa repeated.

"I am sorry it had to be the Gillbridges."

The sentiment pinched at her and she wanted to scream that Madame Orinna had made the choice, that it could have been any family. But the argument was tired and silly so Thessa only said, "I will survive it."

"As you do. I mentioned it briefly last night—I'm not sure if you remember, what with all the emotions about your lodging— but I find myself wary of a member of Woolhill's household." Thessa nodded and tried not to be offended at the suggestion of her failing memory. She'd never let *anything* distract her from her duty. "Campbell Moore is the name. Untrusting of anyone who dares get too close to Woolhill. Thinks every visitor wants to take him away."

"Will I be taking Woolhill away?"

"No," Madame Orinna assured her. "He thinks I'm sending some good-faith ward to facilitate a relationship between our industries. But, do keep in mind his recent loss. I would not be surprised if he confused your business venture with a romantic one."

Thessa was floored. "Madame, am I courting Alastor Woolhill?"

"Don't be silly," Madame Orinna laughed, knowing it was unlike Thessa to be silly at all. "But to anyone else, surely it will look to be so."

"And what am I to do? Go along with it? Shut it down?" Her chest grew hot, panic swimming up from her veins. "Will Campbell have me removed from the estate as soon as I walk through the doors?"

"Thessa, I wish I could give you those answers. But my meetings with Woolhill have been brief and every ounce of information I have about the inside of his estate has come from Sabina's trysts with Cecil. I cannot guarantee what you might face in these meetings. I've only set them up."

That only made her stomach turn more. Last night, she'd assumed this job to be the easiest she'd ever perform. How foolish it was to think she had been offered something easy. Not only was she going to have to avoid the Gillbridges' inevitable probing questions, she was now also responsible for fighting off Woolhill's staff for a chance to speak with him. How was she meant to find out what he knew about their friends in the sea if there were eyes and ears attuned to every conversation they had? An aging man she could convince was misremembering, but an entire estate?

They had just swung the last corner of Woolhill's property and Thessa had taken to wringing her fingers in ugly anticipation of what she was meant to accomplish.

"There's just one more thing," Madame Orinna said as they approached the Gillbridge home. Thessa choked. "I'd like to know if there's any truth to the gossip I've heard around the District."

"What are they saying?"

Madame Orinna's response was cut off by the door of the

buggy slamming open, its hinges practically ripped apart. Samuel Gillbridge stood outside, flinching at the noise he had made.

"Madame Swither! Forgive me," he boomed, the dialect of his district dripping out in his warm voice. "We just couldn't help ourselves when we saw you was pulling up!"

Thessa resisted the urge to peer around Madame Orinna at the "we" Samuel referred to. The longer she could stay out of sight, the longer she could feel like her breath came to her naturally.

"Oh, that's quite alright, Mr. Gillbridge. Consider our excitement matched." The Madame faked a darkening of her mood and her tone. "Thank you again for your immense hospitality. I only wish I could offer Miss Clemen the same. Surely you understand that I wouldn't have left her with you if I had any choice? It's just that I must keep my rooms for my employees."

"Miss Clemen?" A feminine voice sounded from behind Samuel. "Thessa Clemen?"

"Why, yes!" Madame Orinna exclaimed. "You know of her?"

Thessa watched Lorelai push her way around her husband, a star twinkling in her pale eyes. "Know of her? We adore her!"

Lorelai reached out for Madame Orinna's arm and used what little might she possessed to try and wrangle the woman out of the buggy. All to get to Thessa that much quicker. Madame Orinna let Lorelai test her strength before exiting the vehicle of her own accord. Finally, Thessa was face-to-face with the dreaded Gillbridges.

Still, she let a smile lift her features.

Lorelai dove into the buggy, landing half on Thessa's lap with her feet hanging out. She squeezed Thessa and Thessa was surprised at the power behind her grip, wondering if perhaps it wouldn't have been so much of a feat to pull Madame Orinna from the car, if only Lorelai was determined enough. Thessa patted Lorelai awkwardly on her back until Lorelai scooted back out of the buggy and beamed at her from the road.

"If we'd only known it was you," Samuel began as Thessa

finally existed, her bag thunking against her hip as she dropped to the ground. "We'd have let Huxley know to stick around."

"He's gone?" Thessa spoke for the first time and hoped they could not hear the relief in her question. How much she wanted him to be gone.

"'Fraid so," Samuel shook his head. "We sent him downtown to the market to gather up a few things now there's another mouth to feed."

Thessa wanted to kick something but she thought better of it and dug the toe of her boot into the dirt. Once again, she had dared to hope. How many times would she make that mistake?

"Ah! I appreciate your reminder," Madame Orinna told Samuel, pulling his gaze off Thessa. She reached into the stitched pockets of her skirts and produced a pouch. "I may not be able to house the girl but I won't hesitate to pay her way."

Madame Orinna tucked her arm in Samuel's and led them apart from the group to further delve into the discussion of payment. Thessa heard him refuse the coin and heard Madame Orinna refuse his refusal. Her cheeks flushed as she then heard Madame Orinna's ramblings about getting Thessa into the Woolhill estate and how Thessa would be out of their home in a fortnight or so.

"Let's get you inside, shall we?" Lorelai asked, attaching herself to Thessa in much the same way Madame Orinna had just done to the woman's husband. "But before you even step foot through that door, I must have answers, young lady."

"Answers?"

"Where on earth have you been?" Lorelai demanded and stopped Thessa in her tracks. She adjusted her body so she faced her, though Lorelai had to bend her neck backwards to look into Thessa's eyes. "Whatever Huxley's done to keep you away for so long...is there nothing we can do to solve the issue?"

Thessa softened to Lorelai. None of this had been Lorelai's fault and if she was going to be staying with the family, it was high time she got over her discomfort.

"I've been trying to make a living, Mrs. Gillbridge and I know Huxley's been doing the same. Seeing as neither of us seemed to be having much luck, it wasn't time for, um, those sorts of distractions."

Lorelai resumed her walking and turned her attention away from Thessa, whispering under her breath. Forgetting entirely that whispers were meant to be quiet. "Luck'll be changing soon enough."

Thessa's boots were sinking into the beginnings of sand before they reached the house. Really, calling the structure a house was entirely too generous, as the rickety sides and small size made it look much more like a wayside shack. Even so, the Gillbridges' house was plenty big for their purposes and Thessa knew Lorelai liked to spend her afternoons strolling the beach anyway. She didn't need to offer a tour, didn't need to bother with formalities. Instead, Lorelai just nodded her head in the direction of what Thessa had predicted would be her room and walked away.

She'd only just set down her bag when Madame Orinna knocked to announce her presence. "I'll be heading back now," she told her before lowering her voice. "Luck to you and keep your visits to the House at a minimum."

"Luck," Thessa repeated, the response instinct. "But, Madame—"

The Madame was gone, leaving Thessa with a lot of questions and even more worry. She still wasn't sure what rumors she was meant to verify. What if it was something as simple as a new pet at the estate and Thessa didn't think it was important enough to report back? She plopped on the creaking bed and wrung her hands together in her lap. The idleness clawed at her, though, so she jumped to her feet and spent her time unpacking the entirety of her belongings and tidying up the room until she heard chatter in the kitchen.

"Is she here?" a voice asked. One she knew. One she had once liked hearing moan her name. She was frustratingly delighted by the anticipation in his voice until she remembered he would have no idea it was her cooped up in this room. He thought Madame Orinna had simply dropped a young woman off at his door and he was excited by the prospect of meeting her.

A new match for him, perhaps?

"Yes," Lorelai responded. Thessa could hear her satisfaction. "You'll be surprised to find a familiar face, I think."

"Familiar?"

"*Intimately* familiar, I'd say."

Thessa's eyes widened from her stance at the door. So, Lorelai wasn't as oblivious to their relationship as she'd seemed.

"You mean—?"

Thessa retreated, expecting him to shoulder his way through in mere seconds, itching to see her for himself. She wanted to act like she hadn't been listening, like his presence was the furthest thing from a bother to her. She wanted to act like he didn't matter. Like her heart didn't contract whenever she thought about him and what she wasn't able to give.

The door didn't open and Huxley did not come bursting through for her. Not right away. Thessa sat on that bed for hours, tracing the path of a spider web that reached from the upper corner of the room to the window. She knew it was rude to stay locked away, away from the Gillbridges and their smiling faces. Madame Orinna wouldn't be pleased. But Madame Orinna wasn't here. She had dropped Thessa off at the epicenter of her pain and—

She should really go out there.

Straightening her skirts, she realized she probably should have changed into one of the pieces Madame Orinna had procured for her. She'd just count on the Gillbridges' innocence. Surely, they wouldn't be so acquainted with the fashion of whores. And besides, she needed to save her new wardrobe for Woolhill.

Lorelai grinned at her from the basin that acted as their kitchen sink when Thessa emerged. "You must have needed that rest," she said, politeness weaving through her tone. Thessa didn't think Lorelai actually thought she'd been sleeping.

"Yes," Thessa said anyway.

She cast anxious glances around the common area, holding her breath so she wouldn't be caught by surprise when she finally saw Huxley's face. He wasn't there.

"No worryin'," Lorelai said. "He's not run out again. Just popped into his room for a moment."

"Oh, I wasn't—"

"Yes, you were. And that's alright. You two've got some unfinished business to handle, I'd think. Go on." Lorelai pretended to whip her towel at Thessa.

Her knock on Huxley's door was strong, offering him no sign of her quickening pulse and no indication she wanted to escape to the Draca. When the door did swing open, Thessa was surprised to find that Huxley's face was not how she'd left it. The ruddy-faced, freckled boy she had once known had been replaced. Or—not replaced but somehow sharpened and defined. His jaw had an edge she hadn't seen on him before. His clothes, a tightness she'd never thought he'd achieve. But it wasn't just the shape of his body that had been altered. It was the stance and the atmosphere of his presence. While her Huxley had always felt like a cushion of safety, this one made her feel as if there was more to him than simply a kind heart.

She wasn't sure why she felt this way now. Thessa was no stranger to the parts of him that were twinged in desire. It was only that, this time, his body seemed an outward reflection of it all.

Mostly, though, she was surprised to find him with a smile.

"Thessa," he breathed—even his voice taking on this new quality. He scooped her off her feet into an embrace. "You look... well, like you've always looked, I guess."

She pulled out of his arms, disappointed by his words, knowing now that he had been given the space and opportunity to grow once she was gone but she had remained the same. He was not taken aback by her, as she had just been by him, and that only served to deepen the downward turn of her lips.

"Not that there's anything wrong with looking the same!" Huxley rushed to explain. "That is, you look beautiful. Always have."

"Thank you," she said slowly. "You mother thought we should talk. I'm inclined to agree."

"Yes, of course." He ushered her into his bedroom. She had the unsettling thought that she would be able to navigate this space even on the darkest of nights. In fact, she had. "Ma didn't tell me it was gonna be you."

"I don't think she knew, Huxley. I didn't—not until last night."

"Why is it you?" he asked her. "What business do you have with Orinna Swither?"

She ignored the accusation in his voice. "I was just looking for work," she lied. "Same as you. She turned me away. Felt sorry for me, I guess."

"If you were having trouble, you should have come to us first! I shouldn't only be hearing about it after you've tried to strike a contract over in the District."

"How is that your business anymore?"

"You're the only reason it isn't, Thessa. I would have had you here in a heartbeat if it was what you wanted."

Thessa wrinkled her nose, trying to rid herself of the tightness behind her face. The one that told her she was about to start crying. She hated to lie to him. Hated it from the very moment she met him and knew he could never know who she was. She wanted to tell him that being here had been the very thing she *didn't* want.

It would only make him ask more questions when wanting didn't turn out to be enough. It had broken his heart, the first time she'd ended it. She hated to be forced to do it again.

"It isn't what I wanted," she told him anyway. "This isn't what I want."

"Then why are you here?"

"I'm here because this is where Madame Orinna put me." She

wanted to laugh at the truth of the words that Huxley would never know. "So I'll be here until she says I can go."

"Ma says you're lined up with meetings at the Woolhill estate."

"Yes."

"Is it some kind of interview—?" Understanding settled into his brows as he flitted his eyes to meet Thessa's. "That's why you're here? To get closer to him? Closer to that?"

She didn't answer, all out of truths.

"Gods, you couldn't have picked another family to help you get rich? That's not who I thought you were."

Perhaps there was another truth inside her.

"You don't know who I am," Thessa said. And she meant it.

CHAPTER SEVEN

Wyna wasn't sure how many sets of eyes stared at her from the hallway but she was afraid to count. Too many. She met their gazes with a confidence she wasn't sure she had until they finally spoke.

"What House?" one of the sailors asked.

"The Whips," she answered without hesitation.

The answer seemed to please the sailor and a grin settled over his sun-soaked face. Another one Wyna couldn't see piped up behind them. "Oh, I've heard they're positively bad."

"Only if you mean dangerous," another disembodied voice chimed in. "Have you seen the state of some of their patrons? They go in a whole man and come out in pieces!"

"I'd let her tear me to pieces at any time of day."

"I'd return the favor."

"Is she new? Haven't seen her 'round the District."

"Spend an awful lot of time in the District, do ya? Memorize all their faces?"

"Their faces ain't what's needing memorized."

"As if we haven't all taken a tumble into the Houses a time or two."

"'Cordin' to the wife, I haven't!"

"Oi, I'll keep the wife busy while you're running 'round the District, if you please."

"You won't lay a hand on 'er!"

"Bet that's what she says about the whores."

Violence crashed through the hallway, a few of the men's voices fading as they wrestled each other to the deck of the ship. She found herself relaxing slightly, now that she knew she was left with fewer men than before. But there were still too many gazing at her through the doorway.

"Now, lads, let's think about this logically. We can all have a go at some point but never too many at a time or the Houses won't let us bring another on."

One of them scoffed. "Woolhill's pockets are plenty deep to afford another." He turned, enough so Wyna could see his face. He had dark hair, shorn closely to his skull, and she noticed a knick taken out of one of his ears. The intensity of his black eyes scared her. "What's he paid for? All access?"

Wyna stumbled and pretended it was sea legs. She wasn't prepared for the question and was unsure of how Madame Orinna might have instructed her to answer. She decided to push her luck. "He's left me with the choice," she told them, then added, "Overheard him tell Madame if I don't make it back in pristine condition, he'll dock the dee from all your pay."

A few of the sailors groaned and stalked off. Wyna was glad to be rid of them. The sailor with the dark eyes stepped into her room, his chest suddenly too close to her for her liking.

"I'll make your choice for her," he purred at her. At least, she thought he tried to. The effect was more guttural.

Wyna decided to match his energy and took a step towards him, pressing herself into his chest in a way she hoped was imposing. "Like hell you will."

In her proximity, she lifted something from his pocket and tucked it into the waist of her skirts. She was unsure exactly what it was but she was thrilled to know he wouldn't have it anymore. The sailor didn't back down.

"That so?" he sneered. "At your size, it feels like your choice is to either go with it or throw a fit."

She laughed, making impressive work of pretending she wasn't frightened. She slid her hand along his trousers until she reached his crotch, giving it a gentle squeeze until she tightened her grip. "Right now," she said, "it seems like I have the power to make *your* choices. You either get out of my room, or I—"

A hand ripped the sailor from her. "Get off her, would you, Zachariah? What are you? An animal?"

The newcomer shoved Zachariah out of the room and turned to face whatever men remained, giving Wyna the back of his shaggy blond head.

"I think this one's mine," he told them. "Better luck with the next."

This declaration received a chorus of dissent from the other men. "You can't hog her! We've only got one!"

"I can hog her and I will. All night long if I have to. The whole time we're on the ship. Doesn't matter—I'm staking my claim."

"You can't—" Wyna tried to interrupt the sailor but he shushed her to address the protests coming from his compatriots. She narrowed her eyes.

"Felix isn't gonna like this."

"I don't give a shit what Felix likes. He knows a man's territory when he sees it."

"He's the captain!"

"And?" The muscles in the sailor's back pulled at each other as he crossed his arms over his chest. "We're done here."

He backed into the room, slamming the door shut with a dramatic thud and turned to face Wyna, a hyena's grin threatening to split his gorgeous lips. "Well?"

"Well, what?" she demanded, practically roiling now that he'd deigned to let her speak. "You have no more right to me than any of them."

"Oh, that? No worries, love. Won't touch you until you beg

me to. These guys don't respect anyone until they've earned it. Staking a claim on a Whip? That's earning it."

She was skeptical, wondering if this were some kind of game he was playing to earn her trust. But she also couldn't deny the dread Zachariah had woken up in her. She could pretend she had what it took to fight his advances but she remembered the second mate she'd had issues with only the night before. Then, she imagined what might've happened if she tried to take on a dozen of those second mates at a time. Perhaps this sailor's ego trip would benefit her in the end.

"They'll leave me alone?" she asked. "Because they're scared of you?"

He flopped onto her bed, bringing his arms up and crossing them behind his head. She saw that his eyes were the same color as some of the cedar planks of the ship and begrudgingly admitted to herself that the color paired nicely with the sand of his hair. It reminded her of the pier behind the House, midday in the height of summer. She wasn't sure if it was nostalgia tickling her insides or something else entirely. "That's the plan."

"And what will the captain say?"

"Felix? Ah, much as he wants ya, he'll back off if someone's gotten to you first. Kinda old-fashioned like that."

"And you're someone that's gotten to me first?"

"I am the first—and only—one in your bed, am I not?" He raised his eyebrow at her in a challenge, shooting it underneath the sweep of his hair.

"And here I don't even know your name."

"Do you know the names of all the men you let into your bed?"

She thought she might list all the names of the men she'd harmed while they were trapped in her room but she thought better of it. She didn't want to be connected to them. Instead she said, "I'm not sure if that's your business."

"Hey now, I'm just trying to get to know my girl for the next few weeks."

She marched over to the bed and took his ankles in her hands, throwing them to the floor before dropping onto the thin mattress beside him. "I'm not your girl. Not in any true sense of the word."

"That's not what they think," he said, nodding to the closed door.

"And that was your first mistake," she told him triumphantly.

"How's that?"

"You've given me the power to tell all your little friends about the mediocrity of your manhood. Not to mention, if I decide I like any of them better, they get the pleasure of thinking they've outwitted you—that they've won."

He only laughed. "You're evil!"

"And you're arrogant."

"That's not a bad thing." The sailor sat up, leveling his face with Wyna's.

"I can't wait for someone to prove you wrong."

"Are you that someone?"

"I should be so lucky."

"You could make me lucky, if you wanted."

"I don't know you. Don't know if you deserve luck."

"Do I deserve you?" he asked.

"No."

"That's probably true." The sailor got to his feet and turned to face Wyna. forced her to look up to see his face. "Tell me something."

She feigned disinterest. "What?"

"What've you taken from Zachariah?"

Her cheeks flushed, horrified at having been caught thieving. Madame Orinna would have her head. Had she already made a mess of this? Before they even got out to sea?

"I don't know what you mean," she told him, standing in an effort to make him retreat. Give her some space.

It didn't work. The sailor held his ground, letting his chest bump Wyna ever-so-slightly with his intake of breath. He reached his arm around her body and Wyna feared he would pull her even closer before she felt the pressure of his fingers sliding into the waist of her skirts. He only swiped the object she'd stolen from Zachariah with ease and Wyna saw that it was only a weathered brass astrolabe.

"Uh oh. I think we might need this," he sang. "You can't just go around putting your hands on whatever you'd like. Unless you like me—then you can put your hands wherever."

"Around your throat?"

"Dirty," he gasped.

"Watch your mouth."

"Rather watch yours." She stared. "Saying my name, of course."

"But you won't tell me your name."

He stuck out his hand like an eager boy, ready to impress. "Brennan Friswell. At your service, love."

She let his hand hang between them. "At my service?"

He glanced at her mouth and shoved his outstretched hand into his pocket. "Indeed."

"Then get out of my room, Brennan," Wyna said, the saccharine quality of her voice impressing even her. She found herself surprised by how much she liked the feel of his name pushing through her lips.

"It's only fair I get your name as well, love."

"Seems you've already picked a name for me."

"You're sorely mistaken," Brennan told her. "That's just what I want to do to you."

"Charming."

"Indeed. Your name?" He asked again.

"Wyna."

"How fitting!" He placed his hands over his heart, clutching at his chest as he pretended to swoon. "Always a winna' when I'm with you."

Wyna bit her lip to keep from laughing at his sad excuse for a joke. She shook off the impression that she liked being around him and decided to focus instead on the qualities she wasn't particularly fond of. His arrogance, his presumptions. The fact that she couldn't be sure if any of those disturbing words exchanged earlier hadn't come from his mouth.

"Not one for puns?" he asked, frowning.

"Not one for those who overstay their welcome."

Brennan threw his shoulders up and down in a sigh. "I suppose you're right. I can't use up all my time here on our first meeting. What'll be left when you finally decide you want me?"

"Goodbye, Brennan."

"Say it again," he begged as she opened the door, ruffling his hair and grabbing his tunic here and there to produce some wrinkles.

"Goodbye," she said and slammed the door in his face.

She heard his audible moan through the wood.

WYNA HAD to catch her breath before she emerged from her room. She told herself it was to prepare. Really, she just had to psych herself up. But every time she laid a hand on the door, she recoiled like it'd burned her. It was a vicious cycle and one that, unfortunately, lasted until morning. When she did emerge, her sickles a comfort tucked away, she sought out Felix immediately. She wanted to believe Brennan's ruse might be enough to keep the other sailors away from her for the journey but she wanted to be sure the crew saw her parading around with the captain as well.

Wyna had terrible timing.

The ship, somehow, was only just now leaving Keresa and Felix was much too busy at the helm to give Wyna her welcoming tour. Though she was confident Brennan would have stepped up at her request, she'd be damned if she ever had to ask anything of him.

No, she would give herself the tour.

She made a show of slinking back to her cabin, ensuring they'd all believe she was uninterested in the workings of the ship. Not that any of them seemed to notice, too caught up in their tasks.

Perfect.

Wyna wound her way back down the hallway, climbing not all the way up to the deck but one storey up to the captain's quarters. His cabin was massive compared to Wyna's. She supposed it paid to be important. He had candles set around the room, perched in weighted bases to keep them from sliding about on surfaces as the sea shuffled the ship. He'd have no need for them at this time of day as the windows over the desk provided him as much as light as he could never need. Wyna did her due diligence in checking the rest of the room—noting a small, unimpressive cot much like her own and a few rifles and swords locked in a glass cabinet above it —before heading directly for the desk.

Her eyes skimmed over nautical maps, maps of cities they planned to port, and numerous copied lists of all the cargo they were keeping below deck, as well as a document that detailed the ration logistics for every member of the crew. Wyna frowned when she saw that whoever had drawn up this document had decreased her portion size. Perhaps she could pilfer some of Zachariah's. Or Brennan's.

Not finding anything of interest, she moved onto the shelves Felix had behind the desk, on either side of the windows. She saw that one of the shelves had been crudely labeled "scrap," the other "smooth." She racked her brain to try and parse out what that could mean, very badly wishing she had had time to ask Madame Orinna more questions.

Gods, she probably wouldn't have even known what to ask.

The shelves had had a simple bar installed across the front of each tier. It made getting the items on and off the shelf a bit more cumbersome but Wyna understood this kept Felix's quarters quite tidy if they might hit the larger waves or, gods forbid, a storm. She maneuvered one of the logbooks from the scrap shelf and thumbed through it. The words and the numbers blurred together before her, appearing to her to be completely in order. One by one, she took the logs from the scrap shelf and, one by one, they provided no interest to her.

A shout above deck drove her eyes to the door, a bolt of anxiety launching through her in anticipation of Felix finding her in his cabin. As long as she was careful, she could perhaps pretend only to be waiting patiently for his return, a beautifully-clad reward for successfully departing from Keresa. But no one came down and she went back to her investigation with new vigor.

The last of the logbooks on the scrap shelf was a tiny, flimsy thing. Its pages were wrapped in what was likely the softest leather Wyna'd ever touched. When she opened it, she was delighted to find its pages blank and decided it would be a perfect record-keeper for her assignment—her very own logs.

Tucking the journal into her waistband, she moved onto the "smooth" shelf and set to work on their contents. It was only after the third book, when the numbing deja vu seemed less due to the nature of the content and more to the content itself, that she came to an understanding: the logbooks on this shelf were merely tidy, updated replicas of the ones on the previous shelf. She suppressed a groan, having hoped to find something scandalous to report back to the Madame but Felix clearly wasn't the type to skim the books. Still, she went through the remainder of the logs on the off-chance she might find a mention of a beauty with a tail.

No such luck.

The more she considered, she supposed the *Volia* had already been docked in Keresa for a few days. Madame Orinna had probably already sent the Whips out to check on his books. It was now Wyna's job to make sure nothing otherworldly was added in.

Rummaging around the captain's quarters further offered her nothing and, eventually, she returned to his desk to set about finding a bit of graphite she could use for her log. As she reached for the drawer, the ship lurched, sending her off balance and into the desk. Her elbow caught the corner and she bit her tongue to keep from crying out. When she attempted to rest her aching arm on the desk for some kind or relief, the maps and plans shifted, revealing the weathered wood beneath.

A deep scratch in the desk snared her attention. Felix wasn't, she thought, a gentle man but she didn't peg him to be so careless with his things. Feeling silly—convincing herself the scratch was likely the result of a similar such accident as she'd just had, even while her fingers moved forward—Wyna reached to shift the papers.

So it was not a scratch, then, but a rough-hewn image carved into the desktop.

Her heart stopped, remembering the image on the table in Madame Orinna's secret chambers. This, it seemed, was a rushed replica of that work. The tail popping from the waves, the faintest etch of scales. Questions blurred across her vision. Did Felix know? Did anyone else? If not, why hadn't he told? Was he a danger?

Would Wyna have to kill him?

"No." The word restarted the beating of Wyna's heart and before she could even register the speaker or how he had read her mind, she shifted the papers on the desk to conceal the image. She blinked, her eyes returning to the world around her. Brennan stood in the doorway, halfway between shame at being caught and glee at catching her. "What a naughty little mermaid," he cooed, slinking the door shut behind him.

"What?" she asked, panicked. Her eyes flitted down to check she had covered the mermaid—that he hadn't seen.

"I knew you were trouble when you lifted that astrolabe off Zachariah. Didn't know you'd have the guts to come for the captain next."

"I was waiting for him," Wyna lied. She knew, to anyone else, her lie would be convincing. Not to Brennan. She hadn't absolved herself but continued anyway. "Figured he should be the first one to get a crack at the Whip."

She flinched at her wording and Brennan raised his bushy

blond brows back into his hair. "That's shit. What are you actually doing?"

She crossed her arms over her chest. "I should ask you the very same."

"Then ask me."

That threw her off guard. "Um, what are you doing in here?"

"Oh, same as you. Wanted to give Cap a bit of love." He crossed the cabin, coming around the desk until he was only inches from Wyna.

"That's shit," she said, echoing and backing away from his body. Drawing his attention away from the desk. He followed.

Whatever he meant to say to her next was cut off by the creaking of the cabin door.

CHAPTER EIGHT

Another buggy sat waiting outside the Gillbridges as the house began to wake. Thessa had already been up for hours, had neatened her bed and sat on the edge of it when she could find nothing else to do. Despite Lorelai and Samuel's generosity, she felt suffocated in those walls and she knew it had everything to do with Huxley.

She had been furious last night after their discussion and had stormed out of his room—of course, without the stomping or the slamming of doors her mood called for. She hated to know that Huxley thought her to be after Woolhill's money. But, even yet, the more she sat awake and thought it through, what would it matter if she was after his money anyway? To her, it seemed like quite the advantageous move and she wouldn't blame a single woman in Keresa if that were their goal. So long as she had no ill will toward the man, marriages had been built on less.

But it wasn't so much that she felt shame in what Huxley thought. It was that *Huxley* thought it to be shameful. That infuriated her more than anything. It was almost enough to send her crawling back to Madame Orinna to beg for a different assignment.

Almost.

Even if Thessa thought Madame Orinna would give one to her, they still needed a Whip at Woolhill's and they couldn't send two separate girls to stay with the Gillbridges. It was too much suspicion.

Thessa had waited too long to beg.

So when she heard the horse's hooves on the dirt, she readjusted one of her new dresses in the small, circular mirror and left the Gillbridges as quietly as she could. The buggy driver was kind, if quiet, and when she tried to offer him coin for his service, he only shook his head and assured her that her fare had already been paid in full. In fact, he told her, he had been given a schedule detailing when to pick her up and drop her off for the full month —all paid ahead of time. She smiled at Madame Orinna's organization and asked the driver for a copy.

The Woolhill estate was a sprawling thing with ten-foot walls surrounding it on all sides. Each side had its own gate: the West Gate providing easy access to the outskirts of Keresa if he ever needed to disappear, the North Gate providing easy access to the shopping district and downtown Keresa, the East Gate providing easy access to the tip of Keresa—though he would claim the gate rusty and hardly used—and, finally, the South Gate, which provided Woolhill and his staff easy access to Woolhill's shipyard.

The Gillbridge property was closest to the West Gate but Madame Orinna thought it best for Thessa's first entrance onto the property to be from the north. It was all about first impressions, she had said, and if Woolhill's staff saw her coming from the west, there was no telling what judgements they might make of her. Thessa had argued the point, insisting the noble's staff would surely appreciate someone of a lower societal stature. Madame Orinna disagreed, counter-insisting that she could be anyone she needed to be if she came from the north, from town, but she could only be one type of girl if she came from the west or the east.

So, the North Gate it was.

The guard stationed at the North Gate wore Woolhill's colors and it struck Thessa as funny. They wore jackets the color of blood but she had never seen one of Woolhill's men in a true fight. She wondered if they had ever bled at all.

She sobered when he peered into the buggy and met her eyes.

"Business?" she heard him ask the driver, the question muffled slightly by the walls of the vehicle.

"Have to ask the lady," the driver answered, his dismissal evident.

Thessa remained composed when the guard opened the door, stuck in his head, and repeated the question. "I've a meeting with Mister Woolhill. He should be expecting me."

"Name?" he huffed, his eyes having hardly left her since that first glance.

"Thessa Clemen."

He nodded, perhaps recognizing the name from a list he'd been given. But he did not look away. She watched his eyes trail over her body. Watched them land on her chest and light on fire. "Don't I know you?"

She leaned forward until her forehead almost touched his, offering him a brief peek down the front of her dress. "No," she said and pushed him firmly from the buggy. She swung the door back shut.

Thessa watched through the window as the guard cleared his throat and straightened his coat. She felt a twinge of regret, wondering if perhaps she should have played nice with the man. See what he might have given her later. She sighed at the idea that she might have to make it up to him somehow.

He waved them through the gate, his attention still trained on the window for another look at her. The expression on his polished, handsome face was not one of resentment but of keen interest. Perhaps she hadn't sullied this after all.

Woolhill's grounds splayed before the mansion but there still wasn't quite as much ground as there was house. The mansion itself sat closer to the back end of the property, almost riding the wall that held the South Gate. Though, she knew the wall at the back of the mansion jutted out and ran into the ocean, giving Woolhill his own private beach. Thessa couldn't see that facet of the property as they rode up the circular driveway. All she could see was house.

Another guard stood in front of the wide-set french doors, lazily watching the buggy come to a stop in front of the stairs. He didn't start jogging down to meet Thessa until she was already climbing out.

"Morning, miss." He nodded to the driver as he took Thessa's hand and led her up the stairs. Thessa twisted her neck only to find the driver already trotting from whence he came. "Your name?"

She told him. "I've a meeting with Mister Woolhill," she said again, wondering how many times she would have to explain herself, how many layers of guards Woolhill had stationed about the estate. She did not let her annoyance show. "Should be expecting me."

"Of course, Miss Clemen," he said, already adjusting to her name and, thankfully, choosing a neutral title. "Right this way."

The guard swung the doors to the estate open, revealing what Thessa had come to understand as the taste of the rich. Everything was too big and too much, thought to be some statement of status and tradition. Even if she knew nothing of Woolhill, it was clear to her his design senses stank of old money and an empire that had been around for ages. She fought the urge to wrinkle her nose and turned back to the guard.

"Thank you," she told him. She shined one of her brightest smiles. "I didn't catch your name."

"Only because I haven't told you," he blushed. "William."

"Oh, thank you, William." She forced a breathy quality into her words and leaned in to kiss William's cheek. Perhaps it wasn't all too proper for her to go around kissing Woolhill's staff but she wasn't blind to the power a door guard held. He was truly the only one standing in the way of Thessa getting into the mansion, should she ever need to do so without an invitation. Getting over the walls would be easy enough, sure, but she wasn't going to scale a building.

Guilt prodded her organs around when she pulled away. She was sure he was a decent enough man and she hated to manipulate him so blatantly. She wondered if she should offer him a bit more than a kiss on the cheek but that only confused her further. Wasn't that just another manipulation? William's face grew hotter regardless of her intentions. He stared at her, replacing her guilt with panic.

He cleared his throat. "Sir Woolhill is this way, Miss Clemen," he said, turning from her. She nestled her arm into the crook of his and let him lead her toward the belly of the mansion. She had the abstract impression this estate would be more of a den of debauchery than anything over in the District.

She knew the kind of men good money housed.

William led her through the maze of the Woolhill house, taking her deep enough she wasn't sure if she could ever find her way out. Thessa suspected this was on purpose. That Woolhill wanted his callers to feel as though they had to work to speak with him. Such subtle ways to stroke an ego.

"Right here, Miss." William thrust Thessa into the room, pulling the double doors closed behind her and leaving her to the wolves.

Faces turned to stare at her, interest piqued by the noise. It wasn't a full room but it was enough to knock Thessa off her guard, if only briefly. A member of Woolhill's staff stood quietly to the right of the room, his hands folded behind his back and his back to the opulent floor-to-ceiling curtains. He wasn't a guard, that much she could tell. She figured he must be some sort of butler to Woolhill—a personal assistant.

In the center back of the room, two people were situated behind a large, square desk. The heaving wooden thing reminded her almost of Madame Orinna's, strewn with papers and logbooks, and Thessa was surprised Woolhill seemed to be managing his trade himself, rather than delegating all the work to others while still reaping the profit. It made her happy to know that at least an inkling of integrity lived in this house.

Woolhill sat behind the desk, his office chair rising behind him like a throne. To Thessa, his eyes seemed kind. Certainly not the eyes of a bloodthirsty business mogul and certainly not the eyes of any man Thessa had ever seen about the District. His suit was crisp, though even from so far away, Thessa could see the gold threaded through the black material. She was unsure if the black was his usual attire or if it was merely a symbol of the mourning he still did for his dead wife.

The hair on his head had not yet gone completely gray and she could tell the color that had been there once before must have been the sweetest brown. Just like his hair, his face only showed the earliest signs of aging—wrinkles and pock marks here and there—and his body had grown bloated and rotund with comfort. Even so, none of it subtracted from the peculiar, almost-handsomeness that preceded.

Standing over Woolhill's shoulder was perhaps one of the prettiest girls Thessa had ever seen, though Thessa wasn't sure "pretty" was the exact right word. The hard lines of her face, the fierceness they provided, made her look like she might step on Thessa's throat, like she might enjoy doing so. But the high cheek-bones and the full, pouting lips were softened by the reddened whiskey hue of her hair and the rosy flush it gave to the girl's paler skin. The girl fixed Thessa with a glare of a caliber Thessa wasn't sure she could ever achieve.

She checked her dress to make sure she hadn't committed any social crimes yet.

"May I help you?" the girl asked Thessa.

Thessa cleared her throat, flustered at having been addressed. "Yes, Miss..." She trailed off, waiting for the girl to provide her with a name. She didn't. Thesa moved on, pretending to be undeterred. "I'm here for a meeting with Mister Woolhill."

Woolhill's face brightened and he clapped his hands together. "Ah, Miss Clemen! Forgive me; time got away from me this morning." He got to his feet and moved from behind the desk, rushing forward to greet Thessa properly and physically. She curtsied as he approached, adopting the formal method, but Woolhill wrapped her in a firm embrace as soon as she straightened herself out. "Please, call me Alastor."

"My apologies, Mister—Alastor," Thessa said, her gaze flicking back and forth between Woolhill and the girl. "I wasn't aware you already had visitors."

Woolhill let his small, soft belly shake in a laugh. "You can't possibly mean Campbell!" He gestured for the girl to come forward and she stalked slowly towards them, her eyebrows raised. "Miss Clemen, this is my daughter."

Thessa's fears of Woolhill entertaining women while Thessa tried to do her job left her all at once. She was relieved, to be sure. "I wasn't aware you had a daughter, Alastor. I suppose even the gossips of Keresa don't know everything."

"Then you'll have something to lord over them! Wait until they hear she isn't even mine."

Thessa tried to smile through her confusion as she assessed the situation. Did Madame Orinna know Campbell was his daughter—or, something like a daughter? She tried to recover from the stumble. "In any case, I don't mean to interrupt. Please, tell me, when is a good time for me to return?"

"Nonsense! Come on, sit." Woolhill gestured to a grouping of seats in the center of the room, a curved sofa and high-backed, overstuffed chair. Yet another throne for a man with a manufactured empire. The man ambled to the chair, practically throwing himself into it, and laid his hands over his lap in polite excitement for the chance to converse with Thessa. She hated to admit it but it made her feel quite special. She sat on the sofa across from him, leaning forward and angling her body towards Woolhill's in a gesture to earn his trust.

Campbell scoffed audibly before coming to rest gingerly on the edge of the cushion next to Thessa. Thessa could feel the heat of the other girl's body with only the small distance between them. It sent blood to her cheeks but, somehow, it was chilling.

"Orinna spoke quite highly of you, Miss Clemen," Woolhill told her.

"Do you two know each other well?" Thessa asked in response, trying to gauge how Woolhill truly felt about the kind of woman in his presence.

"Oh, we're merely acquaintances. Met her at a party a few months back. She offered up her services on one of my ships." He hesitated. "My captain insisted I take her up on the offer."

"That was quite generous."

Campbell shifted so she was facing Thessa. "And how do you know Orinna Swither, Miss Clemen?" Her question sounded as if it had been spit in Thessa's direction.

"I lost contact with my family," Thessa replied and she wished desperately to be lying. "Madame Swither's face was the first I saw after—I'm sorry." She pretended to choke up. "It's still too difficult for me to discuss. But she's found me lodging with a lovely family and told me you would be a wonderful friend."

She blotted at fake tears, trying to ignore Campbell's steady gaze of rejection. Rejection of her story, as if the other girl knew it was a lie. Thessa did not bow and taste fear at the inquest, as she was sure Campbell wanted.

Woolhill, oblivious to Campbell's silent objections, clutched at his chest. "I do hate to see a child parted from family. And Orinna is not wrong—I have a soft spot for orphans." He nodded to Campbell.

Thessa didn't want to take her attention off Woolhill but she would not risk him writing her off as rude. She pivoted to look at Campbell expectantly, waited for elaboration. Campbell said nothing, which felt awkward to Thessa but she supposed it might be strange to lay out your trauma for a near stranger. She pivoted back.

"Yes, Campbell's mother perished only a few years after Campbell's birth, her father taken from us mere months prior to her arrival. I took her mother in, of course. One can't expect a pregnant young woman to look after an entire estate. It only seemed natural to take Campbell in, as well, once the time came."

Thessa could tell the discussion made Campbell uncomfortable and, though she was sympathetic, she couldn't help but think that living in such luxury with a man who did not create her and yet loved her as if he did was not the sob story they were spinning. Nonetheless, she feigned the appropriate expressions.

"My condolences," she offered Campbell.

"Yes, Alastor is the picture of generosity," Campbell said, a note of warning in the kind words. "But it is nothing to take advantage of."

Thessa ignored the barb, pretending as though it could not possibly have been aimed at her. "Absolutely. I couldn't imagine who would do such a thing."

Woolhill blushed and brushed off the girls' comments. "Stop, stop. I cannot handle the attention!" Thessa thought he very much could. "But Miss Clemen, tell me, how can I be the friend you need?"

She straightened her back with resolve, hoping to Campbell and Woolhill it would seem as though she was resolved to honesty and hard work. In actuality, she was resolved to nail the character she played. "Now, Mister Woolhill—Alastor—I do not expect any handouts from such a respectable man. I see that you have a lot on your roster and I could never ask you for something I do not deserve." She paused and enjoyed the way he seemed to hang onto what she told him, eager to hear what she *did* want. "I only ask that you give me some time. Time to get to know you and your staff. And only after you are sure you can trust me and my heart, I do hope you can find a place for me in your home."

The last bit of her speech had been painstakingly crafted by Madame Orinna and herself. It was the perfect phrasing, they thought. Ambiguous enough that it could read just as much like looking for a job as looking for a husband, leaving it up to her audience to decide which they preferred. It was a speech that would give Thessa enough time to make friends with his staff and make a partner out of Woolhill. Even if he found no place for her here—and, truly, she hoped he would not—it would be the perfect opening for the Whips to do business above the table.

No more stealing.

Except when it was necessary.

She applauded herself later, when she was leaving the estate, at her performance. She knew she'd hooked Woolhill exactly as she intended. She descended the front steps of the mansion, shooting poor William a wink as she left, proud and not at all dreading her return to the Gillbridges.

Not even a little bit.

"Stop her!"

CHAPTER NINE

Wyna landed on the bed with a painful thunk and she was furious that not even the captain of the ship was allowed the luxury of peaceful sleep. She shook off the lint that had flown into her face and tried to get her bearings.

"What are you doing in here?" Felix asked her, staring into her eyes with a look she didn't quite like. She glanced around the cabin, wondering why he'd chosen to zero in on her when Brennan was just as much at fault as herself.

But Brennan was nowhere to be found. No slivers of clothing visible behind Felix's shelves. No pieces or parts mobile and shaking in the breeze his body should have created. His disappearance made her almost as frustrated as his arrival. She would cover for him, though.

Wyna was a lot of things but she was not a snitch.

"I was waiting for you," she said, dropping her voice a couple octaves like the Whips had taught her. This confused Wyna immensely. Sabina had told her, in public, men liked it when their voices were high and soft but, in the bedroom, they wanted to hear a girl purr. "I felt just awful about not taking you up on your tour."

Felix cleared his throat. "I coulda gotten you from your own chambers."

"Sure," she shrugged, "but then I never would have seen your face like that."

She rose from the bed and strode out of the room, hoping whatever he had come to his chambers for was more important to him than following her out. She couldn't stand to be in his bed with his eyes on her like that. She may be ready for this mission but she was in no way ready for that part of it. Madame Orinna never said she had to make good on that sort of promise.

Felix followed her anyway.

"Where should we start?" he asked, raising his eyebrows when Wyna glanced back at him. "Above or below?"

She took barely a moment to decide. "Above."

Felix stepped around her, rushing down the hallway to get to the narrow stairs that would take them to the deck. The sailors were bustling about, just as they were when she first boarded the *Volia*. As she thought of how they all had crowded her below, she found it hard to believe anything they were doing could be all that important. Surely not if they could afford a break to harass Wyna.

She kept her ear open as Felix droned on about the ship, about all of the things that made him proud and all of the things he still wished to improve. She thought it admirable and perhaps a little pathetic for Felix to be so committed to property that would never be his.

She did her best to remember the names as they were introduced to her but many of them escaped her as soon as they entered her ears. Remembering Madame Orinna's warnings, though, she made sure she paid special attention when Felix introduced her to his Crow.

"Wyna, this is Solomon. You won't see him too often on his feet. Spends most of his time up in the nest." Felix's face lit up as he introduced this particular crew member and Wyna capitalized on it.

She stuck out her hand for Solomon to shake. The sailor blushed and took it. "You're a special one, huh?"

His grip loosed in her hand and Felix laughed, obviously thrilled at Wyna's observation. "He's a remarkable one, that's for sure. Never seen a sailor volunteer for sole Crow duty. The man would sleep up there if we let him."

"Oh? And what does Crow duty entail?" It was innocent enough to be discarded as polite inquiry.

Felix pointed to the top of the mast where a little bucket-shaped platform rested atop the sails. "That there's the nest. The Crows stay in the nest. Watch the seas and the sky." He paused, searching. "They're like an early warning system for what we can't see here on deck."

It was suddenly very clear why Madame Orinna had made a point to watch for Solomon.

"That must get quite boring," she said. "Maybe I could come up with you sometime?"

Solomon blushed again but Wyna could tell it was not for the prospect of being alone with her in the nest. No, it was in anticipation of Felix's next words.

"That won't be necessary. Solomon's the best. Never lost focus. Never fallen victim to the hypnosis." Felix winked at Wyna. "He's like our secret weapon."

She shifted uncomfortably. "Against what?"

Felix only laughed again. "Alright boy, up you go."

Wyna watched as Solomon masterfully maneuvered his way up the mast, strapped to nothing with only the sea and the ship to catch him should he fall. He settled into the nest and Wyan saw the change in how he held his body, as if he pressed some button that would turn him into a finely-tuned and perfectly-engineered automaton.

Wyna didn't expect to feel sad for the Crow. He was nice and he was quiet and he seemed to be quite good at his job. She only hoped she would never have to punish him for it.

Felix had moved on while she stood, gawking at Solomon up

in the sky, and when she finally lowered her head, she had to hustle to catch up with the captain. She slowed, though, when she saw with whom he was speaking.

"Where is it, Zachariah?" Felix whispered, furious and loud. "We've already had to delay."

"I don't know, sir," he responded, clearly cowed. "I've had it in my pocket since we took off. It must've fallen out."

"Fallen out where? On deck or in the Draca?"

"I—"

"I'm not interested in hearing your excuses, boy. You had best find it."

A hand brushed the small of Wyna's back and she turned to see Brennan approaching the men.

"Morning, fellas!" He singsonged. "Aye, Captain. You'll never guess what I found this morning." Felix faced Brennan, visibly annoyed by the interruption. He softened when he saw the astrolabe in Brennan's hands. Zachariah released what Wyna could only describe as a squeal and rushed forward to snatch the device from his crewmate. Brennan threw the astrolabe into the air, eliciting a gasp from Felix, before catching it in his other hand. "Easy there, mate. Couldn't be trusted to hold onto it the first time. Might as well go straight to the captain."

Brennan presented the astrolabe to Felix with the casualty of someone who didn't hold a vital piece of navigation. Felix tucked it into his breast pocket before it could go sailing.

"Where did you find it?" the captain asked pointedly.

"Yes, pickpocket, where did you find it?" Zachariah demanded.

Brennan placed his hands on his hips, squaring and puffing his body in front of the larger man. "Now don't you go calling me names when you're the one who lost it!" He turned back to Felix. "Found it near the bowsprit. Guess Zach's ass was more important than getting where we're going."

Zachariah's cheeks turned as red as Solomon's had earlier but Felix only grunted and called for Wyna to follow him away. She lingered, watching as Brennan lifted himself to his toes to whisper in Zachariah's ear.

"Guess you had better think twice about coming after my girl."

Zachariah raised his gaze to Wyna. "You want the whore? You can have her." He stepped away, his arrogance preventing him from showing just how much Brennan's threatening tone unnerved him. Brennan winked at her before the boys parted ways and returned to their tasks.

The rest of the tour was dreadfully boring, compared to what Wyna had already seen. And when Felix finally slowed down and returned to his quarters, Wyna knew what was coming next. She tried to think of another excuse to distract him.

"Do any of the other rooms have windows?" she asked as he opened the door and ushered her inside. "I would really like to be able to see the water."

"'Fraid not. But you're more than welcome to stay in my cabin as long as you'd like. Sleep here too, if you'd prefer."

"That's a shame," she said, pitching her voice to sound upset before changing her tone completely. "But I like my cabin really well."

"I should think so. You disappeared there all last night. Didn't see you come back out."

She decided to grow reserved, like she hated to disappoint the nice man. Scared. "Well, I was going to. I was going to come find you but they were all crowding me. And I got nervous." She lowered her voice, put a bit of a quiver in it and shook the bounce of her hair into her eyes so he couldn't see she wasn't completely genuine. "I've never done this before. I've only just started with the Whips and I—well, I—"

Felix cut her off and she could tell her act had been successful. She may not know exactly what kind of man Felix was but she had taken a gamble and couldn't help but feel like it paid off. With Wyna acting scared and small, she hoped Felix no longer really viewed her as a sexual object. At least not yet. Not right now. She took the place of a daughter and now she could only hope the man wouldn't confuse the two.

"Listen, Wyna," Felix said, grabbing hold of Wyna's shoulder. She flinched when his fingers made contact and he let her go. "If any of them lay a hand on you that you don't want, you come to me. I'll toss 'em overboard for you," he laughed.

Wyna was grateful for the kind words but she thought of all the young women she knew who'd never had someone fighting for them. She wasn't sure punishment for that kind of thing was any laughing matter. But Wyna didn't think he would understand that so she just gave him her thanks.

"Shall I return you to your cabin?"

"Please."

When they arrived at her door, Wyna tried to make her body big enough to cover the entry. Even if she was pretty sure she'd appealed to Felix's paternal side, she didn't want to open the door to her quarters and take the chance he would come in. So she said her goodbyes outside and waited until she heard the clunking of his boots on the stairs to enter. Still, the tension didn't leave her body.

She tried to ignore the feelings of failure. The ones that told her she should be above deck, getting to know the sailors and parsing out their weaknesses. The ones that told her she should have tried harder to get Solomon's attention. The ones that told her she shouldn't have turned Felix off of her so quickly.

It's only been a day, she reminded herself. *Plenty of time to see mermaids.*

She heard the mild brush of fabric against wall and had her sickles in her grip in an instant. A surge of adrenaline blinded her as she shoved the unwelcome party back into the wall he'd pushed off of, the hinges of the door digging into his back. She pressed her body up against his, stepping on his toes and using her elbows to pin his chest. With her free hand, she whapped the sickle into the wall with a thunk, trapping the neck of the man. She dared him silently to move or to swallow. Anything would be enough to draw blood.

And when she took her eyes off of the pulsing, frightened veins in her assailant's neck—though, she supposed *she* was technically the assailant—she met his own, unphased to see that it was Brennan.

She knew he could tell when she realized who it was but she did not release him.

"You seem to spend a lot of time in cabins that aren't yours," she grunted at him.

"Would it help if I told you I was sorry?" he asked, his throat flexing. The sickle was practically shaving him. She wondered what that stubble felt like and she was almost tempted to release her hold. Would be a shame if she were the reason she'd never find out.

She did not relax.

"No."

"Can I tell you anyway?"

"Could I stop you?"

Brennan's eyes traced her lips, even as she threatened him. "I could think of a few ways."

Like a wave shooting up and hitting her face, she was all at once aware of the way her body pressed against him. The lean tendons of the sailor shifted under his skin slightly as he wriggled, trying to relieve the pressure of the blade against his throat. Eventually, Wyna noticed how he leaned into her, like he was trying to touch her body with as much of his as he could.

But she wasn't about to be manipulated into letting him go. He wasn't the first to try it and she could almost guarantee he wouldn't be the last.

"Stop moving," she ordered. "Tell me what you're doing here."

"I came to see you, little sea witch," he laughed. "What did you think I was doing here?"

She ignored his question, knowing he could just as easily try to distract her from his real intentions. What if he knew the truth about the Whips? "See me why?"

"Oh, because I missed your kind face and your sweet voice." She glared. He sighed, "Well, I have to make a show of coming here, do I not? No one's going to believe you're mine if I'm not sneaking off with you all the time."

"I'm still not sure I want them to associate me with you," she said, adjusting her grip on the sickle. She saw the flare in his eye as she did so and stiffened her shoulders in preparation for retaliation. He didn't move. "Why are you really here?"

"I've already—" She cut him off, increased the pressure of the blade at his throat and drew a few beads of blood. "I'll admit I'm curious about you, Wyna. Curious about your pickpocketing. Curious about why you were in the captain's quarters. Curious about how you've seemed to manipulate him. What's your game? Maybe I want to play."

"I should ask you the same. You might remember your own presence in Felix's quarters," she scoffed, trying to steer the conversation away from her own motivations. "And you pretended the astrolabe was your own discovery!"

"And you're quite welcome. Easy for me to blame it on Zachariah's irritable bowels than it would be for you to explain."

"I could have said he dropped it in here when he dropped his trousers."

Brennan stiffened his body. Had the audacity to shift his arm so that it held Wyna's. "He was here? You let him in?"

"Of course not. I'm only saying I can lie just as well as you can, Brennan."

He grinned but she still felt the hardness of his torso. "Say my name again."

The request was what made her finally let him go. She backed away from his body. "I don't need you to come to my rescue." She eyed the blood staining and drying around his neck. "As you can well see."

He lifted his hand to where her eyes rested. "What if I told you it was just as much for me as it was for you?"

"This again?" She rolled her eyes.

"C'mon, Wyna." He stepped towards her, lowering his eyes in a manner Wyna was sure he thought was sultry. She wasn't sure she didn't agree. "Help me out."

Trust was not a feeling that came easily to Wyna. And she didn't trust him—not yet. But he had seen her in Felix's cabin and he had seen her pilfer the astrolabe. And here he was, offering her a mutual lie. She couldn't help but feel the stakes were much higher for her and she considered telling him to put his efforts into a portly walrus. But the thought of his body up on that wall and her sickle on his throat—his life had been in her hands. She could perhaps return it there should things go sour.

She hoped she would never have to.

Wyna wiped the blood off her sickle on the darkest part of her skirts. He took it as her acceptance. Her defeat, maybe. She wasn't sure. Brennan whooped and bounded past her, landing squarely on her bed, his dirty boots still on and digging into her blankets. Her blood curdled when she thought of how cumbersome it would be to wash those on the ship. He must have seen the darkening of her face as he made himself comfortable.

"You'll have to get used to having me in your bed, sea witch," he told her, his grin splitting the skin of his lips in a way she found both adorable and annoying. She pretended like she didn't imagine how they would scrape against hers.

"If you want a witch, I'll introduce you to one," she said and thought of Theo's harsh features. The way men feared her. The way they liked that.

"We've already met."

She rolled her eyes and tucked her sickles back into her waistband, angling her body away from Brennan before placing herself gently on the edge of the bed. She warred with herself over whether to keep a close eye on him or to avert her gaze entirely.

She settled on somewhere in between, refusing to meet his eyes but keeping him in her peripherals.

He nudged her with the toe of his boot and whispered loudly. "Why don't you moan a little? Make a show for whoever's listening."

She latched onto his foot and bent it forward, stretching his ankle as far as it would go. A little bit farther. He yelped.

"That wasn't quite a moan," she told him and tightened her grip on the foot. "Why don't we try again?"

CHAPTER TEN

In typical circumstances, Thessa would have ducked away, concealing herself from whoever wished to stop her. But these were not typical circumstances and Thessa had to save face. She wiped away her annoyance before turning to bewitch Campbell with her sweetest smile, contriving polite confusion and a proper amount of outrage at having been detained.

"Yes?"

Campbell stood at the top of the front steps, her stance evidently wide, even under the mass of skirts, and her hands braced against her hips. She seemed mildly out of breath, like she'd had to run to catch up with Thessa. William stopped his light jot towards her and looked back at Campbell, waiting for the other girl's response to Thessa's question. Thessa attempted to share a conspiratorial look with him but it seemed Campbell was not, in fact, their common enemy.

"Miss?" he asked Campbell.

"Bring her inside for a moment."

Thessa danced around William as he reached for her and stomped back towards the house, furious at having been treated like a child or some piece of property the Woolhills decided they

97

simply must have. But she would not take her frustration out on William and she would not yet say anything to make a sour impression on Woolhill's right hand.

Campbell did not move or shift or make way for her as she approached and Thessa knew the other girl was probably well-schooled in intimidation. How fortunate that Thessa had been running a house full of lethal women and besting the worst of Keresa for years now. Threats and violence, she could handle. And when their chests practically touched, Campbell stepped back and heaved open the door, gesturing for Thessa to go inside before leading her to a small parlor to the left of the door.

Thessa did not sit, though the sofa looked like heaven. Instead she stood by the door, her back straight and her eyes following Campbell as she closed them in. Trapping Thessa.

"Listen," she sneered, "I'm unsure of what plans you have for my father and—"

"Plans?" Thessa interrupted.

"Yes. Plans. I've seen your type here. Ever since his wife died, there's been one of you in this house every hour of the day."

Thessa ignored Campbell's implications. "And do you detain all of those women, as well?"

"Yes. I've overheard Alastor mention your benefactor. He's not interested in sponsoring whatever you're caught up in and he's especially not interested in you." Campbell stepped closer to Thessa, the curl of her fire gently licking Thessa's bare skin. "I will not see him used for his fortune."

Thessa's breath hitched but it was not for Campbell's tone. She hoped the other girl would not notice and mistake it for that sort of weakness. "I appreciate your concern for him," Thessa told her. "How warming it is to know he treats his wards well. But I'm not here to scrape his pockets and I'd greatly appreciate if you would refrain from making those sorts of accusations."

The pout of Campbell's lips deepened. "You're not nearly as good a liar as you think you are."

Though slinging insults was a game Thessa knew well how to play, she clenched her jaw. Campbell's intentions were easy to read. Either intimidate Thessa away, or provoke her into violent acts or violent words that would ruin her chances with Alastor anyway. She wanted to think all the other girls this tactic had worked on fools. But she could see how Campbell could be persuasive.

"I'll ask you again to reconsider your attack on my character," she said finally. "You know nothing of me."

"I know the kinds of people Alastor attracts and I know the kinds of plans they have."

"Tell me, then. What's my grand plan?"

Campbell bristled at the challenge. She stepped back to create space between them. "You come here and you tilt your pretty chin. You shake out the hair, letting him get a whiff of your soaps. Telling him you're clean. Pristine. And do not think I haven't noticed the way you push out your breasts. The way you've overexaggerated your breathing so he can see the way they move." Thessa *had* been doing those things. Not that she would ever admit it to Campbell. "You titter and you laugh and you pretend to be interested in what he has to say. Maybe he'll take you to bed. And then you're left to imagine a life of luxury. Well, he's not the man to give it to you," she snarled.

"It sounds to me like you're the one who's taken note of me. Not your father."

"I've been trained to watch for threats."

So have I. "I'm no threat to you, Miss Moore. And I've no interest in your father's money."

"Good. I'll make sure you never get the chance to spend it."

TEARS WERE a rare thing for Thessa but, especially lately, there were reminders that even she wasn't immune. Back in her room at the Gillbridges, she tried her best to quiet the little choking sobs. Nothing that had happened to her that day had been so objectively bad but she was frustrated. Frustrated at having to play the perfect lady. At having to do a silly diplomatic tango with a woman who'd hated her the moment she set eyes on her. At being ultimately unable to effectively combat all the accusations she was merely hopping widowers in search of a comfy life. Accusations from Campbell. From Huxley.

It wasn't the accusations, so much, that hurt her. She understood women who did what they could. Money and marriage were an armor and so many of the men who had money deserved every dirty trick. No, it was that they meant to hurt her when they said it. It was that they thought less of her because of it. She didn't care if they thought she was money-motivated—she cared that they hated her for it.

She found herself cursing Madame Orinna for forcing her into this. The Madame knew what she could do. She was more than reconnaissance. And she hadn't thought she still needed to prove that to her mentor. Thessa wondered what she could have possibly done to warrant this punishment but then she remembered the way she'd covered for Wyna. The way she'd lied. Oh, it was just like her to ruin things for herself just to keep another out of the trenches. Even though Madame Orinna had caught her, Wyna walked free for her mistakes and Thessa would be paying for it every day.

She tried her very best not to resent Wyna for it.

Though she probably could have stood to wallow in her feelings for a bit longer, she knew what always cheered her. She could no longer hear the bustling of the Gillbridges and she wagered they were asleep in their beds and wouldn't notice their charge sneaking out. And in, sopping wet. She slipped off her skirts until she wore only the trousers underneath and switched her binding top for a light, flowing one she had stolen from Huxley a long while back.

Well, she hadn't so much stolen it as he had left it behind. She'd devolved into uncontrollable giggles imagining Huxley stumbling home half-naked so she'd stashed the shirt to keep hold of the memory. It didn't fix her mood tonight.

She was still hiccuping and wiping her eyes when she opened the door to Huxley, preparing to knock. She tried not to enjoy the way his eyes raked her body. Yet, the expression on his face wasn't one that said he needed to have her. It was concern.

"Can I come in?" he asked, his voice just a whisper. She considered simply moving past him and leaving anyway. He could follow her to the shore, sure, but she could probably lose him in the water.

She wouldn't put the mermaids at risk like that. She stepped aside.

Huxley crossed the meager room in two steps, twisting and landing on her bed with a huff. He leaned back, extending his torso and putting his weight on his elbows. Staring, his eyes half-lidded in that position. It wasn't a sultry sort of look. She didn't think Huxley would ever be capable of that kind of energy. Rather, he looked like a comfortable school boy. Someone who had gone to the inland university and never had to worry about his place in the world but still, for some reason, worried about her.

Abruptly, he sat up again, folding his torso in the other direction and hunching his shoulders. "I'm sorry."

"What?"

"I'm sorry for what I said to you. It's not my business anymore what you do with...what you do with other men."

"Was it ever your business?" she asked.

"I should think so," he said, pushing out a humorless laugh. "But you know what I thought."

Thessa sighed and threw her head back against the wall with a satisfying thunk of pain. "I wasn't ready for marriage, Hux," she whispered. "I'm still not."

"Shit, Thessa, I wasn't trying to take you to the chapel right then and there. Gods know we didn't have the money for a wedding." He shook his head, like he couldn't believe he had to explain this to her. "I wanted to know we were on the same page. We just...weren't."

Thessa thought that now was probably not the time to tell him she *had* wanted the idyllic picture of a wedding Huxley had painted for her. But with that desire came complications. She didn't think Whips were meant to marry. Didn't think they were meant to bring a partner into that life. And she wouldn't pursue that with someone if they didn't know every part of her. If they did not know her soul and love her anyway.

"Did you come in here to talk about our past?"

"I came to apologize," he insisted. "But then I heard you crying." She didn't bother denying it. She was sure her eyes were still puffy. But she didn't like that he knew. "For a minute, I thought it was because of me. I suppose that's selfish, though. So...what's wrong?"

Thessa had to laugh at his straightforward approach to comfort. From anyone else, the inquiry would have been disingenuous. But she knew Huxley had a good heart. She knew he wasn't asking for the sake of asking.

Even so, she couldn't tell him.

When she didn't answer his question, he raised his eyebrows. Critical. No malice. "So we're back to this, then?"

"Back to what?" she sighed.

"You avoiding every question. Disappearing. Pretending it's normal to skirt around topics that clearly affect you."

"I don't owe you my feelings, Huxley."

She watched his jaw flex and his eyes pulse, hurt by her words. Watching his face fall sent the tears right back out of her own. She felt selfish, crying after saying something so mean. Though she felt her words were true, that wasn't the kind of relationship she wanted with Huxley. No matter how often she tried to convince herself she wanted nothing to do with him anymore, she still felt there were strings tied around her fingers, connecting her to him. Her secrets had tried to saw through those strings and she had let them.

Huxley stood from the bed and took Thessa into his arms. He tucked her into the cavity in the middle of chest, surrounding her on either side by the small puff of his hard-worked pecs. She used to know them well but they were firmer now. Bigger, maybe, but almost imperceptibly so.

She'd always been so aware of his body.

She didn't have a right to be anymore.

His mouth moved against her hair. "Tell me what's wrong?"

Maybe it was her current fury at Madame Orinna that made her tell him. Maybe it was her sadness at having to go about this particular mission so privately. Alone. Maybe it was just that she missed him. But she spoke into him the words she never wanted him to hear. "I'm a Whip."

He pulled back, snaking his finger under her chin to help her look up at him. "What?"

"I'm a Whip, Huxley," she said. "That's why you couldn't come around. That's why I never told you what I was doing. That's why Madame Orinna dropped me off. I didn't leave because I didn't love you. I left because you were looking for an apprenticeship. For work. I couldn't ruin that for you."

Again, she watched his face for the changes she knew were coming. The scrunching of his nose as he realized exactly who she was. And that was probably the worst of it. Having to reveal a secret. Feeling the anxiety and release of it all when she hadn't even told the whole truth. She didn't care if he thought of bodies slapping together because he would never imagine the squish of bloody hands and sharp weapons against weathered skin. He would never imagine the difficulty of cutting through the muscle of a tongue. He would never imagine the feeling of bones shattering under her pressure.

But Huxley didn't let go of her chin. He bowed his head until his nose pressed into hers, tilting until they fit together. And when he spoke, he spoke in a way that brushed his lips against her own. "I don't care."

She closed her eyes, unsettled by the prolonged eye contact and the way it sped her heart. She tried to turn her head but Huxley held fast.

"I don't care," he said again.

Only then did Thessa let herself look at him. Truly look at what she had thrown away. For the first time, she let herself wonder if she didn't have to throw it away at all. Before she lost her nerve, she pushed herself onto her toes, letting her mouth find his. He tasted salty, like he was covered in a layer of ocean spray that didn't want to scrub off.

Just like she remembered.

He broke the kiss with his lips pulled tight in a smile. "I've missed that. I've missed you."

She pushed him back towards the bed until the corner of it hit his calf, sending him falling into the mattress. "This means nothing," she told him, knowing, right then, it meant everything to her. He was familiar. What she knew. She may not know what was to come with Alasor. Campbell. But she knew what to expect with Huxley.

And she would drink that in while she was sure he wouldn't change.

She climbed onto the bed after him, on top of him. Without her skirts, she was able to straddle him. Hold him tight between her legs. She saw the smirk on his face as he registered his shirt on her skin and the way he was able to slip his hands right up under the fabric.

"You kept it?" he asked her. "That means something, I'd think."

She silenced him by crashing her mouth back into his. Thessa let herself linger over him, let him feel her the way she wanted to feel him. She sat back up, shrugging her shoulders. "It's comfortable," she argued. "That's all." Before she could feel badly about dashing his hopes, she peeled the shirt over her head and held it over him. "Would you like it back?"

Huxley snatched the garment from her hands and tossed it across the room. "No."

He made it easy to believe her only worries were Samual and Lorelai waking to the sounds of a Whip being exactly what everyone thought she should be.

CHAPTER ELEVEN

"I was under the impression you had work to be doing."

"Hmm?" Brennan opened one eye to peer at Wyna but he shut it upon finding her gaze on him. He had fallen asleep curled up on her bed once she'd decided to let him stay. It had been some time since he had woken up but Wyna knew he wanted her to think he was still asleep. "Can't hear you. Too sleepy."

She smacked him with a pillow that had migrated to the end of the bed. "I thought sailors were supposed to be working constantly. Keeping the ship afloat and all that."

"I like to think we stay afloat with a little bit of magic."

She snorted. "If by magic you mean everyone else on this crew, then you'd be correct.."

"Hey!" He launched the pillow back at her. "If you want me to leave then you have to prepare to answer me about why I caught you in the captain's quarters earlier."

"Or what?" You'll tell on me?" She raised her eyebrows at him. She could see the faintest hint of his iris peeking through his lashes. "I've already paid my dues with Felix. But I could still let him know you were with me."

"You wouldn't."

"Why not?"

He frowned, his mouth making almost comical lines. "Because," he said. "That would be rude."

"I'm not above blackmail, you know."

"Is this the part where I tell you my entire life story and then—"

"This is the part where you tell me why you were in Felix's cabin," she interrupted.

Finally, Brennan sat up on the bed, bending his knees and angling his legs so he looked like a schoolchild, staring at Wyna like he would a crush across the room. She shifted, trying to keep the way that affected her out of his sight. She didn't want to be anyone's crush but, even though Brennan infuriated her, she may have decided she didn't mind being his.

She told herself it gave her power over him.

"Would you believe me if I said I'm not above blackmail, either?" he asked.

"Yes." The answer was easy. Easy enough that she didn't have to consider why. "So you were trying to blackmail Felix?"

"That was the goal."

Wyna knew she should probably think poorly of him after admitting his disloyalty to his captain but she merely tilted her head and tried to stare into his brain. "Don't blackmail plots usually form after you already have your leverage?"

He smiled, the expression opening his mouth in the corner so she could see his teeth. "How much do you know about blackmail, sea witch?"

She rolled her eyes. "Why are you trying to blackmail him?"

"Because." He leaned forward. "I figure there has to be a way to get a little power on this ship. It's slow-going at the moment—getting the crew to respect me. But I don't need it from them if I have it from the captain."

"I'm not sure I'm following the path that took you from blackmail to respect."

"Respect is respect," he shrugged. "Even if it's fabricated."

"Are you important enough to get respect?"

He grunted. "I'm trying to be."

Wyna laid back on the bed, keeping whatever distance she could from his body, and understood what he hadn't yet said. That he had spent a majority of his life as nothing. She saw the way he carried himself. How his over-the-top gesticulations and boisterous voice meant only to distract people from truly looking at *him*. At the way he looked over his shoulders. At the way he fluctuated between making himself big and making himself small. Big to intimidate others. Small to hide when he was finished being seen.

The boy showed all the grit of Keresa's southern edge. Of the people that were hardy because they had to be. She wondered absently how he came to be on this ship and on a Woolhill crew. It made sense to Wyna that he would be desperate to prove himself worthy among these men. She imagined they latched onto what they could read from his past, wanting to feel better than someone.

That was enough to soften Wyna, incrementally. She understood. The possibility that she was pressing on a soft spot did not deter her from asking him how he came to be where he was.

"I walked down the stairs and opened the door, Wyna," he said patiently.

"I'm serious."

Brennan stretched his body out, losing the schoolboy charm of his previous position. His body stretched only slightly further than Wyna's and, though his feet hung off the meager bed, he placed his head right across from hers.

"I can tell you know where I grew up. People always know." She didn't deny it. She just hoped he couldn't read her as well as she could read him. "The little orphan that never quite grew out of poverty."

"I'm an orphan, too," she lied. She wasn't sure why she did it. Perhaps to feel less alone. To make him feel less alone. But he didn't comment on her false revelation. There was a vacancy behind his face. Something hollow and sharp in all the places where he should have still been round. It was like he was lost in the sucking pain of his memories.

"I wasn't very old when they died. Old enough to remember to miss them." She didn't offer her own experiences this time. "Old enough to resent them for leaving me with nothing."

Bitter resentment was a feeling with which Wyna was intimately familiar. "How did they die?"

He shot her a look that said *I'm getting to it*. "They sailed for Woolhill once upon a time. My father was only a swabber but I heard my mother crowed pretty well. She was supposed to stay with me but they needed her one last time, they said. So she went."

She couldn't tell if he was taking a dramatic pause or if he just wanted to leave Wyna wanting more. She bit. "And?"

"They didn't come back. The ship did. Just barely. But it was a skeleton crew and a skeleton ship," he said. "Only bones."

The lilt of his voice as he told the story made it sound rehearsed. She wondered how many times he had opened up like he did. How many times he'd had to tell employers or lovers or friends his greatest tragedy so far. How many times he had gone over it in his head so the tears didn't come when he finally spoke it aloud.

"But what did you do then?"

"I survived." His laugh was mirthless. "I should be dead. But someone in my family had to live. And if they had to die...well, it had to be me."

Brennan's words chilled her, shaking her spine, but she couldn't understand why. She straightened her back, her joints popping and cracking, as she tried to shake it off. "How did you end up on Woolhill's boat?"

He smiled, or tried to. It took him a couple times to get the expression right. Like he had to work to land the emotion he wanted to convey. "A lot of fast talking and even more hard work."

"Hard work to get you on the ship but no labor now that you're here?" she asked. Though she meant to tease him, she didn't currently find the same amusement in it as she had before. Some part of his story, tragedy as it was, had soured the atmosphere of the room completely.

"If you saw the hammocks we have to sleep in, you'd understand why I want to spend every possible second in here."

"I am genuinely curious," she pressed, trying to eke out any information she could, "what exactly you're tasked with on this ship."

He shrugged and the motion was awkward in his horizontal position. "Technically, I'm the bosun. I was just supposed to be the apprentice but the real bosun fell off right before we le—can I tell you a secret?" he asked, interrupting himself. Wyna nodded. "They don't know that I was only meant to be the apprentice. Should've been two of us. But the bosun never showed so I just... took over. The other apprentice thinks I'm an expert!"

Brennan seemed pleased with himself over his now-loosed secret. That he had been able to pull off such a feat of deception. And it was now clear to Wyna why he seemed to have so much downtime, as she imagined it was easy to pawn off work to the other apprentice in the name of work experience.

She wanted to revel with him. Really, she did. But the feeling that overcame her when he told his story only seemed to intensify with this new bit of information. It was fine, to her, when the only secret she knew he was keeping was that they weren't what the rest of the crew thought them to be. But Wyna was not left to wonder what else he stored away.

She wasn't sure there was room for two liars on this ship.

Brennan took note of her silence and, seemingly sensing he'd lost her, rushed to apologize. "I shouldn't have told you," he lamented, closing his eyes and wiggling his head like he was trying to rewind time. "You think less of me now. You should. I'm utter shit."

His wallowing confused Wyna. Made her head fuzzy enough

to forget her suspicions and replace them with concerns for Brennan's emotional well-being. He was her only true ally on this vessel and he had just shared his grief with her. It wasn't right for Wyna to harbor nasty feelings towards him when he had been so vulnerable.

"You're not shit," she told him hesitantly. And then, trying to lift his mood, said, "Or maybe you are."

The attempt was weak and she knew it. So did he. "No, I am. I shouldn't have lied. Shouldn't have pretended to be what I'm not." He hopped out of the bed, bouncing on his feet once he landed, hardly affected by the sway of the boat. He leaned over and placed a quick kiss on her cheek before running the miniscule distance to the door.

She didn't have time to register her reaction to the kiss. "Where are you going?"

"To tell Felix. He deserves to know who's on his boat."

"Wait!"

Brennan turned back and looked at her expectantly, which Wyna thought was odd for a man who seemed so determined to go. But Wyna didn't want him to go spilling his secrets to Felix and she was proud of her assessment of those implications. Should Felix think punishment necessary, Wyna would be left without a buffer for the other men. She would have to find a new tale to spin to get them to leave her alone. Not to mention, her association with an outed liar.

She also had to consider the problems that might cause for her assignment. Unrest in the crew would make it infinitely more difficult for her to get a read on how voyages typically ran—though she had to admit that infighting would be a fantastic distraction from her supernatural friends in the sea.

Regardless, no matter which way Brennan's sudden devotion to honesty went, it spelt pure trouble for Wyna. Headaches and ones she couldn't afford, at that. Maybe he could spill his guilty guts to the captain *after* they returned to Keresa but Wyna didn't see the need for it in the middle of the sea.

But how to tell him that?

He blinked, impatient. "Yes?"

She tried to make it sound like she wasn't unsure of her next words. "I was actually hoping you could take me above deck."

"It's the middle of the night."

"I've never seen the Draca at night."

He smirked, cocking his head to the side. "I thought you were from Keresa."

She got to her feet, ignoring the background pinch of her still rotten ankle and the half-silent clink of her sickles as they resettled. They would be nonexistent to anyone who didn't know what she carried but it was a comfort to her and she would be glad for the reassurances of their presence should anyone else try what Brennan had pulled. She shook off the anxieties and rolled her eyes at him. "You know what I mean."

He pulled at the door with a dramatic flourish. "Then come along."

Brennant took her hand as he led her above deck. She felt like a spontaneous youth, sneaking off with her lover. Like someone who had never known violence. Never thought of it.

She enjoyed the feeling.

The moon was bright and large, hanging low in the sky as if it were trying to keep the horizon within sight. It shone on the faces of the barren crew with a muted glow. One that illuminated the sharp angles of their faces and turned the shadows sinister. But the water held its beauty, swelling as the moon pulled it and pushed it back. There was no longer any point in worrying about what kind of monsters lurked below the surface. She might've, once. Now she knew the water held only wonders.

The monsters lurked above.

Wyna wished she could see a mermaid now, again. Tonight. It hadn't been so long that she had forgotten why she was doing what she did. But it had been long enough that she ached to marvel and learn. Longed to feel the magic as she had before. She held her breath, searching for the signs of sparkling scales and the slap of a muscled tail against the water. She imagined the mermaids swimming with the boat, like fish attaching themselves to sharks.

But as quickly as she had fallen into the hypnosis, her trance was broken by Brennan's voice beside her. Reminding her that seeing a mermaid now was likely the worst that could happen. Her blades would see more blood than she had intended.

Brennan shook her, laughing. "Remind me to keep you out of the nest. You'd fall in a second." She offered him a shy smile, feigning embarrassment. Better he think that than guess where her mind had really been. He glanced over his shoulder and his brows knitted together. Wyna followed his gaze to a shadowed corner. "Can you keep yourself from falling if I run away for a moment?"

She nodded, her shoulders sagging with relief at his absence, and she returned her eyes to the sea. As if waiting for the moment she was alone, she saw a tail whip out of the water, sending splashes up the side of the ship. Wyna suppressed a gasp as the tail turned over and a soaking head emerged from the waves. The mermaid registered just as much surprise as she had, her mouth falling open and spilling out a bit of the sea.

She was stunning. Her deep skin, darkened still by the sun breaking through the surface of the water, shone in the moonlight. The droplets on her skin turned into crystals as they crawled over her body, mingling with the emerald scales that traipsed up her neck. Perhaps it was silly but Wyna felt the magic encompass her. Like she was trapped, with the mermaid, in a bubble of awe.

"Are you alright?" the mermaid asked and Wyna strained to hear.

Wyna nodded and placed her fingers over her mouth, trying to communicate to the mermaid that she couldn't speak. That she wasn't alone. The mermaid nodded her understanding but Wyna saw the concern in her eyes. She couldn't explain the sense of camaraderie she felt—that she knew the mermaid felt, as well— but she knew the truth of it. This was an ally. A friend. A sister?

"Tomorrow," the mermaid said, the curls on her head shrinking slowly as they dried in cold air. "I'll follow you tonight but meet me tomorrow. Alone."

Wyna nodded again, furiously this time, as if no amount of enthusiasm could express how much she wanted what the mermaid offered. But she stiffened when she heard footsteps behind her, breaking over the boards of the ship. The slightest shake of her head sent the mermaid sinking back into the black of the sea.

Brennan's hand found the curve of Wyna's lower back, the force of his fingers driving her body into his. She gritted her teeth at the touch, enjoying it wholeheartedly but still unsure about the show they put on. Every skim of his skin against hers sent electricity through her body but there was so much about him that gave her pause. She found his crass attitude to be both hilarious and insufferable and it felt unfair that she couldn't predict which she would feel in the moment. Not to mention the way his unearned entitlement sometimes made her bristle. But could she blame a broken man for mending himself in only the ways he knew?

And every second she was left to wonder if perhaps his words and his touch were only the show he purported them to be. She herself still tried to believe that whatever their connection was, she did it in the name of her mission. She did it because she was... pretty sure...Madame Orinna would approve. If she couldn't expect praise for her quick thinking, she could at least be proud the job had been done. She wanted to tell herself she was doing this for the mermaids and not at all for herself. For that sense of belonging this lonely boy could give such a lonely girl.

Perhaps the mermaid, well-versed in the faults of men, would be able to help Wyna parse it all out.

CHAPTER TWELVE

Huxley's head sat uncomfortably on her chest, pressing and sticking to Thessa's bare skin as he snored softly. She wiggled out from under him, unbothered about the prospect of waking him up. She had done this enough times now to know that, if given the chance, he would romp into unconsciousness for as long as he was allowed.

He would still be here, likely in the very same position, when she returned.

Thessa snatched her clothes from where they had been tossed and pulled them over her head. The night would still offer her cover for a while but she wanted as much time on the water as possible, while still leaving herself a chunk of the morning to bathe off the salt.

She debated trekking all the way to the tip of Keresa to commandeer Madame Orinna's little boat but that would take more time and effort than simply swimming until her friends found her. She figured it was some kind of sense the mermaids had, to know when something was in the water and where. Then again, Thessa thought, if that were the case, the Whips might be out of a job. She made a mental note to ask them tonight.

Though she knew the water should be cold now that there

was no sun to beat down upon it, Thessa felt her blood rushing and her body heating as she stepped into the Draca. She walked until her feet no longer supported her head above the water and then she swam. Until she was breathless and fatigued and Keresa's shores were like a memory. Only then did she let herself sink. No panic coursed through her, not even when she felt the sting of a slash on her leg and a hand clamped around her ankle. She let the mermaid drag her through the water, closing her eyes and trying to enjoy the ride until she surfaced and was lifted onto a rock ledge.

They were in a different grotto this time, this one unaided by any sort of light. Thessa got to her feet, shaking the water from her hands before she searched for the book of matches. It felt lighter than it had the last time she'd been to his particular location and she noticed the wax of the candles had melted significantly.

"You've made some new friends?" Thessa asked, turning back to Rose.

Rose shrugged and smirked at Thessa. "Old ones, more like."

Thessa feigned offense and placed her hand over her chest. "And I thought this was *our* special place."

"You're right," the mermaid admitted, leaning her body back until she lay flat atop the pool. "A whole ocean to play but mermaids are scoundrels when Thessa's away."

"Ah! My very own proverb." She jumped into the pool and sent water splashing. Droplets sprayed over the flames of the candles, putting them out and sending the girls back into darkness. She had no interest in getting out of the water again, though, so she made herself content in the dark. It didn't matter to Rose, anyhow.

"Oh no," Rose fake-pouted. "We've lost the ambiance."

"The dark can be nice sometimes."

Rose circled Thessa in the pool, creating a miniature whirlpool around her. The slime of her tail brushed over Thessa's body and Thessa ignored the pricking and the stinging where the hardy appendage won out against her skin. "I've been meaning to ask how you always know when I'm coming to visit."

Rose slowed her laps and Thessa thought she could sense the mermaid's presence to her right. When she spoke, though, Rose's voice came from only inches in front of Thessa. Her breath was hot and fishy.

"Magic."

"Really?"

"No, silly," Rose laughed. "We patrol Keresa."

Thessa frowned. She knew Rose could see it in the dark. "You shouldn't be doing that. It's a miracle no one's noticed. They're in these waters all the time."

"How else would we know when you need us?" Rose was growing defensive. "How else would we know when to gather so you can show us off to your baby Whips?"

"Is that how you feel we've been treating you?" Thessa asked, her voice small and embarrassed at having been called out right after she'd reprimanded the other girl.

Rose sighed. "Not really. But what else are we supposed to do with our time? It isn't as if we've been born to the sea—we're citizens of Keresa. Is it such a crime to miss humanity?"

Thessa supposed it wasn't. Not a crime, at least, even if it was foolish. She tried not to let the mermaid feel the anger wafting from her, knowing their reckless "patrols" could potentially take more lives than necessary. Could make even more of a murderess out of Thessa. She wanted to say they deserved to feel close to the lives they once lived. But did the tragedies of their past excuse the tragedies the Keresans might face in the future?

Thessa pushed up against the water so she was fully submerged, trying to clear her head. She decided to choose peace by the time she resurfaced. "I suppose it's alright. So long as you stay out of the canals."

Somehow, she heard the way the mermaid scrunched her nose and Thessa couldn't blame her. Even on a good day, the canals were disgusting. "Deal," Rose squeaked out.

They were silent, then. Rose backstroked her way around Thessa and Thessa treaded water. She enjoyed the company. The lack of expectation. Finally, as if she couldn't take another second of it, Rose spoke.

"We don't usually see you so soon after a visit."

Thessa groaned, transported back to her issues on land. "I needed to get away."

"From what?" Something on Thessa's face prompted Rose to rephrase her question. "Or from whom?"

Two faces flashed across Thessa's closed eyelids but neither of them made complete sense to her. Huxley frightened her because, even though she had been able to fulfill her own desires, she wasn't sure she wanted more from him. Once upon a time, her heart would have fluttered at the idea of marrying him. But now that it had ended and begun again, she wanted nothing less. And still, she harbored the fear that some secret part of Huxley she'd never known was just waiting for the moment he could hurt her like she knew she hurt him.

And Campbell. Thessa didn't like what the other girl had assumed about her. She didn't like that she stood in her way of getting to Alastor. She didn't like how Campbell was able to make her feel.

Rose poked her side and Thessa realized she hadn't yet answered. "Does it have anything to do with the Madame?"

"No!" Instinct had Thessa rushing to defend Madame Orinna, never wanting her disdain to reach her boss's ears. But this was Rose. "Yes. Maybe."

"You're offended she didn't send you on the ship," Rose tried to deduce.

"I was at first," Thessa admitted. "But it's more about what she's having me do instead." Ideally, she could stop there but Rose was expectantly silent. "She's sent me to live with Huxley."

Rose devolved into giggles. She knew well Thessa's unfortunate dynamic with Huxley and, though she was supportive of

Thessa's decisions, Thessa knew the mermaid had always held hope for the two of them. "Absolutely rich!" Rose squealed.

"Far from it. But Hux lives right next to the Woolhill estate so Madame thought it was proper."

Rose stilled in the water beside her but it didn't occur to Thessa to think it was for anything terrible. It was more startling curiosity. "What are you doing with the Woolhills?"

"Trying to get into their trade. Madame wants access to logs and schedules."

"That's not necessary."

Thessa was incredulous. Did the mermaid really care nothing for the lengths the Whips went to for them? "You must be kidding! Having the logs and schedules would nip sightings in the bud!"

"I think we do a good job of avoiding them ourselves." Rose's tone had turned mildly nervous. It was the tone people took with her when they had something to hide.

If only Thessa knew what that was.

She tried the direct approach to answers. "What are you not saying?"

Rose ignored the question. "What I *am* saying is I don't think Woolhill is a threat."

"Good. But it's my job to ensure that."

"What exactly is Madame having you do?" Rose asked, clearly trying to shift away from her secret.

Thessa bit. "I think she wants me to pretend to court him. But...ambiguously?"

Rose's laugh trickled over the water again. "I'd imagine you're not having much luck."

Thessa frowned. She wanted to run her hands over her now-tangled hair. She wished she could be grateful for the lack of light but Rose's vision pierced through the shadows. "You think I can't court him?" she asked defensively.

"I think you can court whomever you want." Rose placed a

friendly, wet kiss on Thessa's cheek. "I've just heard his daughter is protective."

"To put it lightly."

"Quite lovely, though. I've heard."

"If only she had a heart to match."

"I think," Rose said, suddenly serious, "you'll find her heart is for who she loves. Just like yours."

Thessa was uncomfortable with the turn this conversation had taken. "You speak as if you know the girl."

"I've heard stories."

"From?"

"The others."

"And they know her well?"

Thessa heard the splash as Rose disappeared into the pool and, for the first time, was surprised at the grip of Rose's fingers wrapping around her ankle and pulling her under. She let out a scream—one she would have denied had anyone asked her later. And as she did it, she felt the water enter her lungs. Startled by the sound, Rose released her ankle, leaving Thessa to thrash in the Draca.

Panicking, the mermaid lifted her to the surface. Thessa sputtered and coughed and tried to expel the sea but every movement only sent more of it in as she fought to stay above the surface. Finally, Rose swung her tail under Thessa, suspending her in the water so that she no longer had to tread.

"I'm so sorry," Rose cried. "I didn't mean to harm you."

Thessa looked around her at the water. At the flickering lights that made up Keresa in the distance. Beside her was one of the hollow, protruding rock that made the mermaids their grottos while keeping them out on the open sea. They hadn't gone very far but, even though Thessa was used to their magic by now, the speed at which they'd gotten here still surprised her. She would have admired the effortless way Rose moved through the water if she wasn't still feeling the reverberations of fear shooting through her, electrifying her bones.

"I'm sorry," Rose said again, pleading it seemed.

"Why?" It was a whisper, Thessa still trying to find her voice. "Why did you..."

How did one approach such a question?

Rose shook her head without losing the desperate panic. "I can't say anything."

Thessa tried to remember what they'd been discussing before Rose had almost killed her but her mind was drawing a blank. Perhaps water had gotten to her brain. "About what?"

"Don't ask me!" Rose snapped at her. "You keep secrets for a living, Thess, don't make me spill someone else's."

Thessa stiffened and she knew Rose felt the tension in her tail. "Someone's making you keep a secret from me?"

It was Thessa's turn to worry. Was someone threatening Rose? Gods, what had they been discussing? Was Woolhill threatening the mermaids? Campbell? She twisted on Rose's tail and took the mermaid's arms in her hands.

"If you're in danger, you have to tell me."

"I'm not in danger," Rose insisted. "None of us is."

Thessa wanted to believe her. But, just as Rose could feel the changes in Thessa's body, Thessa could feel what hadn't changed in Rose's. The mermaid hadn't relaxed when she implored Thessa not to worry. She hadn't steadied her heartbeat and her breathing and she hadn't released her tightly-corded muscles from themselves. The knowledge pulled at Thessa's chest. There was a very small group of people she felt she could trust. Madame Orinna. The Whips. The mermaids. But Thessa didn't believe Rose and she didn't bother to stomp out the anger that sparked in her. It was supposed to be them against Keresa. Against the world.

Who had pitted Thessa's only allies against her?

"Say something."

"What would you like me to say?"

"That you forgive me for almost killing you."

Thessa eyed her. "Can I trust that you won't do it again?"

The hopeful expression of Rose's face washed away as a small wave pushed over their heads. "I swear it."

She wasn't sure she wanted to be around Rose much longer, even though she trusted the mermaid like she would a sister. Sometimes, though, sisters let you down. Or so Thessa had heard. But as much as she wanted to get away, she dreaded going back to the Gillbridges. Back to Huxley in her bed unaware of everything that made her who she was.

It was a lonely revelation to feel she didn't have a soul on her side. A soul that would fight for her. For her health and her happiness and her peace of mind. Did she truly have so little in this world?

She didn't want to believe it.

Thessa noticed the twinkling of a sunray on the horizon. With a sigh, she asked Rose to return her to shore. They went slowly this time, as if Rose were terrified of breaking her. Thessa wanted to tell her she wasn't a fragile child but she remembered how she had screamed. It wasn't the first time she'd been frightened in her life and it certainly wouldn't be the last. It wasn't even the first time someone she loved had been the source of it all.

But it was the first time she felt guilty for it. Knowing what all those men must feel when her blades whipped across their throats. The thought was not enough to encourage her to change the course of her life. It was, however, enough to feel the weight of knowing the mermaids may take what the Whips did for them for granted. They knew tragedy. They felt tragedy. But rarely did the mermaids Thessa knew try to inflict it.

No, that was her job.

"I'll earn your forgiveness if I must," Rose said when they reached the shallows. The morning light sat upon her features and lit her scales. She placed a hand on Thessa's face, letting her fingers form to the curve of it. "The last thing I want for you is death."

Thessa offered Rose a tight smile. She wasn't ready for forgiveness yet. Her next words were bitter and unfair. "Don't worry. I won't let it interfere with my duties."

She began to swim away, feeling somehow both good about herself and very, very bad. She turned to find Rose still staring. She couldn't tell if it was the Draca or if it was tears wetting the corners of the mermaid's eyes. Guilt caught in her throat.

"I'll come back in a few days," Thessa told her. "Will you be here?"

She expected Rose to turn away. To tell her she didn't want anything to do with her anymore. But Rose nodded furiously before sinking back into the waves, leaving Thessa to swim back to shore on her own. The sun continued to climb, letting her feel the first tingling of heat on her back.

She sprinted back to the Gillbridges' and she knew she should crawl back into bed beside Huxley so he would never know she was gone. But she prepared to bathe. Prepared to wash her troubles off her skin as if they were stubborn flecks of dirt.

She groaned at her own dramatics. She was lucky, really. Madame Orinna had thought of everything. Not only were the Gillbridges close to Woolhill's estate, they were less than a mile from the cleanest pond in Keresa. And Madame Orinna had procured some fine soaps from an artisan in town. If she could not be nobility, she would smell of it.

Efficiency was nearly always at the top of Thessa's list of values. But even as she scrubbed her skin and lathered her hair and the sun still had some ascending to do before morning, she let herself splash around for a bit. She imagined herself to be the one and only freshwater mermaid, kicking her legs together under the water and deciding her scales would be an amalgamation of all the best greens found in nature. Deep and beautiful and earthy in a way her mermaid friends could never achieve.

Despite the pleasure she took in imagining she was no longer of the land, the guilt soon snuffed it out. What would the mermaids think of her perspective? Would they relive every betrayal to keep their tails? Would they mind the wrenching victimization if it meant they could keep the magic alive in the Draca?

It was easy for Thessa to wish to be a mermaid but she didn't think it would be as effortless to actually become one.

She reminded herself to apologize to Rose next time she saw her. Apologize to all of them. The mermaids did not owe her gratitude for the things she did for them. For the crimes and the sins she continued to commit in their names. They did not owe her for the resentment she felt and they did not owe her for her pride. They owed her nothing.

But Keresa owed them.

It was up to the Whips to settle the debt.

CHAPTER THIRTEEN

The *Volia* made its first stop by the next day. When Wyna had been rifling through the captain's things, she'd seen that Felix planned to sail to the farthest port at the start of the journey before turning around and docking at the trading cities on the way back. That port, Adalis, had access with traders on the other side of the known world that Keresa could never hope to reach. Woolhill and his staff and his captains always scheduled their shipments to arrive directly after a drop off in Adalis. Though they would make little coin in the actual port, Woolhill's ships would trade a portion of their goods for the others and deliver the more foreign items on their way back. Wyna had to admit it was a clever system.

But with every plan comes a hiccup and Woolhill seemed to have made this hiccup work for him. The *Volia* was not yet at Adalis and instead anchored in Nazren. Nazren had no interest in the spices and the cloth from Adalis and beyond. Rather, they took interest in the supplies Keresa had to offer. The metals and the wools they imported from the neighboring inlands. Nazren was not a city built on luxury. It was built on labor.

Woolhill's ships, then, stopped to offload some of their goods and acquire supplies for the final leg of the journey to Adalis.

Sailing with only half of what was necessary to keep the crew alive made more room for goods to sell. It made for more profit.

It was quite an empire to be built.

Wyna had never been to Nazren, had never desired to go to a city everyone had deemed stuffy and void of fun. And though the sea-facing side of the city fronted workshops, from her vantage on the ship coming in, she could see the beauty beyond. A beauty that had not been marred by profiteers combing the land for resources.

She watched from the deck railing as the *Volia's* crew brought the ship in. She watched the corded muscles meld with the corded rope, flexing and pulling taut with the work. She watched the cream sails, freckled with Woolhill's colors, roll back into themselves. She watched Solomon stretch his limbs and pop his joints before jumping from the nest and skittering back down the mast.

And then she watched Felix climb out of the boats to check in with the harbormaster.

Wyna allowed herself to feel pride as the two men talked. She knew she was still a long way from her home in Keresa—a long way from completing her time on this ship—but she had made it from land to land without a scratch. Without incident. Now, she only had to count her days and her luck until Adalis. And then the next port. And then the next. It comforted her to break up the journey into its separate chunks. How easy it seemed when she only had to consider her next few days—a week, perhaps, at most.

She tried to ignore the tickling on the back of her neck that told her, even though they had made it to land, this land didn't have Madame Orinna's protection. She no longer had the forceful matron helping to fight her battles.

This was all on her.

She felt a male presence sidle up behind her. It was too tall to be Brennan. Too nimble to be Felix. She twisted her neck just enough to see Zachariah in her periphery.

"Why don't you go explore Nazren?" he asked her, loud and

insistent. Instantly, she knew he didn't speak to her for her sake. He had something he wanted the crew to hear.

"I think I'll stay."

"Shame. Thought we'd trade you out for a whore who does her job. If Friswell's that feral for you, he can go as well." Zachariah turned to see if Brennan was listening. He wasn't. "Sure there's a bosun worth his salt somewhere in this town."

"And what do you do here, Zach?" she asked sweetly. His eyes flicked down to her chest. Some may have found empowerment in their body's ability to entrance but she found no pleasure in the way he leered.

Zachariah straightened his back, peacocking for the others. "I'm the navigator. As you should know."

"Do navigators 'worth their salt' frequently lose astrolabes in the toilets?"

His wind-whipped skin turned red before her as he grew defensive and his voice dropped a few decibels. "I got us here, didn't I?"

"So you've found Nazren," Wyna agreed. "Do you think you can manage to find your own replacement?"

Zachariah's embarrassment rolled to the back of his brain as his fury took over. He lunged for Wyna and she was unsure whether he meant to pull her to him or push her from the ship entirely. She didn't stick around to find out, sidestepping his grasp and letting him crash into the sturdy railing. She heard the shouts of other crew members—the ones who had no love for Wyna but wouldn't watch Zachariah harm a woman. A crewmate whose name Wyna thought was Judah stepped forward and pulled Zachariah away, whispering something. She couldn't catch everything he said but it sounded to her as though he was warning the other mate to not cost them a port with disorderly conduct.

Wyna acted as though the encounter hadn't bothered her but it sent her mind on an odyssey of its own. Perhaps Zachariah only meant to get under her skin this time but she still felt the path his eyes had taken over her body. She still remembered the plans she had seen forming in his mind in her cabin when they first met. Perhaps he wouldn't do anything too serious yet. In front of everyone else. But she didn't like the thought of what he could do to her in the dead of night.

Out on the open sea.

Madame Orinna would tear them apart looking for her Whip but would these men do anything in the meantime when they realized she was gone? Would Felix reprimand his men? Would Brennan fight for her?

Something closed inside Wyna when she realized she didn't know the answers to her questions. Perhaps all she wanted was for something to miss her dearly, to notice when she was gone. She wasn't sure she could remain open long enough to wait until the answers pointed to yes.

THE DAYLIGHT ABANDONED HER AS QUICKLY as it had come but she couldn't feel sorry for it. The mermaid's face had swam around her head all day so Wyna was appreciative of the *Volia's* timing. Not only would the ship be mostly empty as the crew drank their way through Nazren that evening but Wyna no longer had to worry about finding her way back to it out in the open, with no way to tell how far she would have drifted.

She was glued to the deck, her fingers wrapped around the railing until her dark hands turned as white as the foam crusting the waves. Her breath didn't even hitch when she saw the tail zipping through the water because she had been holding tension in her body all day.

Carefully and quietly, ensuring her eyes landed on every inch around her to verify no one lurked, she climbed onto the railing at the back of the ship and leapt. Luckily, the water was deep enough here that she didn't crash into any rocks. When she surfaced on those night-blackened waters, the mermaid's face was only inches from hers.

"May I take you somewhere?" the mermaid asked, her voice carrying a mild accent and, though it was familiar, Wyna couldn't place it. Wyna had barely nodded her agreement before the mermaid told her to hold her breath and yanked her under, dragging her through the water.

They emerged in a cave lit only by the shine of the moon and its stars. She was still catching her breath when six more heads rose from the water.

"She's who we've been chasing?" one of them asked.

The mermaid who'd brought Wyna nodded. "Trading ship from Keresa. I'd recognize Woolhill's colors anywhere."

A waif-like mermaid to Wyna's left grunted her disappointment. "I had hoped it was a pirate ship. Their women are always so..." she trailed off, as if a fond memory stole her voice.

"Beautiful?" one of the other mermaids supplied helpfully.

"Gay," Wyna's mermaid confirmed.

The waif tittered and rested her body against the wall of the cave. "Yes, that's the one." She turned to Wyna, staring intently. "You—"

Another cut her off. "Now's not the time, Ibot."

Ibot crossed her arms over her chest. "You say that as if I've no control over myself. I'm not some animal!" She faced Wyna once more. "I was merely going to ask what you were doing on a trading ship. I know they don't employ women."

Wyna's mermaid grunted gently. "Not in the usual way, they don't."

Ibot flashed her pity at the other mermaid. "Adrie..."

Adrie ignored her. "Are you alright?" she asked Wyna. "Are you on that ship against your will?"

Wyna shook her head.

"Are you there why I think you are?"

"Yes," Wyna admitted. "But Madame Orinna bartered my spot on the ship—"

"Orinna Swither?" Adrie asked, turning steely. "You're a Whip. Don't worry. We'll get you off. Send you back if you want."

"No. Wait." Another mermaid swam forward to get a better look at Wyna. "I've heard of the Whips. That Clemen girl—what was her name? Constance? She told me the Whips helped her."

"Clemen?" Wyna bounced in the water. "Thessa Clemen is my sister! Or—she's a Whip, too."

"What do you mean?" Adrie demanded. "Helped her how?"

"You know what the Whips are called back in Keresa, don't you, Adrie? You lived there all your life!"

"Just tell me, Evelyn. Don't have me guess."

"They're the mermaids," Evelyn laughed. "This one's likely known about us her entire life." Wyna didn't correct her. It hadn't been nearly as long as Evelyn suggested. But compared to many back home, it was a difference that didn't matter. "I don't think you two are the same," Evelyn finished softly, directing the last part to Adrie.

"You're from Keresa?" Wyna asked her. "How'd you end up all the way out here?"

Adrie wouldn't meet her eyes now that she knew what Wyna was. It made Wyna want to shrink into herself. "I thought—my brothel did the same to me."

Wyna reached for Adrie, trying to rest her hand on the mermaid's shoulder. Adrie pulled away as if she were recalling a different sort of touch. "But your brothel was real."

Adrie blinked away a few tears. "I didn't make it quite as far as you did before I jumped. And I didn't know about the mermaids when I did."

Though Wyna wanted to drink in the stories of the other mermaids, wanted to make them feel heard, she wouldn't ask them to reveal their deepest hurts to her. She wouldn't ask them to relive it, as she had the others back home. She had regretted it ever since.

"Do they know what happened to you?" she asked Adrie. "I can tell them when I return."

As soon as the words left her mouth, she placed the accent she'd heard on the mermaids. It was more of a dialect, really. One of the tortoise girls. Wyna knew the way Keresa treated them on land. She couldn't imagine the kinds of violence Adrie had seen on the sea, with no ruling body to keep up appearances. She didn't try to embrace her or touch her again but it was clear to her now why Adrie had been the one to appear to Wyna the night previous.

She'd been trying to protect her.

Wyna was happy to offer her protection in return.

"Thank you," Wyna told her. "Thank you for checking on me."

Adrie nodded and sunk back under the water, only to pop back up in the middle of the pack. Wyna tried to tell herself it wasn't that she wanted to get away from Wyna, that perhaps she just wanted to get away from the spotlight on the worst portion of her life.

"So what are you doing on the ship?" Ibot asked. "If not pirating or living a nightmare?"

"I'm there for you all. Making sure they don't see you. Taking care of it if they do."

"Our hero," Ibot deadpanned. Wyna wasn't sure where the hostility came from.

"Hey!" Evelyn snapped. "You saw what they did to Godelena. You should be thanking her for making sure it doesn't happen again."

Wyna was afraid to ask—it was against the rules she'd just set for herself. But how was she supposed to prevent something she'd never imagined? She was afraid of the answer, yes, but more afraid of what might happen if she never asked.

"What did they do to Godelena?"

Evelyn gave Wyna a quick shake of the head. Apparently Godelena wasn't up for discussion. Horrors of what might have befallen her flitted through Wyna's mind. Perhaps, in her time on the *Volia*, hiding from the men and from her duty, she'd forgotten the real reason she was there. She had forgotten why it was so important that the Whips monitor the safety of these women.

Everything that had been taken from them could never be returned. But Wyna would give them what she could.

EVELYN SWAM WYNA back to the *Volia* this time. Now that Adrie knew Wyna wasn't in immediate danger, it seemed she wanted to stay as far away from the trading ship as she could.

Wyna didn't blame her.

"We'll keep pace with you until you get back to Keresa," Evelyn assured her.

It was a gamble to have the mermaids following the ship. One careless inch could reveal their presence to the crew. And perhaps it wasn't a fishing ship—not a whaler—but that didn't mean they wouldn't try to kill the magic they found in the sea. Without Madame Orinna and without her Whips by her side, Wyna felt naked out on the water. Perhaps they couldn't intervene but she felt comforted knowing they were there should she ever need them.

It was selfish and it was dangerous but she didn't want to give them up.

"Thank you," Wyna breathed.

"You'll have enough time to dry before they return?"

"I'll be fine."

"Be careful." Evelyn placed a tiny kiss on top of Wyna's head.

A feeling of contentment exploded through Wyna at the touch of Evelyn's lips to her hair. Maybe she didn't have the Whips out here but she had found a new sisterhood. One that could follow her on her journeys away from Keresa. Unconditionally welcoming.

Evelyn watched from the water, taking great care to ensure Wyna made it back onto the ship without injury. And when she again stood on the railing, she turned to wave furiously at the mermaid, a goodbye that would convey her intense joy at having visited with them and her even stronger melancholy at having to say goodbye, however briefly.

The smallest sound hit her ears. One made up of the hollow of grating vocal cords. The sound one might make if they were choking on their own surprise. Trying not to be heard. Wyna turned in horror, frantically searching the deck of the *Volia* for signs of a crewmember she hadn't seen. One she hadn't had the care to look out for. But the ship was just as empty as she'd left it. The harbor, too, housed not a soul.

With a calmness that surprised her in her current state of panic, Wyna lifted her head. Bent her neck, inch by inch. Past the nest and straight to the pair of wide green eyes that pierced her even from the distance.

Solomon's gaze flickered back and forth. Falling from Wyna to the water and back again. He had no words to offer. And, quite frankly, neither did Wyna. She had no lies to satiate him. She had nothing to exchange with him for his silence on the matter. But even if she had, deep in her soul, she knew that was not the Whip way. Whips did not barter and hope their offerings were enough. They did not depend on others to keep the secrets they held close to their hearts.

The first strands of morning peeked at the two of them from the horizon. Muted sunbeams hit Solomon's face as he stared and they stayed, locked. Homed in on one another and waiting until the other made the first move. Wyna knew she could not wait until the man decided to descend from his post. She could not risk a fair fight on solid standing. No, she didn't think he would provoke her. That he would attack her first. But she imagined him to fight back when *she* did. They always fought back.

Already, Wyna mourned the Crow. The shy man, so valuable to Felix and so clearly deserving of praise. Indeed, Solomon was the skilled, focused observer Felix claimed him to be. It would be impossible to spare him his life, she decided. Not when his position on this ship was so dependent on his ability to communicate. And if she left him with that ability, it would only follow that he would communicate what she'd done to him. And when she was gone, the search for her ethereal friends would begin.

She wanted to think it a shame he had been at his post. A shame he had remained on the ship. But she would not pretend that this was entirely her fault. Closing her eyes to expel the grief from her body, she stalked towards the mast. And when she opened her lids, his gaze followed hers, oscillating between the set of her jaw and the step of her feet. She lost sight of him as she gripped the rungs of the mast and hauled her body up towards the nest. She counted on his shock to keep him in place. To keep him from jumping out to the arms of the mast that held the sail.

She counted on him not to shout.

He didn't scuttle from her when she entered the nest. Didn't fear her the way she thought he should. But that was only because he didn't know just how much she could accomplish. And as she freed her sickles from her waistband, his eyes returned to the water where Evelyn had been. As if he were willing the mermaid back, desperate to see the beauty of the creature once more. Desperate for what else, exactly? To admire her? To kill her? To share her?

Wyna thought he should focus on the mermaid in front of him.

The one who had no choice but to clean up her mess.

CHAPTER FOURTEEN

Thessa could not boast success her second day at the Woolhill estate, seeing as it'd gone much like her first. Introductions to people she'd already met who hadn't bothered remembering her. Hostility from the ward and flirtation from the guards. A complete absence of notable staff and a rushing sort of travel from entry to room that left her no opportunity to slip away and explore. Her third day, she vowed, would have to be better.

It was a laughable notion, really. Alastor was caught up in meetings when Thessa arrived and, after a few too many inquiries, she knew why. Campbell, it seemed, had taken it upon herself to run Alastor's social calendar, meaning the older man had only time for business meetings. Nothing in the name of pleasure or pleasantry.

Thessa would not be daunted so easily.

She stuck around when William had told her the news, the forthcoming doorman quite unsettled at the thought of Thessa going so quickly. She told him she had some business to attend to with the master's ward, assuring him she would not be going until she spoke with someone in this house of the noble variety.

William had sighed wistfully and Thessa knew he wished to be noble, if only to get a sliver more of her attention.

She didn't enjoy toying with the boy and, indeed, found him quite an agreeable addition to the Woolhill estate. He did his job well. Obeyed Alastor and Campbell effortlessly. But he was still not immune to the charm of a Whip.

William had officially made the list of trusted parties. Should the Whips ever truly get their hands in Woolhill's trade, they'd no need to worry for the doorman. However, Thessa was still wholly unsure of the rest of the household staff and this was entirely because she couldn't get in long enough to speak with them. It was time, it seemed, to try to wield her social leverage.

"William," she began, standing on the top step with him, her hands gripped impatiently around her waist, "will you pass along a message for me?"

"Yes, Miss." His reply was quick. Easy.

"Will you see to it that Miss Moore is aware of the slight she's bringing upon Orinna Swither's name?" she asked sweetly. William blanched. "Madame Swither, as you know, holds a prominent place in Keresan society. Her pockets may not run as deep at Woolhill's but her influence is perhaps just as broad." Thessa took unfortunate notice of the bead of sweat that appeared on William's forehead. "If Miss Moore continues to deny me access to Mister Woolhill, I hate to think of the offense Madame Swither might take."

"Miss—"

"Now, I know that I, myself, am not the most important member of society. But if Miss Moore pays no heed to Madame Swither's personal guarantee of my character then I cannot promise my benefactor will have any desire to continue a working relationship with Mister Woolhill or any of his employees."

Perhaps it wasn't the smartest move to pit the head of a trading empire against the matron of a House in the Sin District. But Thessa knew Madame Orinna's influence was greater than her reputation might suggest. Woolhill might have control over trade—over financials. But Madame Orinna had control over the people. Over their feelings. Over their bodies.

And everyone knew it.

William nodded, understanding completely the meaning behind Thessa's threat, before disappearing into the house for a moment. It wasn't the first time Thessa'd had to use Madame Orinna to get her way and she was sure it wouldn't be the last. But Madame Orinna had insisted it be that way. That was, after all, exactly why she'd built her reputation as it was. To ensure her girls had a standing to fall back on so she could extend her tentacles in every direction throughout Keresa.

Thessa wasn't waiting long when William returned, a tousled and annoyed Campbell stomping behind him.

"Follow me," Campbell barked. Two words and she was spinning and immersing herself once more into the shadowed recesses of the Woolhill estate.

They took a different path than Thessa had taken previously, through a separate wing of the manor, and Thessa tried to shake off the prickles of annoyance. So she wasn't going to meet Alastor, after all. She cursed Campbell behind her back, making subtle-yet-obscene gestures with her hands when the other girl wasn't looking.

As they went deeper into the den of beasts, Thessa caught the sounds of construction. At first, she'd assumed they came from outside the manor—some part of the mansion Thessa had yet had a chance to look upon. But as she listened, she followed the source of the sound to a basement entrance. So...underground construction.

Could that be the rumor Madame Orinna had mentioned?

By the time Campbell finally settled her gait, she and Thessa stood in a room themed for the Draca. A luminescent, scaled drake swam over the moulding of the room, watching over its rich blue walls with narrow precision. Thessa noted the dragon's body had been crafted with a mermaid in mind and smiled to herself. The Woolhills were closer to the truth than they realized. Fortunately, not in the way that sent Thessa's nerves sparking.

A desk of sturdy, well-crafted wood sat in the middle of the room, covered in calendars and parchment that Thessa would have given anything to finger through. Unfortunately, now wasn't the time for gleaming information from Woolhill documents. It was time to crack through Campbell's shell. Thessa was nervous a hateful creature might linger under the surface.

And what a shame that would be.

"I'll ask that you not resort to threats against my family," Campbell clipped—politely—at her once the desk was safely between them.

"And I'll ask that you not resort to threats against my character."

"I've said nothing of your character, Miss Clemen."

"Perhaps not directly," Thessa admitted. "Or out loud."

Campbell was unphased and it was not lost on Thessa that the girl might think it an insult to accuse her of it, once again. "Again, I'll ask what you want with my father."

"And I'll answer just as I did before." As Campbell rolled her eyes, Thessa made her bid on distraction. "What happened to your family?"

"What happened to yours?" she countered.

Thessa answered with a broken sort of honesty. The kind that saw no reason to lie because to lie would hurt more than simply laying the truth bare for another to see. "My father murdered my mother. I never saw him again."

Campbell, to Thessa's credit, was startled by the honesty. Just not startled enough to reveal her own history. "I'm sorry," she said, using kind words for the first time with Thessa. Likely the last, as well.

"I trust you had no hand in it," Thessa said wryly in an attempt to pry out a bit of the hostility. The Whips would never infiltrate the estate if they couldn't trust Campbell. "And you?" she asked again.

"You're familiar with Ellis Moore." It wasn't a question. Thessa nodded. "Ellis was my father. A good friend of Alastor's. I didn't know my mother when she still walked the earth. Alastor claims I'm just like her." Campbell smiled like she agreed. "But my mother wasn't noble. And after Ellis died, Alastor was the only one who kept me in good standing. So I'm sure you can imagine why I'm put off by the prospect of women traipsing around this manor as if Alastor owes them something. If he feels a debt is owed, he'll ensure it's paid ten times over. But"—she made her way around the desk—"I feel it's my duty to ensure you never make the mistake of entitlement."

Thessa gritted her teeth, growing weary of the cyclical conversation. Always coming back to how untrustworthy Thessa was. Campbell seemed to hold fondness for her mother, a nameless girl who'd fallen into a noble's bed, and yet she hated Thessa for the same things. She felt a growling frustration.

"I'm not sure how many times I can tell you I have no interest in your father's money, Miss Moore," Thessa said. And then she changed the subject because she was determined to milk even the smallest stream of conversation out of Campbell. Something to show her Thessa was a person. "Is your office a shrine to the sea?"

"I've always felt quite close to it," Campbell answered, shifting easily with Thessa. The amber of her eyes followed Thessa as she gazed around the room. "I've heard it said that the Dracan Sea is a body of magic rather than water."

Thessa felt now as if she were being toyed with. "And do you agree?"

"It has a magic to it, to be sure," she answered. "I'd be surprised if Madame Swither hadn't mentioned the lore of it all to you."

"Why would she do that?"

Campbell laughed. "It isn't as if she hadn't named her whole operation after the lore of the Draca."

Thessa wanted Campbell to continue. To push further down this avenue. She wanted Campbell to say the word. There was a reason the Whips were called mermaids and no one Thessa had ever met had come this close to speaking it aloud. No one alive, at least. But Campbell said no more about Dracan lore. She did not wax poetic about the creatures hiding beneath its waves. Thessa could have challenged her. Could have played dumb and made note of the drake riding the moulding of the room. But she, too, said nothing.

"I heard sounds of construction," Thessa said instead, not bothering to ask the question she knew Campbell had already gleaned.

"Indeed. It should be an asset to the trade. But," she said, "we've decided not to unveil it until we're able to determine its success."

Thessa leaned against the desk, the edge of it cutting into the tops of her thighs, her back now to Campbell. She couldn't stand to watch the way the other girl's lips moved. Not when she was trying so hard to focus on her words.

"And you have influence in Alastor's trade?" Thessa asked. "Surely his daughter must play quite the part if she also manages his social calendar."

"I do enough." But she did more than enough. Her office and her manner were effective in telling Thessa that much.

Perhaps she needed very little from Alastor. Perhaps all she needed was Campbell.

"Will you see Madame Swither anytime soon?" Campbell asked abruptly and Thessa heard her rifling through the papers on her desk.

Thessa wasn't sure which answer Campbell wanted from her. She played it safe. "Hard to say. Why? What is it?"

"Just this morning I got a report from Nazren regarding the *Volia's* docking. I thought she might be interested in inquiring after her employee."

"I'm certain I could get the message to her, if you'll trust me with it," Thessa assured her, turning around. Deadly curious to know how Wyna fared.

Campbell lifted her shoulders in a half-hearted shrug that conveyed more emotion than she intended. "I can't say much about her well-being but the harbormaster's report lists her presence on the ship, at the very least."

"Was there a chance she might not be?" Thessa challenged, trying to hide the center of her concern, watching Campbell only from the corner of her eye.

Campbell did not balk at her own mistake. "Of course not," she said. "But assurances are always nice."

"And yet you seem immune to my own assurances that I'm not who you believe me to be."

Campbell lifted the corner of her plump lips, sending her cheekbone right into her eye. "Oh, I know you're not who I believe you to be. I just don't know who that is yet."

It was clear to Thessa that the young women were caught in a game of hunter and prey, each of them taking their turn as the hunter and neither admitting to taking on the role of the prey.

"You could find out," Thessa told her. "If you cared to."

She desperately wished Campbell did.

"I will."

Thessa was unable to respond before the door to Campbell's office glided open—there was none of the creaking of time in this manor. As she still faced the door, she saw Alastor's confident, if slightly hobbled, entrance felled by his surprise at finding Thessa inside.

"Miss Clemen!"

She lit her face in another of her best smiles and strode forward to embrace him before Campbell could step between them. Perhaps it wasn't proper for her body to touch his in this way—she knew it wasn't—but it was familiarity that she wanted and it was familiarity she would deliver.

"Alastor!" she exclaimed, matching the excitement of his tone but wedging in a bit of despair. A well-placed implication that her absence from him had nothing to do with her.

He wrapped his arms around her shoulders and held her to

him a little longer and a little tighter than Thessa would have preferred. But she did not pry herself from him. She told herself this was the kind of embrace the man would offer his daughter. Casting a look at Campbell behind them, Thessa decided that was exactly what she wanted from Alastor. The affection and protection and trust he extended to Campbell.

She let herself wonder, for only a moment, what might've happened had Alastor known her father. Had he been left to care for *her* as a child. Would she turn out as cold as Campbell? Would she still be as cold as she already was? As...violent?

No, she decided. She knew the whole of her character had been woven around her past. Around Madame Orinna. Around the Whips and the mermaids.

She pulled free of him in a way that made it seem as though she merely wanted to look at his face and not that she could no longer stand to be pressed against his chest.

"I'm so glad to be able to see you today, after all," she told him. "I was worried you might be caught up in meetings for the whole of the afternoon! Miss Moore's been so kind as to entertain me."

He beamed, full of pride, at his daughter over Thessa's head. "Ah, yes. She's always been my savior when it comes to entertaining my guests."

Thessa's chest hollowed as he said it. Surely, he couldn't have meant to say something so brazen out loud. Her face fell as she turned back to Campbell but Campbell's eyes were focused on a groove in her desk. She tried to watch the way the other girl's chest constricted and expanded. Tried to find hitches in its movement that would show if Alastor's suggestion had affected her or if she was merely bored.

Alastor was oblivious to the spikes in Thessa's blood pressure and continued speaking. "I'm delighted you're here, actually. I've been in correspondence with Madame Swither and she suggested I arrange to have you at a dinner I'm hosting tomorrow evening." He straightened his back, still pulling himself up on that pride.

"There'll be dozens of Keresa's upper echelon in attendance. I imagine that'd be wonderful in the name of making connections for you in this town. It'll be like your presentation into society!"

"Is she not a bit old to be presented to society?" Campbell asked.

Alastor only *tsk*ed. "It's never too late to make a proper entrance. Why don't you stay for the afternoon? I'd planned on taking Campbell for a walk through the estate. It'd be wonderful to have your shining face there as well." He clipped Thessa on the chin as he finished his invitation.

She knew she couldn't refuse.

"That—"

"I'm certain she has more important engagements to attend to," Campbell chimed in, knowing full well no engagement could offer anyone in Keresa more opportunity than an afternoon with Alastor Woolhill.

Thessa grimaced and tried to speak again. "That sounds lovely."

But Thessa did not say so for Alastor's sake—though she *was* glad to spend time that would get her closer to the end of this assignment. In truth, after Alastor's comment about Campbell entertaining his guests, she suddenly found she couldn't stand the man. She would believe him to be a wolf until someone assured her of the contrary.

As well, something tickled Thessa about her earlier exchange with the ward. Something that said they each shared a secret and were carefully exploring to see if the other knew. A part of Thessa wanted to simply burst and demand Campbell tell her everything. That she put Thessa out of her misery.

But if Thessa was wrong about the breadth of Campbell's knowledge...well, that was a dangerous mistake to make. One that could cost the Whips any sort of relationship with the Woolhills. She would have to ensure her own knowledge about the mermaids never made it past Campbell.

The thought of bringing harm to her somehow made Thessa

lurch even more. She'd grown to like the game the two of them played and, though she'd never say it aloud, Thessa had a healthy respect for the firmness of Campbell's convictions. For the strength Campbell had no intentions to hide from the world. Or, at least from Thessa.

Sure, she was bitter and she was mean but Thessa felt she had every right to be. Especially if the undercurrent of her entertainment career was what Thessa thought it was. The only piece—well, perhaps not the only—that Thessa couldn't put together was why, if it were all true, Campbell was so keen on protecting him from the likes of *Thessa*.

Accepting Alastor's invitation to walk the estate likely wouldn't answer all her questions right away. But it was a jagged little shard of the puzzle.

She only had to find the rest.

CHAPTER FIFTEEN

Wyna hated to lose the garment but she stripped off the blood-spattered over-clothes and shoved them through one of the holes in the bowsprit, braving the horrific stench. She was in and out before the smell could stick to her and ran with purpose across the deck to the other end of the ship, hoping to get in fresh, dry clothes before the sun brought back any of the crew.

She debated with herself whether it might be better to pretend she had hid in her room the entire night or if she should pretend to notice the body once the others returned. No one ever suspected the shocked damsel.

A part of her thought she would cry at having killed the man. She'd never actually delivered the final blow. But the skin of his throat was really no different than the packed muscle of a tongue or a sinewy tendon. It was tissue that she had to pierce and cut and she had done it.

She didn't bother telling him she was sorry and it was too late now, anyhow. She would make her apologies when she joined him in the afterlife. She'd never been overly religious but she did hope the gods would take his soul somewhere nice.

Wyna could hardly follow the train of her thoughts as they

jumped through the hoops of all her disjointed anxieties. A Whip would be strong. A Whip would not be cowed by what she must do.

But had Wyna actually *had* to do it?

This wasn't a case of the Crow spotting a school of mermaids while he was at his post. He hadn't gone to tell the others because there'd been no one else to tell. No one but Wyna and Evelyn. Perhaps she should have tried to spare him. Should have shown him mercy for what he had no wish to see.

Would Thessa have shown him mercy?

Thessa never would have gotten herself into this situation in the first place. She would never have dared to be so brazen in meeting with the other mermaids. She would have swam out to sea, Wyna thought, and let the mermaids come to her. And then, when she had finished, she would have had them return her far from where they would be seen. That was what she would do. That was what a Whip would do and Thessa, Wyna well knew, was everything a Whip should be.

Oh, how she wished she were more like Thessa.

For the first time since setting her feet on the deck of the *Volia*, Wyna questioned if maybe Thessa should have been the one on this mission instead. Yes, Wyna had her fears about not being everything Madame Orinna wanted her to be but she had never thought she was simply undeserving.

She did now.

Or...or perhaps Madame Orinna would praise her for what she had done. She would be reprimanded for endangering the mermaids, to be sure, but she had been able to solve the problem rather quickly.

Wyna was getting ahead of herself. Nothing had been solved yet. Nothing, save for removing the mouthpiece for Wyna's secrets. She wouldn't count herself lucky until every soul on that ship had discounted her as the culprit of Solomon's death. She would have to get crafty in how she did so. No matter what story she decided to spin regarding where she was when his death had taken place, she would need to begin planting the seeds of a frame. Someone to pin the deed on so, down the line, no one could unravel the threads of an unsolved mystery.

But she certainly couldn't be too vocal about her opinions on the matter. No one suspect could catch her eye and be the brunt of her blame. No, that would inevitably lead to suspicion against her.

Who to pin it on, though?

Zachariah made a tempting choice. But he'd been in a Nazren. And Wyna couldn't verify his whereabouts that night. Certainly not enough to say he slipped away long enough to off Solomon and return. And what if he had spent the night in some-one's bed, far from sleep? The longer she considered her list of faux suspects, she realized she couldn't account for any of their whereabouts.

So what did that mean for her?

In her panic, Wyna began to weep. She wasn't equipped for murder. Not like this. Not without Madame Orinna having already laid the perfect trap. Without her having every detail mapped, right down to years in the future when those who hadn't been there started to ask questions. It was a frustrated sort of weeping but one that opened itself to all of Wyna's other bottled emotions. The tears filled her pits of loneliness until those pits overflowed and set off torrents of their own.

How could anyone love her after the things she'd done? She wasn't sure if the mermaids would still welcome her with open arms when they knew she'd killed a man just for having eyes and using them. And she began to see quite clearly that she could never dream of opening herself romantically to someone who would never be privy to how quick and light her fingers were, whether they were plunged into pockets or wrapped around her blades.

She heard the commotion above deck as she was securing the last of the ties around her skirts. It made her tears fall harder knowing that comeuppance was so near. Wyna had no time to dry the salt streaks or soothe out the puffiness on her face before her door crashed open, slamming and rattling her walls.

"Wyn—oh, thank the gods." She turned to find Brennan standing in her doorway, his chest heaving as if he hadn't expected to find her here. She watched as his gaze fell over the planes of her and when he finally saw the redness of her own eyes, he fell. "You know," he said.

She did not have a chance to revel in the feel of him checking on her—or knowing his concern for her well-being had rocked him completely. Rather, she let the tears fall and nodded, rushing forward to push herself into Brennan's chest. He wrapped his arms around her instantly, as if enveloping her in the safety of himself. A comfort, maybe, but really the only way to ensure she was physically real and unharmed. The streaks on her face wet the fabric of his shirt and maybe she wasn't crying at having found Solomon but no one could ever accuse her of faking it.

"Why didn't you come get anyone?" he asked her.

She wasn't sure what she found in his voice. Perhaps that was just one of those questions people asked when something tragic happened. A question that, on the surface, was meant to help them understand but really only conveyed their desire to find something or someone to blame. Perhaps it was one of those. Or perhaps Brennan had a tightened grip on skepticism.

"I didn't—I—" she babbled, as if she didn't understand why she hadn't. Like she thought his question as a great one and, oh, if only she had thought of that in her state of shock. "I don't know. I was so, *so* scared."

He stopped rubbing her skin as she said it and gripped her shoulders harshly before pulling her from him. "Have you seen who did it?" he asked. "When you were up on deck?"

Wyna found herself supremely annoyed by his questioning. As if he were trying to catch her in a lie. No, she wanted to say that she hadn't seen who'd done it. But she knew the body was still fresh. That the blood likely hadn't even stopped in the nest.

She tried to think quickly. If the blood hadn't stopped pooling, then how had they known of Solomon's death at all?

How could she explain how she knew?

Shit.

She played dumb. "Have I seen who did what?" she cried. "I heard a wretched sound as I was climbing the stairs to find you all. It frightened me so badly that I ran back here! I've been hiding ever since."

He set his mouth harshly. "Do you have a weak stomach?"

The character she'd created would have told him that she did. And a Whip would have, as well, as a sort of insurance. Too many eyes on an act were sure to pick it apart. But Wyna wanted to see the damage. She shook her head.

Brennan laced his fingers through hers, his arm utterly stiff and pressed close to his side to keep her from wandering away from him. He led her to the deck and, with each step they ascended, she could feel the tendons of his wrist flex as his fingers folded into her skin.

An earth-shaking thump sent Wyna recoiling, almost back down the stairs if Brennan hadn't been holding her so tightly. The stomach she'd just claimed wasn't weak turned inside her when she saw what had made the noise. It seemed as if the sailors hadn't had any wise ideas about how to get Solomon's body out of the nest and had sent someone after him. Only, with all the gracefulness of a toddler, Solomon's rescuer had merely tossed the body over the edge.

Though it horrified her and it made her sick to think of someone treating her lifeless body that way, Wyna was secretly glad for the crew's solution. Sure, the killing blow was obvious and there would be no question Solomon had had his throat slit. But the journey from nest to deck would surely leave some marks. Ones that made it less obvious there hadn't really been a struggle.

And no struggle meant they were less likely to assume a woman could hold her own against a sailor.

"Why did you bring me out here?" she asked Brennan, letting her voice tremble.

"Because I don't want you out of my sight until we leave Nazren."

She nodded and he pried his fingers from her hand like he never actually wanted to let go. She rubbed where he had touched her as he joined the rest of the *Volia's* crew in propping Solomon's body up for inspection. Sidling up to the corpse, Brennan bent over. Put his face only inches from the gashes in Solomon's neck. Wyna wished she could understand what might be happening in his mind as he looked. What kind of conspiracies he crafted just by looking at blood and flesh and bone.

He glanced back at her for only a second. Not nearly long enough for anyone to notice. Not long enough for any of the crew to see where his loyalties might lie.

He stood, brushing his hands on his trousers even though he hadn't touched anything, and stepped back so the other crewmates could have a gander. And when they had all looked and loudly whispered, Brennan finally spoke.

"This wasn't done by one of us," Brennan announced, stalling the gathered crowd. "I've seen the work you men do and those lines are too clean for the likes of any of us."

The *Volia's* crew silenced, on the brink of explosion. They didn't appreciate the insult Brennan had extended to them. But to defend their skill was to admit they were capable of the crime. Wyna wouldn't have been surprised if one of the men did actually incriminate himself in the name of preserving manhood and skill.

But these men were shaken.

Solomon hadn't died by taking on some dangerous part of duty. He hadn't died in a brawl and he hadn't died for lack of survival resources. Solomon, they saw and they thought, had been targeted and any of them could be next.

Zachariah, committed to being the villain, stepped forward and pointed an accusing finger towards Brennan. "How do we know you aren't just saying that so you look innocent?" he demanded.

Brennan's expression had a healthy mix of boredom and distaste. "Because I've been at Cap's side all night, pissant."

Wyna wondered if he was telling the truth until Felix confirmed it.

"So we stay in Nazren," Judah suggested. "Report it here and wait for trial."

Felix shifted, discomfited, before moving to the side of the boat and peering over the edge with the dredges of first morning light. They were supposed to have been off by now, long before any of the other ships boarded, and they didn't have long until the harbor flooded with the Nazrenes. Turning back to his crew, he pitched his voice low and deep.

"We're already behind schedule," he told them. "If we stay in Nazren we'll miss all our ports and all them other leeches will have stolen our partners. You know we ain't the only ones with our goods and our only advantages have been getting to Adalis before the rest. We need to go."

"But what about Solomon?" asked Judah.

Felix shook his head. "Woolhill'll have our heads if we don't meet projected profit. Or Campbell will." He shuddered at the mention of Campbell and Wyna couldn't imagine how terrifying he must be. "We can't afford the delay."

Judah's body tensed, brimming with outrage at Felix's disrespect for Solomon's life. For his body. To leave Nazren now would be karmic injustice. But to defy his captain, Judah himself would have a death wish. And if there was one thing Wyna learned about these men in her short time on the *Volia*, it was that self-preservation was the primary concern. They didn't yearn for brotherhood and family like Wyna did. They yearned for coin. Yearned to finish the job as quickly and as easily as possible until they could return home and explore other pleasures, biding time until they set out once more.

Judah stormed away, prepared to relieve his fury in other

tasks. The others followed, meandering away like they'd only been dismissed from a meeting, not at all like they'd just been instructed to ignore the law in order to meet their boss's monetary demands. Wyna almost felt bad for Solomon. For the way they cared so little to see whoever had murdered their friend brought to justice. But then she remembered it had been her who'd murdered the man and she had no interest in serving herself justice for something she'd had to do.

The apprentices returned to Solomon's body with an old tattered sail that had been stored below deck and wrapped him loosely in the fabric. They would toss him overboard once they made it out to sea and Wyna hoped they would see to it before the body started stinking and rotting. Felix observed the young men, his arms crossed over his chest to keep himself from wringing his hands. Guilt and worry were eating the captain from the inside out but Wyna didn't feel bad for it. His guilt was for his own wrongdoing. Not for hers.

As if he could sense her staring, he turned and found her with her back pressed against the railing of the stairs that led to the upper deck and she saw every emotion that crossed his face until he landed back on worry. His crew he could trust to keep his secrets. They were motivated by the coin Woolhill could provide. By their fear of punishment should they defy their captain.

But Felix had no jurisdiction over Wyna. Wyna's pockets were not to be filled by Woolhill and there was nothing stopping her from running and tattling on their deeds the next time they came to shore.

She wondered if she should play into his fears, like any good girl would do. Surely the urge to tell of their misdeeds absolved her of her own. But Felix's fear of her exposure would mean more attention on her. And that sort of attention had been why Solomon had had to die.

Felix was in front of her before she decided what to do. "Why are you on deck?" he asked harshly. "You weren't meant to see that."

She wasn't sure if Brennan had flaunted his claim on her in front of the captain yet, so she lied. "I heard the voices," she said. "It felt safer here."

"Our crew is innocent," he bellowed, taking her by the shoulders. "Do you understand? We had nothing to do with his death."

She nodded, just like he wanted.

"No one on this boat is going to hurt you, Wyna. And everything we do is to keep you—and all of us—safe." Felix was merely spewing shit now. He cared little whether or not Wyna was safe, whether his crew was safe. He cared if he was safe and if he wouldn't be fired by the time this journey was through.

"Yes, sir," she told him. "I understand."

He didn't beg her now to keep her quiet, though she was sure she would get his spiel before they landed back in Keresa. But she would say little—do little—to catch his notice until they returned home.

She knew this was no longer just about keeping the mermaids safe.

Felix stalked off, still muttering to himself about everything he needed to do to ensure this...obstacle...was taken care of. She searched the deck for Brennan, finding him hovering over the wrapped body, the creamy sails already turning red against their treasure. He watched Wyna watch him before striding towards her. He did not stop when he reached her but took hold of her wrist and dragged her behind him as he descended the stairs once more. Behind her, the crew was preparing the *Volia* to continue towards Adalis and, once again, Brennan seemed to think they didn't need his help.

He swung her in front of him when he reached her door, shoving her less than gently into her cabin. She stared at him in outrage as he looked behind him—making sure they weren't followed—and secured the door shut behind him.

Alone now, he ran his hands over her body, touching every inch of her exposed skin and letting his fingers press through the fabric where it billowed and where it hugged her. She wasn't sure what he was looking for. Injuries, perhaps, but his hands were too fast for her to stop them.

"You said you were on deck when you heard it?" he asked, his hands still roaming.

"Yes," she insisted. "And I—well, I—what are you doing? Why are you asking me this again?"

His hands flew from her body as quickly as they'd assaulted it and the absence of them felt wrong. Like she was missing a weight that was meant to be there. And when she looked at his hands, she saw why.

"Because you're a liar," he said, twirling her sickles between his fingers.

CHAPTER SIXTEEN

Keresan summers were nothing if not scorching and the sun glared on Thessa's back, calling forth beads of sweat that dampened the wisps of hairs at the base of her neck before trickling down her skin into her dress. She cared nothing for the unladylike display as she had a perfect view of the phenomena of both Campbell and Alastor in front of her. Her face twitched in annoyance that she could see it at all.

Alastor had bustled forward, as if the stroll was a task he was set on completing and not an outlet for relaxation. Campbell had rushed past Thessa to take Alastor's arm and block her from both view and conversation and Alastor was so preoccupied with placing one foot in front the next that he had no clue how Thessa had been snuffed.

To her credit, Campbell refrained from turning her head and sticking out her tongue when Alastor wasn't looking.

From her vantage, Thessa could see the slight imperfections in Alastor's gait and the brief sucking of air every time his left foot made contact with the hard ground. Perhaps, Thessa dared to think, Campbell took his arm not to ignore Thessa's presence but because Alastor needed her to.

Feeling bold, Thessa strode to Alastor's other side, slightly off the path and into the grass, to take Alastor's other arm. She would not do him the disservice of pointing out his ailment and she felt the best way to keep him feeling manly and strong was to ignore it completely. He grunted in acknowledgement of her presence but said nothing more.

Thessa didn't mind. Alastor's attention was no longer 0on her list of priorities. Her discussion with Campbell had sent a new task straight to the top.

"Miss Moore seems to be quite knowledgeable about Dracan history," Thessa began, addressing Alastor rather than her target. "Did you have a hand in teaching her? Of course, you'd know the sea with your business."

"I taught myself," Campbell said, unamused. Flat.

"That's wonderful! May I ask what sparked your interest?"

It was a throwaway question. Of course Campbell wasn't going to outright say she had taken an interest in the Draca because of the creatures—the women—hiding inside. But even cheap shots were successful every now and again.

"I think you've already answered your own question." So Campbell assumed she knew. And she thought she did. But Thessa needed confirmation. "Now that Alastor has given me stock in the business, it's pertinent I know the waters."

"Forgive me, Miss Moore. When you mentioned it, it had seemed like a childhood interest rather than a pure business venture."

"Why don't you ask your benefactor, Miss Clemen?" Campbell asked. Thessa didn't like when Campbell addressed her by her proper title. She wished the other girl would just use her name. Did she feel the same when Thessa referred to her as "Miss Moore?" "I've heard she refers to her ladies as mermaids. If that's not rooted in Dracan legend, I'm not sure what is."

"Oh, I won't pretend to know much about her trade," Thessa lied. It was a lie that was familiar to her now. One that had marred the only other joy she'd had. She'd twined it through fine copper locks but, now, she knew how it'd look when woven through fire.

Taking an inconspicuously deep breath, she distracted herself with a risky approach. "I don't ask because I want to know more. I, myself, am enthralled by the waters that surround our home."

"Best to be careful in the waters," Campbell told her. "Much of the sea is unknown."

Alastor scoffed, deciding for the first time to chime in. "Surely not so near to home. My ships have never had a problem in Keresa's waters!"

Campbell shot him a tight smile. "Of course. I'm positive that's by design—having been in business as long as you have."

Was it by Campbell's design? She thought of the dragon that lined Campbell's office, of the scales and how closely they resembled those of Thessa's fishy friends. Thessa was almost certain Campbell knew more about Dracan magic than she was letting on but she was still unsure if that meant she was a threat. And how could she know if the other girl never spelled it out to Thessa? Thessa would surely not be the first to say what she knew.

"What sort of trouble does your trade prevent?" Thessa asked sweetly. "Trouble for your men? Or trouble for those who make the Draca their home?"

Alastor frowned. "Well, both, I suppose."

"How wonderful," Thessa mused. "Do you consider yourself something of an environmentalist, Alastor?"

It was a silly thing to ask the trader, Thessa knew. She wasn't blind to the toll manufacturing goods took on the inlands adjacent to Keresa. And she wasn't blind to the industry's exploitation of labor. But that wasn't what she was after.

"I've no interest in the hunt," Alastor told her. "That's certainly why we've never gotten into the whaling or the fishing." He laughed a bit, as if he were about to admit something that might be an embarrassment to him. "I like to tell people it was Campbell that kept me from it—and she certainly did oppose the opportunity when it arose. But, to be truthful, I'm not sure I have the stomach for killing."

"Not many do," Thessa admitted before lying once more. "I certainly don't." With her free hand, she stroked Alastor's arm. "I find it quite admirable that you'd refrain. The creatures of this world are worth protecting."

Thessa looked up to find Campbell's eyes narrowed in her direction. Studying. "Indeed," she said.

Alastor smiled to himself, relaxing his pace as if he were falling into the purpose of the stroll. "How nice of you to take an interest in the trade, Miss Clemen."

"Now," she teased, "if I'm to call you Alastor you *must* call me by my own name."

Alastor didn't respond immediately and Thessa wondered if she had offended him until Campbell whispered Thessa's name loudly into his ear. Thessa's nostrils flared.

"Thessa," he repeated. She nodded. "Yes, it's nice that you seem to be so invested already. Our trade is our life."

The corner of her mouth—the one Campbell couldn't see—raised. It seemed Alastor had welcomed her already. If he didn't already see her as part of his inner circle, he had plans for her to be there. Never mind that their proximity was starting to give her hives.

"Oh, I'm more than devoted to learning your trade," she told him.

"Have you ever been employed by Orinna Swither?" Campbell asked, quite suddenly, making Alastor choke on his own spit.

"Campbell, that's not—" Alastor tried to correct his daughter.

"It's a fair question," Campbell interrupted. Thessa might have been offended by the way Campbell asked if she didn't know what the other girl truly wanted to know. But she couldn't very well admit her employment with Madame Orinna without compromising her current good-standing with Alastor. How clever Campbell was, knowing Thessa had been trying to glean the very same information. Knowing, only to put Thessa in a position that would damage her relationship with either one of them, no matter the answer.

Lying to Alastor meant lying to Campbell. But telling Campbell the truth only meant spinning another lie to Alastor. One that would cost her.

"I think I've been quite transparent regarding my relationship with her," Thessa answered finally.

Campbell's amber eyes burned into Thessa's. "Do you entertain Orinna Swither's clients?"

Thessa thought the wording of the question felt strange before she remembered Alastor's earlier comment about the duties Campbell performed for his guests. So it was true then. Thessa knew what she had meant by the question and she wouldn't have asked it in that manner if she hadn't meant to reveal the nature of her own interactions. Thessa fought the urge to rip her arms from Alastor's as her stomach roiled.

"She's never required that of me in the time I've known her," Thessa answered, seething.

"That's quite fortunate," Campbell said.

Alastor had gone quiet, leaving Thessa and Campbell to wonder about each other privately. About the purpose each of them served to those that acted as their parents. Thessa had never felt used by Madame Orinna. Had never felt that Madame Orinna exploited her in a way in which she was opposed. Sure, every now and again she had her complaints about her assignments but she was never reluctant to do the job at hand.

It seemed, to Thessa, that Campbell could not say the same. But if Alastor truly used her as he had implied, why was she so loyal? Why did she still treat him as a father who could do no wrong to her—nor others? She was hesitant to pass judgement on a relationship of which she knew little about but she had seen the tendrils of abuse before. Had seen the way they wrapped around the hearts of their victims and ruined every chance of leaving.

And Thessa knew what it was to still harbor love for those who had none for her.

"We should get back inside," Campbell said, breaking the silence and steering Alastor back down the path towards the manor.

When they had pushed through the doors, Thessa stood with uncertainty at its threshold. William flashed her a sympathetic smile, as if he knew what storms swirled inside her mind. Alastor retreated into the recesses of the house and Campbell went with him for a time before angling her neck and showing Thessa her stunning profile.

"Come with me."

It was duty that had her following, she told herself.

Campbell led them back towards her office but she veered off where Thessa had first heard the banging and clashing of tools. The doorway led below the house and Thessa thought briefly that Campbell might be leading her straight into the belly of the Wool-hill beast. The impression was washed away when she landed on the rock at the bottom of the stairs.

She could see now that the manor had been built on sea rock and below the house was a freshly carved cave. The tools of the working men remained and it was clear there was still work to be done. Thessa let a shudder run through her.

"What is this?"

"Is this not what you've been trying to find out all day?" Campbell asked in response.

"Is it?" Campbell said nothing. Still, it seemed, reluctant to speak aloud what Thessa suspected. "Has he sanctioned this?"

"I told him it was a private project," she said. "He's no interest in braving the stairs."

"It seems risky."

"I've lived in this house long enough to know the risks I take," Campbell snapped.

In the middle of this carved cave there was a pool of seawater. It was too dark down here to truly see how deep it went but Thessa could guess. She tried to peer in, tried to find a tunnel that might hint to the direction of its source.

"It doesn't lead to the harbor," Campbell told her, immediately understanding the information Thessa was after. "I didn't want them coming in through the shallow waters. Not when they risked the boats and the hull scrapers. It goes down to the shoreline. You know how it becomes more cliff-like the closer you move to Keresa's borders? I was trying to keep them deep. Reduce the chance of swimmers finding it."

"Smart," Thessa relented. "But why?"

"You're not the only one who keeps eyes on these waters, Thessa."

"How long have you known? About the Whips?"

Campbell laughed, hearty and full but without amusement. "As long as I've been alive. I wasn't sure about you, at first. Wasn't sure if you had that sort of relationship with Orinna. I was... distracted by your advances on Alastor."

"If you've been aware of the Whips, why've you made no move to help us?"

"Sharing a secret with me does not entitle you to my help. And besides, I couldn't very well go join the Whips as if I had no standing in society."

"But you could have *offered* your help!" Thessa exclaimed. "You've had access to the books. Access to the reports from the ships. You didn't think it might save us some hard work to let us know when we needed to do our jobs?"

"You seemed to have been doing alright thus far."

Thessa groaned. "Do you not understand that that's the whole reason I'm here? So we don't have to scheme our way into getting the logs? So we can put Whips on the ships and keep our secret from leaking? And all this time you've sat here and you've *known* what we know and you've *known* what we do and you did *nothing*?"

"I haven't done nothing!" Campbell defended, her voice raising. "I've got a handle on the sightings."

"If you had a handle on it, we'd be out of a job." Thessa was pushing now. "Is it that you're just a coward? That you don't want to get caught breaking the law?" She stepped forward, getting close to Campbell, her foot riding the edge of the pool. "Is your reputation more important than their lives?"

She saw it coming when Campbell slapped her. She did not anticipate the momentum of it knocking her into the pool. Though it startled her and sent seawater straight up her nose, she reveled in the coolness of the Dracan water, usually warmed by the heat of the sun.

Campbell showed no remorse and bent down over the edge. "My reputation and my upstanding in Keresa is how I keep them alive. How I keep them hidden. Don't pretend to know what I have or haven't done."

Thessa would not submit herself to the humiliation of lifting herself over the edge of the pool and climbing out of the water like a soaking feline. She tried to keep her rage in check. The rage that was mostly frustration and having had an ally all this time that was so unwilling to extend a hand. She asked questions to calm herself.

"How did you know? How did you find out?"

Campbell hadn't expected more from her than insults and Thessa thought it was surprise that prompted her to answer. "My mother. They loved my mother, I think—Alastor and my father. But they didn't love her enough. My father made her lots of promises he never intended on keeping. Ones she thought Alastor would enforce."

"And he didn't?"

Campbell raised her shoulder. "Everything I know about it, I've learned from her. I don't know the details but I know it was enough for the Draca to take her."

"Your mother's a mermaid?"

"Yes," Campbell said and Thessa watched some of the tension leave her body at finally being able to admit it. "Alastor may have raised me on land but she raised me in the water."

"That's lovely," Thessa told her. She would not tell the other girl that her mother was a mermaid as well. Because then she would have to tell her that her mother didn't care to raise Thessa in the same way. She would have to admit that she'd run from Keresa almost as soon as she hit the water and that not even Thessa could have gotten her to stay.

Thessa told herself she didn't reveal this part because she didn't want to soil the fond memories Campbell had of her own mother. But really, she didn't want to encourage anyone else to find her just as unlovable as her mother had.

Thessa crossed her arms over the rock on the edge of the pool. "Why do you stay with him? After what he's done?"

Campbell clammed, stepping back from Thessa. "I don't want to talk about Alastor."

"Then talk about the Whips," Thessa said, trying again to lead them into a partnership now that she had settled herself. "Help us."

"I don't know, Thessa," she said.

And even though her words were disappointing, Thessa thought she loved the way they sounded coming from her. Well, maybe not all of them. The last one. Campbell said it in a way that made Thessa feel as though they had a long-standing history. Like they knew each other well enough to grow weary of the other's quirks. And though Thessa knew the feeling she got was only illusion, it showed her a closeness she'd not ever achieved. Not with the Whips. Not even with the mermaids, and she considered them to be her closest friends.

She asked herself if it was the same kind of feelings she got when she saw Huxley. When he took her to bed and told her all that he wanted to do. The bad and the whimsical. The now and the far, far future.

No, this was different.

Campbell returned to the edge of the pool and extended a physical hand to Thessa. "We'll need to get you new clothes." Campbell looked her up and down to assess her sizing. "You can borrow mine."

She did not take Campbell's hand to lift herself from the

pool, preferring to rely on her own strength to propel her body upward. And if Campbell was offended, she brushed it off when she led Thessa quietly back into the house and let her slosh all over the floors and up the stairs.

Campbell's bedroom was decorated in the same hues as her office, the blue of the walls enhanced and enchanted by the light of the sun. She reached into her wardrobe and studied it for a moment before producing some frilly thing only the wealthy would ever put on their bodies.

"I grew too tall for this one years ago. It should work for you. There's no quick release, though, and you'll have to lose the trousers unless you want an ugly rash."

Thesa cocked her head to the side as Campbell explained to her how to dress and moved behind Thessa to aid in peeling the soaking clothing from her body. Her face flushed completely at being cared for in the way she usually cared for others. At having someone attend to the little details that would make her more comfortable.

"Bring this back with you tomorrow. I'll lace you back in."

The nausea that curled through Thessa was not the unpleasant variety she usually felt after she heard or saw something upsetting. It was a turning inside her that made her feel ashamed and embarrassed at how her body responded. Thessa was not unfamiliar with her bodily desires. But she was unfamiliar with the sense of vulnerability that now accompanied them.

Ruefully, she marvelled at how easy she'd once thought this assignment to be.

CHAPTER SEVENTEEN

"Excuse me?"

It was a reflex for Wyna to say. A reflex to play dumb and deny when confronted. But the sickles in Brennan's hand told her how useless it would be to say she was innocent. She remembered the way he'd leaned over Solomon's body. The way he'd convinced the crew of something that would have been impossible.

"I wasn't sure until I saw the body," he shrugged, sauntering the few feet around her room. Around her. "But I have to hand it to you. Those cuts were clean. And then I asked myself what could have possibly made such *clean* lines in Solomon's flesh and then it hit me! My little sea witch has some pretty blades. I've felt them myself."

"Okay," she stared, making sure to go slow. To think. To not incriminate herself if she didn't have to. "If you're so sure, why did you tell them it was someone in Nazren?"

He flopped onto her bed and Wyna started to think the mattress was shaping to him, rather than her. "We orphans have to stick together, you know?" He lifted her sickles into the air, letting them hover over his face as he studied them. Admiring their curve and their point and how they didn't quite fit his grip as well as they fit hers.

"And if I told you I didn't do it?"

He let his hands fall back to his sides, effortlessly careful to not let the blades nick him. His head bobbled towards her, his eyes knowing beneath his lashes. "I'd admire your dedication," he said. "And then call you a liar again. A semi-convincing one. But a liar nonetheless."

Wyna didn't have a retort for him. She didn't see a point in digging herself into a hole she wasn't confident she could claw her way out of.

"So what now?"

"I was going to let you squirm for a bit. I think it would be pretty cute." He smiled to himself, imagining it. "But I decided against it. And no need to worry about blackmail."

"You'd blackmail me?"

He *tsk*ed. "I just said I wouldn't! No, that would cause just as many problems for me as it would for you."

"So what are you going to do?"

Brennan sat up with the speed of a predator and got to his feet. So close to Wyna. She hated how it set her on fire even as he held her crimes over her head. He was dangerous and she was pretty sure she liked it. Because she could be dangerous, too.

"Thank you," he whispered, his breath hitting her ear as he pushed his face right past her lips and pulled her into an embrace.

She took a deep breath before stepping back but his arms did not fall, only loosened. "You're going to thank me?"

He pulled her back to him, their faces almost level, and nodded. His forehead bumped hers and she couldn't get over the niggling feeling that he was just trying to distract her. She brought her arm up to meet his and latched her hand onto his elbow before pushing it gently away from her. She wouldn't risk harsh movements or harsh words just yet, not when she was still so unsure of the game he tried to play.

"Why?"

"I won't pretend to know why you did it. Though I'm sure you have your reasons. What kind of whore gets on a ship with secret knives and never opens her legs? None that I've seen so far. And to be honest, I don't much care. What I *do* care about is that you've just opened some opportunities for me." He grinned at her as if she should already know exactly what she'd done. Like the secret he was about to share with her wasn't a secret at all. "You know Solomon. Always there and always silent. I don't know about you but I don't much like being watched. Not like that, anyhow."

"You think he deserved this because he watched you too much?" *Yes.* Wasn't that exactly why Wyna had killed him? Because he'd been watching when she'd done something she shouldn't have? Still, she led Brennan away from that conclusion. "I'm not sure that's reason enough to die."

"But it is," he insisted. "Felix loved the bastard. He would have never given anyone else the opportunity to get up in the nest because Solomon was always willing. Always able," he drawled, as if that were a crime. "I think everyone is entitled to a bit of privacy in their lives. And I think it would serve us all well if we got someone in the nest who wasn't so sure of what they were doing and seeing."

"I'm not sure I follow."

Brennan sighed. "I guess, to put it plainly: Solomon was getting in my way. The captain only has room for one favorite and Solomon was taking up too much space. Too much space, and I'm sure he'd seen too much. I might've had to do it myself if you hadn't beaten me to it."

Wyna's heart was beating loudly and quickly and plainly. She knew she wasn't having the proper reaction to Brennan's admission. She should be asking him what he had done that he needed so much privacy for. She should have been asking him why he was so keen on being Felix's favorite—and why that desire had to lead to murder.

She should be frightened of him. At how quickly he had

turned from a knave and a scoundrel to a monster of flesh. And she should be frightened of what he could do to her, should he ever tell a soul what he knew about Solomon.

She wasn't frightened of him.

She was...excited.

Hadn't she just been wallowing that she could never share that part of herself—the violent, impulsive part—with anyone? And here he was, standing in front of her and revealing his to her. Perhaps Brennan wasn't the best man but she knew, with everything that now lay between them, that he might be the best for her.

But she wasn't ready to let him know that yet. She squared her shoulders. "You can't expect me to always do your dirty work for you," she told him. And then decided to push her luck. "*What were you hiding from him anyway?*"

He returned to her, pressing his body against her and pushing her into the door as she had once done to him. "Now, now, sea witch. I don't ask for your secrets and you don't ask for mine."

She inhaled his scent, finding it pleasant despite the sweat of labor and sun. The filling of her lungs pressed her chest against his and she felt one of his hands grip into the coils of her hair.

"But I'll happily devour anything you'd like to share," he said into her neck.

She breathed again, hoping to push herself into his mouth without having to be the one to initiate the contact, and he happily obliged, pressing his lips to her exposed skin. Sucking and nipping at her as if she were the most delicious morsel he'd ever tasted.

She would make sure that she was.

Wyna felt him start to whisper his pet name for her and she stopped him. "If you want a witch, I've no problem being wicked."

She pushed him from the wall, her body never losing its precious contact, and let him topple on the bed before climbing over him. He smirked, unsurprised by her sudden boldness. *She* was surprised, unsure from where this floodgate had burst and when. Unsure of how she knew so clearly what her body wanted and how to get it. Once, she might've been afraid she'd be unable to stomach the fallout of giving into these kinds of desires but her concerns seemed so trivial to her now.

Maybe she would remember them when she was done. When she had drank her fill and let the hurricane inside her wear itself out. But she remembered nothing now. Nothing, save for the last instant of feeling and how much she never wanted the feeling to stop.

Brennan whispered things to her that made her push harder and harder at the wall blocking the last bit of pleasure she sought. His words, it seemed, were the final encouragement she needed to break down the barriers within herself. She would never, she vowed, let those barriers fall into place again. How empowering it felt to her to know herself so truly, when the world around her demanded her to go blind. She had never been sheltered from the darkest parts of life and she would not let herself be sheltered from this, either.

She certainly didn't think Brennan was her savior from her own self. And she wasn't silly enough to believe that a man or a woman or any outside body was the key to the truth she'd stumbled upon. It wasn't that she needed another to unlock it all. She'd just needed to be told she could.

And, gods, she could.

TOGETHER THEY CONCOCTED A PLAN, laughable in its simplicity: Wyna would convince Felix to let her crow. The idea thrilled Brennan, now able to do whatever it was he needed, knowing his ally was the only one with eyes on him. And though she kept her reasons to herself, she would use her time in the nest to watch for the mermaids and ensure no one else did.

As they discussed and rejoiced in their genius, Brennan worked to soothe Wyna's guilt. She let him. After all, Brennan was right. Solomon had to die. He'd seen too much, yes, but beyond that, the Crow took up space on the ship that simply better served others. She needed the nest, she decided. It was quiet and private. Far from the eyes and ears of the other crew members she hadn't warmed to. She could write her reports for Madame Orinna while she was up there, fully basking in the wonders of the sea.

Felix was haggard when she cornered him with their idea, his uniform off-kilter and his face in disarray.

"Are you alright?" she asked as she approached, careful to move slowly and talk loudly to alert him of her presence.

He still flinched. "Hmm? Yes, fine."

"Are you thinking about Solomon?" Her question was tentative, born not of scheming as her exchanges usually were but of true concern for the state of the captain.

Felix closed his eyes in a long blink and she wondered what visions might be flashing across his eyelids. She pretended not to notice when she saw the tear slip out and catch in his lashes. "He was a good friend," Felix choked. "I was sorry to see him go."

"We all were," she told him.

He nodded and began to turn from her, back to whatever task he'd been ignoring, but she grabbed his arm and made him face her. Wyna had been struck by an inspiration hiding in grief. "Why don't we give him a funeral?" she asked. "A proper, sea-borne funeral."

She didn't tell him that the body had already started stinking and that it had been making the rest of the crew nauseous every time they got within feet of it. And she certainly didn't tell him that having a body on board was a discomfort to her. This wasn't about her, she decided. This was about easing the pain she'd caused.

Felix considered. "Wrong not to bring his body back home," he said. "Maybe that's what he'd'a wanted."

He'd have wanted to not die at all.

"Yes," Wyna agreed. "We can't subject his family to him at his current state. And if they know anything of his love for the sea, they'd likely take him right back out."

"We're saving 'em a trip?"

She nodded. "I think so. But I didn't know him as well as you."

"No one did," Felix admitted, the words catching on the phlegm in his throat. "But I think you're right. We'll have a funeral for him."

Felix demanded the crew dress in their best clothes that night on deck. For the sailors, it wasn't much. But it was enough to show they cared. They laid Solomon's body over the railing, a few of them keeping hands on it to prevent the body from falling in before they were ready.

At Felix's command, they began a wailing song. Wyna had thought it to be some version of a shanty before Brennan corrected her. She tried to keep up and sing along where she could, as the song returned to the chorus, over and over again.

She listened to the story it told, of the sailor sent out to provide for his family. Of the success he had on the water before his greed kept him at sea and away from them. And after it was greed, it was lust. She tried not to react when they began singing of the mermaids that had seduced the sailor, sealing the separation from his wife. And yet, in all the unfortunate choices the sailor had made, the chorus insisted the gods and the waves granted him luck. Luck, it seemed, to be able to continue his debauchery in the water.

Wyna didn't feel the song was very respectful of Solomon as a person. Of what he stood for. But she didn't think it was her place to stand and say so. Solomon's blood was on her hands and she would not tell his friends how to grieve him.

As the crew of the *Volia* sung the final chords of the song, the hands holding Solomon's corpse released him, sending him into the sea. She thought it was perhaps supposed to be a graceful show. One that sent him home. But the shape of the ship and the lack of momentum on their part rather sent Solomon rolling down the side of the frame, clunking heartily each time his body hit. And the fateful, impacting splash that should have sent tears from the eyes of his companions was instead small—smaller than the sound of his body hitting the deck.

He would not, Wyna decided, be swimming to the afterlife after a display like that. He would be sinking to the bottom of the ocean, right where they left him.

It was selfish but she wondered if the others would have given her a funeral like that had it been her body they found aboard. She hoped they wouldn't treat her form with as much apathy and disrespect but she had to admit that having an entire crew sing and mourn for her was a tempting offer.

And what might the Whips do, should she not return? She had not yet experienced the loss of a Whip, though she was sure it must've happened at some point. She imagined the Whips and the Madame gathering in one of the mermaid's grottos, candles lit and water calm. Singing for her. She imagined a whole sea feeling the pull of their grief and coming to Wyna's farewell.

Perhaps it was a dark thought. She knew she shouldn't imagine herself dying—that even thinking of it might bring it upon her. Might bring death to her. But the idea of this family of hers feeling so strongly for her flipped her stomach over itself and set her body aglow. Those were the kinds of feelings she wished her original family had felt for her when they left. Though, she supposed, if they'd had any inclination to feel that way, they wouldn't have abandoned her in the first place.

She stood staring at the water as the crew dispersed around her, their bodies like the physical manifestation of her swarming thoughts, her mind the ship itself. She told herself to get over it. To give up on the pity and the longing and the guilt and the grief. There was a reason she was a Whip.

She just had to find it again.

CHAPTER EIGHTEEN

The dinner was dreadful. She supposed she should be counting herself lucky that Madame Orinna had arranged the meal and not Alastor himself. Had Alastor extended the invitation of his own accord, Thessa ran the risk of encountering those more intimately familiar with the Whips. She couldn't have a noble recognize her as a brothel member when she'd told Alastor she'd never been employed by Madame Orinna a day in her life.

It was a very fragile lie, she felt. More fragile than anything Madame Orinna had required of her before.

Alastor sat Thessa down between himself and Campbell, a choice that caused discomfort in both of the girls. She had no desire to be close to him and she had no desire to steal his attention away from Campbell. But, he insisted, all the other VIPs in attendance would be scrounging to have his ear to discuss business and what better way to get into those conversations than to be close to him? Thessa could think of a million better ways but none of them were appropriate to say aloud.

Eventually, the dinner fell apart. The guests excused themselves from the table and milled about the expansive dining room, more interested in impressing each other than impressing the young unknown. Thessa was surprised to see that very few of them acknowledged Campbell's existence, let alone made eye contact with her. Though, it occurred to Thessa much later why that might be. Even so, it left no man to notice the absence of the two girls when they slipped out the side door and rushed across the estate.

Campbell had a small boat tied up at the back of the estate, where the walls met the water instead of enclosing the land. She told Thessa she didn't want to risk the mermaids coming in through the cave entrance when there were so many people at the estate and any one of them could wander below and catch them. Thessa wanted to point out the possibility of that happening any time and that Campbell should probably invest in some sort of lock or security to aid in keeping the cave undiscovered and inaccessible to anyone besides her.

And perhaps Thessa.

Like an extension of the sea, a tail rose from the water and slapped the side of the little boat once they'd pushed far enough away from the shore. The girls flinched in surprise, their shoulders knocking into each other. They didn't shift apart when they realized the tail belonged to Rose.

The mermaid flipped herself in the water so that her head was now above the surface and she rested her hands and her chin on the lip of the boat.

"My friends are friends!" she squealed.

Campbell lifted the side of her mouth but did not argue with the mermaid about the status of her and Thessa's relationship. "You're playful today."

"You two were the ones who made me keep secrets," Rose pouted. "Dinah and I were just laughing about it—both of you hiding us from the other."

Had Campbell also come to the mermaids to complain about Thessa? Thessa hadn't thought she'd made much of an impression on Campbell's life until yesterday. What could she have possibly said to the mermaids for them to realize what they were keeping from each other?

"If you knew we both knew, why didn't you say something?" Campbell asked. There was no frustration in it.

Rose deepened her pout. "That would be picking a side."

Campbell reached into the water and splashed Rose. "That's ridiculous."

"What exactly did you think splashing a mermaid would do? As if we don't spend every second of our lives in the water."

"Then you shouldn't mind much," Campbell told her, beginning her splashing anew.

Thessa was too stunned to speak. Stunned at seeing the friendship between the two. At seeing Campbell's lively side, when she wasn't sneering and putting all she had into protecting a terrible man. Thessa was still silent when they calmed a bit and Campbel adjusted in the boat so that her face was closer to Rose's.

"How's my mother?"

Rose's eyes flitted to Thessa before she answered and Thessa remembered Rose had been there when her own mother had left. She remembered the way Rose had wrapped her slimy arms around Thessa while Madame Orinna had pet her hair. She remembered the way Rose had described her mother as a mermaid because—for some reason—it comforted Thessa to know she was beautiful. Her tail had looked like strings of onyx, Rose had said. The scales had sparkled even in the dark, matching perfectly her mother's hair and her mother's eyes. Rose told her she imagined her mother leaving a trail of exquisite, shining darkness on her way back to wherever she was going.

Thessa had known then where it was she'd gone. Home. To the other side of the world where her father had first seen her. Where he'd first laid his hands on her and promised to take her back.

Then, knowing what she'd known even at her small age, Thessa vowed never to mistake a threat for a promise.

Hearing Campbell ask after her mother sent tears out of

Thessa's ducts. She'd never felt the loss of her mother quite as sharply, not even when Lorelai had pressed quick kisses to her son's forehead and Huxley had pondered aloud about the coloring or temperament of their future offspring. No, she did not let her emotions overtake her when others spoke fondly of their own parents but, to know Campbell's history aligned so closely with Thessa's, and to be reminded there could have been a different ending, was too much.

"She's well," Rose answered Campbell, unaware of Thessa's emotional state. "Handling things at the other ports."

"What ports?" Thessa wiped at her tears furiously before either of them could see.

"All of them," Campbell said, making Thessa feel foolish because she didn't even bother to look. "She checks in for me."

Thessa marveled at how the Whips even had work if Campbell had been taking care of everything as she was. "How long have you had your hands in his trade?"

"Not long," she admitted. "He hardly trusted me before this last year so the systems are all new."

"The Whips could help you," Thessa said.

Campbell's muscles seemed to shrink and tighten as she crossed her arms over her chest. "We have it handled."

"If you had it handled, you wouldn't need the Whips."

"I *don't* need the Whips."

Thessa turned her gaze to Rose, her eyes wide so she could share her disbelief. "Not that I don't trust your capability," Thessa snapped, "but the time you take to handle it—if you truly ice out the Whips—is time in which everything could be ruined. Madame Orinna has spent years creating a machine that allows us to do what we must to protect the mermaids. You don't get to have growing pains when their lives—Rose's life, your mother's— are on the line."

"So what are you proposing then, Thessa?" she demanded. "Because you've done a lot of talking but you haven't actually told me what your precious Whips would be *doing*. For us, or for them."

A far-off splash sounded in between the boat and the shore and the three of them stiffened, hardly daring to breathe. Rose disappeared under the waves to retrieve the anchor they'd dropped and threw it back into the boat before dragging the girls into deeper water.

"Let's go somewhere more private," she suggested, and waited for the girls to follow her into the water.

Thessa looked down at Campbell's dress, annoyed at the prospect of riding back to shore in something so heavy. When she looked back at Campbell, she was working on the clasps and hooks and ties of her own attire.

"What are you doing?"

Campbell glanced at Thessa as she peeled her bodice from her body. "What does it look like? I'm not going back home weighed down like that." She studied Thessa, up and down. "And you better not, either. That dress may not fit me anymore but that doesn't mean I want it ruined."

Once she'd stripped completely, Campbell wasted no time diving into the water, leaving Thessa stranded and blushing on the boat. Rose wagged her eyebrows at Thessa when Campbell resurfaced.

"Let's give the girl some privacy," Rose suggested.

"We don't have time for privacy."

Campbell watched her expectantly until Thessa began on the dress, fumbling. Because she hadn't been the one to put it on, she told herself, despite managing it the night before. Every inch of skin she exposed turned hot under the persistent glare of Campbell's eyes. Thessa didn't want to feel like her body was something to be ashamed of and she never had before. But when the last piece of fabric fell from her, Campbell looked away. Like she had no interest in seeing.

Thessa jumped.

Rose took one of their hands in each of hers and guided them to another one of their safe spaces. None of them made a move to correct the darkness.

"So talk, Thessa."

Rose squeezed her hand in encouragement, giving Thessa the confidence and the space to present and propose. And she did. Well, too. Campbell was quiet until there were questions to be asked and, when there were, she asked many of them. Questions Thessa hadn't considered but could see the answers to clearly. It made Thessa feel as though they had every right to do what they did. It made her feel like the mermaids—her friends—were in perfectly capable hands.

And best of all, Thessa felt she would never have to lay eyes on Alastor again. Not before she returned to Madame Orinna and told the other woman of what she'd accomplished. Perhaps Madame Orinna would allow Thessa to run this wing of their operation. Give her something beyond the violence and the gore.

This was an opportunity for expansion the likes of which the Whips had never seen before. It became truth in Thessa's mind: this was now her whole world. Something to sink into infinitely more, she thought, than she had ever sunk into her work before.

But with that truth came another.

There was no room in her life for people that weren't privy to her work. And it hurt her heart to think of the jagged scar cutting them out might leave.

Rose made promises to gather Dinah and Edonie sometime soon, as if they were making plans to go to tea, before returning Thessa and Campbell to their abandoned boat. The night air hit their soaking bodies and sent shivers through the both of them, raising the flesh on their arms with every kiss of the breeze. Thessa had no more energy to be shy but she laid the dress Campbell had lent her over her body as a makeshift blanket, unwilling to expose the surface of her to the air long enough to put it back on.

"You look silly," Campbell told her.

Thessa risked a peek at the other girl in the moonlight, the red of her drying hair sitting atop her head like a crown of blood. She looked as though she were born of the nighttime sea. Born to defend it. She would be silly if someone else—someone like Campbell—would just take the daggers from her hands.

She decided she was quite happy with their union.

"I'd rather be silly than cold."

"Well, you'd better put it on before we get too close to the shore."

"Why? I'm a woman of th

e Sin District. What difference does it make if I run around naked?"

Campbell had no response for her but Thessa took note of every hint of a glance that came her way.

"So what now?" Thessa asked. Not because she truly needed direction and not because she was unsure of what path lay ahead but because she wanted to hear what ideas turned in Campbell's mind. She wanted to look for a hint of excitement in Campbell's words at the prospect of continued engagements with Thessa. She wanted to hear Campbell tell her she wanted to keep seeing her.

"Now you go home," was all she said.

"I didn't mean tonight."

"Then what did you mean?"

And all at once, Thessa was back in Alastor's garden, playing a game of give and take, neither one of them wanting to say what the other wanted to hear—even if they both knew it to be true.

"I don't think I want to play this game anymore," Thessa told her, her voice low. She stood in the little boat, blocking Campbell's view of Keresa, and began to redress. Her eyes did not leave her as she went through the motions of putting back the layers but, while she covered herself, it seemed to her that the layers of Campbell's facade fell away.

Like little sparks, Thessa watched emotions burn and sizzle and die. A smirk and a fall and a heartbreak, one-by-one.

"I see."

"We've already put forth the depths of our knowledge. What do we have left to be vulnerable about?" Thessa reached around herself to close her bodice, turning to face away from Campbell. "I'm tired of guessing at what you want from me."

"I want nothing from you."

When she spun back around, ready to call the other girl a liar, she was standing, too. Close to Thessa. Their boat meandered over the water with nobody to steer and no anchor to hold it down. Thessa felt like that, too. Now. Like her anchor had never met the seafloor and she only went where the Draca deemed to take her.

She let her little boat crash into Campbell's rock.

THESSA THOUGHT she might blame giddiness for her delay in returning to the Gillbridges. An excitement that could simply not be contained until she told Madame Orinna all she had learned and all she had planned.

She told herself her delay was, in no way, an avoidance of Huxley. It was not a way for her to put off telling him that she was sorry. That she adored him but she musn't go back to what they'd been. It was time for her to stop pretending she wanted what Huxley could give her. She thought she might've once, when what she could not have had taken up more space in her mind.

But what she could not have was coming ever closer.

It was time.

After, of course, she went to see Madame Orinna.

The Sin District was alive under the moon and she dodged hands and limbs and laughter as she wove her way through the crowd. The House of Whips stood tall but it was a shadow over the District. Its blackened windows like a reprimanding mother, expressing its distaste for the disturbance of the other Houses. But as Thessa well knew—and as the rest of Keresa knew—the House of Whips was never as vacant as it seemed.

Maren lounged about the desk in the parlor, her slippered

feet propped, sending her skirt up her leg to expose her skin. Sultry, a visitor might think. Thessa knew Maren just overheated easily.

"Is Madame in?" she asked Maren.

"Thessa!" Maren exclaimed and Thessa remembered she'd been gone longer than usual.

Thessa shushed her. "I don't want anyone to know I'm here yet. Is Madame in?" she asked again.

Maren nodded her head towards Madame Orinna's closed office. "In there."

Thessa smiled her thanks at Maren before knocking firmly, twice on the door. She didn't wait for a response before she entered. Madame Orinna held her focus on a sheet of parchment in front of her that Thessa couldn't quite see from her position in the doorway. Without looking up, Madame Orinna called for her to shut the door.

"Have you decided to move back?" Madame Orinna asked it like it was a dare. "That's quite bold, Thessa."

"No, Madame. I'll return to the Gillbridges' this evening."

"Quite the walk."

"Yes," Thessa admitted, trying not to groan.

"I'll arrange transportation once you've told me whatever it is that brought you here."

Thessa strode forward and leaned over the Madame's desk, disturbing the documents lining the edge. Madame Orinna's brows pushed higher up onto her forehead.

"Campbell knows."

Madame Orinna's body stilled and Thessa observed as she clenched her teeth and rose a finger to her lips. Thessa followed her into the secret chamber once she had it open, appreciating the stiller, waxy air.

"Explain," Madame Orinna demanded, composed, as the wall slid behind her.

"His advisor. Campbell. She knows about the mermaids."

"You told her?"

Thessa shook her head, feeling frantic as her still-damp hair whipped her in the face. "I didn't have to."

"And the rumors?"

Thessa hesitated, still unsure of what exactly these rumors were. She admitted as much to Madame Orinna. "But she's contracted a cave to be built under the Woolhill manor that extends out to the Draca. And she has her mother reporting on Woolhill's boats as they make port along their route."

"Her mother…"

"Is a mermaid," Thessa finished.

She devolved into her old self, she felt, as she revealed all she knew of Campbell and as she reasoned with Madame Orinna about the plan she and the other women had concocted. She was free from pretending. Pretending as if she had an interest in coming up in Keresan society. Pretending she wasn't trembling at the thought of working with Campbell. Pretending she wasn't the killer Madame Orinna had raised her to be.

In front of Madame Orinna, Thessa had been laid bare. There was no facet of her to hide because there was hardly a facet of her Madame Orinna hadn't called to creation.

And as she settled into the warmth of knowing she had nothing to hide, she found herself dreaming of the rush she felt when Campbell looked at her—her expression giving away that Campbell knew much more of her than she had revealed. She imagined the way her skin heated at the prospect of protection and tingled under the knife of Campbell's gaze.

She drowned, imagining the sensation of her comfort turning into Campbell.

CHAPTER NINETEEN

It was only Wyna's second time in the nest but she already knew she despised it.

It hadn't been terribly difficult to get Felix to agree to give her the position, though the crew had been much harder to convince. What right did an outsider have to crew their ship? But the reminder of her presence and her tears at Solomon's funeral won them over in the end. If she could grieve with them, perhaps she could be useful. Yet even as the allowance to enter the nest pulled her into the fold of the *Volia*'s crew, it isolated her all the same. In the nest, she sat above it all, watching them go about lives and tasks in which she had no part.

Though she knew there were Whips who preferred a good vantage and the comfort of height and shadows, it was of Wyna's opinion that a good spy—a good Whip—did her best work in the middle of the crowd.

To be fair, she didn't mind the views of the water as much as everyone told her she would. And perhaps she hadn't been in the nest quite long enough yet but she hadn't fallen victim to the hypnosis. To Wyna, the ocean was not an expanse that kept her from land and the people she loved. What she loved lived in these waters.

She was horrified when she hadn't been in the nest but an hour before one of the mermaids swam far ahead of the ship and waved at her. She knew the crew couldn't see her—the mermaid would never have attempted such a thing if she hadn't been confident she was hidden—but a terror now lived in Wyna at the prospect of having to kill another member of this crew.

The playfulness of the mermaid sent Wyna reeling for a different reason, too. How had they known Wyna had taken a spot in the nest? Had they been close enough to overhear—close enough to be seen? Or was this perhaps a regular practice for these mermaids? To make a spectacle of themselves for whatever eyes might watch them from above?

Had they done this for Solomon?

Had Solomon already known of their existence?

She tried to tell herself that line of thinking was ludicrous. Solomon couldn't have already known about the mermaids. The only reason she knew he'd seen her was because of that little gasp. Why would he gasp if he already knew?

Unless he'd only been surprised by Wyna's involvement with the mermaids...

Each passing moment, it seemed, only served to convince Wyna she should have never taken her blades to his throat.

To distract herself, she watched the crew below, making up silly stories about what they might be saying and what they might be doing. The other bosun, the apprentice, whose name she could never remember sat on the deck with his hands on the ropes that suspended the sails, reinforcing the knots. She imagined he sang a little song to himself to remember how to tie them, using some dirty metaphor regarding the movement of his fingers.

When her eyes fell on Zachariah, stomping around, she whispered to herself, "Ooh, look at me. I'm the prick of the sea." And she comforted herself by thinking of him chanting the line, over and over.

And finally, she found Brennan, flitting through the crew. Putting his hands both on and in everything. Pretending to oversee his apprentice. Doing just enough to be helpful and never break a sweat. As if the crew of the *Volia* was a plank of harvested wood Brennan was set on smoothing out, splinter by splinter.

He was successful.

Wyna understood now why he was so unbothered by Solomon's death. No one had to know what he said behind closed doors to incriminate him. All one would need is to be up in the nest.

Much as Wyna despised it, she would keep the position.

But she would not admit to herself how frightened she was. How volatile her life felt. Every time she looked Brennan's way, she was dazzled by him. Thrilled. But her inner Whip knew the power he had over her. Perhaps she had seen the parts of him he wasn't willing to share with anyone else but he had also seen hers. He knew she was capable of murder. And they both knew one word from him—one spark—could ruin her forever.

Perhaps even end her life.

Even so, when the sun fell and the crew disappeared below deck and Brennan called up to her from the base of the mast, she felt the blood rush through her in delight.

"Oh, sea witch," he crooned below her, "won't you grace us with your presence?"

"No," she called back.

"Then I've no choice but to come up!" He threw the rope he'd been holding—a prop he'd no intention of using—over his shoulder before scampering up the rungs to the nest. Once inside, he grinned at her before pushing his mouth against hers, his bared teeth scraping the sea-chapped skin of her lips. "So," he said, pulling back, "how does it feel to be mine for real?"

"It feels a lot like being not yours," she told him and clenched the muscles in her belly. "Just with more physical contact."

He said nothing of her comment and peered over the ledge. "How do I look from up here?"

"Like a scoundrel."

He frowned. "No changes, then."

"Not even one," she whispered.

"I've been thinking," he said, turning as if he had not heard her. "The more I weave into this crew, the more work I can convince them I'm doing, I could probably collect Solomon's pay."

"What about his family?"

He scoffed. "His family isn't on this ship. What stock do they have in what he does? Did," he corrected after a moment. "But if I collected his pay, I could build a life, you know?"

"What kind of life?" she asked, skeptical.

"One for both of us." He took her hands in his own, swirling the nerves under her skin. "My pay will be larger than the apprentice pay I was expecting. And if I can get Solomon's pay, as well... well, we put the money away. We convince them you're the best Crow the *Volia* has ever seen—woman or not. Get you a wage of your own. A couple more routes and then we have enough to leave. To start a life and start a family."

Brennan moved to close the short distance between them, sending Wyna's heels into the wall of the nest. She didn't think she could manage to return to the nest again and again—and even if she could, she had no desire to. But Brennan's dreams called to her like a siren. She'd never heard anyone plan a future around her. For her. And she'd never felt so close to the promise of family. How could she refuse an offer of something she'd never had? It would be absurd.

...But what of the Whips? What of the wage she already earned, maiming and killing for Madame Orinna and her mermaid friends? Wyna's mermaid friends. Ibot and Evelyn and Adrie and Rose and Dinah and Edonie and all the others she hadn't met yet.

Could she forsake them for what Brennan promised her?

She came dangerously close to wanting to.

"Wyna?" Brennan asked, in a rare show of actually addressing her by her name. "Doesn't that sound great?"

"I've always wanted a family," she told him. She knew he

would think she meant children and a legacy. All she really meant was that she wanted people in her life who would never think to leave her, never think to not love her.

"I could save you," he mused. "With Solomon's pay, I could save you from the Whips. From the District."

Something in her hated his choice of words, hated that he thought she needed saving and that he would be the one to do it. But she shook off the distaste, telling herself his intent hadn't been to doubt what she could do.

Gods, she was so confused. She wanted to soak into the navy sky, to disappear before Brennan and make herself deaf to his words so she would have the time to truly figure out what they meant. Every passing second she spent aboard this ship pulled her in a different direction. Towards Madame Orinna and towards the Whips and towards the mermaids and towards Brennan. She'd never been closely associated with the right thing but, at least, she'd always known what the right thing was.

She couldn't say anymore that she was sure.

He leaned forward again, no doubt to press his lips to hers and let his hands wander along the outline of her body but she stopped him as she heard the clunk of a heavy frame listing into the railing of the stairs as it ascended. She peered over the side of the nest to find Felix wandering onto the deck. The captain of the *Volia* had evidently been imbibing—all day from what Wyna could tell—and his movements were uneven, his feet sticky and dragging. The planes of his face drooped not from his age but from clear sorrow. In his stupor, he somehow managed to stumble into the thick railing of the ship, leaning precariously over the edge.

Wyna turned to Brennan, expecting to find him still drunk on his own fantasies, but his eyes were sharp as he watched Felix. And as he watched Wyna watch Felix, staring intently through the strands of salted hair that fell into his face. It was good, Wyna decided, that he was watching her. It was good that he gave no interest to the sea and what it might be hiding that so closely held Felix's interest.

Felix spoke, then. And Wyna could not make out the words he said, from distance or from the sounds he allowed to run together in his state. Wyna held her fingers to her mouth, ensured Brennan saw her and, at the very least, seemed as though he planned on obeying.

"Stay put," she mouthed to him. "Hide."

He crouched in the nest, enough so he could still see over the edge. Wyna placed her palm on the crown of his head and pushed him down.

"Hide," she whispered, daring to make the noise.

Brennan made himself comfortable on the ground, staring up at Wyna and waiting for further directions. She didn't currently have the time to acknowledge that she liked being looked at in that way. And he immediately went to ruin it by lifting the edge of her skirt as if to climb underneath. She batted him away before climbing over the edge of the nest as silently as she could manage. Not that it truly mattered for Felix's sake. She was certain the drunken voices in the captain's mind were enough to drown out anything not in front of his face.

No, it was for Brennan's sake.

She was silent so she could keep up the facade. The one that kept him blind and unaware of what Wyna now sought to investigate. She didn't want the observant little wretch to see her search for glistening tails and she didn't want him to see her push the captain overboard should she find any.

Felix's words grew clearer as she approached.

"Won't you take me, too?" he asked the sea.

The sea had no response, to Wyna's relief.

"The gods won't take me now. Will you?" he wailed.

Wyna stopped her approach, recognizing the grief emanating from Felix. The guilt over what he had no part in. She suddenly felt as though her sickles were at her own throat, slicing through flesh and vein and artery and causing her to sputter out.

"Yes, you'll take me," Felix continued and Wyna could hear the upturning of his lips.

She retreated and gently moved down the length of the ship so she could approach the edge without his notice. She leaned over, her eyes pinned on the black water that held them.

She could see no tails, no hair, no sparkle.

Felix stepped onto the railing, crouching so he could still grip the sides with his slick fingers. An errant wave could send him over the edge and Wyna knew he stood no chance of surviving the water in his state. She looked back up to see if Brennan had defied her and found his eyes narrowed on Felix. He made no move to come help.

Wyna wanted to shout his name, to take his attention away from the call of the sea, but she worried the noise might startle him enough to send him to his death more quickly. She took hurried, silent steps towards him, her focus sharp on the way his fingers unlatched from the railing, one after the other.

"I'll trade my life for yours, Sol," Felix told the water. "If I go in, you'll promise to come back?"

Wyna reached him then, stood only breaths away from his body. As the last of his fingers left the rail and he made to stand, she thrust her own fingers into the waistband of his trousers to try to pull him back in. But Felix was already jumping. His momentum was more than hers, gravity more than she herself could fight. As he fell towards the water, taking Wyna with him, she felt a hot, ripping pain fly up her arm as it was pulled away from the joint of her shoulder. Her fingers were tangled and aching and she was unsure what would give first: her bones or the fabric of his trousers.

As Felix's weight began to topple hers, she tried to wrap her leg around the slats in the railing, a herculean effort to not follow him. The wood of the ship slipped through her skirts and dug into her skin, forming bruises with every passing second.

Wyna strained her neck to look back at Brennan, hoping to find him behind her, ready to pull her and his captain back. She searched the deck, convincing herself he had only gone to get some sort of rope that wasn't decorative. She refused to believe he still sat in the nest, watching her struggle.

Below her, Felix began thrashing. He was unaware of Wyna's part in his suspension and she heard him bellow at the gods to let him go.

Something gave. Fabric or Felix or her. The entirety of her body was hot with pain but she didn't really feel it anywhere. All she felt was the crushing relief as Felix's body escaped from her grasp and all she heard was the crash of it as he reached his destination.

Finally, she looked back up. Looked at Brennan. Saw the lack of emotion or surprise or panic at what had just occurred. She had options, she knew. Brennan wouldn't breathe a word about Felix's departure. He wouldn't blame Wyna. And he would likely try his hand at captaining the ship. She could already hear his pitch to get her into the captain's quarters. Into the captain's bed.

But Felix was innocent in this. Not like Solomon—though she had her doubts of even that. She couldn't let him die, couldn't live with herself for having been the reason.

But how could she save him?

Her mind whirred, searching itself for an answer that would right the world she'd created. She was certain Brennan saw her as she flitted through the scenarios in her mind, was certain he likely knew most of whatever she was thinking. What he didn't know was that there were heroes in the water.

Without breaking his gaze, Wyna deftly untied her skirts and let them fall to the deck below her. She used a stray string to try and tie back the curls around her face as she set her jaw, a silent warning to Brennan not to follow.

And she dove, accompanying the captain into the black.

CHAPTER TWENTY

It was good that she had come, Madame Orinna told her as she made to leave, and Thessa dared to hope a dismissal from her assignment would follow. That Madame Orinna would tell her to rest in her own bed, in her own House, and not have to worry about ever returning to the Woolhill estate as a proper young woman with prospects.

"I have something for you," Madame Orinna said instead, "on your way back to the Gillbridges'."

The older woman stood again and opened the wall to her office, ushering Thessa through. She plucked a small note from her desk, swinging it to Thessa and letting it go so quickly Thessa had no choice but to catch it. Looking down, she saw in Madame Orinna's quick, flourished handwriting the words:

R. Klune

Bracken's Merch Fleet

C: 4 + 7

P. -

LS: Hatchling's

She translated the message in her head. One of Aleksander Bracken's men had reported a mermaid sighting. Multiple offenses—unmistakable. Last seen at Hatchling's bar in downtown Keresa.

Punishment at Thessa's discretion.

"And if one of Woolhill's men sees me at the bar?" Thessa asked, surprised at having been given so mundane a mission in the midst of her breakthrough. Madame Orinna hadn't yet declared Thessa's original assignment finished. It was a risk to go about Whip business when any Keresan could report to Woolhill that Thessa was back working with the mermaids.

Madame Orinna's back was to Thessa as she tidied something behind her desk. "Don't let them."

"And tomorrow? Am I to go back to Woolhill and act just the same as always?" The Madame *mhmm*ed affirmatively. "Even after what I've just told you?" Thessa demanded, careful to keep the details of their conversation quiet with a full House behind them.

Madame Orinna sighed and faced Thessa, keeping her voice low. "You've brought me great information, Thessa. And I'm impressed with how you've handled Campbell. But you haven't told me a thing about Woolhill. Perhaps his daughter has her hands in it but she doesn't control it all. And his staff? You've hardly learned a thing about the staff."

Thessa didn't bother defending herself.

"You've made a breakthrough but the work is far from done."

"Yes, Madame."

"Grab a change of clothes from one of the girls and have Maren arrange transportation."

"Yes, Madame," Thessa repeated, defeated.

And when she had done so, her body shook with the effort to keep from screaming. She had been so proud. Thrilled at what she'd managed to accomplish with Campbell. And she had done so in just a matter of days. How heartbreaking to have presented what she thought she'd achieved only to be shot down by

Madame Orinna. Not enough information. Not enough of herself had been given.

And, truly, she should have known. She should have known the work was far from over. Thessa had been doing this for years and Whips didn't get that far without being thorough. Suddenly, she wasn't so sure she deserved Madame Orinna's trust. Was this why she'd given her this note? To see if she could still manage the basest of a Whip's responsibilities?

She offered a quiet goodbye to Maren as she stepped out of the House and into the buggy the other girl had called for her. The driver gave her a tight-lipped smile and let his eyes linger on her but he did not ask her her destination. They said nothing, still, when she finally emerged onto the grimy stone of the street facing the lines of pubs and taverns, each of them with names belying their seediness or ones that would appeal to the immature humor of a sailor.

It was a perfect place for a mermaid as Keresa knew them.

Thessa eyed Hatchling's at the end of the street, right off the canal, and narrowed her eyes when a woman's booted foot shooed a few men from the property, muttering profanities and warning them to keep their hands off her girls.

So Hatchling's wasn't friendly to lust tonight.

She slipped into the shadows between the buildings across the street and watched as the exiled men laughed with each other and chose another tavern a few paces down. That was how it usually went with the merrymakers—they started to the west and worked their way through every liquor establishment until they were out of Keresa proper. That was where the ladies of the District usually lay in wait, preying on the men who weren't the least concerned about their wallets.

Wyna had once asked her why they didn't start further up the line of taverns, before the men had already spent every coin they had on their drinks and their lifted spirits. Thessa admired her for the thought. But, she'd explained, it was the same reason the District sat on the end of Keresa's peninsula instead of next to the action. Anyone who could pay for it—*would* pay for it—would trek the journey. If it were too easy, they were simply more likely to get men who promised them everything and gave them nothing.

Still standing in the shadows, Thessa considered the length of her conversation with Madame Orinna and the time she'd taken in getting ready and travelling here. Doing some roundabout math in her head, she landed on a tavern just more than halfway down the strip. Doubloomers. She rolled her eyes, the name never failing to make her question how the business was able to take off in the first place. But she stifled her annoyance and sauntered in, keeping her thin cloak tight around her.

She scanned the dim and stinking bar from the doorway with the corner of her mouth tilted up, as if she were a woman who wished to feel the weight of a fleshed dagger in her hand rather than the steel one tucked into her belt. And they noticed, a good portion of the patrons straightening in their seats and trying to attract her. Desperately wanting to be her prey.

And when her heady gaze finally fell to a table nestled in the back corner of the bar—a large, circular table that still somehow managed to have a head—she knew she'd found her target. R. Klune watched her from that head of the table, his chest puffed and his arm not-so-casually lifted to scratch a nonexistent itch on his head. He contorted his mouth to match her smirk and beckoned her without gesturing to join him at the table.

She would. When the time was right.

Perhaps it was silly for her to make a spectacle of herself in a bar when she was meant to be playing the budding socialite—no, she knew it was. But a man bent on telling his tale of mythical creatures would not be swayed by something quiet and proper against the wall. He wanted an audience and the only way she would be able to get him away would be to provide that for him. If she had her own audience, she told herself, it was only more to add to his.

Thessa approached the bar, drowning out the chatter from

the other tables as she listened to what Klune had been saying to get all that attention.

"Well I'm not going to spoil it!" he laughed. Waited for them to insist he spoil it for *them*, at the very least. They obliged.

"Come on, Robby! I'm not getting on a boat with you in the middle of the night if you're not even going to tell me what's out there."

"For all you know, he could just be trying to have his way with you," another said, elbowing Klune's dissenter in the ribs.

"The only thing I'd like to have my way with is that," Klune sneered. Thessa didn't need to meet his eyes again to know he was talking about her. It was her cue to finally make her way toward them. He continued, "I've got a boat tied up on one of the northern beaches. Come with me tonight." In his tone, Thessa could hear the arrogance and status signals he tried to imbue but she had to keep herself from smirking as those were cut by his flailing attempt at gathering a crew to venture out into the Draca.

"You've got a boat?" Thessa asked once she was close enough to claim to have only just overheard.

"Depends on who's asking," he responded coolly. She gave him something plain to call her, nothing memorable, and played off the rolling of her eyes as flirtatious. She could tell he immediately forgot as he said, "And what's it to you, doll?"

"I've always loved the sea at night," she told him honestly. She feigned embarrassment. "Call it curiosity, I suppose."

One of his companions tilted his head, seeming to consider. "Well, if she's going, then—"

"Invitation revoked," Klune said, cutting the man off. But Thessa knew he didn't want to isolate anyone who might listen to what he had to tell. To show. He tried to correct. "You and I will go tomorrow. All of you."

Klune stood, wiping his hands on the thighs of his trousers before stepping from behind the table and offering Thessa his arm. She stared at it pointedly before turning and allowing him to watch her exit the tavern.

Outside, waiting the few seconds it would take him to catch up with her, she considered her options. There were plenty of dark alleys and plenty of shadows to shield them from the glazed-eyed revelers. She wouldn't have to take him very far. Wouldn't have to keep up this facade for very long, if she would just end it here. But something in her hesitated. Klune hadn't actually revealed anything he knew about the mermaids yet. His only crime was the function of his eyes over the water and Thessa wasn't sure that was enough to take his life. She wanted to give him a chance to convince her not to harm him so permanently.

Her chest clenched. Was she growing soft?

No, she decided, chasing the thought away. It wasn't so much that he deserved a chance to do right. It was that she deserved a chance at dramatics, at making Madame Orinna proud of her again. The justification was weak, she knew, and mostly illogical at that. But she was reaching for anything that would help her fill the hole Madame Orinna's lack of praise had left.

She glanced behind her, peering into the fogged windows of the tavern to see where Klune had gone and found him settling his tab at the bar. When she shifted her view back to the street, she found a freckled face staring at her across the way.

Huxley.

She adjusted her hood to hide her face, enough that she could still see him but he could not see the panic flashing through her. His eyes were narrowed in question. At what Thessa was doing here. At why she would try to hide from him. Nerves fired in her body as she remembered what they'd done. The way their mouths fought and their bodies made up for lost time.

"Thessa?" he called, his voice carrying across to her.

She shook her head, just once, as the door behind her clanged open. When she turned to give Klune her attention, she caught Huxley's form jogging across the street.

"Let's go," she commanded quietly.

It was clear to her why Klune had seen the mermaids as he looked past Thessa, taking in her stance and taking in the man approaching her. He settled an arm around her frame, his fingers digging into her shoulder. Huxley stopped in the middle of the street, his own shoulders sagging. Guilt swarmed her but she stepped forward and Klune moved in time with her, keeping his hands curled into her cloak. She knew his hand had little to do with her own protection and everything to do with his stake on her that night. He was to have her, he'd decided, and he wouldn't let some string of a boy steal her away from him.

"This way, doll," he said, steering her with his grip and leading her to an alley that would take them northwards.

If he had done this with any other woman, Thessa would've sliced his hands from his body without a second though. But he was doing it to her. And she had the tools to make sure those hands never roved where she didn't want them.

Klune made conversation as he led her to his boat, though she supposed it was generous to call it conversation when he had no interest in hearing her speak. That was okay. There was nothing she desired for him to hear. Let him talk himself into the afterlife.

He was a helmsman, he told her, and it was his responsibility to know every detail of what went on in the waters around his ship. *His* ship, as if he had any stake in it at all. She cooed over his supposed accomplishments where appropriate until, as he was untying his little baby of a boat, he told her that once he'd shown her his discovery, it would be her job to congratulate him. She didn't ask how he wanted his congratulations and she didn't have to.

He told her, in wet, sticky details.

She spoke, finally, when they were out on the water. "What is it you want to show me?"

Klune reached a hand across the boat and rubbed it up her leg, bunching the fabric of her skirt as he did so. His hand clenched as he noted movement across the water and gripped her as if he didn't believe she was truly there.

Thessa lifted her eyes to the waves beyond Klune and met Rose's stare, just above the surface. Her slick eyebrow was raised in question. Should she come? Thessa nodded, imperceptible, so that Klune could not see she had a hand in the creatures that were about to emerge.

"Do you believe in fairy tales?" he asked her, not tearing his gaze from Draca.

"Only the true ones."

Klune didn't seem to register what she'd said by the time the tail flipped from the water, splashing them in the boat. He stood and the boat rocked with the movement as he lurched to the side and strained his eyes in the dark. "Did you see that?" he whispered.

She stood behind him and crossed her arms over her chest. Waited for him to turn and address her. He didn't. He did, however, address the three heads that popped out of the water. Thessa smirked at her friends.

"What are you?" he asked, bending slowly. The mermaids didn't answer. "No one will believe me."

"No," Edonie snapped. "They won't."

He bent further, his hand brushing his leg until he reached his ankle and tugged up the hem of his trousers, exposing a knife strapped there. And that was when Thessa struck, expertly wrangling the weapon from him, sad to know the Whip's assumption of mankind had been correct: they would seek to kill and mutilate and make a spectacle of the magic they didn't understand.

Klune yelped when Thessa broke his fingers and he clutched his injured hand to his chest. "What the fuck was that?"

She held the knife in front of his face. "What's this for?" she demanded. "What were you planning?"

"I needed a souvenir!" he shouted, "You dumb whore! Something to take back. Do you know how much they'll pay me for something like this?" He whipped around, searching the water again for the heads that'd disappeared under the waves. When his attention finally returned to Thessa, there was hot rage in his features. "Look what you've done!"

She stepped closer, fighting to keep her balance on the rocking boat and taking pleasure in the way Klune flung his arms out to do the same.

She pitched her voice low as she said, "I know exactly what I'm doing."

She set her ankle into a sturdy crevice to keep her balance as a muscled tail flew from the water and smacked the wood of the boat, splintering it just enough to give a good scare. Klune, to his credit, did not yelp again in fear.

"It was so easy," she continued as he sank to his knees and thrusted his hands into the water, trying to feel for the mermaids if he could not see them. "So easy to get you to bring me out here. You didn't question who I was. Or what I wanted." She crouched behind him so the wave of her voice tickled his ear. "Or why I would ever want someone like you."

Klune just continued splashing.

"I know who you are," she told him. "I know what you wanted to do to me. What you wanted to do to them."

He stood and faced her, abandoning his desperation to touch the mermaids.

"What are—"

Thessa pushed. The force of her body and the unsteadiness of the boat was enough to send him into the water.

"That's your plan?" he spat when he resurfaced. "To just leave me here? I can swim, you know! I'll go back and tell them all about you and—and all about my discovery!"

She held her features in complete neutrality, though she felt she should have some kind of sinister, triumphant smirk. His confidence waned and he thrashed. Thessa knew one of the mermaids had gotten a hold of his feet. And as the other two resurfaced, she felt that guilt again. It was hardly fair to ask these women to deal with the weight of a killing blow. Hardly fair to make them do her job for her.

She nodded to Rose and Dinah and the two of them hooked themselves on Klune's arm as he stared at them in awe. They swam him to Thessa. The lip of the boat was slick in her hand, his knife cold in her other, as she leaned over the side of the boat. She tipped until her face was just above his.

"Nothing," she told him as she slashed, "about these women is yours."

It was too dark to really see the red that spilled into the Draca and washed away. Thessa didn't care to see it anyway. She flung the knife into the sea and nodded her thanks to the mermaids.

"You'll get rid of it?" she asked, already detaching herself from her taking of a human life.

Dinah nodded and Rose pushed herself closer to the boat. "Thess..." A small shake of Thessa's head stopped Rose in whatever she'd been about to say. "I'll pull you most the way back," she finished.

"Thank you," Thessa told her, already forgetting the body as the mermaids dragged it into the murk.

CHAPTER TWENTY-ONE

yna didn't recognize the scream that ripped through the water, especially not as her own. But the water filled her mouth anyway as she called to the mermaids she knew were nearby. Her arm stung as one whipped by her, the scales tearing open her skin.

"Save him," Wyna tried to tell the mermaid. "Save him first."

Though she couldn't see, Wyna felt the presence of the mermaid depart from her and tried to push her way to the surface. She had to know. Had to see if Brennan had followed. When she broke, the moonlight illuminated the *Volia* and she strained her neck to see if that mop of hair hung over the side.

It didn't.

Only then did she realize she may have made a mistake.

Wyna turned in the water, trying to see if she could find Felix or perhaps one of her friends, but all she could see were the roiling waves pushing against her, feel them as the ship pushed them back to her. As she tread water, she began to notice how the ship moved. How it sailed away from her. Away from Felix and the mermaids. Each wave it crept away was only a shortening of the span of Felix's life. Wyna cursed the helmsman for continuing to push them. She cursed Brennan for not rushing to the cabins and retrieving help to drop the anchor until Wyna could return the captain to its ship. Perhaps the captain went down with the ship but what happened when the captain was the first to fall?

Oh, Wyna had really made a mess of this.

Not knowing what else to do, Wyna plunged back into the water. Dove below to see if she could glimpse any sliver of Felix— perhaps a ray of moonlight catching on a button of his coat. Nothing. *Nothing*.

A tail caught her again and shoved her towards the surface and Ibot's head poked through after Wyna's.

"We have him," the mermaid told Wyna while she panted. "We have him, don't worry."

"What do I do?" Wyna wailed, as quietly as she could, not wanting to draw the attention of anyone on the ship. "How do I get him back?" She felt the blood rush from her face. "How do I make sure he hasn't seen you? Oh gods, this is all for nothing if he's already seen you."

"He's unconscious, Wyna," Ibot assured her. "And he was when we found him. If you can get him back to the ship, we'll stay out of sight."

"My—someone saw him go over. Saw me follow him."

Ibot sunk slightly, trying to make herself less noticeable. "Oh, stupid girl," Ibot sighed.

Wyna tried to tell herself Ibot only said the words out of exasperation. Out of the realization their situation was more complicated than she'd originally anticipated. Frustration, Wyna hoped. But even so, the words cut her. Deeper than the slicing tail had.

"What was I supposed to do?" Wyna asked, spitting out the water that somehow kept finding its way into her mouth. "Let him drown? Was I supposed to return to Madame Orinna and just pretend it's completely normal for a ship to be down two men?" Wyna grunted and wanted to bury her head into her hands but she needed to keep them moving to keep her afloat. "Even one is enough to bring suspicion on the Whips."

"Two?" Ibot demanded. "Who was the other?"

"I'm sure you saw us throw him off the side of that ship. He saw Evelyn when I returned that night...I had to do something."

Ibot stared, her eyes narrowed as she studied the panic on Wyna's face. "I can't tell if you're reckless or lucky."

Neither, Wyna wanted to tell her, not sure if that was actually true. Sure, Wyna wasn't always as careful as someone like Thessa but she didn't *think* she'd been reckless. And she certainly didn't consider Solomon's sighting to be lucky, nor did she consider having to jump in after Felix to be. But perhaps she was lucky. Lucky that Solomon's had been the only pair of eyes on her that night and that she'd been able to reach him and dispatch him within the span of a few minutes. And perhaps she was lucky she'd had Brennen to shift the blame from her when his body was discovered. *And*, perhaps, she was lucky she had the mermaids with her tonight, to spare Felix from death and Wyna from Madame Orinna's sure fury.

Lucky, she decided to herself. Maybe she was lucky.

But she wasn't quite ready to count on that luck.

"It hardly matters now," Wyna finally said. "All that matters is getting him back on that ship."

Ibot watched the space behind Wyna. "You'd better hurry."

Wyna turned again, seeing the ship had traveled even farther —far enough that Wyna and Ibot would soon just be flecks above the surf.

"I would hurry," Wyna snarled, "if I knew what I was going to do! You don't seem to have any helpful suggestions." Wyna waited for Ibot to start bouncing ideas off her but Ibot stayed silent, her eyes never leaving the passing ship. It deflated Wyna. "Where are you keeping him, anyway?"

"On shore."

Wyna glared incredulously even as water splashed into her eyes. "You took him *that far*?"

Ibot scrunched her face. "It was a five-minute swim. You'll be docked in Adalis by dawn."

"So he's curled up on a beach somewhere?"

"No," Ibot drawled, crossing her arms over her chest. "We laid him out in a cave. And, gods, was he heavy."

Wyna's panic was enough to stop her from asking why the mermaids didn't have superhuman strength. She just stared, willing the answer to her problem to appear in the lines of Ibot's face, searching for some sort of pattern in the water the water droplets dripped and fell back into the waves.

Nothing came to her, not even an embarrassingly terrible idea.

She was...lost. And that just wouldn't do.

Setting her jaw, Wyna let her eyes find Ibot's again. "Can you keep him? Unconscious? Until I can return to get him?"

"Unconscious?" Ibot asked. "What do you want me to do? Hit him upside the head every time he stirs?"

Wyna flinched but pushed on. "If that's what you have to do."

Ibot studied her as she bounced in the water, bobbing and letting the waves overtake her every now and again. Wyna got the impression the mermaid was trying to determine whether or not she was serious—if she truly meant for them to keep an unconscious man in their cave indefinitely.

Wyna was dreadfully serious.

Finally, Ibot agreed. "Do you need me to take you back to the ship?"

Wyna turned in the water to find the *Volia* nearly a league ahead of them and was dumbfounded. When she was on the ship, she'd felt they were crawling through the sea, one painful inch at a time. And maybe it was that the young women had drifted as well but, from her current vantage point, it seemed as though the ship was racing.

She didn't want to have to rely on the mermaid for anything else but Wyna probably wouldn't catch up to the ship before it docked in Adalis—and she would only manage that if she didn't pass out from exhaustion before then. Even now, she could feel her body tiring from keeping itself afloat.

She sunk, longer than she had while she'd been talking with

Ibot, and the mermaid hooked her arms under Wyna's, pressing the girl to her chest to keep her above water.

"Get on my back."

Wyna obeyed, climbing around her and latching her hands around Ibot's neck. Her clothing caught on the wet skin, her trousers tearing on the scales as she made her way around. When they were secure, they went under.

Wyna could tell they moved at a breathtaking speed, one she wouldn't have thought any creature capable of, but with every pump of Ibot's tail, she felt as though she were in slow motion. She felt every molecule of water as it hit her, every brush of the various fish and debris floating around through the water. It was enough to dispel her panic about Felix, enough to make her forget she would soon be back on that ship, back amongst men who didn't have her best interest at heart.

It was enough to reinstate her wonder.

She grinned, letting the water seep into her mouth in between the gap in her teeth and, though she couldn't see in the dark anyway, she closed her eyes and let herself be hypnotized by the movement.

It was over too soon.

Ibot resurfaced before Wyna could even feel the lack of air and they were back nestled into the ship, close enough to the slime and the barnacles to reach out and touch. She saw the ladder, saw that it was perfectly within her reach, but she could not make herself grab hold. Could not make herself return.

Ibot sighed and shook Wyna off her before snatching her arm and guiding it to the ladder, her fingers working to make sure Wyna latched on.

"I'll find you," Wyna told her, trying to delay. "In Adalis. Tomorrow, I'll find you."

"We'll be watching for you."

"Okay."

"Go," Ibot commanded, splaying her fingers under the curve of Wyna's bottom to push her up onto the ladder.

She went.

The deck was empty when she reached the top. No sign of the crew. No sign of Brennan. It was her and the wood and the sea. Her instincts told her to rush for Brennan. To take him aside and demand his help. But her instincts hadn't done her any favors thus far.

She sloshed across the deck to retrieve her skirts before fumbling down the stairs to her cabin, wringing out her curls as she went and leaving a trail of salted water behind her. She didn't care. Everything was always wet on this godsforsaken ship. It was only when she had sloughed off her sticking clothes and replaced them with one of her last good outfits that she sought out her companion.

She searched slumbering faces in the crew's quarters, glaring away any surprised gazes. But Brennan's curious, attentive one wasn't among them. She searched what passed for a kitchen and she searched among the supplies, clenching her jaw when he didn't appear around a single corner.

And finally, finally she remembered where she'd caught him when they'd first arrived. Or, rather, where he'd caught her.

She stalked towards Felix's quarters.

Brennan did not look towards her when she threw open the door, nor did Wyna notice even the faintest hitch of his breath. He stayed crouched behind Felix's desk, rifling hurriedly though the papers littering the top. He was searching for something—something he evidently needed quite badly—and he wasn't finding it. Wyna stood in the doorway. Waited for him to speak to her.

To address her.

To embrace her.

"You're back," he said simply, his concentration still unbroken.

"Yes."

"Where's Felix?"

She hesitated. She didn't want Brennan to think his captain

dead—she knew the kinds of things Brennan could be capable of. The kind of power he sought. But she couldn't very well tell him she'd left the captain of the *Volia* with a bunch of mermaids.

"Safe."

He grunted.

"That doesn't please you?" she snapped. "You'd rather he be dead?"

He glanced up at her, finally, before returning to the papers in front of him. "Of course not."

"Then you'd rather I be dead," she announced as if she knew it to be true. She punctuated her statement with a little stomp of her foot. "Because I can't think of a single other reason why you wouldn't have cared that I jumped overboard."

Brennan straightened his back out slightly and stared up at her, a fire now burning in his eyes. The tilt of his head made the look frightening to Wyna but she didn't regret what she said. She crossed her arms over her chest, indignant. The action brought forth a twitch from Brennan's face and he prowled forward before grabbing her shoulder.

"You already know I'm doing this all for you, Wyna," he growled. She started at the use of her name. "You killed a man on this ship and then helped throw his funeral. Forgive me if I thought you could handle yourself."

"What about Felix?" she asked him. "He couldn't handle himself. But you didn't do anything for him."

"I don't care about Felix! I care about you! And don't you wonder why I'm in here? Why I'm going through his desk?" She didn't want to tell him she did. "I'm making sure we can dock in Adalis without trouble! Gods, Wyna, I'm covering our asses."

"He could have died. You think I care what happens in Adalis? What does it matter if the ship doesn't have a captain?"

Brennan tightened his grip on Wyna. "This ship *has* a captain," he told her. Then added, "If that's what I need to be."

"You're lucky."

He cocked his head. "Lucky?"

"That that's what I was coming to ask you."

Brennan slumped as if he'd been preparing for more of a fight. Really, she wanted to fight more. While she was glad he'd been ready to step into the role, Wyna found herself mildly irritated that Brennan had gotten to it before her. It was like the plan wasn't hers anymore, like her opportunity to save the day had been stolen right from under her.

Resigned, she said, "We'll retrieve Felix in the morning."

"We?"

Did she want his help? She thought of the weight of Felix and buckled at just the thought of dragging him to shore, let alone waiting for him to wake so she could talk him back to the ship. No, she didn't think she could do it alone. But she wasn't ready to get Brennan so close.

There could be no "we." Not yet.

"I'll handle it. You handle the harbormasters." He nodded his agreement and she went on. "Does the crew know? What did you tell them?"

Brennan let her go and returned to the desk, shifting a small box Felix had been using for a paperweight, and exclaimed to himself. He'd found whatever it was he'd been searching for. As he leafed through the hard-won papers in his hands, he answered, "I told them he was ill. They all saw how much he was drinking."

"Will they believe he's entrusted the ship to your care?"

"No."

"But they'll have to."

"You're catching on, sea witch."

She didn't fight her urge to grin at the nickname. So they were okay. He didn't begrudge her for going after Felix or stomping into the cabin like the world was ending. As she watched him, she felt her smile growing. He hadn't come for her because he *trusted* her. Brennan thought she was strong, capable. All of the things she wanted to believe about herself.

It was exactly what she wanted in a partner, she decided. Someone who would not stop her from flying—who would fly with her when she asked—but always be the nest she came back to.

"Why are you staring at me?" he asked, not looking up from his study of the plans.

She turned to the door. "No reason."

"Where are you going?"

"I...don't know."

She didn't have a plan. Couldn't think of anything that needed her attention. Her scramble to find Brennan and solidify the half-formed scheme had taken up the entirety of her mental capacity and, now that it wasn't a worry, she was lost again.

"Stay."

She turned again, finding his eyes on her. The papers forgotten, he sidestepped the desk. The boat lurched on a powerful wave but his footing was firm. He was intent. On her.

"You're incredible," he told her. "The things you can do..."

Wyna felt her cheeks heat at his attention. She didn't thank him but she certainly didn't argue. It was good that he found her incredible. Good that he recognized her potential. Calm swelled in her, knowing if she couldn't make Madame Orinna proud, she was enough for him.

"Don't you see?" he whispered, coming ever closer. "This world is ours for the taking."

She wasn't sure she wanted the world. "Ours?"

"Ours," he confirmed.

"What do you plan to do once you have it?"

He squinted at her, having not anticipated her question. As if he hadn't thought far enough ahead to know how he wanted to use the things he acquired.

He shrugged. "Rule."

CHAPTER TWENTY-TWO

Huxley would come to her, Thessa knew. He hadn't come home the night before and she'd given him the day but he was here now. There was no reason for her to sit outside of his bedroom door with her hand raised, poised for a knock that would sound through every wall of this house.

But she did, if only for a moment.

She held her breath, thinking the lightheaded effect would give her the courage to go through with it. But she hadn't done anything wrong. There was no reason to crawl to him and beg for forgiveness or to give an explanation that would be untrue and never satisfy anyway.

She cursed herself. Thessa should have known better than to open her heart back up to this boy. She should have kept his heart just as broken as she'd first left it.

Thessa dropped her fist and slinked to her own bedroom. She hadn't been there but a moment before the door squeaked open and Huxley entered. He held none of the apprehension that usually saddled him in Thessa's presence. None of that timidity of worship. Now, he was blank. A state of shock.

She found herself angry at his attitude. As if he had any right to shock—any right to the girl he thought he'd known. Her actions, of which he'd seen very little, should not have made this much of a difference to him.

"So?" he said impatiently. "Are you going to explain yourself?"

She sighed and busied herself with arranging her cloak so the material wouldn't crease. "What do you need explained?"

"Oh, I don't know. Maybe why I saw you leave Doubloomers with that...that—"

"Whatever insult is about to come out," she interrupted, "won't really communicate what you're trying to say. Don't bother."

"What did you do with him?" Huxley growled at her and Thessa's heart stopped beating in her chest for a moment. She had never heard that tone come from the boy, had never been privy to the jealousy that now plagued him.

"And what does it matter to you?" she demanded. "Why should you have any say in what I do with other men?"

Huxley deflated. "I thought—after the other night, I thought we were going to go back."

"Go back to what, Hux? Go back to being two people who shouldn't have anything to do with each other?"

"No! Go back to how we were before."

Thessa caught herself before she could rip him apart in a way he might never recover from. She didn't want to do it this way. Didn't want to break it off in a way that would destroy him, even if she should. She should poison herself to him—make him hate her.

But, gods, she didn't want to.

"We can't go back," she said quietly.

"We can't? Or you don't want to?"

She closed her eyes and tilted her head towards the ceiling. Anything to prevent the tears from falling.

"Both." The word stuck in the wetness of her mouth, the sounds congealing. She wasn't sure if he had understood her so she said it again. "Both."

"That's shit, Thessa," he heaved.

She looked at him then, confident she had stopped her dripping eyes, and set her jaw. "Believe what you will."

"Oh, I *believe* that you're too much of a coward to face what you feel for me so you push me away." He stepped towards her. "I *believe* that when you screamed that man's name, you wanted to say mine."

He was bold now. More bold than he'd ever been before. It wasn't the gentleness she'd come to know when she'd had him as a lover, nor the gentleness of the caress he'd had on her heart.

She couldn't stop herself from the defense. "I didn't scream his name."

Huxley lowered his head so his breath blew back the hair around her ear. "Then you whispered it, like this, and you wished it was my body."

"No." Thessa shook her head. "No, I didn't."

"Then what was it?"

"I killed him."

She imagined time itself stopping as the sound of her voice traveled to Huxley's ear. As he let it seep through his skin. She didn't know why she said it. Didn't know why she bothered to defend herself to him when he had no right to be angry—even if she had been intimate with Klune. Huxley saved her from having to explain further.

He laughed, mirthless. "Very funny."

"What do you want me to say, Huxley? Do you want me to tell you I'm sorry and get on my knees? Do you want me to tuck myself in your bed every night and pretend that's the life I want?"

"*Yes.* I thought that was what you wanted."

"I wanted comfort!" she screamed, as loud as she dared. "I've no interest in changing myself to make you feel better."

"I'm not asking you to change, Thessa!"

"Then what are you asking?"

"I'm asking you to love me."

Her chest heaved as the two of them imploded. But she did not let herself hesitate before she said, "I can't."

His face twitched, flinching back from her as if her words were a palm across his face. She supposed they might as well have been. But she didn't take it back. She didn't let her own face fall with the realization of what she'd said. And she did not apologize.

Because what Thessa told him was true.

She could not love him. For so many reasons, not the least of which being his disbelief at her ability to kill. She should have known better than to test him like that but perhaps it was easier now. Now that she knew he would never be able to accept the life she'd been leading. The life she fully intended on continuing to lead.

"You can't?" he asked, his voice still harsh. "Or you don't want to?"

"Stop asking me that," she snapped, suddenly tired of the constant clarification he was asking from her. She wished he would just take her at her word—accept it when she told him what she knew to be true.

But with the thought, she realized he'd been right. She *was* a coward. He wasn't asking after the petty difference between *can'ts* and *won'ts*. He was asking if she would choose him. If things were different. If she could have what she wanted, would she want him?

Campbell flashed in her mind.

She wouldn't.

"I may have wanted to love you once," she told him finally. "But that's not what I want now."

"Do you even know what you want?"

"Whatever it is...it isn't you. Not anymore."

"Get out, Thessa."

"What?"

"Get out," he said again.

"This—this is my room."

"And my house," he hissed. "You're not welcome in it anymore."

"And where do you expect me to go?" she demanded, furious at him for acting so childish. "I'm not here for you, Huxley. I'm here on orders."

He stomped past her, leaning under her bed to retrieve the bag she kept packed. She heard the clank of her spare weapons rattling and snatched the bag from him before setting it back on the floor. Huxley was undeterred and moved to gather the dresses she'd hung and her cloak.

As he reached again for the bag at her feet she shouted at him to stop.

"No!" he shot back. "You need to leave."

The movement of his arms caused her to recoil, minutely, her instincts telling her to prepare for whatever was in his hands to fly at her face. She saw the fear enter his eyes as they widened, saw him glance down at the bundles in his arms before dropping them on the floor.

Thessa would have never let him get far enough to hurt her. She had enough training to take him out with the barest hint of effort. But it was the surprise, she thought, that had made her flinch. She had come to know Huxley as gentle and soft-spoken but this person he showed her tonight was quite the departure. If she couldn't anticipate what he said, she could make no guarantees about what he would do.

"Thess, I—"

She cut him off. "Do you think that maybe this is why I won't love you?"

"I never would have—"

She kept going. "I understand you're hurt," she reasoned. "But if my honesty and my wishes cause you to lash out and act like a child then I think it's for the best."

"I'm sorry, Thessa."

"I'm not interested in your apologies."

She knew her coldness was only a facade to make herself feel better. Still, she scooped the bag on the floor, careful not to jostle it too suddenly and set it on the bed. She bent before him to retrieve the fabric at his feet. Folded the garments swiftly and shoved them into the bag without looking behind her.

"What are you doing?"

"Packing." Her voice was clipped. "Hand me my cloak, please."

Once her bag was packed, she slung the strap over her shoulder. Huxley only stared. Feeling mildly guilty for having turned herself into the victim, she sighed and retrieved the cloak, letting it rest over her shoulders without actually clasping it.

"Where will you go?" he asked.

"I hardly think it should matter to you," she sneered. And she was gone.

MADAME ORINNA WAS GOING to have her head. She wouldn't be surprised if her name ended up on one of those little notes she gave to the Whips. She could see it now:

T. Clemen
House of Whips
C: Insubordination
P. X
LS: Gillbridge residence

SHE COULD HAVE TAKEN to the water. Found Rose and the others and had them make her a little bed out in the middle of the sea in one of their grottos. But the look Rose had given her after she'd dealt with Klune was enough to keep her away. She didn't want to explain. Didn't want to tell the mermaid why she'd chosen his death over anything. The Whips had ways of keeping people quiet—they didn't always have to die. And, usually, Thessa was sympathetic.

This time she wasn't.

She had cared little for Klune's life. Little for the Whips and for the mermaids. And, just now, she'd cared little for Huxley. She wondered for a moment if she had been changed irrevocably since she'd left the House. If she'd somehow transformed into a monster of legend with no regard for the humans it hunted.

But then she thought again of Campbell and she knew it wasn't true.

And perhaps it was that thought that led her over the stretch of the Woolhill wall. Led her dropping onto the grounds after her meager luggage and slipping through the landscaping until she stood outside of the estate, looking up at where she now knew Campbell's suite to be. She considered. She could probably scale the wall of the mansion—she'd done worse—but then she'd have to leave her bag behind for the staff to find. She could go through the front doors but they were noisy and heavy and most likely guarded by Woolhill's night shift. She could enter through the staff quarters, bestowing upon them the sweet smiles and kindness and attention they so rarely got from the nobles that moved through the estate.

None of those options would guarantee her a peaceful escape from the violence still roaring within her. As she stared and debated and let the light of the moon flash with the movement of the clouds, her ears perked at the sound of stifled cough. She pressed herself against the rough wall, peeking around the corner to find Campbell, bulbous jar of amber liquid gripped in her delicate hands, skirts splayed across the steps leading to the rear entrance of the estate. She took another swig, choking again on the bitter burn as it slid down her throat.

Sighing, Thessa hefted her items into her arms and rounded the corner, waiting patiently for Campbell to notice her. When the other girl's eyes fell upon her, she didn't start, just took another swallow.

"What are you doing here?" she asked gruffly.

Thessa didn't deign to answer her question. "Are you alright?"

Campbell lifted the bottle towards Thessa. "I'm drunk. Why wouldn't I be alright?"

Thessa stepped forward and deposited her luggage before dropping on the steps next to Campbell. "You don't strike me as the type to get drunk without reason."

"And you know me so well?" she asked. She gulped down more of the liquor and Thessa could tell it was easier for her now. "You think—you...you have no idea why I drink."

As Campbell said it, she stretched her arms out on either side of her, her fingers spread save for the two still gripping the bottle. Thessa lifted the bottle from her and took a swig herself, closing her eyes as it moved over her tongue.

"Hey." Campbell frowned at her. "That's mine." Thessa tipped the bottle back once more before handing it to the girl. "Why are you here anyway? You never answered me."

"I've been kicked out of my lodgings."

Campbell narrowed her eyes at her. "What'd you do?"

"I broke his heart."

"Do you have a habit of breaking hearts?" Campbell asked her, her shapely lips pressed against the glass of the bottle.

"Just his, I think."

"Why'd you do it?"

Thessa was surprised at Campbell's line of questioning. She hadn't thought she'd taken an interest in Thessa's life, let alone who she took to her bed. But this felt to her like the closest she'd get to conversation with Campbell about anything other than what they could or would do to each other.

"I couldn't—didn't—love him."

"Why not?"

Thessa peered at her, holding her breath as she said, "I think you know why."

Campbell didn't comment on Thessa's implication. She didn't react at all. Instead, she said, "Alastor's guests returned today. We left too soon last night." Thessa stayed silent, waiting on the explanation she knew was coming. "He told them to come upstairs and swore they'd be compensated for the investment they'd made in his 'empire.'" The words were drawn out as she said them, as if it disturbed her to communicate them to Thessa.

"And were they?" Thessa whispered. "Compensated?"

Campbell scowled into the rapidly-emptying bottle. "Not in the way they'd hoped, I'm sure. I'm also sure I'll regret it tomorrow."

"Hence the drinking."

"Hence the drinking," she confirmed.

Thessa turned to Campbell, finding her breath catching at the view of the other girl's profile. At the way the lines perfectly captured the soft paths which led to her edges. "Why do you defend him?" Thessa asked abruptly. "Why do you feel the need to protect him? From me, from anyone. What has he done to deserve that when he requires this from you?"

"I don't expect you to understand what it is to owe a debt, Thessa. To know the only reason you're alive is because someone deemed you important enough to save. To care for." Campbell swallowed. "On nights like these, I don't want to love him and I hate that I do. But...I've never been able to stop."

Thessa didn't tell her she knew what it was to owe her life to someone. She owed it to Madame Orinna, she knew. But Madame Orinna had never required anything of the sort from her and Thessa would bet her soul she never would.

"Why are you able to enter the Draca?" Thessa asked her instead. "When he does this to you, over and over again?"

Campbell shrugged before polishing off the last of the liquid, letting it linger in her mouth as if savoring the feeling on her tongue. Savoring the hurt. "Is it really a betrayal if you've seen it coming all along?"

CHAPTER TWENTY-THREE

Adalis welcomed the *Volia* with inviting arms, ushering the ship into its massive harbor. Wyna watched from the nest as the harbormaster stood with his book folded in his hands, waiting patiently for the crew to settle the ship. For its captain to meet him.

Her eyes flitted to Brennan, talking hurriedly with a few members of the crew. She was too far away to hear what he said but she hoped desperately that he was sticking to the script they'd worked out together.

She'd made herself scarce when he'd explained away Felix's absence, wary of garnering the crew's suspicion at their continued partnership. Brennan had returned to her room later than night, giddy at all he'd managed to accomplish. Zachariah had fought him, as expected, demanded to see his captain and get the orders from the man himself. She had coughed through the door, feigning illness enough to send the navigator away. But she knew it hadn't been her efforts alone which convinced Zachariah to drop the matter. She'd heard the hissed consonance of Brennan's threats—his blackmail, perhaps.

The whole of her body had remained flushed long after he'd disappeared from her cabin to finalize the preparations. It was easy to forget about the gooseflesh he'd raised on her arms when he'd proclaimed his intentions to rule and it was even easier to forget about his inaction when she'd followed Felix into the sea. Easy when the memory of his lips on her was so fresh. When his praises of her—her body and her mind—still flowed through her ears. And she was amazed, really, as she watched him work and as he explained to her the depths of his plans to take over the ship. Amazed at how quickly his mind worked to protect himself. Flattered he had chosen to include her in his plans.

Did she have a choice to be flattered, she wondered, or was the only other option to fall to his control?

But a shameful pride flashed through her when she saw him beam at the harbormaster, communicating in a moment's time that he was the one to be reckoned with. The harbormaster hardly spared a blink at the change in leadership and pried open the book in his hands, resting it on his forearms and noting anything he could immediately see about the *Volia*. Wyna yearned to get her hands on that book, yearned to know if it held information that would impress Madame Orinna.

Brennan swung down from the deck of the ship, extending his hand to shake that of the harbormaster, his own ledger rolled at his hip. When they'd finished their small chat, he unfurled the ledger with a flourish and presented it to the harbormaster, pointing quickly at all he planned to declare before rolling the parchment again and tucking it away. Wyna cocked her head at the sight, wondering why the sailor had opted for a sleight-of-hand approach rather than handling the other man with his semi-honest charisma. Sneaking product in or out of Adalis wasn't part of their plan and Wyna wasn't sure how comfortable she was with the prospect of it when their lie was already at risk of discovery.

It was difficult for her to tell if the movement of her heart was a fluttering or a flinching. Harder still when he met her eyes from the dock and winked, the shagged ringlets falling from the tie at the back of his neck and somehow making him look even more charming. He called to the crew, ordering the dropping of the ramp. The crew's compliance came quickly, no grumbling or questioning of his authority to make the order.

Brennan did not retreat with her to the nest once the order was given, preferring to stay enmeshed in the flurry of crew and cargo. The timing of their dock had been planned to perfection, as the daily markets were just starting to open and the wealthy of Adalis dripped into the streets beyond the docks to empty their purses into the pockets of the merchants. The *Volia's* quartermaster stood panicked next to Brennan as the cargo moved from the ship faster than he could track. Wyna knew instantly that that had been by Brennan's design. Was this soon-to-be pilfered cargo the riches Brennan had promised her?

She felt the magnetism of a set of eyes on her head and searched the crowd below her to find whose attention she'd caught, finding the harbormaster's face pinched in the direction of the nest. In her direction. He approached Brennan, clapping a hand on his shoulders before pointing to Wyna. Brennan's body did not stiffen at the questioning but Wyna saw the flex of his jaw that gave away his displeasure. The two men argued quietly with one another, neither of them willing to let their friendly demeanor drop. She could almost hear the pleasant insults they offered.

Wyna's breath caught in her chest as she tried and failed to read their lips. Her mind raced through the horrific possibilities. They would keep her in Adalis, never to return to Madame Orinna or Keresa ever again. They would keep her from Felix and the captain of the *Volia* would discover the truth of the mermaids and she'd be able to do nothing to prevent it. They would declare her unfit to crew a ship and kill her where she stood, gifting the Draca yet another lifeless body.

Even hours later, after the ship was near empty and the harbormaster long gone, she hesitated to release the breath. Brennan had left her without explanation, abandoning her to the onslaught of wind and sun and loneliness. She had no interest in remaining in the nest until they returned so she opened the hatch and slid down the mast with ease.

"Did you get what you wanted?" Zachariah's voice sent Wyna leaping into the air and cursing her continued recklessness. He went on, biting out the words. "Is this ship how you want it now?"

She didn't face him when she responded. "I'm sure I don't know what you mean."

"You've convinced Friswell you're worth the time, it seems. I don't know what you've done with Felix but I'd hate for you to think we've all bought it."

"I'm growing tired of you finding me every time we dock, Zachariah," she snapped, angling herself towards him now.

"That's the only time you're ever alone."

"And you've been itching to get me alone since I boarded."

His face curled in feigned disgust. "Don't flatter yourself, whore."

She stepped forward as if she meant to move around him, anticipating his instinct to block her from exiting the conversation. And when he was still in her way she continued to step forward, making sure the brunt of her foot landed on the most sensitive part of his. Zachariah howled at the pain, his arm whipping up to strike Wyna in response. She blocked the hit effortlessly and sent his arm back to his body.

"I wouldn't," she said, "if I were you." He hopped in place, each landing sending his body careening into her. She kept steady. "Don't you have anything to do? Away from me?"

He stilled at the question. Stopped his hopping and whining. Like he wanted to appear powerful again when he next spoke. "There's plenty I want to do to you," he drawled.

Wyna rolled her eyes. "I know," she told him. "At this point, it's pathetic."

"Not those kinds of things, bitch."

She stepped around him, ducking the arm he threw out to stop her and spoke without turning her head back to him. "Liar."

She disappeared.

It was only when night fell that Wyna had to admit another mistake. Brennan had been at the market stalls all day, overseeing the trade slotted for the *Volia* as they only had two days in Adalis before they began their return trip. The absence of Brennan and the crew would have been the perfect chance for Wyna to slip away to retrieve Felix and then leave him in his quarters for someone else to find. That way, she wouldn't have to explain where she'd gone, she wouldn't have to risk someone following her, and the secret she kept of the mermaids would be entirely safe. The only issue, had she taken this route, would have been in hauling Felix back to the ship.

Wyna hadn't done any of that.

Instead, she paced in her cabin, eagerly awaiting the return of the crew so she and Brennan could get to work putting everything back together. She'd asked for his help in ensuring their docking in Adalis was successful, and so she had assumed every part of this plan hinged on their continued partnership. But now she had to figure out how to get Felix back under the watchful eyes of the crew. And of Brennan, who never seemed to miss a thing.

Brennan, who'd been able to read her since day one.

If she left now, she wouldn't have time to get to the cave and back before the crew returned. And who knew what Zachariah might try if he saw she was the one slowly dragging Felix's body after her? Surely he'd be able to spin some story after the way she'd dispatched him earlier.

No, it was no longer an option to do it on her own. Madame Orinna would be furious.

Wyna tried to work out her plan in her head. She'd swim out from the beach she'd spotted a few miles down and wait for the mermaids to carry her to their cave. She'd enlist their help in getting Felix to the shallow waters where Brennan could wait for her return. She'd shoo the mermaids away before they were spotted and, from there, the two of them could surely manage to bring Felix back to the ship—even better if he woke from the mermaid-induced stupor and walked the distance himself.

She reviewed each step, over and over again, trying to find the flaws she knew must be hidden somewhere, trying to memorize it all so there was no room for her own error, no room for any surprises. Eventually, she'd repeated it to herself enough to be convinced of its solidity. It would work.

It *had* to work.

The door to her cabin squeaked open behind her, Brennan slipping in before it could slam shut once more. He peered at her through his hair, glistening and damp with sweat.

"You'd be proud of me, sea witch," he told her, grinning like a fool.

She elected not to tell him she already was. "And why is that?"

He produced a bag that had been tucked into the lining of the jacket he wore—despite the warm weather—and spilled its contents onto the bed. Coins rained from it, cascading onto the sheets and eventually clanking to the floor. She tried to take a quick count of all the money he'd procured but gave up as it continued to fall and roll.

"Aren't those supposed to go in the ship's coffers?"

He shook his head, laughing. "My hands are almost as quick as yours now!"

"You *stole* all that?" She wasn't passing judgement. Gods knew she'd taken her fair share and would never begrudge the impoverished for skimming a little money off the undeserving. She was just shocked he'd managed to steal so much without notice. "How? From who?"

"From *whom*," he corrected. "We're rich now. We must act like it."

She smacked his arm. "I didn't ask for a grammar lesson. I asked how you got the money."

"Does it matter? Those markets are so packed that people have no idea who's touching them and who's taking from them. All the vendors are so busy with customers that no one ever notices a hand reaching across the displays." He clawed into a pile of the coin and lifted, letting them run through his fingers and tumble back onto the bed. He admired the shine of it before turning back to Wyna. "On top of our wages? I count at least five paychecks we can collect now."

"Five?"

"My original one," he started, a bit sheepishly. "And then the bosun's. Whatever they agreed to pay you, plus Solomon's. And then we'll have to let Woolhill's men know about Felix's incompetence. I reckon we can skim a bit of his wages, too, considering he didn't bother to show his face for one of our biggest docks. That, and all of this money? Gods, Wyn, we're set."

Despite herself, and in spite of her hesitation at exploiting Felix's fragile state, she began to leech some of the giddiness from him. Half-jokingly, she said, "I can only imagine what other positions you'll assume before we get back to Keresa."

"We," he told her. "We're in this together from now on. Always."

Shyly, she agreed. "Together."

He kissed her then, running his hands over her arms before bringing one up to cup the back of her neck, holding her to him. His other hand snaked behind her waist and pushed her against himself. She was breathless when she pulled away and somehow unable to stop herself from ramming back into him, shoving him back until he fell atop the coins. She laughed against his mouth at the noise but he silenced her as he deepened the kiss.

Yes, she thought as he writhed under her, yes, they would be fine. They would make it through this, money in tow, and she would never again have to worry about who might be next to her on her journey. She could dispatch on Madame Orinna's missions *with* Brennan. No, she wasn't quite ready for him to know her secret but surely someday he could be trusted. They'd all done things which the law would frown upon—she knew he'd never turn her in.

And she had faith.

Had faith that, just like he'd been ready to step in and cover for her, he'd be more than willing to do whatever was required of him to protect the mermaids. They would fight the mermaids just like they fought for each other.

The future was quickly stretching itself before her.

It was him.

She broke the kiss and stood, instructing Brennan to pick up his coin and stash it somewhere away from prying souls. He pouted at her abrupt departure but did as she bade, tucking the pouch into the Wyna's bag under the products Madame Orinna had given her for her cycles. Even he seemed to hesitate at touching the unused items and she rolled her eyes at him from the doorway.

"We've got to go," she told him.

He frowned. "Where?"

"Surely you don't expect me to leave Felix for dead."

His eyebrows disappeared into his hair and then his eyes were hidden altogether as he glanced at the bed. "I never know what to expect from you, sea witch."

She threw the door open. "Come on," she said. "I've got it all taken care of. All you have to do is follow."

And follow he did. Right to the edge of the water where Wyna had decided he'd wait. He watched her again untie her skirts and she folded them neatly before handing them over to him to keep while she walked into the sea. Then, remembering she'd have to haul a beast of a man back with her, quickly cut the strings from the waistband of the skirts and looped it around the holders for her sickles.

"Stay here," she instructed, mustering as much confidence into her as she'd seen him use on the crew. "I'll be back shortly." She glanced at the moon and pointed to a rock in the distance. "If

I'm not back by the time the moon clears that rock, go back to the ship without me. Pretend nothing's wrong. I'll be okay."

He nodded and asked her fewer questions than she'd anticipated. Fewer, meaning none. So he trusted her. He trusted she could manage this by herself. Biting her lower lip, she pranced forward through the sand and pressed another long kiss to his lips, letting it linger until he tried to tangle his fingers in her curls.

"I'll be back," she said again, and waded into the surf.

She was sure to swim far enough out that Brennan could no longer see her. Satisfied, she tried to submerge her body as long as possible so the mermaids had time to steal her away. Eventually, though, she grew weary of swimming and bobbing and inhaled before dropping back into the water and shouting Ibot's name. The mermaid was beside her instantly and did not give Wyna the opportunity to take another breath before latching onto her and dragging her through the water. In the darkness, Wyna could make out the streaks of foam they left behind.

Just when she'd been about to beg Ibot to let her up for air, the two emerged in a dim cave, lit only by a singular thread of moonlight leaking into the entrance. The mermaids gathered there, nervously staring at the body of the man who lay unconscious on a cropping of rock above the water. None of them made a noise, frightened to wake him and spoil their existence.

Wyna gestured for them to drop under the water and hide before she poked Felix's body and called his name. Shouted at him to come to. She'd be able to manage him just fine if he was able to wake up and swim. But if she needed the mermaids' help in getting him back, she needed to ensure he stayed unconscious.

He did.

She swatted her hands upwards under the water to communicate to the mermaids they should surface.

"He's out," she assured them.

"Been like that for a while," Evelyn told her.

Wyna turned towards the woman and extended her a wide

smile. "I missed you." The confession was breathy as she made to embrace her.

The mermaid accepted the embrace instantly, wrapping Wyna in her slimy arms and holding onto the girl as if it'd been years since they'd last seen one another. "We've been worried about you. We saw the body your ship dropped into the ocean and assumed the worst. Ibot told us what happened." Evelyn gestured to the other mermaid, who hadn't taken her eyes off of Felix's body. "What happened to this one?"

"He blamed himself for Solomon's death," Wyna admitted, hoping her voice didn't give away that the droplets on her face were actually from tears. "I think he aimed to die."

Evelyn pet her arm and the other mermaids moved in to comfort her. "It was quite brave of you to jump in after him," Evelyn said. "He's lucky to have you on his ship."

"No." Wyna shook her head to keep from wailing. "I killed his friend. And I almost killed him. I"—she took a breath—"I feel like I've given you all more trouble than I have protection."

"You're just a girl," Evelyn said. And when she saw the way Wyna's lip quivered she hurried to elaborate. "You're just one girl. It's unfair to put the weight of a centuries-old secret in your hands alone. You're doing the best you can."

"If...if it's your life or theirs, I want you to know I'll always choose yours."

She thought of Brennan and the future he'd planned for the two of them. Perhaps she could choose the mermaids over the others but would she choose the mermaids over herself? Over the family she'd always wanted? She gazed around the cave at the mermaids. At the friends she'd never thought she'd have. The family.

Did she have to choose at all?

A man's voice startled her from her concentration.

"I called you 'sea witch' as a joke, Wyn," Brennan panted from the mouth of the cave. "I didn't know you actually knew some."

CHAPTER TWENTY-FOUR

The unfamiliar setting had Thessa on her feet in mere seconds once she'd opened her eyes. The quilt that had covered her tangled in her legs as she stood, crouching in a defensive stance as she took stock of the room.

It wasn't her own—she hadn't slept there in some time now —but she'd been here before.

Campbell lay on her side in the bed next to Thessa, staring up at her with a mildly annoyed scrunch to her face. She was casual. Thessa straightened.

"Are you finished?" Campbell asked. "Or would you like to have a go at the pillows next?"

Thessa felt color rush to her cheeks and busied her fingers with combing the knots out of her wild hair. Her head pounded but she couldn't be sure if it was from the sun poking through the curtains into her eyes, the quick movements she'd made upon waking, or the second bottle of liquor the two of them had decided to polish off the night before. She glanced down at the floor, at the pile she'd left of a fluffed pillow with a head-shaped dent in the center and a few mismatched blankets.

So she'd slept on the ground.

Her vision blurred as she tried to piece together how they'd gone from the back steps to here but she came up short. Swallowing, she asked, "What happened last night?"

Campbell raised her eyebrows but refrained from the commentary Thessa was sure burnt the tip of her tongue. It seemed to Thessa that Campbell's mood had already soured. Campbell threw the blankets from her body and stood gracefully before going about putting the bed back together in some semblance of order. Thessa moved to the other side to help.

"We drank," Campbell finally answered. "And then we slept. I offered you the bed but you prattled on about honor. Honestly, Thessa, you aren't nearly as frightening as you pretend to be. As if I really thought you planned to have your way with me," she scoffed.

"Thank you," Thessa told her. "For letting me stay here."

Campbell turned away from her and sat at the vanity on the opposite wall, crossing her legs at the ankle. "Where else were you going to go?"

"I wasn't aware you had an interest in my comings and goings outside of our business arrangements." She was testing her, she knew. Planting the trap for Campbell to fall into. Waiting for her to admit she cared about Thessa the way Thessa was beginning to care about her.

Campbell rearranged her hair so it covered her face. "We don't have much of an arrangement if you disappear into the night. There are some...unsavory...people running about Keresa."

"And I suppose you'd like me to believe you're not one of them."

The blocking hair shifted with the movement of the cheek underneath. "You didn't seem to find me unsavory last night," Campbell said. Thessa blanched. Had she...? "People don't look at unsavory things the way you look at me."

"And how do I look at you?" Thessa managed to ask.

Campbell's eyes shot to a worn book sitting on the corner of her vanity. "Like I'm the fairy tale you just found out was real."

Thessa wasn't sure what she meant—wasn't ready to delve into all the implications Campbell had laid before her. But she'd become intimately familiar with the feeling of her heart lurching into her throat.

"How does the fairy tale end?"

Campbell did not have a chance to respond before a knock sounded and the door to her bedroom suite had opened. A middle-aged woman, small and sturdy, bustled in. She took only the briefest of moments to acknowledge Campbell before setting to correcting the bedding to her own standards.

"Sorry to interrupt ya, miss," the woman said. "Yer daddy's expecting ya for breakfast."

"Thank you, Philippa. Do you have a moment to spare to prepare Miss Clemen, as well?"

Thessa smiled at Philippa. "Oh, no. I can dress myself."

"It's not a bother, miss," Philippa told her. "Do ya have yer own frocks or shall I find ya some?"

Thessa didn't want to argue with the woman so she just said, "I have my own."

Philippa nodded her acknowledgement and moved to the wardrobe to begin pulling garments for Campbell. The woman dressed her with tenderness and efficiency. With love. Thessa could sense the affection flowing between them even from the other side of the room. Even as she averted her eyes to give Campbell privacy while in her state of undress.

Philippa said nothing when Thessa pulled the black trousers from her bag—which had apparently been tossed haphazardly in the corner—and tugged them over her legs. The woman merely snatched one of Thessa's skirts from the bag and ushered Thessa into it. She noted Philippa hadn't chosen one of her quick-release ones. When they were dressed, again according to Philippa's standards, she set the girls down on the vanity bench, side by side, and set to work on their hair.

Taming Campbell's hair was effortless and Philippa kept most of it down so that loose ringlets tumbled over the bare skin of her back while the upper portion of her head was woven into a delicate plait. She had more difficulty with Thessa's salt-hardened locks and managed only to wrangle most of it into a bun at the base of her head that would loosen and unfurl within the hour.

Campbell pivoted on the bench as Philippa made to leave and cleared her throat. "Can we be discreet about Miss Clemen's presence, Philippa? Alastor doesn't need to know she stayed the night."

Philippa nodded easily. "Course, Miss."

"You're close with her," Thessa observed when Philippa was gone, her ass still firmly planted on the bench.

"Yes. Alastor's kept her employed forever. I suppose she was responsible for raising me more than Alastor ever was."

"And you trust her?"

"Wholeheartedly."

"What about the other staff?" Thessa pushed, standing and pulling her daggers from the pocket of her bag and tucking them into the pockets sewn into her dress.

"Yes," Campbell said warily.

"Do they know?"

"About?"

"The mermaids," Thessa clarified, keeping her voice low. "Do they know about the mermaids?"

Campbell crossed her arms over her chest, growing defensive. "Is it a problem if they do?"

Thessa channeled Campbell and raised her brows. "If it is a problem, it's certainly not mine."

"It's not," Campbell snapped. "It's not a problem. And they do know. Most of them. I keep the staff closest to me informed— the ones I've known forever. I require the rest of the staff to be employed for at least a decade before anyone ever thinks of informing them. There are some who have been here since I was a child that still have no idea what lives in these waters."

"I'm not interrogating you," Thessa told her. "I just—"

"You just wanted to know if we could be trusted to keep the

Whips in the loop," Campbell finished. "If this arrangement stands, my people will work with yours. I'm not joining the Whips, Thessa. The Whips are joining the Woolhill operation."

"I'm certain Madame Orinna wouldn't be too fond of that particular verbiage."

"I'm not working with Madame Orinna," Campbell countered. "I'm working with you."

"Well, I," Thessa began, "am working with everyone. With you. Your staff. Madame Orinna *and* the Whips. This is a cooperation that must be established on trust."

Campbell ignored her and stepped towards the door. If she weren't so prim, Thessa thought she would be stomping.

"You can't control everything," Thessa told her, and wondered if the advice might be more for herself.

THESSA FOUGHT the urge to gag when Woolhill embraced her, his arms holding her body entirely against his. She could feel where he'd already begun to sweat as it seeped through his clothes and onto hers. He beamed down at her before letting her go and insisted she sit opposite Campbell towards the end of the table.

He, of course, sat at the head. His makeshift daughter to his left and Thessa to his right. Campbell kept her focus on the flowering centerpiece as Thessa wished him a good morning and inquired about the night he'd had in her absence. He regaled her with the stories he'd stolen from his guests and the idle gossip about the wealthy's affairs. When he spoke, Campbell actually gave him her attention.

Thessa watched as the young woman relaxed, seemingly forgetting what Woolhill had required of her as he went on. She was sinking, Thessa realized, into the role of his daughter. Letting herself be fooled into comfort because his particular brand of comfort was the only one she'd ever known.

Thessa felt sick.

When his attention again fell to her, Thessa almost spit out her food as he asked where she'd been staying.

"I'm staying with a family friend just west of the estate," she told him. She wasn't sure why he'd asked but she rushed to explain further. "Forgive me for showing up so early," she preened. "I just had to get back to you as soon as I could."

Woolhill's face brightened at the compliment and Thessa only felt a great regret. "We'll have you out of that house soon enough," he assured her, placing his hand over hers atop the table.

She found herself relieved that he remained within eyesight of Campbell and hadn't opted to let his hand creep up her thigh. Still, the other girl's knuckles whitened as she gripped her fork, the veins in her neck straining at the sight of their hands together. Thessa stole the appendage back from him and hoped he would just think her hungry. She never felt his eyes leave her as she focused on the meal in front of her.

"I'm sure Campbell would enjoy having you around more often," Woolhill went on. "Wouldn't you, Cam?"

If Thessa hadn't so desperately yearned for a "yes' from her, she might have hoped Campbell would tell Woolhill she wanted nothing to do with her. Maybe then he would distance himself, if only for the sake of his daughter.

How silly to think Woolhill would do anything solely for the sake of his daughter.

Regardless, Thessa couldn't afford to soil the relationship with Woolhill. Not after Madame Orinna had already so clearly communicated her expectations and especially not after Thessa had gotten herself kicked out of the Gillbridges's.

"Indeed," Campbell muttered through a mouthful of food. Even with crumbs dribbling from her mouth, she was elegant. The softness of the mess didn't dampen the hardness of her edges and Thessa thought she liked it that way.

"I'd like you to stay here, Thessa," Woolhill declared, so informal with the use of her name. "A few nights out of the week until you grow more comfortable. Of course, we can't move too quickly—we wouldn't want to be improper—but soon enough you'll be staying here full time. I'll have Campbell and the staff train you on duties you may not have had the chance to learn with your...upbringing." He cleared his throat, clearly uncomfortable with the thought of Thessa's past. "We'll make a Woolhill out of you yet."

Her chest heaved and Woolhill's eyes moved towards it. She told herself she'd misheard him. That whatever she was reading in his words couldn't possibly be true. She tried to clarify. "A Woolhill, sir?"

He chuckled at the use of "sir" and again his hand found hers. "Forgive me, Thessa. I thought I was being clear. Your scheming has won me over," he tried to joke. "Won all of my compatriots over, really. It is my intention to marry you."

It wasn't a proposal. Not like any of the proposals that had sung through her head when she was a girl and still believed settling down was how she'd grow up. Her insides churned as she went over his words in her head. No, it wasn't a proposal. It wasn't even a demand. He was simply telling her what was to happen, regardless of what she felt.

He thought she felt for him. He thought that was why she was here.

She choked a bit and hoped he would chalk it up to his comment about scheming. Before she could swallow it, she asked him, "Why?"

"Why do I intend to marry you?" he laughed. "Well, that's what this was all about, wasn't it? You're quite the attractive young woman—of course, I was assured you would be. And I was so sorry to hear about your family. What was I to do but extend my hand to you, dear? You know I'm quite generous." The laughing had stopped, every word spoken with deadly sincerity. "But think of it as mutually beneficial. You'll be rich, Thessa, and I'll stop having to hear about all the noble daughters."

"I don't know what to say."

He smiled, his cheeks puffing out. "You needn't say a word. I'll take care of everything."

She needn't say a word? Did he truly have no intention of even hearing her agree to his marriage proposal? She thought of Campbell. Of all the things he'd made her do. No, Woolhill had never been interested in hearing the word "yes." Not that he was partial to "no," either. It seemed no matter what answer he was given, Woolhill got his way.

Thessa met Campbell's eyes across the table. Let her read her rising panic.

"Are you finished, Miss Clemen?" Campbell asked her.

Woolhill *tsk*ed. "You must start using her name, dear. Or," he countered, snickering at his own joke, "I suppose you could refer to her as 'Mama.'"

"Are you finished, Thessa?" Campbell bit out without looking at her father.

"Yes," Thessa said, frustrated that it had been one of the first things she'd uttered after the proposal. She never wanted Woolhill to know what it was like to hear her agree.

Campbell stood and gestured for Thessa to do the same. "I've much to show you, I suppose."

Thessa stepped away from the table to stand behind Campbell, waiting for instruction or for her to simply start moving first. Campbell hissed "curtsey" and Thessa dropped before Woolhill and muttered something about seeing him later.

She managed to hold back her tears until they made it to the hallway but she knew her face was flushed and the skin around her eyes had already started to swell. Campbell said nothing and somehow that made it worse. Like Campbell thought she actually intended to marry him. Like she was furious with Thessa for not turning her father down. But how could she have? How could she have told Woolhill it had all been a lie?

"I will not marry that man," Thessa spat, feeling hopeless and that she might very well have to.

"I'll be surprised if you can get out of it."

"I have to go back to the Whips. Maybe leave Keresa entirely."

Campbell's face fell, drooping more than Thessa ever thought the tight, rosy skin would allow. "I'd like you to stay in Keresa."

"And marry your father?"

"I—don't call him my father. Not right now."

"Do you want me to marry him?" Thessa asked, incredulous and inexplicably hurt.

No, that wasn't right. It wasn't inexplicable at all.

"Maybe you should," Campbell said. "Maybe you...because—because at least you'd be around. You'd be here."

Thessa'd never heard her stumble over her words like she did now, not while she was sober. And for the second time, she found herself asking, "Why?"

"You'll truly make me say it?"

Thessa's chest heaved again, for a wholly different reason now. Despite herself, the corner of her mouth lifted in a smug smile. "Yes."

Campbell extended her arm as if to slap Thessa. But when her skin made contact, it wasn't a sting Thessa felt. It was a squeeze as Campbell latched onto her and pulled Thessa towards her.

She never did say what Thessa asked her to but her mouth communicated enough as it pressed against Thessa's. Their bodies shoved together in a way that was both passionate and graceful. Even as she was swallowed by her want for Campbell, she was blown away by her. She, somehow, had enough presence of mind to appreciate what lay in front of her. On her.

Thessa deepened the kiss, urging Campbell's mouth open to accept her tongue. Campbell's met hers in kind and her arms swam up Thessa's body to cup the back of her neck and twine into the hair that had fallen out of Philippa's bun.

Thessa could no better stop the whimper that escaped her than she could the rising tide.

And yet she stiffened, hearing another sort of sound tangling with her own. She broke from Campbell and Campbell did not protest. Her eyes were already open. Already on whatever stood behind Thessa. Thessa spun, her skirts brushing Campbell's in their proximity.

She straightened her back and did not bother to right her clothing or her hair—did not bother to wipe the wetness that still clung to her mouth—as she met Woolhill's wide eyes.

CHAPTER TWENTY-FIVE

The mermaids were upon him before the words had a chance to echo off the cave walls. In the moonlight, there was a flurry of motion and a mad slap of tails as they descended upon Brennan's form. Without thought, Wyna shouted at them to stop.

They did.

One of the mermaids slowly lifted Brennan's head back out of the water and he glared at her. Attempted to shake out of her hands. Her grip was strong and she did not relent. Did not even glance at the boy as she looked to Wyna for guidance.

Wyna didn't bother explaining why she'd stopped them and she had no inclination to defend him to the mermaids at that very moment.

"You followed me?" she demanded of him. "You followed me here? Today? But you didn't think to follow me last night."

His face was blank as he stared, having no reaction to Wyna's fury. Only when he saw a similar fury fly off the mermaids did he have the decency to look chastened. "I was curious," he whined. "I had to know what you were doing. I thought—" He tried to swim towards her but the mermaid holding him did not allow him the movement. He lowered his voice. "I thought we were in this together."

She begged herself not to cry. "Being in this together means trusting me when I say I have it handled. You did last night. What changed?"

"Nothing, I..." He stared at the water like he wasn't brave enough to meet her eyes. "Gods, Wyn, can you give me a minute to process what the fuck's in front of me before you interrogate me?"

It struck her as funny, for some reason, and she exploded with laughter. "Oh, pardon me! Yes, here are the mermaids! Take a good gander and then maybe we can get back to our conversation." She sighed but it sounded more like a grunt. "You don't even know what this means. You don't even know what I have to do to you now."

"What you have to do to me?" he asked. "Why do you have to do anything?"

She didn't answer. Waited for his go ahead to return to their discussion.

"I can't believe you'd keep something like this from me," he pouted. "I really thought you were in this for our future...and you were only keeping secrets."

Guilt slithered through her. Hadn't she just been lamenting that she couldn't share this with him? Hadn't she just wanted to tell him everything and let them face the world together? Why was it so different now?

Just because he had stumbled upon them by accident? Because she hadn't been the one to show him?

She deflated, all of a sudden feeling like she was the one who'd made the mistake. Like it was a crime to keep this sort of secret from him. He had already seen her kill and lie and he had protected her then. She should have trusted him to keep this secret, too.

Perhaps he was the one who had to forgive her.

"Let him go," she told the mermaids.

They did and her muscles clenched with the pain of rejection when he didn't immediately swim to her. She wondered if it would be long before they were okay again.

Would they ever be okay again?

"This is incredible," he said. It stung that he wasn't talking about her. "How did you know they would be here?"

"We brought her here," Evelyn said, her voice harder now. "But we did not bring you."

Brennan ignored Evelyn, finally extending the gift of his attention back to Wyna. "How did you know?" he asked again.

How was she meant to explain this to him? She opened her mouth to speak, willing the explanation to come forth but it never did. Eventually, she gave up and just shrugged. "I'm a Whip."

He furrowed his brows. "I know," he said, like it was the most obvious thing in the world. "But I don't—that's why they call you guys the mermaids?"

Wyna nodded. Slowly. "It's easier," she told him. "If someone sees, everyone will think they're just talking about us. It...gives us time."

He did not ask what it gave them time to do. Brennan was intelligent enough to figure that much out on his own. He schooled his features and Wyna knew he was playing out every-thing that'd happened in his head.

"I knew you were hiding something."

The comment had a shiver traveling down her spine even though the water was warm. "You've got plenty you hide from me."

"I'm not harboring mythical creatures!"

"What are you going to do?" She began to grow anxious and the feeling pulled the frustration out of her. "Now that you've seen them, what will you do?"

He studied her for a moment before squaring his shoulders and swimming towards her. "No need to worry, sea witch," he whispered, blowing droplets of water into her ear. "I don't have a death wish."

So he had figured it out. He knew Solomon had died because he'd seen too much. He knew Wyna had slaughtered the man for less than what Brennan now witnessed.

"I don't want to kill you."

"Don't you trust me, Wyn? In this together, remember?"

She wanted that to reassure her. She wanted to believe him. It was easier than having to realize how badly this could end. If believing him meant she could keep both parts of herself, then that was what she would do.

Turning off the thoughts still trying to rattle inside her, she let a smile creep onto her face. "These are my friends."

The mermaids took longer to come around than she did—especially Adrie. They kept their distance from Brennan, kept almost every scale under the water and out of his sight. Soon enough, Wyna's concerns grew to be less about the ramifications of Brennan's discovery and more about whether or not she could blend her loves together. She found herself rambling through every positive quality she could conjure for him, explaining to the mermaids how he'd so masterfully taken over as captain and cooing over the romance of his plan to take her away and build her a life.

And to Brennan she explained her awe for the mermaids—that they weren't creatures to her. They were people. Her people. But she did not reveal to him why the mermaids had come to be. It wasn't up to her to offer these women's pasts to a man they did not know. Though Wyna wanted desperately to build a bridge between them, she knew trust like she had took time to forge. She, too, had been unsure of the boy when they'd met.

It would come. In time, it would come.

Her body heated as her mind ran with fantasies of the future. Of the two of them, taking a little boat out into the open sea and having a soiree with the mermaids. She'd bring them presents and they'd sing songs as Wyna and Brennan danced in each other's arms under the moonlight. They'd fall asleep, curled up in between the seats of the boat and, when they woke, the mermaids would be ready to start again.

She would know peace.

It was good he was here, she decided. Good this had happened now, rather than later. She could only imagine the kind of reaction he'd have if she'd gone longer with such a secret. There would be no repairing the trust then. Now, when it was still tentative, it would be easy enough to mesh back together.

Brennan kept up his charm as he spoke with the mermaids and Wyna's thoughts turned to Madame Orinna. She'd have to tell her. Maybe the Madame would offer him employment— Wyna had seen how quickly Brennan had been able to pick up tasks and he was nothing if not the perfect spy. But Madame Orinna wasn't a fool. She hadn't been in business as long as she had by throwing out her secrets to anyone who could catch them. No, she'd take a lot of convincing.

But what was family if not something to fight for?

BRENNAN'S SPIRITS were high as they dragged the captain's body back to shore. He chattered to Wyna about the mermaids, about what it meant now that he knew they were real. He had eventually convinced Ibot to swing her tail up to him so he could examine the scales. His fingers were still red from where the edges had sliced him but he didn't seem to mind. All he could talk about was the beauty of it, like it was something even the richest of Keresa's nobles couldn't buy.

Wyna was glad for his attitude, glad he didn't seem to take the mermaids as some kind of trophy but recognized them for what they were—beautiful, strong women and proof of living magic. So she gushed with him, gleeful to be able to share the experience that she'd so recently had. The other Whips who'd known of the mermaids long before would never be able to share the kind of enthusiasm that came with the first discovery.

They grew quiet when they felt the body between them stir. Felix was slow to waking and even slower to reacting when his eyes opened and he saw he was not on solid land. Brennan relaxed his hold so the other man slid into the water, shocking his senses into awareness.

And he screamed.

Brennan dunked him back under before pulling him to his chest and shouting at Felix to gather himself, claiming he would wake the whole of Adalis with his yammering.

"Adalis?" Felix faltered, suddenly even more panicked than he was before.

"Yes," Brennan told him with strained patience. "We docked this morning."

"Then that means—I have to—"

"We've already taken care of everything. All you need to do is rest."

Felix stared at Brennan, seemingly transfixed by the boy's calm. He then looked to Wyna, who tried to match the expression splashed on Brennan's face. She didn't feel the emotions he portrayed but expressing her own would only send Felix spiraling more, she thought.

"Have I not been resting?" Felix asked.

"I don't know if you can call that resting," Wyna said softly. "We need to get you to the medic."

"Why?"

"You took quite the fall. You've been unconscious."

He narrowed his eyes at her and remembered where he was. "Then why am I in the water?"

She went the opposite route as Felix and made her own eyes widen. "You mean you don't remember what happened?"

"I remember...drinking. And jumping."

She nodded. "You jumped off the side of the ship, Felix. We've had people searching for you." She forced a laugh. "It's a miracle you're alive. Brennan and I found you floating about a league from shore.

The story was shoddy and ultimately improbable. She only hoped he would be disoriented enough to believe her. At least for now. She looked up from Felix when her toes finally curled into the ocean floor and she could walk forward. Brennan's eyes were locked on her face. She wasn't sure what he looked for in her but she didn't think he found it.

Once her clothes were back on, Wyna and Brennan each slung one of Felix's arms around their shoulders and allowed the man to lean on them as they made painstaking progress back to the *Volia*. Brennan kept watching. She counted herself a child of miracles that it hardly crossed her mind whether Brennan would spill her secret to Felix or the crew. How lucky she was to be able to trust him. To have someone like him to watch her lie and trick and kill without passing the slightest bit of judgement.

Should she name one of her sickles after him?

Eventually, when they reached the docks and stumbled over the wooden planks to get to their ship, Felix began asking Brennan questions about how the trading had gone in Adalis, inquiring as to whether they'd stuck to their schedule or if they'd need to plan either more time or less. Now that they'd reached their biggest market, their timeline didn't matter so much and liberties could be taken here or there. Their only concern now was making it to their other ports before any other trading company could corner the market.

"You know," Brennan told Felix, "the praise at the market fell on the *Volia* hard. Do you think I might be able to return tomorrow and resume? I'm happy to take over and let you recover from your ordeal."

"Oh, I don't need to—"

Brennan flashed his eyes at Wyna.

"You do, actually," Wyna interrupted and swallowed. "Brennan can handle himself. I'll stay and look after you."

He did not jump on her offer immediately but when she

tightened her grip on him, he conceded. He would stay. But that didn't stop him from rapidly running through everything Brennan would do in order to prepare for the second day, as well as making the boy roleplay vendor scenarios so he would never be tricked into a bad deal.

Wyna found the talk of trade dreadfully boring and let her mind wander back to what had happened in the cave, trying to parse out the fuzzy feelings it had given her. It had been a disaster to have him follow her but even as she ran through the events in her head, she couldn't think of a reason not to be glad it happened. Perhaps the two of them would celebrate that night.

They deposited Felix in his bed after a bit of hollering and clapping from the crew who'd set up various gambling stations on the deck. Brennan ensured Felix was leaning on him quite heavily as they waded through the crew and shot quick glares at all the men who claimed to miss their captain. Wyna could read his thoughts effortlessly—he should have been enough for them. He would make sure they treated him like that someday but, in the meantime, he would ensure they knew Felix was nothing without him.

Once she was back in her cabin, she stripped off her soaked trousers, peeled them stitch by stitch from her skin. It was so freeing she finally decided she was comfortable enough to not sleep in her clothes. She pulled a laced nightgown from her bag and donned it. Waited for Brennan to come to her and hoped to erase any of his earlier disappointment. She had never been motivated to impress anyone like this before.

Tonight was special. It was a beginning.

He didn't speak when he arrived, choosing instead to settle into the small bed beside her and warm her with his body. His breathing had evened before she gathered the courage to ask if they were okay.

"Are we okay?" he repeated. "Why wouldn't we be?"

"You were upset."

"Wouldn't you be upset if you found out I was hiding something like that from you?"

"I would think you had your reasons."

"And I'm sure you did," he snickered. "But I can't be with someone who doesn't trust me."

"I *do* trust you," she insisted.

"It doesn't seem like it."

Wyna scrambled for proof. "If I didn't trust you, I wouldn't have let you stay there! If I didn't trust you, you'd be dead."

"You would have killed me?"

She didn't think she imagined the way his voice wobbled.

"No! But...if it were anyone else, I wouldn't have had a choice."

He flipped over in the bed so his breath hit her face. "Never," he exhaled, "do anything like that again. At least not without me."

She nodded but it wasn't quite enough yet to relieve the weight in her belly. "Promise me," she told him.

"Promise you what?"

"That you won't tell a soul about what you saw tonight. That you won't leave me because I kept it from you."

"You have my heart, Wyna," he told her, "and my word."

CHAPTER TWENTY-SIX

It surprised Thessa how quickly Woolhill was able to move when motivated and, before she had the presence of mind to react, Woolhill's hands were in Campbell's hair and tugging her away from Thessa. Campbell's cry caught in her throat but Thessa yelped for both of them as she lunged forward and detangled Woolhill's fingers from the girl's locks. As she pulled her away, Thessa tried to tuck her into her chest, wrapping her arms to protect her from any further moves to harm her. Campbell shoved away and wheeled on Woolhill.

"What in the gods' names do you think you're doing?" Campbell bellowed, raising her hand as if she were going to slap him. She curled her fists and shoved the hand into the folds of her skirts. Thessa thought she could hear the whisper of tears in Campbell's voice but they didn't fall.

"Quite bold of you to ask me that when I've just caught you kissing my bride," Woolhill snarled at her.

Campbell rolled her eyes back into her head and pressed her lips together. "She doesn't even want to marry you! Or don't you care what she wants?"

"That's absurd. The sole reason she came here was to trick me into marriage. She's getting what she wants!" He faced his supposed betrothed. "Aren't you, Thessa?"

Campbell stepped towards her father. "You have no right to say her name," she warned, the words guttural.

"I have every right. She's going to be my bride whether you like it or not."

Thessa floated a hand to rest on Campbell's arm but Campbell shook her off, opting to let Thessa press her body into her back. A silent promise to support her, should she need it.

"It's always whether I like it or not, isn't it?" she asked him. "It's always about what *you* want—what you need. Never about what it does to me."

Woolhill glanced at Thessa and she could see him prepare to deny. It was fun for him, she was sure, to imply his indiscretions when no one could prove them. Less amusing to have his daughter spell them out for company. But as his eyes met Thessa's, he seemed to remember what it was he'd caught them doing.

"You said you wanted to help me with the business, Campbell."

"It was never about the business!" She was shouting now, her rage filling the emptiness of the hall. "It was about what you could offer your associates that no one else could."

"As if you're something special?" he scoffed. It was a lie and he knew it. She *was* special. Everything about her was special and Thessa knew any man in Keresa would do despicable things to get their hands on her and her wealth. Many of them already had. "I've given you everything, Campbell. And this is how you repay me?"

"A nice home and a promise of money when you die is hardly enough to make up for the years of torture you've put me through." Campbell chuckled to herself, as if the entirety of it all was suddenly comical. "And I've told myself you cared about me! I told myself you just didn't know what you were doing. That in order to be as generous as you were with everyone else, you had to take your liberties with me. I told myself..."

Campbell tried to work through her woven emotions for her makeshift father, did her best to untangle them and show what lay beneath. But the strain was breaking the muscle of her strength. It wasn't enough, not yet. Not enough to unlearn the love she was made to feel for the man who'd abused her.

"And I was supposed to know?" he huffed. "Never a peep of complaint from you and I was just supposed to know you hated it?"

Campbell dug her own fingers into her hair now, clumping it and ripping it from its plaits before turning from him. She needed an outlet, anything to redirect the explosion they could all sense coming.

"I shouldn't need to complain for you to know. That's not how fathers treat their children."

Woolhill rolled his jaw, preparing to say something he knew would wound her deeply.

"Then I suppose it's a good thing you were never really my child," he announced and straightened his back. A dismissal. "Come, Thessa."

Campbell did slap him this time. "I told you not to use her name," she growled.

Thessa stepped between them and took the returning slap, the meatiness of Woolhill's hand stinging more than she'd anticipated. The force of it would have been enough to knock anyone else to the ground and Thessa knew a bruise was likely to form once the redness had gone. She reached up to feel the gouging of her skin where the rings he'd stuffed on his fingers had connected.

Woolhill had the good sense to panic when he realized what he'd done but he did not apologize. "You're defending her? From me?" he sputtered.

"I won't let you lay a hand on her," Thessa told him. "You're done hurting her."

"This disagreement is above you, dear," he said. It was an attempt to regain his composure.

"This disagreement is over," she corrected.

"Ah, I knew you'd see sense. See, Cammy? You can't take this from me, too."

"I won't marry you," Thessa told him. There would be no rebuilding this relationship now. Not between the Woolhills and not with the Whips. No reason to keep up the ruse. She tried not to be selfishly grateful.

Woolhill straightened the cuffs of his jacket. "Yes, you will."

"Over my dead body."

"Well," he scoffed, "that just might be the case once Orinna gets wind of this. Can you imagine what she'd do if she found out her little prize was snogging women and not securing herself a suitable attachment?"

It was time to tread carefully. Madame Orinna wouldn't begrudge her relationship with Campbell—it wasn't in Madame Orinna's nature. But if she shared that truth with Woolhill in her fit of anger, she was certain he'd have questions about why she was there. And it had become abundantly clear to Thessa that even if she could trust Campbell and her staff to protect the mermaids, there was no hope for someone like Woolhill, who hadn't even viewed his own daughter as sacred.

Again, she wondered how Campbell had never sprouted a tail after all Woolhill had demanded of her but she wouldn't focus on the magic of the Draca now.

"You will marry me, Thessa," Woolhill said again.

"Why?"

It wasn't about him liking her anymore. Not about the curves of her body or the drivel or wit she'd performed for him. Now it was about control. About taking back a situation on which he'd lost his grip. And she wanted him to admit it.

"Because I can make you."

"Be very careful about how you proceed, Alastor," she warned. She knew he would hate the way she drew out his name. "You have no idea how dangerous I can be."

"I've an empire, Thessa. A fleet of ships with hundreds of

men and more money than any person has ever seen. You, my dear," he said, "are just a little girl."

She strode forward, using her momentum to push Woolhill into the opposite wall of the hallway, disturbing a heavy frame to their right. She maneuvered his arms so they were behind him and used her knee to drive the rest of him back. With one hand, she ran her fingers over the dagger in her waistband, hoping she wouldn't have to use it. She used her other forearm to press into his neck. The skin there puckered and spilled over her arm as she dug deeper. She was embarrassed at her delight in the shade of red he turned.

"You're right," she crooned. "Just a little girl." She gathered saliva in her mouth to spit on him but was interrupted by Campbell's voice behind her.

"That's enough, Thessa." Thessa turned to catch Campbell's eyes lock on Woolhill's and narrow. "I'm not doing this for you," she told him. "I'm doing this for her."

"You selfish bitch," Woolhill barked.

"Let him go, Thess."

She did, taking great care to grind her knee into the sensitive part of his crotch before releasing him from her hold. He folded over, his body inflating and deflating as he tried to find breath through the pain.

"We should go," Campbell said, tugging her away.

Woolhill coughed. "Not so fast."

"Oh, haven't you said enough?" Thessa snapped.

"No." He fortified. Straightened. "I don't think I have. You still don't get it."

"Don't get what?" his daughter asked warily.

"I'm not giving you the choice, girls. I have too much power to be denied what I want." Woolhill began to stride down the hall. She was sure his ego shielded him from his own limp. The slow movements and the small steps. Different to the careful ones he'd taken on their garden romp. She was satisfied, knowing she'd hurt him. Over his shoulder, he called, "I think it might be time to pay Orinna another visit."

"AREN'T you going to follow him?" Campbell asked when Thessa just stared after the wretch of a man.

"Eventually." Thessa faced her. "Are you okay?"

Campbell shook her hair into her face, thought better of it, and shook it back out. "No. But I wasn't the one who got slapped."

Thessa shrugged and tried to laugh it off but the mention of the strike brought its hurt to the forefront of her mind. She'd had worse injuries, sure, but she wasn't desensitized to violence quite yet.

Campbell cupped Thessa's cheek where she'd been slapped. It was quite high on her face, bordering on her eye, because Woolhill had been aiming for Campbell's height. The girl's hand wasn't cool against her but Thessa held the clammy fingers to her face and revelled in the rare intimacy of the moment.

"Thank you," Campbell told her.

She dug her fingers into Thessa's face and pulled her upwards to meet her lips. Thessa found it within herself to smile against her.

"Last time we tried this, it didn't turn out so well."

Shocking even herself, it seemed, Campbell said, "I don't want there to be a last time."

"I'll give you anything you want," Thessa breathed into her. "Anything?"

She wanted to clarify. *Within reason*, she thought. *I'd give you anything within reason*. But that wasn't quite true. In that moment, Thessa believed her own words. She would give Campbell anything—she didn't even have to ask. Before Campbell could reply, Thessa pushed onto her toes and kissed the girl again, bringing her hands up to cup her face and hold her there.

"Is this what you want?" Thessa asked. Campbell nodded. "Am I what you want?"

Campbell deepened the kiss in answer and it was like Thessa found everything she'd ever looked for in Huxley. A wanting that went beyond convenience and lust. It was preceded by who they were, not what they could offer one another. There was sweetness to it. A sweetness that couldn't detract from the passion if it tried.

"You could tell me you want me, too, you know," Campbell informed her when she pulled away.

Thessa smirked. Turned away and practically skipped down the hall in the direction Woolhill had gone. "Why waste words?" She checked to see if Campbell had followed but the stubborn girl stood in place, arms crossed over her chest, waiting for Thessa's announcement. Thessa sighed. "I want you, too, you insufferable brat," Thessa told her. "But what I really want is for you to come on."

She did.

CAMPBELL MADE sure to have Philippa inspect Thessa's face before she would let her go after Woolhill. It was a tedious process that came with a lot of Thessa swatting away the older woman's hands and insisting she was absolutely fine. The woman didn't seem to understand no one had yet died from a slap to the face, least of all a Whip.

"I'm fine," she said for the hundredth time. "There's no need to fuss."

"If yer important to her, yer important to me," Philippa said, gesturing towards Campbell who was making quick work of gathering Thessa's things.

So she, too, understood it was unlikely Thessa would ever be back here. She met Campbell's eyes in the vanity mirror and the other girl gave her a sad smile that hardly moved the corners of her downturned lips.

"It's important we get going," Thessa told Philippa.

Philippa threw her hands up and backed out of the room, warning Thessa she'd see her again soon. Thessa didn't correct her.

William caught Thessa's arm as she and Campbell made to leave and Thessa smiled at the friend she'd nearly forgotten about.

"I don't know what you did," he said, "but he stormed out here and was so flustered getting a carriage that he didn't leave until maybe five minutes ago. You can probably catch him."

Campbell thanked him and told the boy to put any parcels or letters that came to the estate on her desk. She'd already called for a private carriage and the driver set the horses off before they'd even gotten the chance to close the door behind them.

Thessa tried her best not to feel awkward as they rode but the distance was great and, even if the horses were at a full sprint, it would take quite a while to reach the House of Whips. What else was there to do but worry and plan? Campbell pulled back the little curtain and stared out the window at the empty roads.

"I don't think I want to say goodbye."

"No one's making you," Thessa assured her, engrossed in her own staring at where her knees would be under her skirts.

"Perhaps not now. But soon enough."

"Madame Orinna will understand. She'll take you in if she must."

Campbell looked at her then. "You don't understand, though. Woolhill isn't riding out to the District to tattle on you to your boss. He's riding out there because you—as much as you tried to keep your distance from the House these past few days—acted on behalf of Orinna."

"What are you trying to say?"

"If he can't punish you, he'll punish her. Punish the others."

Thessa laughed. "He couldn't best me. And who do you

think taught me what I know? I don't imagine he'd be able to take on a whole house of us."

Campbell shook her head, the remnants of her pretty plaits slapping into one another. "It's not about the physical fight. He knows Orinna needs the connections he has. He knows marrying you, initially, would have only given her more access." She turned back to the window and clucked her tongue. "Whatever he giveth, he may take away."

"So, what?" Thessa pushed. "He's going to tell her she has no business on his ships? Near his sailors? I hardly think that matters now that you and I will be working together."

"No, Thessa. He'll ruin you. Ruin the Whips."

She wanted to argue. To tell Campbell she was being over-dramatic and paranoid. But who knew Woolhill best? Who knew well what kind of creature lay underneath the merchant's skin?

"So what do I do?" Thessa asked, feeling helpless that she wasn't able to come up with the answer to that question on her own.

"I'm not sure there's anything you can do. He's right about one thing, you know," she added, cocking her head. "He gets what he wants."

Thessa felt her insides boil and she leaned across the carriage. Found Campbell's fierce eyes.

"You have one fight with your dad and suddenly you have no backbone?"

"Excuse me?"

"The Campbell I f—know would never roll over like this," Thessa told her. She sat back and crossed her arm. "Where's your fire?"

"He stamps it out."

"Fuck that."

Campbell glared. "You aren't going to cure me by pissing me off, Thessa."

"I don't want to cure you. I want you to fight. Fight him like you fought me when we first met. Like you fought to keep your secrets."

"I don't want to fight him! I don't think I have the capacity to fight him anymore. I...I don't know if I want to see him fall," she said. "I want to see him learn."

"Then I'll fight him for you," Thessa sighed. "Because men like that don't ever learn."

CHAPTER TWENTY-SEVEN

It had been a lie.

The bed was cold when she woke—as cold as it could be in the sweltering heat of the cabin. But this time she woke with only her own sweat and found herself missing the icky sensation of peeling Brennan's skin from her own. He'd been sweet the night before, if a bit absent, but she'd done her best to return his attention to her. To what she had to offer him and the life that might lay before them. And she had hoped, when they awoke that morning, she could remind him again.

But he'd left her.

She told herself she'd simply woken up too late. That Brennan had already escaped to the market, working the crowd and gathering more coin that was never supposed to find its way to his hands. Even she didn't quite believe that. Something about the air felt...off. As if the ship and the sea were trying to warn her.

Dressing quickly, she moved frantically about the ship, searching for Brennan and hoping to the gods she wouldn't find his body strung up somewhere. A spectacle of a punishment for the boy who'd tried to steal the crew out from under Felix.

He was nowhere to be found. None of them were. Not even

Zachariah, who made a habit of seeking her out when she was alone just to taunt.

She was unwilling to go out into Adalis alone. She didn't trust them not to leave her behind, not now that Felix had returned and Brennan no longer held power in his absence. Who was to say he'd have enough sway to convince them to wait for her? Wyna tried to talk her heart into settling as she climbed the mast to the nest.

So she'd wait.

The crew began to trickle back onto the ship as the sun fell in the sky. She counted them as they came, one after another until each one—even Felix—was accounted for. Other than the one she wanted. Wyna crouched in the nest, trying to piece together what she could read from their lips. They did not discuss her lover but she couldn't be sure if it was because they knew nothing or because he never crossed their minds.

And finally—finally—when the full moon lit up the sky and the stars winked at her, she saw him. A waning beacon in the night with a damp burlap sack slung over his shoulder.

Its weight slowed him as he trudged forward, sinking with every step but barrelling on. Whatever he hid in that bag was still. Lifeless. A feeling she hadn't yet dared to name grew in her.

Brennan called out to the crew, demanding they help him get his trophy back onto the ship. Below her, she heard his bellow for Felix. She prepared herself to make some difficult choices.

Wyna opened the latch in the floor of the nest and used it to watch, rather than pushing herself over the edge. She didn't want to be seen right then. Felix bumbled onto the deck and Wyna pushed her ear down further, closer to the opening.

"What's the meaning o' this, Friswell?" Felix asked.

Brennan finally dropped the sack, letting it clunk onto the deck. Whatever was inside rolled and threatened to expose itself to the crew. "I think you'll want to see this," Brennan smirked, searching the faces of the crew gathered around him. "I don't think we'll ever have to work again. Not after we bring this home."

"Quit talking 'round it," Felix snapped. "Show us."

Zachariah advanced on the sack, bending to unfurl whatever lay inside but Brennan stepped on the man's wrist. "This isn't for you."

The navigator tugged but Brennan did not decrease the pressure. Wyna could only imagine how much he enjoyed wielding that power over him. When he did remove his boot, Zachariah retreated like a frightened animal. Brennan took his time as he reached to finish what Zachariah started and she nearly dropped from the nest onto the spectacle to ensure he never did.

Foolishly, though, she wanted to give him the benefit of the doubt. She avoided directly addressing to herself what might be in the sack. But she knew. And her heart imploded when he finally did release the contents and Wyna watched as an arm flopped out. Then a head. A torso.

That was where it ended.

The crew muttered and gagged at the sight of the body in front of them, severed from its bottom half.

"What," Felix gritted out, "the fuck is this?"

"Take a closer look."

Felix did and so did Wyna, though she already knew who it was. Her eyes did not miss the scales climbing the arms and chest, duller now they weren't moistened by the sea. And she'd recognized Evelyn's slack face even through the bit of bloat that'd somehow already set in.

"It's got scales!" one of the crewmembers needlessly pointed out.

Brennan grinned. "Indeed it does."

As he said it, he flung the sack from him, releasing the remainder of its contents and letting the rich plum of Evelyn's tail fall and roll across the deck. As the crew scrambled back, it occurred to Wyna she'd never actually *seen* this mermaid's tail and now, the first time she did, it was no different than any other fish.

The crew stepped forward again as it settled onto the deck, silent. One of them reached out to run his fingers along it and Wyna heard him hiss as the scales sliced his skin. Still, he tried again, moving his hand with the grain before tracing the paper-thin fins running down its side.

"I knew it was real," Felix gasped. "Where did you find it?"

"There's a whole coven of them just off the shore," Brennan explained, boyish excitement infiltrating his words even as he spoke of blood. "But I think they've been following the ship."

"Could fetch good coin for't in Adalis," Felix considered.

"Not in Adalis. Keresa."

"You want to take this back?"

"It'll stink up the ship!"

"Do you want the coin or not?"

"What kind of coin are we even talking?"

"Stop!" Brennan shouted the command and, just as he wanted, the crew obeyed. "You're all missing the big picture. I don't care about this one. Didn't you hear me? There are more."

"How do we get them?"

Brennan straightened his back and tilted his neck, immediately—effortlessly—finding Wyna's eyes as if he knew she were there the whole time. "You leave that part to me. Let's get moving. You crew the ship—I'll take care of the rest."

He assumed a protective stance over the mermaid's carcass until the crew set about taking off. He would not risk a deeper study of his prize. And when they were dispersed, he gathered the pieces of Evelyn and threw them recklessly back into his sack before dragging it down the stairs. Each relentless thud that sounded killed a piece of Wyna. A step and a death and a desecration of everything she'd thought she'd built on these waters. She'd let it die, then.

But she had something to do first.

SHE WAITED until the *Volia* had traveled a considerable distance from Adalis. She couldn't risk anyone seeing the carnage she planned on leaving in her wake, nor could she afford any of the crew to make it back to land.

This would end on the Draca.

It was easy enough to wait, easier still to understand exactly how much time she had to do what she needed. The crew on the deck would stay until the waters were deep enough. Then they would sleep and it would be quiet until sunrise. Zachariah had already retreated after setting the ship on its course and Felix had returned to his cabin to rest, still recovering from his short coma.

No one else would come up to interrupt her.

There were four men remaining in the open air. None of them had eyes on another, so engrossed in their tasks they likely wouldn't see her coming. Good. Her sickle made a sick ripping sound as she dragged it across the neck of the first and she clamped her hand over his mouth as he began to gurgle his own blood. He fell back into her and it was all she could do to keep him from thrashing. She wondered if she should say a little prayer for him as she laid him to rest. After all, it wasn't his fault Brennan had exposed the secret—it wasn't his fault Wyna had been reckless enough to allow Brennan the opportunity. But Wyna didn't know any prayers and she felt as though the blood wasn't truly on her hands anyhow.

She moved on.

The next two men fell as quickly as the first, though she made sure they were quieter. After the second, she considered dragging their bodies into a neat pile but quickly dismissed the idea when she realized just how much time and strength it would cost her. She'd leave them lying.

Her next victim hummed a shanty to himself, just like she thought a sailor should, the repetition of the verses allowing him some easy entertainment amid the monotony of his task. At least he would die happy. He turned, seeing her blood-splattered clothes and the grimy streaks of gore sliding down her. His gasp did not have the time to escape him before she pounced.

It was getting easier to kill.

When she was done, she did not bother admiring her work—she couldn't afford to. Everything in her called to dispose of Brennan next. He was the threat. He was the one who'd done this. The one at fault. But her heart wasn't ready to face him. She hadn't yet let herself process what he'd done. She knew it was his nature to take advantage of others but she hadn't thought, naive as she was, he could possibly give her the same treatment.

The longer she waited to kill him, the longer she had to convince herself he hadn't done what she thought he had—the longer she had to hope.

So she descended the stairs and found Felix's cabin, playing his words over in her head. *I knew it was real.* Had he been talking about legends? About the mermaids the children all admired in their fairy tale books and discarded when the world told them it was time to mature? Or had he seen Wyna's friends when he jumped into the sea? When they held him in their cave? Had his eyes been open long enough to see the wonder in front of him?

However he'd stumbled upon it, Wyna couldn't allow him to live. Rage built in her, replacing the doubt as she remembered how his thoughts had immediately turned to coin. He'd done exactly what Madame Orinna had always warned he would. He wasn't a victim—not like the others. He was the monster Wyna'd been hired to slay.

His door didn't creak as Wyna slipped into the cabin. A candle had been left flickering on his desk but Felix was curled into his blankets like a child. She did not keep herself from laughing. The captain started at the noise and raised his head to find her standing at the foot of the bed, an apparition of death.

"It was you," he breathed. "It was you."

She stalked closer and shook off the feeling that something had snapped inside of her. She wanted to hear him puzzle together what she'd done. Wanted to hear him realize there were no gods to fear. There was only her.

Keeping her voice low, she asked, "What was?"

"You killed my Solomon," he whispered.

"He knew too much."

"I—"

"And so do you."

"Please…"

She did not care to hear him finish the plea. Truthfully, she didn't know if he planned to or if he expected a single word to be enough to sway her. It wouldn't. Not now. Not anymore. It was too late for mercy, too late for sympathy and trust. She'd given that already and she didn't have an ounce left to offer.

She ignored the tear that slid through the blood as she waited in the silence for the end of a life. When she found it, she blew out the candle and left, let the door swing on its hinges behind her. She was enraged now, hearing Felix simper before her. Because she wished it hadn't been him she had killed. She wished it had been Brennan's perfect, stubbly neck that she'd sliced with every iota of strength she could muster. She wished he'd seen how she cried and she wished he'd known how he hurt her and she wished desperately that it would change whatever had rotted between them.

Had anything rotted? Or had it always been this way?

In her fiery state, she found Zachariah, who'd managed to claim a place private and dry to spend his night. She slashed and she slashed and she charged her hits with every emotion she'd ever felt. He never woke and he'd never get the chance to again.

And she didn't care. All she cared to know was that he was dead and never coming back. He could never hurt another woman. Could never hurt another mermaid.

Could never hurt her.

She sobbed over the ribbons of his body and told herself it was Brennan. She wouldn't be able to do this with him, knowing she didn't intend to leave enough of him to cry over. To touch.

She mourned what she had and what she could have had, cursing and begrudging that tickling refusal to truly believe it was over.

Wyna decided she couldn't wait any longer, that every death that preceded Brennan's was only delaying the inevitable. She needed closure, she told herself, before she could finish what she'd started.

She moved silently about the crew's quarters, searching every face for the one that'd broken her but he was a ghost. She moved to the other side of the ship, sweeping her eyes over the deck and combing every surface.

Was he hiding from her? Did he know what she had planned for him?

Eventually, there was only one room she hadn't touched—her own. She hadn't thought it possible to feel more fury than she already did but the thought of him laying in her bed while she cleaned up his mess only proved her wrong. *Stupid*. How stupid she'd been to believe he would protect her. To believe he truly wanted a future with her. She'd convinced herself he was her family, just as much as the mermaids and the Whips.

In a sick sort of way, she guessed he was just like her family: willing to give her up in order to do what he pleased. Had that been why she was drawn to him? It was generous, she knew, to give even her subconscious the credit of seeing who Brennan was. In reality, she hadn't seen and hadn't let herself see what was in his heart because she'd wanted so badly to believe it was her.

Her body didn't tremble when she placed her hand upon the door to her cabin but Wyna felt like it did. Or, at least, that it should have. She should have been sparking and igniting every-thing around her as her rumbling frenzy burned. But Wyna was the picture of calm. She checked her sickles, barely gagging at the flesh still clinging to them. She tried to shake it off and, when it didn't budge, she wiped it on her already-soiled skirts. It occurred to her she should probably take the skirts off—they'd only get in the way—but the ever-maddening part of her wanted Brennan to see the ruin she'd had to lay before him.

Wyna opened the door.

Brennan laid straight on her bed, his arms folded neatly over his abdomen. His eyes were closed and his head lolled gently to the side as if he'd merely fallen asleep waiting for her. Perhaps he had. He had to have known she would come. Wasn't that why he came here? Or did he just think himself entitled to her space, despite what he'd done?

A putrid scent hit her nose and when she searched for the culprit, her eyes lit on the wet sack in the corner, tossed like an inconvenience. The opening of the bag had fallen open to reveal a sliver of scales and matted, damp hair. Her face contorted at the carelessness with which Brennan had dispatched and discarded her friend. Glancing back to ensure his eyes remained closed, she twisted the sack closed and attempted to heft the body over her shoulder. It was too large, the tail too heavy and packed, for Wyna to carry. She whispered soundless apologies to the mermaid as she dragged Evelyn across the floor.

The sea was her home and that was where Wyna would lay her to rest.

The silence of the ship was eerie and Wyna found peace in the lack of disturbance. Good. She was unable to lift Evelyn over the railing while she was still in the bag so Wyna pulled the top half of her body out by the armpits. Grunting and sweating, she heaved the torso up and over the edge, wincing when she heard it thwack against the ship on its way down. Her tears were falling again but she didn't mind it this time. This was the best funeral she could give her friend and it was only right to cry.

The tail wobbled and tried to slip from her numerous times as she tried to send it after Evelyn's torso. Swallowing the rising vomit, she shoved her hand into the sinew and muscle where the tail had been severed to get leverage and grip. It went over, smacking ungracefully onto the surface of the sea.

Did mermaids have an afterlife? Had one ever died before?

She returned to her cabin, again wiping the gore from herself before she opened the door and again finding herself disgusted at the sight of Brennan in her bed. Stomping would feel better but her steps were light as she approached, pulling her sickles from their hooks. She leaned over him, letting the not-yet-dried blood drip onto his serene face. Even now, even through the shards of her anger, she still found him hauntingly beautiful. This would be a reminder, then. A reminder the world had not earned her trust.

She crossed her blades over Brennan's chest, letting the tips dig into his skin. She knew he'd awoken, if he was ever asleep at all. His eyes, though, did not fling open in panic like she thought they should. They opened slowly, leisurely, and drank in the sight of her in. They offered nothing. Not surprise. Not disgust.

Not love.

"You promised me your heart," she whispered in the dark, the leaking rays of the full moon sparkling on her sickles. "I'll be taking it now."

THE BETRAYAL

Though it was a feat to do so, the underdrake loved the child. Claimed it as her own. And so the child grew, developed and adopted the traits of the underdrake until her tail was as magnificent and her magic just as strong. The upper half of the child did not transform from human to fish as the rest of the body did. Rather, it grew into that of a beautiful young girl, a product of the land if one only beheld her above the waist. And because of her beauty and the strangeness of her form, the underdrake took it upon herself to appoint her child as an ambassador to the human world.

The underdrake had much to study and, as she grew old, even the expanse of the sea was not enough for her. It was her intention to pass all she knew and all she could learn unto the child so that, one day, when the underdrake had passed, the child could harness the underdrake's magic and rule in her stead. Most importantly, she wanted her child to continue to glean what knowledge she could from the world around her. She would never be fit to lord over the sea if she knew nothing of it. She would never be able to ward her creatures from the humans if she had no knowledge of those she vowed to protect.

And yet the child loved the humans very much, braver than

the underdrake had been since its incident with the whaler. She was fearless and charming and her song called many men to her. She brought these men, thrashing and drowning, to the underdrake as gifts so the underdrake might study them from the safety of her caves.

In the child's courage, of course, lay misplaced trust. For the one man she kept from the underdrake, the one she came to love, did not love the child for all the good things she was. Rather, he loved her for the promise of power and the curiosity of bad intentions. This man hungered for knowledge, much like the underdrake, and for this she could not fault him. But his hunger posed a danger to the underdrake's domain. She warned her child of her concerns but the child was blinded by her love for the man and insisted the underdrake spoke only from her fear.

In all her ferocity, the underdrake was brought to icy tears when her child fought her, reminding the creature of the injuries which still pained her. But it was a pain that could never match the loss of her love so she conceded to the child's wishes.

The man was insatiable in his thirst for the sea. He dazzled the child, convinced her to gift him a set of gills all his own so he might explore below. Thinking he only meant to spend more time with her, the child gave them without protest and with many blinding smiles. He brought with him to see the underdrake a spear—a weapon the child thought he meant to grant to the underdrake as an offering of peace.

Give it to the underdrake he did, directly through the heart, through the source of her power, so she had neither life nor magic left to offer. The child, incited by her grief, tore the spear from the underdrake and plunged it into the man's own heart—the one she'd so foolishly believed had belonged to her—so that he might never return to land with his boon and so that he might suffer the same fate he'd foisted upon the child's mother. And when he was dead, the child cried as forcefully as she had when the underdrake had popped her bubble of sea foam. This time, there were no horns or whiskers to comfort the wailing away.

The child tore through the waters, letting her tears and her magic leak into the sea and imbue her wishes into the waves. No other should suffer the same fate as her mother, to die by the hand of a traitorous man. No other would hurt as she did now. And as her ire grew, her teeth transformed into those of her mother's, spiked and sharp like the spear that had undone her. So she might exact her revenge without the aid of a human weapon. The scales of her tail, too, grew into razor-like points, the tips of them hued red to match the blood of whosoever may cross her.

But when the child's anger subsided, so too did her magic, spent from her body and her heart. Without magic, there was nothing left for the child under the water. So she found a quiet cave with soft, sinking sand. She laid her head upon her folded hands. And she slept.

She slept still when the sea foam surrounded her, carrying her back from whence she came.

CHAPTER TWENTY-EIGHT

oolhill's carriage was parked haphazardly outside of the House of Whips when Thessa and Campbell arrived. His driver was still seeing to the horses as they slowed and Thessa knew he hadn't been there long.

Maren emerged as Thessa helped Campbell out of their carriage, annoyance strung across her features.

"I'm assuming you know what that's about."

"Unfortunately," Thessa admitted. "When did he get here?"

"Two minutes ago?"

So they *had* made good time. Thessa shuffled forward, dragging Campbell with her as she went. "Make sure no one leaves the House," she instructed Maren. Thessa stopped, considering how rude she'd been. "Maren, Campbell. Campbell, Maren."

Campbell's greeting smile was thin and Thessa pulled her through the darkened entrance before Maren could respond. The familiar noises of the House hit her ears all at once. She heard the muffled cries of pain and pleasure leaking through the walls of the rooms nearest the parlor and breathed in the coppery scent of blood and cleaner. Thessa checked the clock on the wall behind the front desk and noted it was a bit late in the morning for there to still be customers and clients milling about the House but some days were just like that. There were Whips laughing together upstairs, either winding down from a sleepless night or preparing for the day ahead. To her left, she heard the noxious yawping of Woolhill as he berated Madame Orinna, who surely hadn't yet had a wink of rest.

Thessa went to her left, barging in through the office door. Woolhill did not pause in his tirade against the older woman and Thessa saw Madame Orinna take in the gouge in her face and put together what had happened and who'd done it.

"Did you lay a hand on my girl?" the Madame interrupted. When Woolhill continued speaking as if he didn't hear her, she raised her voice a scant decibel and asked again. "Did you lay a hand on my girl, Alastor?"

Woolhill glanced back at Thessa and briefly inspected her cheek, no doubt assessing what level of lie he might get away with or how much he had to justify. Turning back to Madame Orinna, he scoffed and inclined his head towards the hand Thessa still wrapped around Campbell's arm. "Let's not throw blame regarding whose hands were on whom."

"Answer my question, Alastor."

Woolhill's muddy gaze narrowed at the woman as realization poured over him. "Not just a benefactor then, hmm? Your girl, you say? I could have sworn you told me Thessa had never been employed by you."

"Miss Clemen," Madame Orinna corrected. "You'll refer to her as Miss Clemen until she has given you permission to do otherwise."

She could have explained that she had given him permission but a small part of Thessa sagged in relief at Madame Orinna's words. Though she should have known better, she almost believed the Madame would punish Thessa for all that'd happened. But that was not the woman she knew. Yes, the Madame could be harsh when it was required of her but she had never given Thessa any evidence that she wouldn't move the earth for her Whips.

"Miss Clemen," Woolhill spat, "deigned it appropriate to molest my daughter."

Madame Orinna willfully stopped her eyes from rolling back into her head. "I do not take those accusations lightly, Alastor. You know that. I know you know that, considering how many times I've had to wrangle your men from my girls." She adjusted to face Campbell, who stared at Woolhill with horror set into her frown. "Did you consent to the contact you've had with Miss Clemen?"

"Yes." Firm as ever, Campbell's eyes did not leave Woolhill's.

"Of course she'd say that! The girl has her in a death grip."

"It's not my place to punish a crime when the supposed victim hasn't even confirmed it!" Madame Orinna was steering Woolhill away, trapping him in technicalities to stall for solutions she hadn't yet thought of. "And the House of Whips takes no responsibility for Miss Clemen's actions. I've told you she is her own woman and I stand by those words."

Those words stung but Thessa understood them.

"Even so," Madame Orinna went on, "she is under my care. So if you find yourself encountering any trouble with her, you bring it to me. You do not lay hands on her body. You do not desecrate my establishment. You come to *me*, and me alone."

"What is it, Orinna?" Woolhill demanded. "Is she yours or not?"

Thessa had to admit that she, too, was confused by Madame Orinna's proclamations. However, she took the time to piece them together in her head and she did not trust Woolhill to do the same. Madame Orinna was protecting the House. The other Whips. Distancing herself from the operation at hand so the others wouldn't suffer for what Thessa had done. But Madame Orinna would still go to war for her.

She'd always been a champion of justice.

Why couldn't Thessa make sacrifices like that?

She dropped Campbell's arm and stepped into Woolhill's line of sight.

"Move aside, whore," he ordered her.

"Is that any way to talk to your future wife?" she asked, holding up her hand and making sure his eye landed on the jewelry she'd crammed onto her finger. He hadn't given it to her. Before they'd left the estate, Thessa'd snuck into his chambers and pilfered the ring. She had wondered if she might need to use his late wife to her advantage—it'd only been a moment before that she'd decided to actually wear it.

"Where did you get that?"

She raised her eyebrows, performing Campbell's judgemental indifference and adding a bit of her own puzzlement. She felt rather silly. Who was she trying to fool? Campbell knew he hadn't given her the ring. And what did Madame Orinna care if there was a ring or not? But Thessa counted on the other patrons overhearing their discussion and attempting to listen through the door. She had left it open a crack as a measure of precaution and it would be effortless for anyone to peek through.

"You gave it to me," she lied.

"So you're a whore and a thief *and* a liar?" He sawed out a laugh. "When will the debauchery end?"

Thessa mustered up tears and stepped towards him, throwing herself at his chest, scraping on her way down. "Please," blubbered. "You said you'd marry me. You said you would! I've done nothing wrong."

She drew out her final syllable and caught Maren rolling her eyes from the front desk. The other patrons shared looks and conspiracy in the parlor, their curiosity and pity driving them to community. Perhaps Woolhill had come here with the intention of ruining the Whips and perhaps he would succeed. But she would be sure to ruin him first.

She lowered her voice, slight enough he might think she was trying to speak only to him but loud enough for their audience to continue listening in. "That night," she said frantically. "When you took me to your bedroom. You told me I'd be your wife. If I touched you, you said I'd be your wife."

Thessa couldn't feel badly about the lie, though it pained her to throw that kind of accusation around. She figured he deserved it after what he'd done to Campbell, though. She knew the man had no qualms about coercing young women into sex.

Woolhill crinkled his face and tried to rip Thessa from him. She held tight, wailing as he gripped her wrists and yanked. "You took my body!" she shouted at him. "But you won't take my hand?"

"Stop this at once!" he shouted, matching her in volume. "Campbell, shut the damn door!"

Campbell did not but the patrons moved as if they'd been the ones ordered around. Thessa beat at his chest but the man did not react, letting her do what she needed until the House cleared out. When he was satisfied the four of them were alone, he roared and threw Thessa from him, calling upon the strength with which he'd slapped her. Thessa lost her footing and wheeled her arms in the air in an effort to regain her balance. Woolhill followed her, righting her across the room before shouting at her again of how she was a liar and filthy seductress.

He shoved her again, harder this time, and Thessa wondered where the frail, aging man with a limp had gone.

The breath left her as she slammed into the bookcases behind her. Cracking and splintering sounded through the buzz in her head and she couldn't determine if it was from the shelving or from her bones. Yet, even upon impact, her momentum could not be stopped. She kept going—kept falling—and landed on her back in the chamber connected to Madame Orinna's office. As she tried to catch her breath and will her body into functioning again, into letting her get up from the floor, she heard the door finally snicking shut and Campbell screaming at her father and begging him to stop. Begging him not to hurt Thessa further.

Woolhill refused.

A crash sounded, different this time, and she wasn't sure how she knew—if perhaps she was so attuned to the other girl—but she recognized it as Campbell's body dropping to the floor and her skull hitting Madame Orinna's desk in the shuffle. Another thud, and Thessa thought she could make out the Madame's larger frame smacking against the far wall.

The man was on a tirade.

Woolhill tried to push his way into the chamber after Thessa, elbowing away the edges and shards to get his body through the opening she'd made. Once he was in, he stood over her, shaking and panting. A beast who would not leave without his prey.

"Is it time to reconsider your lies?" he asked Thessa.

And as he caught his breath, he looked up. Took in the room around him. At the shelves lined with logs. The inscriptions of his name and his ships along their spines. He took in the table, lined with plans. And he took in the mural, registering the details of the mermaid painted there. The scales he had perhaps seen some time ago and written off as belonging to some deep-sea fish.

Thessa narrowed her focus and her eyes as if she were trying to peer into his mind, working to catch any realization that struck.

"What is this?" he choked out.

Madame Orinna ducked through the hole, Campbell behind her. Ragged but functioning.

"Alastor," the Madame warned.

"What is this?" he asked again, whirling to face the lady of the House. "Why do you have my records?"

Through her pain, Thessa understood the situation was dire when even Madame Orinna couldn't spin a response. She'd never thought anyone would make it this far. She'd never anticipated the most powerful man in Keresa throwing her prized Whip through the wall. She'd never...

There was simply too much none of them had ever considered. Too much had gone wrong. Slowly—painfully slow—Thessa tried to sit up on her elbows and she had the presence of mind to hope Wyna was faring better, out there and away from this.

Campbell seemed to find herself first as the three of them

stared at one another, silent, hoping someone else would speak and reveal what it was they wanted to know.

"Leave it alone, Alastor," Campbell hissed in a rare use of his first name.

"I won't!"

"You will. You'll leave it all alone. The Whips. Thessa. Me. Why don't you just go home and die?" she screamed before folding into herself, sobbing. Thessa could tell she regretted the words. Campbell didn't want her father to die. But how else could she get him to stop? Thessa hated that she was right. Hated that he would never learn, not even for Campbell's sake.

He ignored her and turned back to Madame Orinna. "I'll ask you once more, Orinna. Why do you have my records?"

Campbell answered for her, her voice miraculously steady despite her state. "What is it to you, anyhow? You've not lifted a finger for the fleet in a year. If anything," she hedged, "your questions should be mine to ask."

"Then ask them."

Campbell crossed her arms over her chest, having given up on pleading to return to the ice she wore so well. "I don't need to."

Thessa admired her for how well she avoided giving her father the answers he sought. She wondered if they just might get away with it all and still have the man be none the wiser. But it was too late. Now, it didn't matter what he knew and what he didn't. He'd already seen enough to be dangerous.

Still catching her breath, Thessa rose from the ground and fixed her attention on Woolhill. "Look around you, Alastor," she spat, just as he'd done to her. "And you really thought it was ever about you? You really thought I ever wanted *you*?"

"You wanted my empire," he gasped, convinced he'd stumbled his way into understanding.

She rolled her eyes. "If that's what you'd like to believe."

"What sort of operation are you running here, Orinna?"

Thessa crept towards him, undaunted by the possibility of his hands on her again. She let an evil sort of smile slip onto her face and had the fleeting impression it might never leave after this night. "The kind that puts men like you into the ground."

"But my records—"

"I was wondering when you'd notice some of your men returned to you without limbs or tongues." She cocked her head, drinking in his fear. "Gods, what do you think that was about?"

His eyes flitted to the mural behind her and she nodded, solemn, before continuing her pursuit. It was Thessa's turn to be the beast. And it was Woolhill's turn to tremble. His thigh caught the corner of the sturdy table and his back bounced off Madame Orinna's braced arms.

"What sort of secret do you think they were keeping?"

"Get back!"

She did not. She hadn't played yet with her prey. And she hadn't in a long while but here she was, twice in a week. Taunting and merciless. Gods, did they deserve it.

Madame Orinna shoved Woolhill off of her, towards Thessa, and Thessa lunged, wrapping her fingers around his throat.

"Help!" he tried to scream. His plea did not stop her. She tightened her grip, feeling feral. "Help me!"

She hoped he choked on more than his words. He would never touch Campbell again. He would never look upon another woman and claim her as his own. He would never allow his friends the luxury of their desires, nor would he ever again entertain his own. He would die and he would rot in Thesss's arms to atone for his crimes and she would enjoy it. If it meant he never harmed another, she would enjoy it.

Thessa spared a glance for the hole in the wall to make sure none of the lingering patrons snuck in to check on his cries. The hole was empty, exposing only the mess of Madame Orinna's office proper. But when she swung her gaze back to the sputtering man in her hands, she caught sight of Campbell, a horrific sort of expression marring her beautiful face.

So Thessa had been right. Campbell didn't actually want Woolhill to die. Her grip loosened and Woolhill threw her from him. She landed on the table, her back smacking and smattering the collection of logs.

Woolhill ran, best he could now that his adrenaline had abandoned him and his stilted gait had returned. He disappeared through the hole and out of the Madame's office. Thessa could not tell if it was the punch of wood to spine that took her breath away or if it was the sight of Campbell dashing after him. She flew to her feet to follow.

"Leave it alone, Thessa," Madame Orinna clipped. "She'll handle him for now."

Deflated and searching for something to say, Thessa pointed weakly to the hole while she panted. "I'm sorry about your wall."

The Madame sighed. "The wall can be replaced. You cannot."

The older woman reached for Thessa and, surprising herself, Thessa stepped into her arms and let herself be comforted. Like she was a child again, fighting the grief of what she'd seen. Perhaps she hadn't witnessed her mother murdered tonight and perhaps she didn't have the same attachment to the Woolhills she'd had to her family but the wounds bled just the same.

Whatever had happened tonight had been her fault and, regardless of the steps taken to reach this end, Woolhill had still seen more than he should have. They had all said words that should never have been spoken. And Thessa—oh, gods—she had transformed into the monster from which she'd fought to protect the Whips.

She didn't know how she'd repay Madame Orinna. How she'd keep the mermaids safe. How she could ever face Campbell again after what she'd done to her father. How she could live with herself knowing she didn't regret the way she'd wanted to hurt him. Knowing she would not mourn him. And she didn't know how to reconcile that with her desire to right the world for Campbell. In fact, Thessa knew very little in that moment save that Alastor Woolhill had to die.

CHAPTER TWENTY-NINE

Wyna held back a cry at the feeling of her sickles digging into Brennan's chest. The puncture, through the shirt and through the skin, was a finality for which she felt unprepared. Even so, she knew she had a few more layers to go, through the muscle and bone, until she reached the heart she'd sworn to take from him. She'd wanted it. She'd been prepared to fight for it and now she would kill for it. If he wouldn't give it to her, she'd retrieve it herself.

A consolation prize for the pain he'd caused her.

She felt Brennan watching her face but he did not move while she pushed her blades further into his skin. He did not flinch and he did not pull away. She wished he would. Anything to make this a fight, to make it a battle in which she could tell herself she'd killed him for his own safety and not because he'd done her wrong. If it were physical, she'd be fine.

But it was as if Brennan knew what Wyna wanted from him and actively chose to do the opposite.

Her blades caught on something firm in his chest and she had to catch her breath before she could plunge them deeper. He moved beneath her and she almost smiled.

"What are you waiting for, sea witch?" he asked.

Wyna flinched at the name. It had been affection before, she'd thought. She didn't know what it was now.

"I'm not."

"Then kill me."

"I am."

But she wasn't. Not really. Sure, her sickles were piercing deeper, bloodying his shirt as she tried to reposition them. Her pace was slow, though, and if she kept to it, she wasn't sure she'd even be to his heart by morning. Through her lashes, she saw his grin.

"You can't, Wyn," he whispered. "You don't want to."

"I've never wanted anything more."

"Liar."

He flipped her so her back pressed against the hard mattress and pushed down upon her, letting her sickles dig deeper into his chest. Still, he did not show he felt the pain of it. Not for the first time, Wyna wondered if the boy were even human.

"Must I do this for you, too?" he asked, the curls on his head falling into his eyes. Charming and childish, nothing like what left his mouth.

"What have you ever done for me?" Her question was stilted and she knew it would be so easy to just put a little more pressure. But her body, her soul, no longer felt like her own. It retracted her arms, clutching them close to her torso. Not enough to allow the sickles to depart but not enough to be the cause of any more pain.

Brennan *tsk*ed and sat back, pulling Wyna with him so their bodies still pressed together at the same angles. "I would have done everything for you if you'd just done as I asked. What do those creatures matter against the riches we would have seen in Keresa?"

"I don't care about the riches," she told him, trying to rip herself away. He held her in place, their proximity growing uncomfortable. He was bleeding on her.

"You should," he said as he shook his head. "We could have taken over Woolhill's fleet, Wyn. We could have ruled these waters.

And what then? Then no one would be able to harm your mermaids."

Her breath caught.

"I thought you understood," he admonished. "I thought you knew the life of one was worth nothing compared to the rest. Isn't that what happened with Solomon? You killed him to save the mermaids, right? Didn't I do the same?"

Her head flopped, side to side. Listless and lost as she was unable to find the words to tell him he was wrong. "Let me go," she said instead.

He ignored her. "Isn't that what you were going to do with me? Kill me to save the mermaids?" Brennan hid those cedar eyes behind his lids and tipped his head back into the moonlight coming from the slit in the side of the ship. She distracted herself by wondering where it'd come from. She didn't remember seeing it there before. And if it had been...well, surely an errant wave would have had her belongings ruined. Nonetheless, it was fitting. A punctuation to Brennan's end. Only, he kept speaking. "If only you could have seen the bigger picture," he lamented.

"The only picture," she gritted, "I can see is a gaudy portrait you've commissioned to show off your coin."

He brought one of his hands up to cover a sickle. "You wound me. All this time and that's the kind of man you think I'll be?"

"I don't know who you are anymore. And I don't know who you'll be."

He clicked his tongue. "I thought if you had it your way, I'd be dead."

She stilled. "Yes."

"Then do it."

Using all her might, she shoved him, abandoning her sickles in his chest. He tumbled to the end of her bed, righting himself as he went, and in her freedom she ran. She should have finished it right there. Should have pushed those blades into him just like he'd told her to. But, gods, she didn't want to do what he told her to. She didn't want to feel orchestrated anymore.

She heard the sickles slick out of him as she ran and she heard him follow. He laughed behind her. It was a cold, dead thing. Born of greed and depravity. But it wasn't different than any other time he'd laughed. So why hadn't she heard it before?

As she climbed to the deck, she stumbled around the felled body of a sailor before turning and kicking it, hoping to displace it enough to force Brennan into tripping. Satisfied, she kept going. She didn't know where. Her weapons were gone. She needed time.

Wyna hoisted a rope onto her shoulder and climbed the mast to the nest.

Brennan did trip on the body. She strained to hear the details of his movement, the smallest clinks telling her he'd brought her sickles with him. Telling her he'd dropped them. And he had not picked them up.

She peeked over the edge of the barrel at him and found his eyes trained on the deck. The surface over which they could easily walk. But without looking up, he called, "You can't kill me from all the way up there."

Bracing herself, she coiled the rope to shorten its length before slinging it over one of the ties for the sails. And she slid. The friction heated her hands and her wrists and she knew without looking that her skin would be boiled and raw. She didn't care. Spying the glint of metal, she let go of the rope and curled her body. Cut through the air before landing deftly on her feet. If only she had time to be proud. She scooped up her weapons and dashed up the stairs to the upper deck, trying to regain whatever advantage she could over him.

What was she doing? Why was she running? Wyna understood her options were limited. She either killed him or, well, she didn't know what would happen if she didn't. Not exactly. But she did know the mermaids would never know safety. She knew the Whips would be compromised. And...

She had to kill him.

Clamping her teeth down, she instructed her heart to make peace with the outcome of this night.

Brennan stood at the other end of the *Volia*, on the stairs to the opposite upper deck. His eyes were on her, having lost their woody warmth and gained the darkest black. She wondered if hers looked the same.

He cupped his hands around his mouth and taunted, "I'm over here!"

"Was it ever real?" she called back. She started descending the stairs once more as she waited for his reply.

"I don't know." He stepped down as well, his pace matching hers to perfection.

His response made her feel like she were the one with a freely-bleeding chest. "I suppose that's all I needed, then."

He went on as if he hadn't heard her. Or as if he didn't care if he had. "Certainly not at first. You were something I could claim. And so, so scared. It didn't matter how much you steeled your spine or whose pockets you picked. You didn't want them anywhere near you. What choice did I have but to become your hero?"

She crouched as she landed on the deck proper, making her body small enough so he would not see her past the supplies and equipment. Through the holes and the gaps, she continued her surveyal, ignoring the electric pangs sparking around her body, wearing her down completely.

"It helped that you're pretty, if that makes you feel better." It did, though in a strange way she would never admit to another breathing person. "And it helped you were keeping your own secrets."

She flinched as he began laughing again.

If she survived this, would she always flinch at joy?

"You know, I guess this is fair! You shared your secret with me, so I'm sharing mine with you!"

"You haven't shared anything," she told him, then darted across the deck so she would not be found where her voice was.

She could hear the frown in his own voice as he responded, his pace unwavering. "I shared my past with you," he argued. "Or at least the parts of it I wanted you to hear. And I shared all the money I stole. And my plans for the future. My plans for us. I guess that was real."

"Did you want *me* in your future?" Wyna asked. "Or did you just want someone you wouldn't have to explain yourself to ever again? Did you want someone who wouldn't pry into your secrets because she had secrets of her own?"

He beamed, the brightness of it rivaling the moon. "I like that answer."

Wyna latched onto her vulnerability. Onto the hurt she wasn't sure she'd ever let heal. "I wanted a family," she admitted.

"Oh, I know," he said. "You should have seen how your face changed when I first mentioned it."

His voice wasn't much closer now and she knew the reckoning was about to begin. Revealing herself from her hiding spot, she faced him. Squared her shoulders. Like predator and prey, they stalked each other, circling the mast between them and giving the protrusion a wide berth. Wyna was glad for it, if only so she could keep her eyes on his body and anticipate the movements. And so she couldn't be distracted by his proximity. She would hope, after all he'd just said, she wouldn't be affected by him still.

But how could she ever trust herself after this?

"It might take me awhile, Brennan, but I'll be glad when you're dead."

Right now, it was a lie. But she was holding out hope. He only laughed.

"I don't know if you've noticed, sea witch, but I always get what I want." He stepped closer to the mast. "And I want to live."

She sprang, tackling him until they were rolling onto the deck, hitting and curving around the levers and pulleys and coils of rope. Her body ached and screamed at her but she leaned into the pain, reveled in it and internalized it until she was filled with so much ire she thought she could evaporate the sea. It was easy to tell herself it didn't hurt anymore.

She scratched as they tumbled, feeling his flesh give and tear under her nails. She loved the sound of his howl, so different from the ones he'd released for her before. She convinced herself she liked these ones better.

Wyna was good at telling herself lies.

"You want the world," she grunted as her back slammed into the railing of the ship. "You want to live. Is there anything you don't want?"

"You."

That was the last word he said to her. Luckily, it was the very last word she needed to hear. There was no salvaging what the two of them had left behind. She hadn't fallen in love with the boy in front of her and it was the greatest betrayal to know the one she *did* care for didn't exist at all.

Wyna claimed one of her sickles in her right hand and, holding him away from her with her left, she swiped. Took care to hit the cuts she'd already made. He tried to slap her weapon from her hand but her grip was tight. Brennan's knee came up to her belly, colliding with a force she should have expected, and it took everything she had not to double over and expel whatever was left inside of her.

With one hand on her waist, he raised his other and tangled it in her curls until he reached the scalp. He tightened his grip before pulling her head down and bringing it to meet the railing of the ship. Her vision darkened and, for a moment, she thought she was on the waves. Fallen over the edge of the *Volia* into the surf, her task incomplete. The thought was enough to clear it.

Wyna kicked out, using her hold on Brennan to steady herself as her legs and her feet rammed into his body. He released her, his hands flying to protect himself. She took advantage of the sturdiness of the ship to list herself into him. The two of them rolled over the base of taut rope and the material cut into the men, the momentum of their battle shaking the sails. Wyna felt the ship careen and she pooped her head up to see an outcropping of rock and stone down their path.

Immediately, she released him and hopped away, sprinting for the upper deck and the help to steer the ship away from crashing. He followed. Tugged at her hair and her clothes to keep her from escaping him. Did he not see? What good did it do to kill her if the ship were destroyed anyway?

For only a moment, she let herself consider crashing the ship herself. Letting the secret of the mermaids die with them. But, gods, Wyna wasn't ready to die.

When she reached the helm, she stood to its side, using both her hands and leveraging her body to pull it in a different direction. Brennan pulled from the other end, undoing all her work.

"Stop!" she screamed in protest. "You're going to kill us all!"

His eyes flew to the rocks and she used his distraction to kick him off of the helm. Once her feet left the ground, the wheel spun towards her, depositing her back on the deck and knocking her breath straight from her lungs. Before she could recover, Brennan had her in his arms and tossed her over the side of the upper deck. She landed next to the sailor she'd picked off and Brennan had tripped over. On her back, her weapons dug into her. The tactic had stunned her into inaction while he rushed down the stairs to meet her.

She was determined to be on her feet before he got there.

Scuttling backwards, Wyna tried to lead him away from the helm and away from the body. She had to get him to come to her. She had to have the advantage because what else did she have?

He was faster than she gave him credit for and met her quickly. Wyna glanced up at the sky, expecting to see the sun rising somewhere in the distance, coming to save her from him. But the sun was nowhere to be found and, truthfully, the events of the night so far had likely only taken an hour or two, at most. There was nothing to save her now but herself.

She sensed him behind her so Wyna whirled and squatted. She had to stop herself from hissing, from singing the war-cried song of a killer cornered. She was glad for the railing at her back so she couldn't step away from his approach. She wouldn't run away again. But she could not keep her head from turning to see the rocks that had felt a far-off threat suddenly impending. Her steering had done nothing to help.

If only she could replace him, perhaps she could send him over the edge and hope the rocks would do what she could not. Yet even as she thought it, she saw Brennan swing low, capturing her legs in the hook of his arms as he lifted her over the railing. She twisted in his grasp, reaching desperately for anything that would save her from the fate she'd wished upon him. Her fingers found purchase through the slats of the railing, slick with the spray of the sea but not slippery enough to dislodge her.

Brennan released a grunt of frustration at her determination to hold on. His eyes softened in his skull and she shushed her heart as it swooned. The boy reached back over the edge and gripped her chin in his hand, pulling her violently upwards in a surprising show of strength. His fingers enclosed on her arm and lifted that, too, until her fingers slipped from the slats. He hefted her up by her chin and her arm until their foreheads were together.

Wyna's breath hitched as he tilted his head and breathed into her, his mouth caressing hers before he let her go completely. The sensation of falling felt right in the moment, much like the smack of water did before she sunk into a perilous dark, unable to dodge the jagged edges of old sediment as they kissed her.

And just as he was hers, she vowed to be his undoing as the rock split her skull.

CHAPTER THIRTY

Miraculously, her tears were not yet spent. It wasn't from the pain of her scuffle with Woolhill, though Thessa knew those injuries would haunt her for weeks. Rather, the sense of unavoidable loss forced the water from her eyes. Even so, she did not let that paralyze her.

She had a job to do.

Thessa did not ask Madame Orinna for permission to go after Woolhill—she knew the matron would gladly see the man pay for what he'd done. But she did ask how she might go about it. Woolhill's murder was likely to be much discussed and she knew whoever dealt the killing blow could expect to be hunted.

It was better they go after her, though. Few could tie her to the Whips without Woolhill's personal testimony, save for Campbell. Thessa didn't think Campbell would betray her like that. Outside of the girls in the House, Thessa had no other attachments. She had no family. She'd broken Huxley's foolish little heart. And she was about to take Campbell's only family from her —a traitorous act the other girl would never forgive.

So she'd sink one of her daggers into Woolhill's chest and then she would leave.

It was easy, she told herself. Simple.

But Madame Orinna would not let her escape her duties so easily. She drafted letters to her connections in Adalis, planned on sending Thessa there after the deed was done. She would have her take a little boat and...Thessa couldn't be bothered to concern herself with the details at the moment.

It was lucky, she figured, that she'd started to build relationships with Woolhill's staff. Luckier still that they'd seen her with Campbell so often. She didn't think they would stop her when she got to the estate. Perhaps they'd even be happy to see their pitiful master gone. She could trust Philippa, she thought, and maybe even William. But did they only trust her because Campbell had? What would happen when that, too, was gone?

Swallowing a lump that appeared in her throat, Thessa left the house. She didn't bother to raid Madame Orinna's cache of weapons. Hers would be enough. She nearly sagged when she saw the carriage she'd ridden over was still parked out front, the driver dozing in his seat. And after the relief came a bubble of laughter that surprised her. The gods evidently wished her no happiness but they had yet to truly fail their mermaid creations.

She bade the driver to go quickly, abandoning the idea of stopping about Keresa to see if she could catch Woolhill sharing his tale with all who might listen. Campbell's love for the mermaids may have been enough to send Woolhill directly back to his estate. It was a foolish hope but she committed and clung to it.

Thessa decided it was wrong for the sun to still be in the sky after all that had passed. And, truly, she felt this was a job best saved for the cover of night. But there was too much risk in letting the knowledge fester in Woolhill's guts. Disgusting herself, she entertained a fantasy of cutting it out. Perhaps she'd pry the large diamond out of the ring she wore and take it to his flesh, his love cursed to hurt him in the end. But what did Woolhill know about love?

What did Thessa?

The tears flowed anew as she thought of Campbell. How silly

she'd been to prepare herself to face the world with Campbell by her side. If this was what their world had to offer, there was no hope for them. She knew the other girl would be furious when she discovered the fate of her father—the man to whom she'd continue to give chances long after he'd stopped deserving them. But perhaps Thessa could settle her just long enough to implore her to trust the Whips. She'd tell her she acted on her own. She'd—

There was no use posturing about what might be once Thessa was gone.

The guards at the gate did not balk at the entrance of one of their own carriages, nor did they feel the need to check who might be hiding inside. The crest was signal enough. She thanked the driver before sidling around the house, landing in the spot where she'd hidden the night previous. She hadn't been able to make good on her determination to scale the mansion but perhaps she could change that now.

Running her hands along her sides to feel her weapons were still in place, Thessa straightened and leapt. She gripped the vines and the ivy and the lattice work all together in one hand. If one gave out, surely the others would be enough to hold her. It did not give and she gave herself the moment to question whether she might not be the first to climb into Campbell's room. Had this climber been someone the girl invited to her bed? Or one of Woolhill's men simply doing everything within his power to take what he'd been promised?

The climb was effortless for her, even with her aching body. She likely had a few hours before her fury wore off and the falls and hits came back to taunt her. But now—now, she barely even noticed when the glass of the window she'd shattered dug into her bruises and cuts.

Her tumble through the opening was graceful and she landed on the floor of Campbell's bedroom in the elegant stance of a killer. Campbell wasn't there, nor was Philippa. Thessa could guess where they were based on the cold shouting echoing through the halls. Slipping out of the door, Thessa followed it like a dog with a scent.

"I forbid you!" she heard Campbell scream.

"*You* forbid *me*? Have you forgotten who's clothed and fed you for nearly two decades? Who's taken you in when your mother didn't bother to?"

They were in Woolhill's study, where Thessa had first met them, the door cracked open enough that the staff gathered in the hall with their faces pressed together, trying to catch a glimpse of what went on beyond. Thessa stood back, not ready to be noticed or announced, and continued to listen for just a little while more. Until they dispersed. Until there were no witnesses to her crime. She slipped into the crevice in the wall, out of sight should any of them choose to look over their shoulder.

"You want to speak of my mother?" Campbell demanded. "As if I do not know her?"

"How could you know her? You were only a babe when she passed."

"She didn't pass. You know what she is now."

The sting of skin on skin rang through the air. He'd slapped her and Thessa hadn't been there to absorb the shock of it. She heard some of the staff gasp before scurrying away. Thessa soon knew why. Campbell stomped out of the study, racing with heavy steps down the corridor towards the front of the house.

Thessa didn't know which way to go. Woolhill was alone now. The staff had all fled so they wouldn't get caught and Campbell, she knew, wouldn't be back. Not after that. But...to leave Campbell, hurting and crying, by herself when she had likely never needed anyone more? Philippa hurried past Thessa's hiding spot and Thessa was grateful she no longer had to make the choice. No longer had to take the chance that, had she gone after Campbell, she'd be turned away. Rejected. Refused the comfort she could offer.

Thessa moved.

Woolhill huffed in his study, pacing and unaware of her

entrance. She stuck to the perimeter of the room as she watched him. Looked for anything that might convince her not to go through with her plan. Woolhill did not notice her as he stomped to his desk and pulled out parchment.

Thessa stood silently over his shoulder and read the letter he drafted.

Dearest Brethren,

I write to you with unfortunate news—news that will rid many of you of your most cherished treasures. I must first insist that any dalliances with my daughter be halted upon receipt of this letter as, effective immediately, she no longer stands as representative to my household. Any favors gleaned from the girl do not reflect on what might come of our business partnership. Secondly, I must advise your men to stay away from the mermaids employed by the House of Whips, as I have been gravely assaulted by both the Madame and her whores. I ask that you aid me in my effort to have the den put out of clientele and, subsequently, coin.

Furthermore, I wish to share with you the boon I have discovered this night. Should you do as I have requested, I will fill your pockets with the secrets of the Dracan Sea and we shall all be the better for it. I do not wish to put this prize in writing, should my letters be intercepted. If you

*do receive this letter, please arrive at my estate no
later than tomorrow eve, at sundown.*

Ever looking forward to our future dealings.

Regards,

Alastor Woolhill

Signing his name with a flourish, Woolhill put his drafted letter aside and fished for another piece of parchment before starting again, copying his initial letter, word by word. Curiosity begged Thessa to wait until he was finished with his letters, just to see to whom he might address them, but practicality told her not to allow too many copies of the document to exist.

With exacting movement, Thessa swept the supplies from his desk, causing ink to splatter and ruin his calligraphy. The man sputtered and tried to save his supplies before he raised his head and saw her, his eyes narrowing in a disdainful sort of surprise.

"*You.*"

She let a saccharine smile light her face. "*Me,*" she sang.

He stood, knocking the contents of his desk further about and approached her. But Thessa had learned from what'd happened at the House. She danced away effortlessly, her movements an instruction to chase. Perhaps she should have been more stealthy. Should have slit his throat without the theatrics. That's what she would have done a week ago, perhaps. But his behavior had stoked a fire within her. One that yearned for the man to do his worst before she ever took a blade to him. One that begged for his suffering like she had never desired before.

"I should have you arrested for trespassing," he told her.

"Yes," Thessa agreed. "You should. But do you think they could get here in time?"

"In time for what?"

Thessa decided she didn't miss the man Woolhill was. The one he tried to show her was sweet and generous. The one that cared for his daughter and longed to see Thessa cared for as well. She didn't miss the breathless idiot he'd been as they'd walked the ground and she didn't miss the happily presumptuous man he'd been as he'd told her his intentions to marry. What a different man than the one in front of her.

Thessa would take this man any day. The man that did not hide behind a mask of beneficence and good-heartedness to obscure the wicked rot. What did he care for Campbell, other than control? And what did he care for who he thought Thessa to be, other than yet another pretty thing to add to his list of possessions.

Yes, Thessa liked to know exactly who she was dealing with. She had no patience for men who pretended to be good.

"In time to save you," she said finally. "From me."

In an instant she was behind him, one hand on his forehead to tip him back, one hand around his neck. His bulbous fingers reached up to pry her off of him but she'd had too much practice to let go that quickly. She knew she was cutting off his air as he tried to call for help.

"Do you want me to let you go?" she hissed in his ear. "Do you want to try to call for someone? Do you think they could get to you? Do you think they'd want to?"

"Why are you doing this?" he rasped instead.

"For the mermaids."

"I'll let them alone. I'll forget about the chamber. Please—just let me go."

She fit her arm more comfortably across his neck. "How delightful to hear you beg for my hand and your own life in the same day."

"Is that it?" he asked. "You want me to marry you?"

"I will never marry you."

Thessa let go of his forehead to reach for her daggers. She had to finish this soon, otherwise hearing the man plead might churn her will. She was unsure how long this version of her would last.

In quick, careful movement, Thessa switched the pressure she put upon him from her skin to her blade and did not let up until she heard the puncture of it on his neck.

"Is it Campbell you want?" he asked, panicking now. "I can loan her to you."

Thessa dug deeper into his neck.

"You can have her," he went on. "If you let me go, she's yours. To do whatever debauched and unholy thing you'd like. She's done it before. I'm sure she won't begrudge me another."

Thessa's eyes flicked to the doorway where Campbell stood, a shard of broken glass clenched between her delicate fingers. Her back was straight as she watched the two of them, her lover and her father, and she did not flinch when the glass in her hand drew blood.

Thessa grew self-conscious as Campbell watched her with her dagger to Woolhill's throat and considered Woolhill's words. Did Campbell think Thessa had asked for his permission? Did Campbell think she'd wanted that bargain all along? Thessa shook her head and closed her eyes.

"I'm sure she won't," she told Woolhill. "But I'll be damned..." She pressed the dagger harder and felt the man in her arms choke on his blood, losing whatever it was she'd been about to say. Her eyelids sprang back open and she met Campbell's gaze. "Her body isn't payment for your debts, Woolhill. Your blood is."

Thessa dragged the dagger across him, knowing it sliced true. He would never respond to her, never mock her further. He would never use Campbell and he would never take another breath.

Campbell choked, her shock and her grief catching, and the sound mimicked the last of Woolhill's as she watched her father drop to the study floor. Thessa said nothing as she ran and dropped beside him. As her fingers flitted to the wound. Campbell's hands grew even bloodier as she tried to make herself understand the sight before her.

With a sigh, Thessa stepped away from the two of them and returned to Woolhill's desk. Her usual efficiency had her collecting the letters he'd drafted. Stacking theme in a neat pile. And carrying them across the study to the small fire that had been glowing in the hearth. The letters went in and the heat wafting towards Thessa's face told her they burned.

She should stay, she knew. Stay so Campbell would not be caught with the man's body. The staff had been witness to their fight and Campbell had come running back to the study with a sharp tool in hand. Had Thessa not had a part in the murder, she would draw the unfortunate conclusion. But Thessa also knew which of the two of them had the staff's allegiance and she knew not a single one of them would turn her in for what had to be done.

That would not be what kept her here.

Again, she wondered if she should stay and comfort Campbell. But Thessa thought of watching her mother die and, very suddenly, knew she would not have wished to be comforted by her father. By the monster that was her downfall. She would have pushed him away, cursing and kicking, until she'd released the sorrow inside her. No matter what he'd done to Campbell, Campbell had loved Woolhill. And Thessa had taken even that away.

So, once the pages had finished their burning, Thessa left. She walked from the study, through the estate. She took no time to reminisce on what had passed there. And once she had pushed her way through the giant double doors, she ran.

CHAPTER THIRTY-ONE

It was dark under the water and Wyna told herself that made sense. It had been night when she fell, after all. What didn't make sense, however, was the consciousness that washed over her as her body mended the split in her skull and her legs morphed and fused.

She was meant to be dead.

But the pain she felt in that moment was the pain of someone very, very much alive. If she were dead, she would not have had to live through the excruciating hurt of the change. She wouldn't feel the bones crash and crack as they worked to accept one another. She wouldn't feel each individual scale poke out of her skin. She wouldn't feel the rippling as gills grew into being or the crushing of her unused lungs under the pressure of the deep.

Yes, Wyna was alive. But she was no longer as she had been.

Her eyes were the last to adjust and, as they did, she was awed by the scene around her. The silky midnight blue of the water was the stuff of dreams and she couldn't believe she'd ever thought it to be so ordinary and black. And the fish...the rock...the coral. It was a beauty she loathed to know had never been hers before. But, gods, it was hers now.

Her trousers had tattered and ripped once the tail had fully formed but her skirts and her bodice remained in place. She stripped off the trousers at the waist, relieved to feel her sickles somehow still attached—did she still need them down here?—before running her hands down her tail. *Her* tail.

She was surprised to find the normally razor-sharp scales did not cut her as she touched them and she held her hand up to inspect. It certainly looked the same but when she prodded at it, she could feel the change in thickness. She wondered if it was only to protect her against herself or if she might need the extra layers for something that hid in these waters.

Wyna tried to push herself up off the seafloor, figuring out the kinetics of the muscles as she tried to propel herself upwards. Or, at the very least, forward. But her movements were rough and she quickly discovered the weight of her clothing would do nothing for her here. So she removed it.

And finally got a good look at her tail.

Wyna gurgled a gasp at the sight. Her tail was a rich, yellow-y gold that complemented her skin quite nicely. It shimmered, even in the dark, as if the sun were trapped inside her. Like she was the most precious, most valuable gem in the world. She'd thought the other mermaids were beautiful—she still did—but they were nothing compared to her. She hoped it wasn't terribly vain to think so but her tail was her own. Her prize. It was only natural to be proud.

Once she'd removed her bodice, Wyna knew she would not miss the clothing. She felt no shame at her new nakedness, though she wished her hair might flow down long enough to cover her breasts. It might take awhile to get used to that level of bareness. But even in her confidence, Wyna hesitated to rid herself of the clothing entirely. Without a waistband, she had no place to hook her sickles. And without her sickles, she was utterly defenseless. Certainly, she couldn't just hold them?

Spotting a small sprout of seaweed, Wyna kicked off with her tail, the force of it sending her flying into the water and right into the seaweed within a fraction of a second. So that was how the mermaids were able to move so quickly. She'd have to practice.

She tugged a strand of seaweed from its root and measured it around herself before forming two loops on either side of her waist and securing it behind her back. It wasn't a permanent solution, she knew, but it would have to work for now.

So. She had her life. She had her tail. She had her sickles. But... what now?

Using the rock that had killed her—sort of—as her guide, she swam to the surface. When she popped out of the water, she felt her lungs kick back into action, her gills going dormant, and she marvelled at the feeling and the instantaneous way her body acclimated to her needs. Her human body never would have. It hadn't even been able to handle a twisting ankle.

She searched the water around her, noted the placement of the still-full moon as if it meant anything to her. Noted the *Volia* was nowhere in sight. Nothing was in sight. And she had no idea how to get home. She thought of returning to Adalis but she wasn't sure she could get there, either. She hadn't learned how to navigate while she'd been on the ship. She certainly never anticipated having to know. But she cursed herself now as she looked around her for any hint of what step to take to push herself forward.

Eventually, out of options, she dropped again below the surface and started off. Perhaps it was irresponsible to trust her instincts to carry her where she needed to go but she didn't know what else she could do.

What if this was her life now? A nomadic and lonely existence, in which she was more powerful and more beautiful than she ever had been but damned to never find another with which to share herself. Cursed to never find a family. It was punishment, really. For not stopping Brennan. For letting him kill Evelyn. For letting him kill her. If she had known this was her fate, she would have just crashed the ship.

But Wyna hadn't wanted to believe Brennan was what he was.

And it wasn't naivete that cost her her life. Should she ever get the chance to right her wrongs, she wouldn't make the same mistake again. She would fix it.

Hazarding a guess, Wyna swam towards what she thought was Keresa. If she went fast enough, perhaps she could catch the ship. She wasn't sure what she might do when she found it but, at the very least, it might guide her back home.

The sun graced the sky before she came upon the shadow of a merchant ship. It was a feat to gather the courage to poke her head above the waves and see if the sails bore the Woolhill livery—there could be mermaid killers on that ship. But she did. As she broke the surface, the morning air washed her skin, the slight wind blowing the heavy curls back from her face. Wyna leaned back her head, closing her eyes and basking in the sensation before she returned to her task. She was too close to the ship to see the sails so she pushed herself back from it, swinging to the side. Just as she tipped her head to catch a final glimpse, hands wrapped around her tail and yanked her back under the surf.

Wyna's human instincts had her flailing and fighting to return to the air, had her screaming and letting bubbles flow into her. Her sickles were in her hands before she realized she wasn't drowning.

"Calm down!" Ibot shouted at her.

The sound of her voice gave Wyna pause. It wasn't the same as she'd come to know. It was muted and distorted—very slightly, but distorted all the same.

"We can speak," she said, a vocalization of her wonder just as much as it was a test of her own abilities. "Underwater, we can speak."

Ibot's hands were still on her. "Yes. Now, are you done?"

Wyna stilled and Ibot let her go only to capture her hand and pull her along.

"You almost got yourself caught," the mermaid admonished. "That bastard's eyes are peeled for us ever since you dumped his treasure over the side of that ship."

Evelyn.

"Has he hurt any more of you?"

Ibot glanced back to her. "Only you."

The words were lamenting but they filled Wyna with a sense of fuzzy pride. She was one of them. Ibot even thought so. And she *cared*. Cared that Wyna had been hurt by Brennan. That she'd been betrayed so fiercely.

Wyna considered how Ibot had found her. "You're still following that ship."

Ibot didn't look back this time. "We didn't see him kill you. Didn't know where to find you. We figured you'd come back for revenge."

She wasn't positive that was what she had been doing but she didn't correct Ibot. "We?" Wyna asked.

"Where do you think I'm taking you?"

She stalled any further questions, content to know they'd be answered soon enough. Ibot led her around the other side of the rock outcropping where she'd been dropped and Wyna had to command herself not to laugh. They'd been right there. Right next to her as she'd perished and changed. And they hadn't seen.

The other mermaids welcomed her with embraces that definitely felt less slimy now that she was covered in her own layer. The hugs were hard and firm, each one of them feeling for themselves that Wyna was really in front of them and really was a mermaid. They complimented her tail, which begged her cheeks to heat as she accepted the praise and cooed over it herself. She whipped it for them so they could see it in motion, the fins sprouting from the end catching what little light they could and refracting it into fire.

But they sobered quick enough as Wyna told them she was sorry. She regretted how she'd been the cause of Evelyn's death. Brennan would never have known enough about the mermaids to take a blade to them if Wyna hadn't led him right to that cave. If she hadn't insisted he was good. That he could be trusted.

"Did you see how he did it?" she ventured to ask. "Were you there when she died?"

The mermaids shook their heads. No, they hadn't seen. They told her Evelyn had always been more trusting than the rest of them, always willing to extend a hand she didn't need. Wyna got the impression the other mermaids thought her foolish. Thought she hadn't learned from whatever had made her a mermaid in the first place.

"Trust kills," Ibot said with finality, willing away the conversation about their fallen friend.

"I trust you," Wyna pushed. "I trust you all. But I understand if you have no trust in me."

Adrie shushed Ibot before the other mermaid could tell Wyna she didn't. "There's nothing to do about it now."

"Are you sure?"

Adrie cocked her head, her hair slinging slowly through the water. "What do you mean?"

"Are you sure there's nothing to be done? Or might we go back to the *Volia* and finish what we started?"

"I think it's best if we leave well enough alone."

Wyna shook her head furiously. Both an emphatic refusal and an attempt to emulate the weightlessness of Adrie's hair. "Just because I got rid of the evidence doesn't mean he doesn't know anything. He knows you exist. He's seen you. It's only a matter of time before he tries for proof again."

"How can you ask us to risk our lives for you again?" Ibot snapped. "How can you ask us to return to the man who killed our sister?"

Wyna ignored the shame that ate her at the insult. "Because he's likely to kill more. He's a danger to every one of you. Either here, on the open water, or back in Keresa. There's only so much Madame Orinna can do once he has one of us on his hook."

"Wyna..."

"I may not be able to go home now. But that doesn't mean I'm not a Whip." She moved her gaze beseechingly through the eyes of the mermaids in front of her. "I have my assignment. You don't have to help me but I've got to see it through."

The mermaids didn't protest after her speech but neither did they agree to aid in her task. So she let it go. She let them teach her how to be a mermaid. What to eat and where to swim and how to find caves and grottos and allies. They showed her how to swim just under the surf, so she could see everything that transpired above without letting them see below.

They showed her how to use her anatomy as a weapon and they laughed at her makeshift holster. "You won't need those," they told her. "You have teeth now," they told her.

And Wyna's fingers flowed to her mouth to feel for the teeth inside, mostly the same save for the sharpened points. Perfect, she knew, for gripping her kill and tearing its flesh from its bone. She was beautiful but she was more of a monster than ever.

She loved it.

But she did not rid herself of the sickles, not yet. They were a comfort and a reminder. A reminder of the life she'd been forced to leave behind, yes, but just as stern a reminder of what she still had to accomplish. The sickles had been a gift—a generous one— and she would be damned if she didn't use them for their intended purpose.

Besides, how bad could it be to keep something sharp at her side?

She was loath to tell the mermaids about the bloodlust that rose inside her as she sat with them. One that begged her to sink her teeth into something soft and fleshy and alive and make it known she was something to be feared. With her fangs and her blades, she would make herself known. And in the final shuddering breaths of whatever she might kill, she would no longer fade into the shadows like a perfect spy. She would be a reckoning.

And the mermaids would love her anyway.

Now, there was no one to leave her. Nowhere they could go should they even desire to. Sure, they had the whole of the sea as their playground but the mermaids *enjoyed* each other's company. Their differences were moot, if not celebrated.

She would have love and she would have death and she would not hide.

A part of her, which grew louder with each passing second and each waft of seawater through her gills, felt this was always what she was meant to be. She would mourn what it might have been like to have the future she'd been promised but she would not begrudge what stood before her anew. The rest—everything that had pushed her and pushed her until she finally found closure with that rock—was only a necessary stone on the path to this new creature. A creature born of lust and betrayal and beauty.

Her existence was hers now, she felt. And she would not waste it.

CHAPTER THIRTY-TWO

Thessa wouldn't have been surprised if the soles of her thin, slipper-like shoes had worn through by the time she reached the tip of the peninsula. Each crash and pound of her feet on the pavement sent shockwaves through her already strained, bruising body. But she paid the pain no heed. She hadn't liked what she was in Woolhill's study. The creature yearning to take a life away and ensure the man felt each moment of his passing.

Was that what her love had done to her? Turned her into a vengeful sort of monster? A monster that cared not for the opinions of her ward, only for her own desire for blood?

She'd never felt such a need to protect before. Sure, she felt a strong responsibility to the mermaids and the other Whips and she would have gladly laid her life down for them if they'd needed it. And her love and debt to Madame Orinna would have her plunging her daggers into her own heart if she required it. But never before had she been so wrought by desperation to see another thrive. Never before had she felt so acutely aware of Keresa's crimes.

She didn't know where she planned on going. Not to the

House, surely. She could not soil their reputation further, should it come out Thessa was the one who'd offed the head of Keresa's mercantile industry. And she could never return to the Gill-bridges. Huxley would never offer her the comfort she needed and she wouldn't submit herself to asking for it. That was a cruelty to which even she would not stoop. But she'd already known that. She'd already run in the opposite direction.

Evening crept upon her as she ran, the night finally coming to claim the life Thessa had offered it. The moon, though still bright and bestowing just enough light to see what lay in front of her, had started slowly waning. Another cosmic mistake, Thessa thought, that the passing events had not occurred under a full celestial omen.

But it was not for her to predict her own pain.

She was surprised when her shoes began to sink into the ground, the sand of one of Keresa's beaches falling over her slippers. She wished to feel the gritty softness underneath her so she kicked the shoes from her feet. She wanted to ground herself before her panic stole her away. And when she looked up from her feet, she saw the sea.

The Draca was as enchanting as ever under the moon, its waters calling to her like a siren song. The sea would take her, then, if Keresa wouldn't.

With slow, dragging steps, she moved towards the water. Thessa could not pinpoint a betrayal which might grant her kinship among the mermaids. She had been in the Draca many times after her father committed his sins. And none of the men she'd killed had performed their crimes against *her*. But did the sea call to her for Woolhill?

Had he betrayed her?

Yes, she decided, though she couldn't put into words how she knew.

She kept walking.

Thessa ears felt detached from her as she heard the vague crunching of feet and screaming behind her. It was of no consequence to her. She, instead, focused on the roar of the seaside wind and the whooshing of the waves as they met the shore. She focused on the bubbling and crashing of water to wood as the Draca kissed the docks, and the knocking of boats as the tied-up dinghies floated to one another. They were sounds she knew and they made it so, so easy for her to ignore the thundering in her head that told her to go back.

To Campbell.

Delicate hands tugged her arm but they were not enough to break her from her trance. She shook them off and continued forward. Almost...almost to the sea. Waves presented water to the beach until it was a breath away from washing over her toes. It receded. She kept going.

But then she wasn't looking at the Dracan Sea. She was looking at the sky and fighting for breath as it had all been knocked out of her. She was looking at stars. At locks of inferno hair as they hung over her.

She was looking at the hand that came down swiftly and ripped across her face, opposite to where Woolhill had slapped her before.

Trance, broken.

"What are you doing?" Campbell demanded, still on top of Thessa. "What in the gods' names are you doing?"

"Leaving," Thessa grunted out. "I'm leaving."

Campbell flicked Thessa on the temple before sitting back. Still straddling her.

"No, you're not."

"I should."

"Says who?"

"What's left for me here?"

Campbell stood. "I see." She backed away from Thessa and gestured to the Draca. "Well go on then. Go ahead and waste away in the water since there's nothing here for you. Go ahead and forget me."

Thessa didn't move.

"Well? What are you waiting for?"

Thessa blinked at Campbell. "Now I'm not as sure about it."

Campbell crossed her arms. "Good."

The other girl reached out a hand for Thessa to take and Thessa did not let a moment pass before she did. Campbell's hands, though small and usually soft, felt crusty against Thessa. Thess looked down at the two of them joined together, each of them covered in their own layer of blood. Campbell's was darker. Deeper.

"We're disgusting," Campbell told her.

Thessa pointed to the Draca. "There's a very large bath behind you."

Campbell scrunched her perfect nose and looked instead to her feet. "I don't trust the sea right now. Not after what he did."

"You came for me," Thessa said stupidly.

Campbell let her gaze shoot back up to Thessa. "You killed my father and then you ran away."

"I won't apologize."

"I'm not asking you to."

"Then why did you come?"

"Apparently to save you from yourself."

To save her. Campbell had wanted to save her. Thessa couldn't dwell on it.

"What did you do with the body?" she asked.

"I left it."

Thessa gripped Campbell's shoulders. "You left it? With whom? Just there?"

"What was I meant to do? Give him a funeral and just hope to find you later? Then I'd have lost two people I love."

"You loved him?" she asked. *Him*. Thessa asked if she'd love him. Not her.

"At least once in my life."

"And me?"

"At least for now."

She soared. And then she cried, crumpling to the sand.

"I had to," she told Campbell. "I had to do it. He would have ruined everything. He would have ruined you."

Campbell crouched next to her. "I know you had to do it. I'm not upset with you over it." She sat back on her heels, sighing. "I wish there'd been another way. But it was probably for the best. You're right, you know." Thessa could tell it took quite a bit of nerve for Campbell to admit as much. "There was never any hope of change."

"I never would have done it if I thought there was."

"I know." They each readjusted so they faced the water. "I've known for a long time he didn't love me like he should have. I knew he loved me. But...Alastor only knew how to love things that put more weight in his coffers. He didn't love for the sake of loving. But I let him love me like that. And I told myself he was everything he told me he was. Everything he wanted people to believe. I told you that, too. But, really, I just wanted you to go away. I didn't want you caught up in him. Not like I was. Not like the other girls were."

Thessa did not ask about the other girls.

"But you..." Campbell punched Thessa's arm without any real force. "You don't know how to back down."

"Guilty."

"I wish you would have learned."

"I've no desire to take it back, Campbell. If he stood in front of me again, alive and well, I wouldn't hesitate to rip out his heart."

"Bloodthirsty."

"For you, I will be."

"I can take care of myself." Campbell shrugged. "I don't need you to do it for me."

"But I will."

"I know."

"Thank you," Thessa whimpered, cursing the words as they

left her and how they betrayed the strength she meant to portray. "For stopping me. I thought you'd hate me for it. And I wouldn't have blamed you." She barked a cold, short laugh. "Madame Orinna was going to set me up in Adalis."

Campbell scrunched her nose again. She was always doing that, like the world disgusted her. "I'm glad she didn't. My mother tells me they're snobs." She paused, considering. "Though I suppose you'd fit in. You're very full of yourself, you know."

She knocked her shoulder against Campbell's. "I believe I was supposed to say that to you."

"Watch yourself, Clemen."

"No."

They fell silent for a moment, the whole of Thessa's body thrumming at their proximity. The sky sparkled above them as the stars awaited whatever was to happen next. She considered jumping into the Draca merely to ease the tension—to make something, anything break. But then Campbell spoke again.

"I'm unsure if I can go back home now. Perhaps I've never belonged there, truly, but it isn't as if I belong anywhere else."

Thessa wanted to tell her she would always belong to her but she didn't think possession was the way to win the girl's heart. She wanted to tell her she could have a home with the Whips, that they would protect her if she only wanted them to. And she almost suggested running away together, just as she'd wanted not very long ago. But though Thessa was many things, she was a coward least of all.

"They would fight for you, I think," she said, biting back all the alternatives that ebbed through her mind.

Campbell fought a scowl. "His murder won't go unpunished. If it's not me, it's Philippa or Cecil or William or...or it's you."

"No one saw me," she said absently, unhelpful.

"Then it's me or it's them."

Already, Thessa's mind was spinning with plots and lies and seductions that might beg the council to overlook Woolhill's murder. Some scheme which might allow her to swing their perceptions. She wouldn't ask Campbell for a hand in arranging it, not with her unfortunate history of sneaking and bedsheets. But she would handle it. She would take the burden away because that was what she did.

But even as she thought it, she imagined the scope of what she might have to do. Whatever she told the council about Woolhill, it wouldn't change the fact his fleet was now parentless. Without the coin to fund it, there would be no sailors willing to crew the ships. And without the ships, there would be a gap in trade. A gap, she was sure, other merchants would be itching to fill. And as they grew their own trade, they grew as a threat to the mermaids. To the Whips.

Thessa ignored her urge to ask Campbell to continue running the empire as she had. It was one thing to wrangle control from her father. It was another to be left alone with the responsibility.

"Go home," Thessa told her. "It's my problem to solve."

"Your problems are solved with knives, Thessa. My problems are solved with lots and lots of paperwork."

Thessa shook her head. "Any problem can be solved with the right lie and a sharp knife," she declared, repeating the phrase she'd overheard Madame Orinna utter once before.

"You're such a Whip," Campbell sighed.

"You're welcome."

Campbell flopped gracefully back into the sand and huffed at Thessa, staring at the girl through her light, abundant lashes. Her cheeks and her nose grew pink with the night air, rivaling the hue of her pouting lips. It was strange, perhaps, but Thessa had no desire to see the ends of those lips curl into a smile. The pout was what she'd grown to love and love it she would.

"Do you think you'll ever get over yourself and kiss me?" Campbell asked, startling Thessa. "Or will I always have to do it myself?"

Thessa raised an eyebrow before leaning over the other girl and pecking at her lips with efficiency. It wasn't a good kiss, she knew. It wasn't even the kiss she'd wanted to give. But it gave her an embarrassing sort of pleasure to tease her.

When she pulled away, Campbell said nothing and stared angrily at Thessa. And when Thessa did not return to finish the job, she growled an *mm-mm* with a shake of her head. Simply communicated instructions, impossible to misinterpret. Thessa swallowed her smile and resumed her position over Campbell, capturing her mouth. She pressed and worked to fit the two of them together, parting her lips to let the other girl in. At the flick of her tongue, Thessa suckled on Campbell's lower lip, grazed it with her teeth, before returning her tongue to its work.

Campbell's arms flew up to Thessa's and gripped her as she arched her back, aligning their bodies. And with a force unexpected, Campbell flipped her until Thessa was on her back and Campbell had returned to straddling her, all without breaking the connection of their mouths.

Thessa began to feel a fluttering she hadn't felt in a long while. Sure, she'd been aroused enough to pursue a tumble or two with Huxley but her body hadn't been as enamored as it was now. Now, her body listened to what her heart told her to want.

If only they'd done this before Thessa had set her blade to Woolhill. Only then would she have had no doubt about Campbell's feelings. Because with the way she kissed her now, there was no possibility that Campbell was not pouring as much of her soul into their embrace as Thessa was.

With a frustrated moan, Campbell hitched up her skirts to gain stability and comfort over Thessa and her hands explored her over her clothes. She gathered the fabric of Thessa's skirts into her fists, yanking and pulling it up before remembering her skirts had ties. Campbell did not fumble with the ties as Thessa had expected but deftly released them and let the skirts fall to the sand as a sort of blanket under them

Campbell pulled herself from Thessa briefly. "I think it's time you stop wearing these godsforsaken trousers."

Thessa laughed. "I don't know that it's proper to invoke the gods when you have that look on your face."

Campbell pressed her mouth to Thessa's again, evidently to silence her, and stuck her fingers into the waistband of the leathery material of the trousers. She pulled, slipping her arm under the small of Thessa's back to lift her off the ground and get the skin-tight material to release from her bottom.

Thessa knew she should take more care of her surroundings. She knew this was no place to do what they did. But she also could not bring herself to spare even a moment to concern herself with the prospect of someone seeing them. Let them see. And let the two of them never face the pressure to hide themselves from Keresa again. She met Campbell's eagerness with a fervor and finished lifting the girl's skirts to her waist. They fell again and Thessa gave up and reached for the buttons and clasps around her back.

Thessa pushed Campbell away to pull the loosened fabrics over Campbell's head. Her breath stalled in her chest at the sight of her, at the expanse of perfect skin. More beautiful and ethereal, she thought incredulously, than even the mermaids. Campbell's lips turned at the expression on Thessa's face and Thessa knew she'd been wrong. She *did* need to see Campbell smile. Especially if she smiled like that.

Campbell leaned back over and whispered against her mouth. "Your turn."

Thessa pushed herself up and helped Campbell pull her bodice off. She felt her skin flush at her gaze and it was a look she'd never been given before. It wasn't the same hunger Huxley had watched her with, though there was certainly hunger with it. And it wasn't worship, though she could tell Campbell appreciated what she saw.

Rather, it was an honoring and an adoration and a settled sort of thing that calmed whatever was within, fearing for an end. It was a taking without possession.

And it was enough.

They fell back into each other, furious in the movements of their tongues and their lips and their fingers and their bodies as they explored, neither one of them inexperienced but neither one of them familiar with the other.

It was fun.

It was love.

And it was almost enough to allow her to forget what she'd done.

CHAPTER THIRTY-THREE

Wyna watched the distant bodies tangling on the beach with a reverent sort of longing, the two of them somehow representative of what she would never have again. Thessa, a Whip she would never be again. Able to love and touch as freely as she desired, with permanent access to the parts of her that brought her pleasure. Surely, her new body brought with it new erogenous zones but she hadn't learned them yet. And perhaps, given the circumstances of the tail, whatever magic made the mermaids did not take into consideration a personal motivation for sexuality, choosing instead to protect its prizes from those who might take advantage of them.

There was still so much she didn't know.

But watching them, seeing their faces light even in the dark, hearing their expressions of their glee, it was difficult to ignore the envy banging through her chest. A constant, insistent ache.

She hid under one of the more spindly docks, the wood half rotting and the planks tilting this way and that. She had chosen it because she knew not many bothered to walk to the end of this one, at least not far enough to see her. Perhaps it was foolish but she had wanted to return home, at least once, before setting back off with her sisters. It was true that Keresa's resident mermaids might welcome Wyna to them without question but she was rather drawn to Ibot and the others. She felt bonded to them, in a way, if only through the means of their shared trauma.

She cursed under her breath as footsteps sounded on the dock above her and sunk deeper into the water, grateful for the night and its inability to catch the gold of her tail. The person above walked to the very end of the dock before plopping down, their feet hanging over the edge.

At the glimpse of a familiar shoe, Wyna ducked under the surface and pushed forward through the water. She poked her head out again once she was beyond the dock.

"Madame?" she said sheepishly.

To her credit, Madame Orinna did not appear surprised by Wyna's presence. Rather, saddened. And deeply so, the lines of her face drooping and her eyes losing their usual calculating glean.

"Oh, Wyna," she whispered. "What's happened to you?"

The question pricked tears into Wyna's eyes and she hoped the Madame could not distinguish them from the water still dripping off of her.

"I failed," she told her. "I'm so sorry, Madame, but I failed."

Madame Orinna shook her head. "Just tell me what happened."

So Wyna did. She told the Madame her story from start to finish, first with the initial aggression of the crew so she would understand why Wyna had clung to Brennan. She told her all of the things she was proud of—of her assessment of the logs in Felix's cabin and her adoption of the nest and her performance in Adalis. But she did not leave out the details of all she had done wrong. Her misplaced trust. Her reckless, silly kills. Her ultimate failure.

Madame Orinna grew alarmed when Wyna arrived at her demise, both concerned with Wyna's own state as well as fraught with concern over whether Brennan might return with news of mercreatures and bodies in tow.

But Wyna had more to tell.

"Once they taught me a bit," she began, "I convinced them I had more to do. They didn't want to join me—not at first. But they decided I was one of them now and that I deserved to have their loyalty."

It had taken much convincing from Wyna to get the mermaids to agree to her plans. They had no desire to chance their lives for that crew, not ever again. Already, they had said, too many had died. And Wyna had agreed. She had lamented the deaths of those she should have prevented and she'd assured the mermaids she would grieve still for the deaths to come. But they could not be avoided.

The turn, she thought, had been her pleading for the mermaids of Keresa. The ones who lived so close to Brennan's home that it would be too tantalizing for him to avoid them. No, she knew he would hunt. And the more he hunted, the harder the Whips might have to work. The more lives they might have to take.

Though she knew she was right, she'd hated that her argument had sounded so very much like the one Brennan had given her. A fraction of the lives taken so that they might save many more. The line of logic had stung her, hissing its justifications in her ear. But she had also known then Brennan had had no care for the lives of mermaids. His words had merely been a pacifier for Wyna—and, if not a pacifier, a taunt.

As the memory coursed through her, Wyna closed her haunted eyes. Pretended away the pain in favor of the cheery girl she'd been at the House, and went on with her story to Madame Orinna.

"They took me to the *Volia*. It was right before they were meant to dock at the next port. The ship had just begun to enter shallow waters and the port was more cliffside than anything else. Ibot helped me steal a bit of rope from some of the ships tied and anchored around the dock and Adrie showed me how to string it through the figurehead—she said some ships have a mermaid as a figurehead. Did you know that? But she insisted they usually have no idea how close they are to the truth," Wyna hurried to say. "When they slept, the mermaids helped me pull the ship by the rope, away from the ports. Gods, it was heavy."

She could still feel the strain of her muscles. It had taken every one of them, and though their progress was slow, she'd known it was much faster than she could have gone had she still been human.

"It took us all evening to get it away. We dragged it to the other side of one of the cliffs, far enough away so no one in the other port could hear what happened. And then...we, sort of, crashed it?"

Madame Orinna gasped. "How?"

"Adrie told me nothing would happen to the ship if it didn't have any momentum. So while we dragged it, we pulled it away first, a ways out into the water, to see what kind of speed we could manage. And when we were far enough away, we turned it back around and rushed the cliff."

"And it worked?"

Wyna nodded solemnly. "The momentum crumpled the wood. I hadn't thought it would work but the planks folded in on one another and made enough cracks to start the sinking. Some of the crew woke up and tried to jump overboard but the other mermaids were able to catch them all."

She heard the deafening splintering of the ship as she told her story and how it mingled with the ensuing screams. She had killed and she had maimed but she had never in her life heard such fear as that which streamed out of the living quarters. The smacking of their jumping bodies on the water had made her flinch but it was not enough to deter her.

"And did they dispose of them?"

"Yes, Madame."

"And what of your Brennan?"

Wyna's face crumpled, as if the memory plagued her. "He was the last to leave the ship because he spent so much time gathering his coin. It weighed him down when he jumped into the water.

And I think he soiled himself when he saw me. He dropped his bag, at least."

Wyna turned and swiped something from the seafloor before holding it out to Madame Orinna. She felt her chest heave with the lungs she now barely used, taking in air through her nose that seemed to be tainted and stained with the metal of blood and coin. It was a breath that flashed a face in her mind, one who had not even done her the service of screaming.

Cocking her head, she jingled the boon. "I brought this for you. I was just going to leave it on the dock but I suppose it's better that you're here."

Madame Orinna reached for the soaking bag and took it from Wyna before gesturing for the girl to continue.

"I didn't hesitate this time," Wyna announced proudly. "I didn't even let him speak. I smiled at him and showed off my new teeth. And then..."

And then she had ripped him apart, newfound strength and teeth tearing into him until he was no longer the color of wood and sand but a rich, diluting scarlet. She was unsure why she didn't want to tell Madame Orinna what she'd done. Perhaps it was because Madame Orinna had never taught them to delight in violence. It was simply a task that must be accomplished. For efficiency and protection. Never revenge, not really. Especially not one so personal.

"You killed him," Madame Orinna supplied.

"Yes."

"I hope you do not begrudge me, Wyna," the older woman lamented.

The words confused her to mere blinking. "Why?"

"I have taken you away too soon. Placed you on a journey you had no hope of returning from."

This time, Wyna prickled. "I'm not incompetent," she snapped.

"I know. I meant not to insult your skill, Wyna. You've done well with what you were given. I fear the *Volia* was cursed from the start. I was bound to lose one of my Whips, no matter which one I sent." She leveled her gaze at Wyna. "But not many would have come back to me in such confidence of a secret kept."

"I did my best, Madame," Wyna said, her voice shrinking. "I'm sorry I cannot be a Whip anymore."

The Madame laughed. "If you wish me to relieve you of your duty, all you must do is ask."

Her ears perked. Of course she wasn't going to beg Madame Orinna to let her go. She was only trying to save herself the humiliation of being fired. Or dismissed. She wouldn't blame the Madame if she'd dismissed her but that didn't mean she wanted it. Perhaps she could be an honorary Whip. Retired.

"What?" she ventured to ask.

"I will not bring you another assignment if you don't want one from me."

"And if I do?"

Madame Orinna's lips curled into a smirk. "Then I'm certain I can find use for a mermaid."

"Does it have to be here? I quite like the coven I've been traveling with."

"The sea is yours to explore, Wyna. I'll not keep you here."

"Thank you," she breathed. "Thank you, Madame.'

"We will miss you in the House."

"You will?"

The Madame nodded and turned, looking to where Thessa and her lover still lay in each other's arms. "We'd hoped you were having more luck than us." Madame Orinna shook her head, her curls begging to spring loose from where they were wrapped tightly to her head in fuschia silk. "Ah, but I'm sure the tide will come back around."

Wyna lingered, inquiring as to what had passed while she'd been away, discovering Thessa's run-in with Woolhill and a few various juicy tasks the other Whips had attended to, each with their very own dramas and missteps. She'd always assumed Madame Orinna ran quite the tight ship and it was comforting to know she was not the only one of them who was only human—or, at least, that she had been.

Before she parted, Wyna swirled back to Madame Orinna. "I'll return every now and again. But, please, tell them I love them all dearly."

Madame Orinna smiled, one that lit her face and bared her pearly teeth. "And they, you. In your journey, just know the House of Whips will always be a home to you."

Wyna nodded and again faced the expanse of the Dracan Sea before she could cry again. But it didn't feel as though she'd traded one family for another. She was not leaving the Whips behind for the mermaids, nor would she have abandoned the mermaids had she been given the chance. Instead, she basked in the embrace of both of her worlds. Very suddenly, she felt no desire to grieve the loss of what she'd thought she had with Brennan.

This love, she knew, was infinitely better.

And as she swam, she gave thought to the violence in which she'd partaken in recent weeks. Of the consequences that had given her fear and made her stomach turn and twist with guilt. And yet, those feelings hadn't been enough to deter her from it. Truly, if she spent time considering and peeling apart everything she'd felt in the moment, she would find she hadn't really minded the actual killing. That she'd only been numbed to it in favor of her anxieties. Perhaps she enjoyed it. She'd certainly enjoyed toying with Brennan before things had gone completely sour but she'd not yet explored it. What if that was to be her calling? A mercreature of deadly justice.

Perhaps, she thought, it would take a few more sinking ships for her to know.

THE END

ACKNOWLEDGMENTS

First and foremost, I want to thank all of the incredible women at Indie Forge. This book wouldn't be where it is if you all hadn't taken the chance on it *and* taken a chance on me. I know I wasn't the perfect client and am what we in the biz call Bad At Social Media but the love and support you continually showed me and the herculean effort you put into getting this project published and distributed means the absolute world to me.

Speaking of social media, I also want to thank all the other authors signed with Indie Forge for the way you all welcomed me with open arms. If you hadn't been so kind and inclusive as I re-wet my toes in the online waters, I'm certain I would have been too discouraged to continue.

I'd also love to thank all my pre-publication readers (who were 90% my friends). Haley, Kelsey, Caleb, Jaycob, and Morgan—I would probably still be telling myself no one would actually like this strange little book if you hadn't fallen for my desperate pleas for compliments. And Josh and Joanna, I know you're waiting for an audiobook but you've always been the loudest and the proudest of all of my creative endeavors and I love you more than you know.

To my family: I was trying to be so chill about this and none of you let me and I'm obsessed with you for it. Lisa, I'm humbly awaiting your review as I truly look up to you and admire your lifelong passion for all things bookish. Amy (or Mom, if you prefer), thank you a million times over for all the help you provided me in getting graphics together for my social media. I love being a graphic design nepo baby. As a reward, I might let you read this one.

To Jaycob in particular: I don't think I ever would have been brave enough to tell anyone in my real life about these projects if it wasn't for you. To have found a partner so encouraging and supportive is one of the luckiest things that's ever happened to me. And if anyone reading this thinks that the bare minimum, I'll just very casually drop that he literally picked up his life and moved across the country for me. Honey, you've taught me so much about love and I can't wait to keep learning with you.

Finally, to whoever picked up this book: whether you liked it or not, you made it to the end. And I love you for it.

www.ingramcontent.com/pod-product-compliance
Lightning Source LLC
Chambersburg PA
CBHW021213310726
48971CB00006B/1548